THE EYE OF VALERIA
The Valerian Chronicles – Volume 1

T. R. Rankin

THE EYE OF VALERIA
The Valerian Chronicles – Volume 1

CAST OF CHARACTERS

BALAZAR-Son of Valerius, king of Valeria

CHUBAR-Lawgiver of Kantar

COLINUS-4th Battalion Subaltern

CORMIN-Chief Royal Guard, Army Chief

COXIUS -8th Battalion Chief

CROSSEUS-Half-Breed King of Kantar

DELCINIUS-Advisor to the King

FABRINAN-Advisor to the King

FANTAR-Emperor of Inland Sea, Conqueror of Valeria

GAFTON-Sergeant of Guard

GALDOMERE-Chubar's wine steward

HARADIN-Merchant of meat

HUDARIN-Army Chief

KALA ATAR-Kudanim God of Death

KALNIS-Bath woman

KOLTAR-Aristocrat, inventor, intellectual

KOLTUS-City Administrator

MACIMUS-2nd Battalion Subaltern

MALTINUS-Chief Engineer & Architect

SALIA-Bath woman

SALONIS-Queen

SERIS-Attendant to Queen

SIMPLINIUS-4th Battalion Chief

TARMIN-Advisor to the King

TEUKONIS-A Bard

THORNGERE-A barbarian of mysterious lineage

VALENCIUS --Hudarin's Chief of Staff

VALERIAN-Traditional name of heir to Valeria's throne

VALERIUS-Dead King of Valeria, Balazar himself

WETANIS-Bath woman

ZAGREB-Fallen King of Zagorbia

PROLOGUE

Amidst the vast and barren reaches of the mountains south of Zagorbia stood a single chimney of rock so smooth, so cylindrical, and so lofty it might have been carved by the hand of man. Formed in the vent of a long extinct volcano, it had emerged inches at a time over the millennia as softer, surrounding rock was worn away. Now it stood, lofty and alone, like the last remaining column of a once grand and opulent palace. Around it, for as far as the eye could see, spread a vast panorama of jagged peaks with dazzling caps of snow and plunging valleys, blue with afternoon shadow. No men made cities here, none even came to keep sheep or goats. So far as was known in Zagorbia and the other cities of the north, no men had ever even been here, let alone returned. The mountains, all agreed, were impassable. And this pillar was unknown.

Atop it now, however, stood an ancient and seemingly enfeebled mage, his robes whipped by the wind and the twin streams of his hair and beard flapping like pennants. How such a figure could have ascended that height-indeed, how he could even have reached a spot so utterly remote-only the gods might know. Yet there he stood, as stiff and rigid as the very stone.

Overhead, the sun pursued its normal course, but the mage beheld it not. For in his withered hands, cupped before him as if in prayer, he held a large red gem. It was on this, and only this, that he bent his wizard's eye. A deep, fiery red, the gem pulsed and glowed like a thing alive. And like a man in a trance, the mage gazed deep into its heart and marked not the passage of natural time.

Evening came. The wind, which had blown full from the west and the distant sea, dropped, then changed, then dropped again as the sun dipped into a distant haze, and all was still. And still the mage stood, his shadow now lengthening to infinity, the rock rising in the gathering gloom like a beacon, tipped with a ruddy glow. Yet it was not quite night. Still the tip of the sun shone above the world's rim when, of a sudden, the gem seemed to explode in a brilliant red flash. The force of it knocked the mage back. He staggered, stumbled, teetered briefly on the edge, and then, flailing his arms and loosing a long, high pitched wail, he plunged into the abyss below.

Thorngere stopped to draw a ragged breath and wipe the sweat from his brow. It was hot. Overhead, the noon sun stood almost still. Yet here, on the north east slope, snow still clung in the shadows and under the corners of jagged rock. Rivulets of water cascaded down the steep gradient and in spots, formed rushing streams ankle deep. Thorngere kept to the dry rock as much as possible and wound his way upward, ever upward towards a distant mountain pass.

For days now he had been climbing. Why, he did not know. The month before, in his ship's haven far to the south near Dulcai, a dream had come to him, bidding him take ship and sail. Six times it had pulled him from sleep, leaving him with but a fading image of an ancient face and a distant trail, before he had summoned his crew and gone. Ten

8

days he had been at sea and the dream had remained the same. Then, one night as they lay at anchor in a hidden cove south of Zagorbia, it had changed. Leaving his ship and crew, Thorngere had marched inland. Two days through trackless brambles and across tortuous ravines he had marched with naught to guide him but the sun. Then there had been this trail. And the dream, coming on him now like double vision, guided him upwards.

He went. On and on, up and up, following a trail a goat would shun, day after day. He went without rest, almost without sleep until now, his great strength drained and the muscles of his legs-long inured to hard climbing from a youth spent in the mountains-turned to pulsing sap, he was nearing the point of complete and utter exhaustion. But he was also nearing the peak. Loosing a heavy sigh, he started up again.

"Whatever it is," he muttered, "it had damn well better be good."

Dusk found him at the pass. Or, to be more precise, inching his way around the edge of the pass on a shelf of rock hardly wider than his foot and with his back tightly pressed against a wall of stone. Following the face as it curved around to the east, the shelf widened at last into a broad plateau. In the center of this and hitherto hidden from view, rose a huge pillar of stone. It was a startling apparition; a smooth white column rising like a tower into the night, and Thorngere was momentarily stunned to find it there. Following its flank upwards with his eye, he was even more startled to see a stiff, angular figure, all bathed in a deep red glow, standing at the top.

It had to be, he thought and let out a wild yell.

But the figure paid him no mind. Frowning, Thorngere approached the base of the column in search of a means of ascent.

No sooner had he reached it than the mage-for that, thought Thorngere, he must surely be-let out a long piercing wail. Looking up, Thorngere saw a flash of brilliant red, then a body plummeting. Stretching out his arms, he caught it like a child.

The mage was still alive, but he had plainly suffered from the blast. His eyebrows had been burned away, and the uppermost hairs on his cheeks were singed and crinkled. Around his eyes the skin glowed a deep red, like iron heated in a forge and his eyelids fluttered spastically. Gradually, the red glow faded and the man opened his eyes.

"So," he said as if nothing unusual had occurred, "you've come."

"Aye," said Thorngere, "I've come. But if it was only for the saving of your scrawny hide, you'll wish you'd called a closer neighbor."

"I am Volkmir," said the mage, once the two were comfortably ensconced before a cozy fire in his nearby cave. "Formerly Chief Advisor to His Majesty, Valerius Everreigning, King of Valeria and all the Inland Sea, and Royal Tutor to His Highness, Prince Valerian, heir to the Throne. Lately I have been merely Keeper of the Eye. My servant here is Chad," and he indicated a small, dark complected man shuffling about the fire. "But to answer your question, young friend, from what I've just seen-or rather, been forbidden to see-you were not summoned here for an idle exercise in gymnastics."

10

"Forbidden?" said Thorngere, coming up reluctantly from the depths of his mulled wine. He was weary. Very weary. The dance of the fire, the heat of the wine, the deep cushions of his chair all seemed to lull him, seduce him into slumber. Looking vaguely about at the rich furnishings, thick tapestries, racks of scrolls and other oddments about the cave, he wondered how on earth-or in spite of it-the mage had managed to get everything here. But that, he reminded himself with a shake, was not the point. "What forbidden?" That was the point.

"Sight, my boy. In case you didn't notice, the Eye has struck me blind."

"Blind?"

The mage drained his wine and, sighing heavily, settled himself back in the chair. "Yes," he muttered, "quite blind and quite fast-though perhaps not fast enough." Then, louder, "But I wouldn't worry, my boy-it usually passes in a day or so."

"It's happened before, then?"

"Oh, yes. Several times. But never like this. This was like getting hit with a club."

"Looks it, too. But, what do you make of it?"

"The best, my boy. The very best. I take it to be a most encouraging sign!"

The warrior raised an eyebrow. "Encouraging, you say? I can see how that makes sense. Why don't you have some more wine-it will sober you!"

"Ah, Thorngere," Volkmir chuckled, "there is much you do not understand about this stone. For it simply to knock me off my perch and dim my eyes is gentle treatment indeed. It could have done much worse. Look at Fantar!"

"He had the stone?"

11

"Briefly. It was for the Eye he sacked Valeria. But all it got him was a nickname."

"'One-Eye'!"

"Precisely. And if you ask me, the only reason he got off that lightly was because he was a bastard son of King Valerius. Anyway, after that one little episode, he threw the stone into the sea."

"So, how did you get it?"

"Oh, we wizards have our ways. But, actually, I think it was more a case of the Eye coming to me than me to it. It was looking for a steward, you see: someone to look after it until such time as it could return to its rightful master. And in return for my services these fifteen years-or perhaps to better enable me to serve-it has allowed me some little use of its powers.

"So, do you see now why I say this blindness is encouraging? That those powers are now withheld can only mean that the time for The Return has come. That too, I believe, is why you were summoned."

"What 'Return'? And what about me?"

"You have been summoned to undertake a mission of vital importance. A mission only you can perform. It is one which has been in the hands of the gods, lo, these fifteen years, ever since the fall of Valeria. Now the time is ripe and you must summon the king!"

Had he his wits about him, Thorngere would have spat at talk such as this. Now, however, with the urge to sleep swelling in him like a malignant mushroom, he only asked, "What king?"

"*The* King," intoned the mage, his voice chanting the phrases: "Valerius Everreigning, High

12

King of Valeria and all the Inland Sea, Valerius Everreigning, Master of *The Eye*."

"Thought he was dead."

"He who Ever Reigns never dies," said the mage. Men may be mortal but the Eye lives on. Now is the time when it must pass. It is the son you must seek-he who was Valerian but now IS Valerius."

"Thought he was dead, too," said Thorngere. He was beginning to wonder just how sane this old windbag was.

"So thinks the world and so thinks Fantar One-Eye. And so, I believe, it was meant he should think."

"Look," said Thorngere, "I've had a rather hard day. Can we just get to the point?"

"You know the tale of the fall of Valeria: how king and heir were counted among the slain...?"

"Yes, their heads were left to rot on pikes before the ruined city. I've seen them there."

"So you were meant to see. But you interrupt me. How the king was found on the field of battle but how the son, being too young, was found later with the women?"

"Yes, and how, despite his youth, he put up a valiant struggle. I've heard it, I tell you."

"Well, that young man who wore the prince's armor and died protecting the honor of his city was not the king's son."

Suddenly, Thorngere no longer felt tired. "What? Who?"

"The real prince disobeyed his father and went to the battle dressed as a common soldier. Early on, he was struck unconscious and did not return to his

13

senses until late that night. Then, seeing that all had been lost, he made good his escape.

"Now," Volkmir went on, holding up a cautioning hand, "why this should have been I cannot say. I know not all the powers of this stone, and of the powers behind it, or their motives, I know even less. But I believe that time was not ripe then. Fantar's power was ascendant. It could either not be denied or was not meant to be denied: I know not which. But I believe that, had the stone passed then, the boy would have died. Instead, it came to me. And the boy-though I am sure he himself knows not why and probably even wishes at times it were otherwise-the boy, as I say, survived and has been living since under another name. That's where you come in: you must go and fetch him."

"Why me?" said Thorngere, up and pacing now. "Why don't you just summon him yourself? And why now? I mean, if Fantar's power could not be broken when he was just starting out, how can it now when he is master of the whole Inland Sea?"

"To answer your questions in reverse order," said the mage, "I know not how the stone, or the powers that rule it, intend to oppose Fantar, or even if that is their intention. It has not been given me to see things as they will be, only as they are. But I do know that in all things there is a certain cycle-a rising up and a falling off, an ebb and flow, if you will-and that while Fantar would certainly appear to be much more powerful now, that may not actually be the case.

"However, that is mere speculation on my part. I only suggest that the wisest course is to trust the visible promptings of destiny.

14

"As to why I do not summon Valerius myself, three things: first, one does not 'summon' such a king; second, I am a very old man and the promptings of my own destiny in no way suggest I go tramping around the countryside; and third, the stone summoned you for the job."

"But..."

"As to why that should be," the mage interrupted, "I can think of several things. The first, of course, is your backstairs relationship to the royal family. Second is the nature of the task. As I shall explain, this is not simply a messenger's job, but one which will require a great deal of tact, subtle diplomacy, quick wittedness and even, if I may use the term loosely, a bit of deceit-all of which traits, my dear Thorngere, you possess in excellent measure."

"Deceit? Volkmir, you sting me! I've always considered myself as having the very soul of honor."

"And so you have, my good man, so you have! Fortunately, though, you have not let it taint the rest of you! But seriously, there is one final, overriding consideration which I suspect will come as quite a surprise to you. That is that King Valerius has for many years now been one of your boon companions."

Thorngere, who had resumed his seat, jumped up again. "A friend of mine? I'll be damned! But then, it would make sense, I suppose. I mean, the true king would never submit to Fantar, and with so few of us left fighting against him, odds are I would know him. But tell me, who is it?"

But the mage held up his hand. "Not so fast, my friend, not so fast. If I tell you now, you won't listen to another word I have to say, and what's left is the most important part. So, just sit you down, lad, and pay attention."

Thorngere sat.

"Now, as I was saying, this is a ticklish business. You cannot simply dash up and announce the news. Quite the contrary. Just as the Eye has chosen its time, so must the king choose his. Keep in mind that there is more to the forces at work here than meets the eye-at least yours or mine. We are dealing with a man who has had the highest honor and power-indeed, his very identity-stripped from him. And if I know anything of the King's character-and I do for I was his tutor-he will not place the blame for that elsewhere, but will have taken it into his own heart. No matter the facts of the situation, he will have been condemning himself for the very existence of Fantar's empire-and for every act of cruelty and inhumanity committed under it-for lo these fifteen years.

"Kingship is a mystical, sacred thing, Thorngere, and for the man who bears it, it can be an onerous thing. There is no appeal beyond the king, no higher authority in this world. And when there is failure, there is no more ultimate shame than that borne by a king. His cannot be the petty emotions of the common man. A wave of his hand can raise up a temple or crush a city, a nod of his head can bring riches and fame, his slightest frown can send a man-a whole nation of men!-to the depths of hell. It is awesome to be a king!

"And yet he is mortal, too. His heart is as yours or mine, he laughs and he cries just as we and yet, it is so... so magnified. Can you imagine, then, what such a loss could do to a man?"

"Oh, I'm sure," said Thorngere, who tired of hyperbole rather quickly.

"I doubt it! I doubt it very much indeed! He must be deeply wounded, deeply scarred. And what effect that might have on his ability to assume the weight and responsibility of this stone, I know not. I do know, however, that he must come to it of his own volition. To have it handed to him or thrust upon him now would only serve to make him a mockery to himself. No, he must take it. It must be an act of will, a conquering!

"Do you see what I am getting at, Thorngere? It is a tricky thing, even to try and explain."

"King or no, Volkmir, every man must face his demons."

"Well, I suppose-though that's a very crude way of putting it. But the point is that in fetching the king you must under no circumstances reveal your knowledge of me, of the stone, or even of his true identity."

"How can I reveal his identity, Volkmir? You've yet to tell me who he is!"

"Nor will I, if you persist in treating the matter with such levity."

"You're right. And I am sorry. But it just seems so strange to think of one of my friends as, well, not just a king but The King of the Eye! I can't imagine any of them who could possibly measure up... except one, of course. But he's been dead these two years and more."

17

"And what if... ," said the mage, smiling like a cat, "what if I told you he was not dead? But come, you need rest. You've a very hard journey ahead of you."

BOOK ONE
A BUTCHER'S BUSINESS

CHAPTER ONE
A Butcher's Business

Under the hot, forenoon sun, Balazar strode downhill towards the wood line and halted about fifteen yards away. Though it was high summer and the foliage thick, he could still see through the brush and trees the glint of arms and an occasional shape darting. The Kudanim were in there, of that there could be no doubt. And they would attack. Of that there was no doubt either. All Balazar had to do was stand there long enough and they would come. It was a curious thing, this making war on the Kudanim.

The woods stretched along one of the many streams which coursed through the hills and led, eventually, to the cultivated plain around the city. There they joined the river which flowed through Kantar and on out to sea. From the wild country up river, the Kudanim followed these arteries on raiding parties, traveling along them by day, striking at night, and returning the following day. They were marvelous infantry, these Kudanim, although not much as fighters. Rather, they relied on stealth and surprise and avoided open combat. But they also had curious tempers and by making use of them, Balazar had good success in his war making.

Standing in the knee high grass, he waited while the sun passed its zenith; a huge man, thickly muscled and fairly covered with dark hair. A great tangle of black beard sprang from his face, and from under his battle cap equally black and wild hair hung to his shoulders. His dark eyes smoldered as he squinted against the sun. In his mailed hauberk, with his round buckler at rest on his arm, his great curved falchion at his side, and with his massive greaved legs, he was an awesome figure to behold.

Yet, he stood at ease, watching the stealthy movement among the trees much as a farmer would survey a crop nearing harvest. He was a professional, hired by the city and paid by the head. He fought alone, going out for days at a time with his cart, and watching among the hills for raiding parties. It was much like hunting and though quite lucrative, it was also often exceedingly dull.

Curious too. Not like any other war he had ever fought in. In fact, it was hardly like war at all, except that both sides wore armor of sorts and killing was done. The Kudanim were strange. They had a quixotic sense of honor which made the making of war and consequent killing of them a matter of the utmost simplicity. At least, it was so for Balazar.

All he had to do when he located a party of them was march in and wait. At his approach, the Kudanim would freeze and take cover. Though they knew full well that Balazar was more than a match for any number of them, they would not flee. They would just hide. And Balazar would stand there and wait until, finally, they got mad, or got their courage up, or felt heroic, or desperate-or whatever it was they really did-and attacked.

20

They always attacked. If there were many, the waiting was short. If a few, long. But they always came, and always in the same ragged manner. Once, when he was new to the business, Balazar had waited most of a day and all through a night only to be attacked by a scrawny pair of warriors in the morning. He had, of course, learned to make more profitable use of his time, but he had yet to fathom the reason for their behavior.

They also had no tactical sense or were simply fanatical about revenge, for they never attacked *en masse* but in driblets of twos and threes, and once one attacked, or three or four, they all seemed bound to it. It was as if the deaths of the first necessitated the attempts of the rest. Or, perhaps it was the honor thing again: no one individual could show any less courage than another, even if that courage was suicidal.

Curious. However, it made the business quite profitable and Balazar nearly always returned from an outing with his cart overflowing.

The party he had this time appeared fairly large for already they were making signs of attack. He could hear them scurrying about in there now and see the glint of shaken spears and raised swords. Then came the murmur of voices, rising like a gust through autumn leaves. The tongue was foreign, of course, but it was plain they were cursing him and daring each other.

Suddenly, there was a loud screech followed by a tumult of yelling. Then three warriors broke from the underbrush in quick succession.

They were small and frail, these Kudanim, not half the size of Balazar. Dark-complexioned and

21

with little body hair, they were armed only in crude leather jerkins and battle caps and carried small swords or spears and flimsy shields of twigs and hide. When Balazar struck the first of these, his sword cleft the shield like brushwood and hewed the Kudanim in two from shoulder to hip.

The second attempted a spear thrust on the run but Balazar parried it easily on his buckler and spitted him in return with a quick thrust of his falchion. The third lost his head and crumpled spastically under a geyser of blood, but by now others were rushing from the wood in increasing numbers. Balazar met them steadily, moving with extraordinary grace for such a large man, leaping, parrying, slicing, stabbing, and hacking. He slaughtered them as fast as they came. It was no contest, really, and soon the hillside was strewn with bodies, whole and in parts, and the tall green grass was dappled with red.

In half an hour, it was done. Not a scratch did Balazar sustain. Their blows, the few that had reached him, had not even been sufficient to pierce his armor. Balazar waited until he was sure there were no more, then wiped his great sword on the nearest torso, brought his cart and horse around from beyond the hill and began loading. Then he walked to the stream in the woods, and washed from himself the blood and gore of battle.

Balazar was not a native of the city, nor was his war making on the Kudanim a work of choice. Both, rather, were the result of accident and necessity.

He had come only two years before, the sole survivor of a shipwreck. And though this land was part of the continent, was in fact, separated from the known world by only a few hundred miles, two things kept him as effectively marooned here as if he had fetched up on some deserted isle in the midst of the sea. The first was that those few hundred miles consisted of a range of impassable mountains which completely encircled this land. The second was that the Kantaran, the people of the city, knew absolutely nothing of ships and held no commerce with the world outside. Indeed, as far as Balazar could discern, they did not even know there was an outside world. Nor did the outside world know of Kantar. It was as cut off and isolated as the end of the earth and, unless one knew the way, about as hard to get to.

The coast along here was merely a narrow ledge backed by sheer cliffs rising thousands of feet. Though ships from Zagorbia to the north and Dulcai to the south passed often, all aboard-and their countrymen as well-believed the cliffs were part and parcel of the great barrier range which separated their two lands. None had any idea that between the northern and southern ranges, and just behind those cliffs, there lay a huge basin of habitable-and inhabited-land.

There was, in fact, only one means of access: through some freak of nature, the great river which was formed by all these mountain streams-and along one of which Balazar now guided his laden cart-had forged a channel for itself beneath the cliffs; a huge, cavernous channel leading to the sea.

Chance alone had guided Balazar to it. Half unconscious from exhaustion, and clinging to a length of spar after his ship had broken up in a gale, he had been adrift for two days and was in imminent danger of being dashed to death on the rocks when, suddenly, a tidal current swept him into a cave. Astonished at finding what appeared to be a river flowing out of the mountain, he was even more surprised to discover that along its edge, a roadway had been carved into the over-arching rock.

For miles he had stumbled along it in utter darkness, sliding his hand along the slimy wall to keep from tumbling off into the river, all the while wondering if he really had been dashed to death and was now on the road to hell. Finally, however, he had spied a tiny glimmer of light in the distance which had grown brighter and brighter until, suddenly, he found himself at the edge of a vast cultivated plain, staring up at the walls of a city.

Had he his wits about him then, he would have been more circumspect in his approach; have lain in hiding for some time and observed what manner of men the inhabitants were or, better yet, have grabbed one and questioned him. But after his long ordeal, all he had seen was refuge and, trusting to the God of Wayfarers, made for it.

At the gate he was immediately assaulted by six raggedly dressed guards. They were small men-the largest did not top his shoulder-and filthy, but weak and unarmed as he was, Balazar was quickly overcome and carried a prisoner into the city, bound to a pole like a stag.

He was brought before the Law Giver, an emaciated, snake-eyed devil named Chubar who at first blithely consigned him to the flames. But then, as they were dragging him off, this Chubar had changed his mind.

"Tell me first," he had hissed, "how you came here and why it is you have been spying on my people."

"Spying?" Balazar spat. "Do spies usually approach your gate openly, in the middle of the day? Are they usually half dead from exhaustion and caked with salt from the sea? And are your enemies-whoever they are-such fools as to send a man of my size to spy upon your people? If so, then I think you need fear neither your enemy nor his spies."

Chubar stroked his greasy beard and cocked an eyebrow. "You certainly are a large one, I'll give you that. Tell me, then, who are you and how do you come here?"

"I am called Balazar, Lord-Balazar the Butcher by those who have fought with me-and I am a warrior, lately mate aboard a galley cruising this coast. My ship broke up in a gale. I come to your land as a wayfarer and claim the protection of that God."

"We honor no such God, Outlander," Chubar sneered. "But you say you are a warrior-whose warrior?"

"A free warrior, Lord. I fight for him who can pay my wage."

And so it was done. Balazar-the "Butcher" part had been a spur of the moment boast which had since proven prophetic-was hired by the city to make war on the Kudanim, and in two short years, had raised himself from absolute penury to a position of considerable prominence.

25

But he had found the residents of Kantar to be an ignorant, primitive lot, a people sunk deep in sloth and indolence. The men were crude and stupid, cutthroats seemingly by nature, and their city was a heap of decay. Of the finer arts-poetry, music, philosophy-there was no evidence and even the written language had fallen into disuse except among certain merchants and palace scribes. The women were squat and ugly, the wine very often sour and the food, well, the food spoke for itself. So, even though the work was easy and the rewards munificent, Balazar longed to escape.

Guiding his cart and its grisly cargo along a gently sloping valley, Balazar shook himself free of the creaking, hypnotic monotony and looked about through the ambience of late afternoon light. The trees, the grassy hills, the very air were as still as an image on a tapestry. Only could he hear, above the cart's creak and the horse's snort, the swishing gurgle of the stream as it danced along towards the river and the sea. It would be an hour yet, he noted, before this stream joined the river and his own path met with the cart track that stretched across the plain to the city. That would be a smoother ride for him, but being level instead of downhill, a harder pull for the horse. As this was a heavy load and he would have to rest the horse often, he doubted he would reach the gates of Kantar before the beginning of the mid-watch.

But the people of Kantar were not the only reason Balazar yearned for escape. There was also Fantar and the futile but obsessive war Balazar and an ever shrinking number of his comrades had been waging against him all his adult life. For fifteen years this power mad regicide had been ravaging city after city all around the Inland Sea to the north and reigning terror over an ever widening empire. And for all of those fifteen years, beginning with the hopeless defense of Valeria, his native city, Balazar had been fighting against him.

He fought for revenge. On Fantar's hands, long ago encrusted and flaked away but staining still, was the blood of Balazar's family and that of his entire city: the blood of all he knew and loved.

That first battle before the towered, crenelated walls of Valeria had been merciless. It was Fantar, then, who sought revenge. The bastard son of King Valerius, and a megalomaniac with sadistic tastes, he had been denied by Valerius and, ten years earlier, had run off into the mountains where he had gathered about him a motley horde of brigands and scoundrels. In the summer of the year in which young Balazar, then fifteen, was to reach his majority, Fantar swept down on the city. Scorning the safety of his walls in the face of such an enemy, Valerius marched out against him only to be routed and utterly crushed.

Brought down by a blow to the head before he even had a chance to bloody his sword, Balazar awoke to find the battle done and Fantar's troops looting and razing the city. Dragging himself out from beneath a pile of bodies-to which he owed his very life-he was sickened to see the extent of the defeat. Mangled bodies lay everywhere, singly and in grotesque heaps. No quarter had been asked or given and vast mounds of dead lay piled against the city walls where the last remnants of the army had made its stand.

27

Even as he watched, Fantar's madmen danced and cavorted atop the walls, putting children and ancients to the sword and flinging them down onto the piles below. Flames and smoke towered heavenward from the depths of the city, illuminating the ghastly work like a scene from hell, and everywhere the air was filled with screams of anguish and terror. Losing his nerve, Balazar had turned and fled toward the dark bulk of the eastern mountains.

But horror had not quite done with him yet. Scurrying across the littered plain in the quickly lowering dark, he had tripped, and sprawling onto his belly, skidded to a stop, face to gory face with his own father's severed head. Its glassy eyes stared accusingly and its mouth seemed to utter a silent curse.

Even now, after years of battle had hardened him to such sights and after reason had asserted time and time again that it could not have been his father's head; that the odds against it were tremendous; that the light was bad; that the thing itself was so gory as to be virtually unrecognizable; that, in short, it was much more likely to have been his horrified imagination that saw his father and not his eyes... even now he could not recall that moment without a shudder. The shock of it had ripped him open and scarred him more than all the other horrors of that day combined.

He was only a boy, after all, had not the first down upon his cheeks. Yet, at that moment, staring into those vacant, sea-stone eyes, his youth had been consumed in rage and shame: rage at Fantar and what he had brought upon the city, and shame at the fate such a great and proud city had suffered, at the pitiful role he had played in defending it, and most of all, at the fact that he alone had survived it. In the face of inexorable death, his own youth had passed away and when he arose from the pool of his own vomit and tears, it was with dry eyes and a grim, determined chin. And as he stalked away, no longer heeding the gore or the flames or even the screams, he vowed never to rest, never to lay down his sword until either it had tasted Fantar's blood or he himself had joined the ghostly host of his people.

Nor had he lacked opportunity for using that sword, for it soon became apparent that Fantar's appetite for blood would not be satiated by one city alone. Palmania was next along the coast and when Fantar came, Balazar was there; then at Palmeria, Bangorum, and Durumkae; at Telos, and before the fabled walls of Dunskol; at each of the numberless cities and towns which filled the years since, Balazar had fought in the vanguard, had placed himself directly in the path of Fantar's oncoming tide. Yet in each, in town after town, city after city, year after year, while other men died in their thousands, he was simply swept aside, utterly crushed, but miraculously unscathed, and left to march on and begin the struggle anew. In the last great battle, before the walls of Zagorbia, some four summers ago, Fantar had completed his circuit of the Inland Sea and Balazar, along with a few diehard companions, had been swept completely off the continent and into the Outer Ocean. Even there they had carried on, preying as pirates on Fantar's ships and making futile plans for an overland assault. But then came the gale and Balazar's descent into Kantar.

Even here, however, he had not given up. The fact that this hidden valley would make an ideal base for operations was not lost on him and he had no sooner concluded arrangements with Chubar than he had turned his thoughts to escape. Could he but reach his friends, he reasoned, and return with a few seasoned troops, the place would be theirs to do with as they would.

But he never got the chance. Ever wily, the evil-eyed Chubar had played him like a cat with a mouse. Three times Balazar had constructed rafts up river, in forested areas well hidden from the city, only to have a laughing Chubar and his minions swoop down on him just as he was making his final preparations. Twice more he had sought a path over the mountains, once to the north and once to the south, only to be dragged back by Chubar after fruitless days of search and exposure. How that viper had laughed then, when an exhausted and emaciated Balazar had been tossed at his feet, how he had laughed and offered again the choice between immediate death and "continued labors at a munificent wage."

Turning his cart onto the westward track, Balazar squinted into the setting sun which crowned the distant cliffs and set the river ablaze like a path of glowing coals. Turning his face away, he shook his head ruefully. 'Maybe I really did smash up on those rocks,' he thought. 'Maybe that cavern really was the road to hell.'

CHAPTER TWO
Like Thieves in the Night

It was past midnight when Balazar halted his cart before the barred, landward gate of Kantar. He was weary and sat hunched over on the seat, his elbows on his knees and the reins slack in his hands. Behind him rose the great shadowy mound of his Kudanim cargo. From the wall above, a sentry's voice challenged.

"Who dares approach Kantar like a thief in the night?! State your name and business or I'll have your heart."

"Good grief," Balazar muttered, looking askance at the figure on the wall, "what kind of dolt have they put on the guard now?" Then, aloud, he called, "It's Balazar, fool! Who else would be coming in at this hour of the night with such a load? Open the damned gate!"

The figure disappeared and Balazar heard footsteps thumping down the inner stair. But instead of the great gate swinging inward, only the small portal on its face creaked open and the guard, bearing a lighted torch, stepped out. He was a young man, hardly more than a boy, and one whom Balazar had not seen before. He came forward and thrust his torch into Balazar's face.

"Balazar, eh?" he sneered. "I've heard of you. You ought to learn more respect when you talk to a Man of the Guard!"

"Man? What's the matter with you, boy? Are you crazy?" Balazar batted the torch away. Though the lad was big for a Kantaran-and larger than the

Kudanim by half-Balazar, sitting atop his cart of gore, towered over him. "Get in there and open that gate before you rile me."

"I'll hear no such talk from you, cur!" snapped the lad. He reached for his sword, but before his hand even touched the hilt, the huge outlander vaulted from the cart and, with both feet, kicked him square in the chest. When they landed, it was with the boy spread-eagled and windless on his back and with Balazar's foot on his chest and his great falchion pressed against his throat. Only the hurried arrival of the sergeant prevented the blade from biting.

This man, rushing from the gate with terror in his eyes, clasped Balazar's arm in both of his and, pleading with him, tried to pull it back. "Please Balazar," he wailed, "spare him! He's only a boy. He didn't realize!"

"Who is he, Gafton?" Balazar growled, his arm firm despite the tugging. "And what the hell is such a half-wit doing on the wall?"

The sergeant was shamefaced. "He's my son, Lord. He... he just started. Oh, great Balazar, let him live to learn, I beg you!"

Grunting in disgust, Balazar stepped away. "Because he's your son, Gafton-but only because. Now!" he yelled, slashing the air with his sword and advancing on the portal where by this time, a score of guardsmen had gathered, "open that damned gate before I murder you all!" The onlookers scattered like chaff and, in seconds, the great doors swung inward. Balazar climbed back to his seat.

"It's a fine haul you've got tonight, Lord," squeaked the sergeant as Balazar took up the reins.

"A day's work," he mumbled, "a day's work," and rattled on through the gate. From behind he could hear cuffs and curses as Gafton reiterated the lesson to his son. "Boys!" Balazar spat. "All bravado and no brains."

Horse, cart and cargo clattered on over the uneven cobbles through the dark, twisting streets. The way was narrow and rutted, lined each side with clusters of sagging adobe dwellings and shops. Few lights shone at this hour and even the numerous taverns were quiet. Here and there along the way, skulking figures melted into door and alleyways like wraiths. Twice, his path was blocked by coarse, thick limbed 'ladies of the evening'-which, in Kantar, might mean any 'lady' at all-who attempted to entice him with their charms. One even hoisted her skirts, the better to promote her wares, but both jumped out of the way before the cart rolled over them, and their catchments turned to curses at his back. Oblivious to all, Balazar sought his way by moonlight, the clacking, creaking, clopping sounds of his progress echoing off the walls.

Finally, he stopped at a large building-one of the few with more than a single story-which was surrounded by a walled courtyard. It, too, was dark and the gate barred. Jumping down, Balazar took up a large mallet which swung from the gate post on a cord and struck heavily three times on a knocker plate secured to the gate. In a few moments, a light was struck in an upstairs window and a portly figure threw open the shutter and leaned out.

"Who's there?"

"Balazar."

33

"Ah, Balazar! I've been expecting you. Just a minute and I'll be down."

Balazar waited, leaning against the gate and watching the light spread from window to window as the man shouted for his servants. "Up! Up!" he yelled. "Get up, you louts. It's Balazar." In a few minutes he appeared alone at the door and came to the gate, the house all alive behind him. Unlocking it, he stepped out and shook Balazar's hand. "How was your trip?"

"See for yourself, Haradin. A good kill." Together, they walked around the cart, surveying the cargo. Taller by a head and more massive, Balazar was the younger of the two by a good fifteen years, but the other, though gone to fat and bald as an eel, still walked with a sturdy, vigorous step. "Fresh, too," said Balazar. "Only killed this afternoon."

"Ah, good! Good. A fine lot, Balazar. What's your count?"

"Thirty three."

"Fine. Excellent. Bring them in." Leading the horse, they passed through the courtyard and around to the back of the building where Haradin's men were already lighting lamps and readying their tools. Haradin helped Balazar unhitch and stable his horse and when they returned, the work of unloading was well underway. Working with assembly line precision, pairs of men were hooking the corpses through the heels and hanging them on a long rack while others systematically beheaded and gutted them.

"Come into the office," Haradin said after surveying the operation for a few moments, and led

Balazar in through the shed and the back entrance to a large, pushily furnished room with a fireplace and shelves lined with scrolls. A servant raked up a fire in the grate, and when the two men were seated across Haradin's large work table, brought them wine. Stretching out his long legs and leaning back in the softly cushioned chair, Balazar drained his mug at a gulp and held the cup out for more.

"Ah," he said as the servant poured, "it's been a thirsty day."

"Well, you brought in a good load for it," said Haradin. "I hope they're heavier than they look, though. I don't know what the trouble is this year: all the Kudanim are thin as rails. They must have had a hard winter. Several of them. Used to be you could count on forty, forty five kenos a head. Now we're lucky to weigh thirty or thirty five. And their stringy, too. Even the choice cuts are tough."

"That's your business, Haradin. I just bring them in."

"I know, I know," said Haradin, holding up his hands. "I'm just trying to tell you it's not so easy to turn a profit anymore..."

"I take my pay by the head."

"I'm not talking about you."

"I am."

"Yes, I know. Thirty three, you say? Do you mind if we wait for the count?"

"Suit yourself, Haradin. I've never cheated you yet, have I?"

"No, no, of course not. I didn't mean to suggest you would, Balazar. It's just business, you know. Just business." Haradin motioned for the servant to fill their cups again, then dismissed him. "We had

35

another raid just last night. Carried off four. You think it was this bunch?"

"No, there were no bodies with them. Besides, these were fresh troops, coming downstream."

"Well, no doubt someone will be thankful for that. You know, you've got quite a good thing going here, Balazar, do you realize that? You'll be a rich man before long."

"I earn it. And besides, there are more things in this world than riches." Haradin began to reply but at that moment a clerk entered, handed him a small tablet and departed in silence. Adjusting the candle, Haradin bent and studied the figures.

"We count thirty one and two partials."

"What do you mean 'partials'?" Balazar snapped, sitting up indignantly. "I cleaned that field!"

"Maybe you dropped some on the way in. You want to go over it together?"

"No, I'll take your word for it-two partials are not worth arguing about."

"Good." Haradin pulled a massive ledger of clay tablets from a shelf behind him, opened to a fresh page and began scratching figures. "Let's see, thirty one at two is sixty two and ..."

"Sixty two! What the hell are you talking about, Haradin? My price is three cunae a head, not two. You know that." Balazar's eyes narrowed to slits and he leaned forward in his chair as if ready to spring.

"Ah, Balazar," Haradin sighed. "It's the weight, I told you. And there's just so much meat on the market as it is. I can hardly make my costs. You'll have to take less."

"You don't set the price, Haradin," said Balazar, half rising out of his seat. "Chubar sets it: three cunae per head, payable on delivery."

"Ah, but Chubar is not here, my friend," said Haradin, spreading his hands upon the table and smiling coyly. "And you are not exactly in a position to argue." Balazar followed his glance to the door where one of Haradin's minions stood holding a spear, poised and ready to throw.

"Haradin, you're a swine," Balazar sighed. "But I guess you've got a point." Apparently resigned, Balazar sagged back onto his seat and let his great arms drop listlessly between his knees. Beneath the chair was a heavy wooden footstool. Eyeing the spearman from under his brows until he relaxed just enough, Balazar flung the stool backhanded with all his force. It struck the man flush in the face and knocked him, spear and all, back through the doorway and onto the floor in a clattering heap. Following quickly, Balazar slammed and bolted the door, then turned on Haradin, falchion in hand.

"Now who has the point, eh, Haradin?" Advancing, Balazar thrust the table into Haradin, pinioning him against the wall, then pressed his blade tightly against his throat. "Would you like more of this point?"

"No, no!" Haradin gagged. "I beg you! Don't kill me-I'm sorry, Balazar. I've been a fool!"

"We'll see, Haradin. Now mark down the full price: ninety three and four for the partials." Picking up his stylus, Haradin shakily scratched out the first figures and entered the others. "All right. Now, count them out." Pulling a bag of gold coins from a chest against the wall behind him, Haradin counted.

When he got to ninety seven, Balazar again pressed the blade against his throat. "Now," he said, "count out a hundred more."

"A hundred! Why, that's ....," but the cold steel checked his protest.

"That's right, Haradin. A hundred more. This will just be between you and me-a sort of bonus for unexpected risks. Agreed?" And he gave him another little poke. Haradin counted.

The transaction complete and the coins safely deposited in his purse, Balazar grabbed Haradin and held him hostage as far as the gate. There, he dropped him like a sack and started off up the street.

"No, Balazar, wait!" Hastily, Haradin scrambled after Balazar, catching him by the arm. "Listen, Balazar, I ... This ... I mean, it was all a mistake, all right? I was wrong. I apologize. We've a good arrangement here, Balazar. Don't let's spoil it with a minor disagreement. Tell me there are no hard feelings."

Balazar wiped his hand across his face in utter weariness and cast a glance at the heavens. "You're the only dealer in town, Haradin."

"Yes, yes, but you know I'm fond of you, Balazar. This tonight was only-only a matter of business. Say you forgive me."

"Aye, and a butcher's business it is! All right Haradin. But you listen now," and with this he grabbed the smaller man and hoisted him up by his shirt front. "You try another stunt like that and I'll slit you open from asshole to eyeballs. Do you understand me?"

Haradin quailed under the glare of Balazar's fierce black eyes and his intended reply came out as a squawk. Tossing him aside, Balazar once again started off up the street.

Haradin coughed to clear his throat. "When do you go out again?"

"Few days," Balazar grunted. "I need some rest."

"We'll have your cart ready and waiting. Good night, Balazar."

Balazar spat. Haradin watched him until he rounded a corner and was lost to sight. Then, he too spat and hurried back to the slaughtering shed.

Striding steadily uphill through the darkened, garbage-strewn streets, Balazar made no attempt to conceal his presence, though his purse contained coin enough to feed a dozen Kantaran for a month. He did, however, keep an eye on alleys and doorways and an ear perked for sounds of approach from behind. His right hand hung hooked in his belt, close to the hilt of his great falchion and his buckler was at the ready on his other arm. Though his size made him an easily recognizable figure and his reputation was enough to ward off attack by all but the most foolhardy, the streets of Kantar were infested with fools, especially by night. A score of times before this he had been attacked in these very streets, several times by a single man-if men such half-starved, babbling jackals could be called. Once, some poor wretch had tried to leap on him from a roof top but, dolt that he was, had missed and broken his spine on the pavement. Balazar had slit his throat out of pity.

But despite the reality of danger, Balazar's precautions were more the result of lifetime habits than fear. For more than half his years he had been forced to tread such streets by night and was more than capable of defending himself. And this night the few shadowy figures he did catch sight of slunk off at his approach. The putrescent reek in the air and decomposing slime underfoot bothered him more than they. Besides, he was still angry over Haradin's attempt to cheat him and angry, as well, at his own reaction to it.

Of course, he had behaved on principle: the price was agreed to beforehand and should have been paid without question (though he had little doubt that Chubar had approved of Haradin's scheme and he planned a little conference with that Worthy first thing in the morning), but it was the implications of it, the way it reflected back on himself that bothered him. What were a few more cunae more or less? Had he not a chest full of them at home? And precious gems as well? Had he not a house grander than any in the city save the palace itself? Had he not a horde of servants, a stable of fine horses (or, at least, what passed for fine in this neglected corner of the world), an armory filled with battle gear? In just two years he had become a wealthy man and was quickly becoming a very wealthy one. That was the problem: he was becoming a slave to gold.

Idly, Balazar fingered the heavy purse at his belt and chided himself. A few cunae. He had maimed one man and been prepared to kill another over a few cunae. Not that Haradin did not deserve killing, but how did that make him, Balazar, compare with these thieves who lurked all around? They at least had need to argue for them. He had no more need of these cunae than of another foot.

But it was not just that. It was that he feared he was becoming as crass and greedy as Haradin, as if he were no longer a warrior at all (and, in truth, could what he did be called warring?) but some kind of perverted merchant. That was it: here he was, paying lip service to his supposed desire to return and take up the old struggle against Fantar when all he was really doing was rolling in gold like a hog in slops. He was an idle dreamer. Worse! He was a base hypocrite!

When he demanded harshly of himself as he stomped along, now at a furious pace-when was the last time he had really tried to escape? Those trips to the mountains? They were vacations. Had he not gone believing they were impassable? Had he not taken Chubar's word? If not, why had he not carried more provisions; why had he given up so easily? When he built the rafts? The first one, maybe. That was well built, could have endured the sea. But the others; were they not tossed together more for appearance than use? Had he not secretly believed the attempt futile from the start? Yes, yes, and yes again! And since that last trek to the south, what had he done? Nothing. And how long had it been? Months. Months and months, almost a full year since he had made any attempt at all.

No, he had not tried. He had gone on, accepting his exile as the workings of irrevocable destiny, had gone on chopping Kudanim up like vegetables and fancying himself a great warrior for doing so. He had settled in to sit on his piles of gold like a fat, lazy dragon in a cave!

Suddenly, he wished a band of thieves would attack, so filled was he with self-loathing and contempt. Bah! Snatching the purse from his belt, he whirled and flung it as far as he could back down the darkened street. Then, his frustration vented, he laughed aloud.

"Balazar, old boy," he chuckled, "that was really dumb." Shaking his head, he started back to retrieve it, but, already, a host of shadowy figures had converged upon the spot and a great melee was in progress, the sounds of blows and shouts swelling in the fetid air. Snorting, he turned and resumed his homeward trek. Let them have it. Poor buggers, they needed it more than he.

On reaching his own house, however, which sat grandly within its walled courtyard on the hill adjoining the palace, he was again filled with a sense of revulsion. He lifted the mallet to knock but let it fall again, unused. Though he had been three days in the field with hardly any sleep and was so weary his knees wobbled beneath him, he suddenly did not want to enter this house, did not want to be fawned over and pampered by perfumed servants. Rather, he was seized with an urge to go back down into the bowels of the city and sleep in some slime coated alley with only his cloak for shelter as he had in days of yore when he really was a warrior. But that, too, was stupid. In those days he was usually on the run from Fantar's victorious troops and had little choice in accommodation. In those days he would have gladly entered this house, whether he owned it or not. So why spurn it now? Again he raised the mallet and again hesitated as a new bit of mania struck him.

Why bother to rouse the servants at all?

Chuckling to himself, he slung his buckler over his shoulder by its thong, and jumping up, caught the top of the wall, deftly scaled it, and dropped down on the other side with only the faintest rattle from his arms. He felt silly but oddly pleased with himself; entering his own house like a thief in the night. He would sneak around and climb into his chamber-no! He would not go to his own chamber. He would go to the guest chamber and then, in the morning, raise holy hell with the servants for sleeping through his summons and threaten to chop off all their heads!

It was such a silly, childish thing to do. In the morning, once his exhausted brain had regained its quota of sense, he would probably be so embarrassed at these antics that he would say nothing at all to the servants. Nonetheless, he chuckled with glee now and loped off along the shadow of the wall and followed it around to the rear of the building.

The main guest chamber took up the rear corner of the first floor, directly behind his own. All was dark and silent in the house as he left the wall and darted through the shaded garden to the window. The sill was only chin high and he was quickly over it-with hardly a sound-and into the room.

He was just tiptoeing across the darkened chamber towards the bed when a heavy arm grasped his head from behind and a dagger pressed against his throat.

"Be still now, thief," a voice hissed in his ear, "or you'll soon be still forever."

43

CHAPTER THREE
An Irreversible Journey

Reacting with cat-like reflexes, Balazar grabbed the dagger arm and attempted to flip the man over his shoulder. But, whoever he was, he was large and heavy, nearly Balazar's size, and the effort only succeeded in dislodging him sideways. Jerking himself free, Balazar snatched out his falchion and faced his invisible foe. "You'll find yourself pretty still in a moment, dog!" he snarled into the darkness.

"Balazar?" said the voice. "Is that you?" There was something about it ...

"Thorngere??"

"Balazar!"

"Thorngere!" Dropping their weapons, the two men embraced with howls of laughter.

"You're lucky I didn't slit your throat, you fish spawn!"

"You? Slit my throat? Why, in another second I'd have split your skull down to your belly button, you wastrel. You never could take a man from behind." Striking a light, Balazar embraced his friend again. "What the hell are you doing here? How did you find me?"

"What am I doing here? What the hell are you doing, sneaking into your own house like a thief in the night?"

"I, ah .... Well, I err ..." An embarrassed flush mounted Balazar's cheek.

"Ha! The guard told you I was here and you thought you'd be cute, didn't you?"

44

Balazar smiled sheepishly at this, then quickly raised a mighty shout to rouse the servants. "Wine!" he bellowed. "Meat! Up, you swine! Up! Is this any way to greet your master? Up, I say! We want wine!" and he stomped from room to room, bellowing and slamming things until the house was ablaze with light and activity.

"But you still haven't answered my question, Thorngere," Balazar said when the two were comfortably seated by the hearth in the great hall. This took up the entire central section of the building and was open to the rafters two stories above. Each clasped a mug of wine and on tables beside their chairs food was heaped on platters. Terrified servants scurried to and fro in the shadowed corners, not sure whether to hide or, even at this hour, begin their next day's chores. "How did you find me?"

"I didn't, actually," said Thorngere. In terms of size and bulk, he was almost Balazar's twin. But his hair and beard were blond and his eyes of a deep sea blue. Also, he had not quite the girth Balazar had accumulated and appeared a year or two his junior. He drank from his mug and laughed easily, his countenance reflecting an affable, easy-going nature. "I was mistaken for you when I approached the walls last evening-the guards hollered 'It's Balazar, it's Balazar,' and opened the gate. By the time they figured out their mistake, I already had them convinced you were expecting me."

"So that explains that young fool tonight," Balazar murmured. Then, aloud, "But I don't mean that. I mean how did you get here in the first place?"

"Well, it was an accident, really. I was aboard ship, cruising along the coast and there was a, well, let's say a slight difference of opinion between the Master and myself, as a result of which I decided that if such was the company I was forced to keep in riding, I would just as soon walk!"

"Ha! So, you got tossed overboard, did you?"

"I wouldn't say 'tossed'; it's such an ignominious word."

"Ah, Thorngere," Balazar chuckled, "how I've missed the likes of you! But go on, go on."

"Well, as I say, after I had gotten rid of that detestable ship and my righteous indignation had been soothed somewhat by the cool waters about my feet-so to speak-I discovered myself to be in a bit of a predicament. The sea being otherwise barren of craft and the shore looking very formidable indeed-but less so than the sea-I chose the lesser of two evils and made for it. Anyway, the closer I got, the nastier those cliffs looked and I was on the verge of becoming a bit concerned when, suddenly ...."

"You got sucked into a cavern, right? I know all about it."

"You too? Don't tell me someone had the audacity to chuck the great Balazar into the sea!"

"No," Balazar laughed, "there was a dispute but I got the better of it. Unfortunately, we were left short-handed as a result and broached in a gale. The ship broke up and, as far as I know, I was the only survivor. But I got here through that same cavern."

"Well, word had it you were dead. But I see you've been doing slightly better than that. How do you come by all this?"

Balazar hesitated, suddenly reluctant to reveal the nature of his business. "Why, by making war, of course," he temporized. "What else have I ever been good for?"

"Ha! You've never even been much good at that. As I recall, the last time I saw you, you were running for all you were worth with Fantar's Imperial Guard hot on your heels!" Thorngere illustrated this with a comic impression of a fat Balazar, holding up his skirts and waddling.

Balazar laughed until tears ran from his eyes. "Why you-the only reason you saw me run was that you were looking over your own shoulder at every step! And still, you outpaced me by a good bit." Both laughed again and Balazar motioned a servant for more wine. "But speaking of dear old Fantar, tell me: how goes the war?"

Thorngere dismissed the question with a wave of his hand and shook his head. "Bah! There is no war. We pick off a fat merchantman every now and then, but it's the same old story. No unity, no cohesion. Our people fight more amongst themselves than they do against Fantar. We're as much of a threat to him as a flea on a dog's ass.

"But what kind of war are you waging here? This city looks too damned poor to do much of anything. Not to mention odd: what the hell kind of people are these, anyway? I never saw such a runty, squirrel-faced lot in all my days! Why, even the guards come barely to my chest and they're bigger than most."

"If you think the Kantaran are small," said Balazar, "you ought to see the Kudanim."

"The who?"

"Kudanim. Hill people. They've had a running war going on with the city now for, oh, generations. I don't know how it all started."

"And what did you do; fall into a generalship?" Absently, Thorngere picked up a chop from the plate by his side and began munching on it.

"Well, not exactly," said Balazar, hesitating. Then, exhaling sharply, he went on: "Actually, it's more like a *Butchership*."

"A what?"

"Butchership. You see that meat you're eating?"

"Yeah?"

"It's Kudanim. I probably killed him within the week."

"Human meat?" Thorngere stopped chewing and looked at the piece in his hand as if it were diseased.

"More or less. They're little, but I guess you'd say they're people."

Thorngere gagged and spit a mouthful into the fire. He had turned a decided shade of green. "But why?

"No beef."

"No beef! Why not, for God's sake?"

Balazar shrugged. "There just isn't. The story is that years ago the Kudanim came down in a great raid and herded off all the livestock. Then, when the townspeople sent out an army to recover them, they were ambushed and slaughtered to a man. So, out of starvation-and revenge, I suppose-the people started to eat their enemies. Then, I guess, they just sort of got in the habit."

48

"But couldn't they get beef from somewhere else?"

"For these people, there is nowhere else. This entire land is nothing more than a great basin sunk into the surrounding mountains. You go to those mountains-and I know because I have-and you run into sheer cliffs, a thousand feet high. And as for the sea, the way we got here, well, the Kantaran simply are not sailors. They have no ships of their own and in the two years I've been stuck here, I've never seen another ship come in from anywhere."

"That's certainly possible. I've been sailing this coast for four years now and had no idea there was even such a place as Kantar."

"Likewise. I don't think anybody does. And I'm sure the Kantaran are as ignorant of the world as the world is of them. Anyway, as far as they're concerned, there is no more beef. They eat Kudanim mostly-except for an odd horse or two roasted up for festivals-and most of the Kudanim are supplied by yours truly."

Thorngere sat for a long moment, alternately staring at his old friend and around his old friend's opulent hall. Then, with an air of decision, he picked up the chop again and gnawed off a large bite. "Balazar, my friend," he said, chewing forcefully and pointing with the bone for emphasis, "you know that when it comes to gold, I've never been squeamish. Take me into your war band and you'll be able to get rid of half your other fighters and still bag twice as many of these little buggers!"

"Ah, Thorngere, my very good friend," Balazar laughed, "if I took you into my 'war band' and got rid of ALL my other fighters, I'd still have twice as many fighters as I have now."

"How do you figure that?"

"Simple. I fight alone." At Thorngere's blank expression, Balazar went on to explain: "The other fighters in town-they're mostly guards working off-duty-always go out in bands. The Kudanim run from them and they end up chasing them for miles and only bagging a few for their troubles. But me, standing out there all alone-I don't know. I guess it does something to the Kudanim, makes 'em feel like they'd be cowards if they ran from just one man. So, they attack and I hack 'em up. There's really nothing to it: most of 'em don't even come any higher than my waist. I even had to make up a set of greaves so they wouldn't scar my legs! So, how they'd react to two of us, I don't know. It might ruin the business. But I'll tell you the truth, Thorngere; if I could get the hell out of here, get back to where I could do some real fighting, you could take the whole operation, house and all, with my blessing."

"What, are you crazy? Sitting here up to your ears in gold that all you have to do to get is chop up some little buggers who run up and ask to have it done, and you want to throw it all up for real fighting? I can see it's been a while since you've HAD a real fight!"

"Oh, it's not just the fighting." Balazar shook his head and sank lower in his chair, his face dark and brooding. "It's like... It's just like I'm a damned merchant here, for God's sake! I go out, kill a few, load 'em on my cart and bring 'em back. That's all. There's no challenge, no excitement, no real purpose other than hauling meat to market. And you're right, they are people. That gets to me no matter how I try to look at it. I don't know. It just gets to me now and then, that's all." Balazar waved his cup for more wine.

"And you don't find the gold sufficient to soothe your ruffled morality?" The sharp look in Thorngere's eye belied his casual tone.

"What the hell good is gold-or morality, for that matter-if you've got to stay here to get it? Have you seen this place? Never have I been in a filthier town! The men are either thieves or cowards or both, the women are as ugly as jackals, and there aren't enough brains in the entire population to make a proper kettle of soup. Gold or no, it's just not worth it."

"Well, you may have a point there," said Thorngere, laughing. "When I heard from the guards how rich and important you were around here, I thought, 'Ah ha! there'll be a serving wench in my bed tonight if I know Balazar!' Then I saw some of them and ..."

"Feel free to take your pick."

"I'd rather pick my nose, thanks."

"Ha! You just wait until they start looking GOOD! But that's only part of it anyway. What about the war? The real war, I mean; against Fantar. Now, I know you said it's a lost cause..."

"I never said that!"

"Well, you implied it. But, damn it, I don't believe it!" Agitated now, Balazar started up in his seat. "Everybody's fighting amongst themselves, you say. Well, I say that one of these days somebody's going to come along who can put all the pieces together. And when that happens, I want to be there. I've been rotting here for two years now, but I've still got a good idea of what's going on. I know what Fantar is like and I know what kind of realm he keeps. Until Zagorbia he was swelling up, riding the crest of a wave, with always one more army to face, one more kingdom to crush. But now all that conquering's done-unless he's fool enough to try invading Dulcai from the sea-and the whole impetus of his movement will begin to falter. He got his start by promising blood and plunder, told his troops he was going to sweep away all kings, all governments. It was going to be a free rein for everybody! And the rogues who flocked to him believed it. They were all scum-never had anything and so had nothing to lose.

"But now-don't you see?-now that's all over. Fantar himself is the government now and instead of whipping his dogs on, he's got to try and hold them back. And if he does that as ruthlessly as he does everything else, they're not going to like it. No more free rein! Now it's Fantar's reign and the people who helped him are quickly going to discover that he's six times worse than any of the old kings." Balazar was on his feet now, pacing back and forth and swinging his fists like hammers.

"Don't you see, Thorngere? The whole thing's rotten. It's like a great big melon festering in the sun. One day-and one day soon, by the gods!-the fellow who can slash it open is going to come along. And then good old Fantar-Fantar One-Eye! -is going to wish he had ten eyes to see his way clear of Hell!"

"And just who, do you suppose," said Thorngere, leaning back with a smile and stroking his beard, "who do you suppose this great hero will be?"

"How the hell should I know?" Balazar replied, snatching up his cup, draining it at a gulp and holding it out for a frightened servant to fill. "I just want to be there, that's all."

"Well! I suppose the best thing for us to do, then, is to pack up a lunch and go find this fellow."

"Yeah, sure. I'll just tell dear Chubar-he's top dog around here-that I want to go visit my sick aunt in Zagorbia. I'm sure he'll let us go."

"Wouldn't hurt to try."

"Be serious. Chubar would have us flayed alive and fed to his hounds. Or, more likely, to his court!"

"I just mean getting out of here. I don't know about your great hero theory, but I've certainly no real wish to hang around here eating people-or being eaten!"

Suddenly Balazar shooed all the servants out of the room and pulled his chair close to Thorngere's. "Listen," he said, a new excitement in his tone, "I don't know if it's possible-I've tried before and gotten nowhere-but if we could manage a raft on the sly and could reach some of our people, we could come back and take this place like nothing. Imagine what a base it would make for our operations! Impregnable overland, accessible from the sea only through a single hidden cavern! Why, we could gather an army in here..."

"Forget the sea," Thorngere said, cutting him off with a slice of his hand, "especially in a raft."

"But it's the only way."

"Well, for one thing, I don't believe that. But sailing out of here on a raft would be suicide."

"We might be able to slip by at night."

"I don't mean that. I mean if and when we get to sea. Do you know what the odds are against us running into a friendly ship? About a hundred to one."

"What do you mean? Our rovers were all over this coast!"

"Two years ago, yes. Not now. Fantar's got his Navy at sea now: fifty fast cutters that will run down anything afloat. What people of ours are left are hiding way south of Dulcai. No, we wouldn't find a friendly ship in these waters and we sure wouldn't get away from one of those cutters on a raft!"

"Well, you were out there, weren't you?"

"Yeah. But that's because of something else you don't know about: Fantar's new amnesty."

"Amnesty? For whom?"

"Anybody who fought against him, supposedly. Last year he came out with a great proclamation of peace and forgiveness, offering to let anyone who was still in arms against him settle peacefully in his realm in exchange for their pledge of loyalty."

"Surely, you don't believe that!"

"I don't, no. I think anybody who surrenders gets a convenient knife in the back. But a lot of our people do believe it. That's what was going on when I 'decided to walk'. I was with old Grumwald-you remember him?-and I thought we were going north on a raid. Turned out he was going to turn himself in. Said he'd had enough of war and if Fantar was offering peace, he'd take it."

"Grumwald giving up? It's hard to believe."

"A lot of them are, Balazar. It's been a long fight and there's no hope left. If this hero of yours came along and things were as you say within the empire, well, it might be different. But unless this fellow of yours happens to be walking along out there-I doubt such a grand fellow as you describe would need a ship!-unless he's out there, I can guarantee we won't find another friendly soul. I say we try the mountains."

"Nah. The bloody things are impassable, I told you. Sheer cliffs a thousand feet high. There's no way."

"Well, I don't believe it. Listen, what do you know about mountains? You're city born and raised. But I come from the mountains, remember? The cold, barren northlands? I know more about mountains than you know about your own ass end. And I can get up 'em just as easy as you can sit on yours. I tell you, there's no such thing as an impassable mountain."

"You think so, eh? Well, let me tell you something: these mountains are not your little northland pimples. I know. I've seen them. And I tell you there's no way."

"Pimples! What the hell are you calling pimples! I'll give you a pimple, you, you...!"

In other days, when they were younger and felt the needs of their manhood more, there would have been a fight over this: a bloody nose, fat lip or a loose tooth. But those days were gone. More mellow now, they simply stared in hostile silence for a few moments, then burst out laughing.

"Ah, Balazar," said Thorngere, throwing his arm around the other's shoulder, "you ever were a stubborn cuss."

"Me!" said Balazar. "You're the great Mountain Man with the brain of granite! But enough. This is no way to have a reunion!"

"That's right. Let's have some good cheer!"

"Wine!" Balazar bellowed. "More wine!" And the servants scurried in to obey.

"Say, do you remember the Falkan war," said Thorngere when they were again seated comfortably before the fire, "when we carried off that monstrous serving wench-the one who beat us both bloody with a tree limb when we tried to have our way with her, then had HER way with us?"

"Oh, Gods," laughed Balazar, "I'm still trying to forget it! We were the laughing stock of the whole camp next day-you with the side of your face all scarred and swollen, me with my arm in a sling-and she mooning along behind us like a great contented cow! Ha!"

Other reminiscences followed, one upon another as the wine flowed. Old battles were re-fought, harried escapes recounted, exploits of daring and foolish interludes enlarged upon: all that repertoire of old comrades who have lived through dark and dangerous times came forth as cup after cup passed away. Soon, they were singing old campaign songs and wrestling on the floor. Finally, too drunk and weary for anything else, they stumbled off to bed just an hour before the dawn.

Gaining his own chamber, Balazar pitched headlong onto his bed and was unconscious on impact. Rolling, somehow, to his back, his mouth fell open and huge, rattling snores filled the air. So deep was he sunk in wined slumber, in fact, that his battle trained senses, usually acute to the slightest disturbance even in the depths of sleep, failed utterly to note the faint rustling as of someone climbing in at the window, or the subsequent footfalls as of someone padding softly across the floor. Only when something brushed against his outstretched hand did he start up like a volcano. But then it was too late: something else, very heavy, smashed down very hard upon his head and he neither heard nor felt anything more.

CHAPTER FOUR
Appearances

When Balazar next opened his eyes, the world had turned upside down. Or at least, seemed that way. Then, as his eyes focused, he saw that it was he who was upside down. He was, in fact, lashed to a long pole like a great worm in a cocoon. Long coils of rope wound around him from ankles to shoulders, pinioning his arms to his sides and holding him to the pole. Only his head was hanging free and the muscles around his throat were aflame with pain. At the back of the pole no fewer than four Kudanim were struggling to bear him along a wooded stream.

The sun was well up by now and from his general surroundings Balazar guessed they were already into the lower hills, quite distant from the city. The Kudanim marched in silence and, apart from their footfalls on the leaf-strewn earth and an occasional grunt, the only sounds came from the water of the stream, hissing over rocks and tiny falls. To Balazar, whose throat was also parched and foul from the previous night's wine and whose head was throbbing, the sound was torture. Some hangover, he thought with grim irony.

Before long they came to a small clearing in the wood. Without a word of command the Kudanim laid down their heavy burden and flung themselves down to rest. One, coming back from the stream with a gourd full of water, splashed part of it in Balazar's face and gave him the rest to drink. "Ahhhhh," Balazar sighed as the cool liquid soothed like a balm, "I thank you for that, lad. Should we meet sometime in battle, remind me of your kindness and you'll be spared." The Kudanim ignored this and turned away. But another voice made Balazar twist and squirm to see ahead.

"Balazar! You're alive then?"

"Thorngere! Are you all right?"

"Aye, but my neck is killing me. You know, this is going to have a terrible effect on your reputation as a host."

"Ha," Balazar chuckled. "I doubt it matters much anymore." Out of the corner of one eye, he could just make out the blurred shape of his friend, similarly trussed to another pole. "I wonder they haven't slit our throats already."

"No talking!" A grizzled Kudanim stepped between them and shook his spear. He was older than the rest and was missing several teeth so that he spoke with a slight lisp. He wore a heavy belt with silver inlay and had several goose feathers secured to the front of his leathern battle cap. Repeating his admonition, he sat down between them to enforce it. Thorngere, however, paid no attention.

"You know what you look like, Balazar?" he quipped. "You look like a great big worm all wrapped up in a cocoon. Do you suppose you'll come out a butterfly?"

"Silence!" said the old one and shook his spear under Thorngere's nose.

"Listen, mate," Thorngere growled, "unless you're prepared to use that spear-and I don't suppose you are or you would have already-I suggest you stuff it."

Spear poised, the old one glared into Thorngere's eyes.

"Wait a minute," Balazar called. "You want us to be quiet? I'll make a deal with you: you rig us a couple of slings to rest our heads and we'll be quiet."

This seemed to strike the old one as reasonable and he lowered his spear. The slings were soon fashioned and when the march resumed, Balazar was able to rest his aching neck muscles and soon fell quite comfortably asleep. He did not awaken until the sun was well overhead and the troop stopped again. This time he and Thorngere were laid side by side. They were given more water and some dried roots to chew on. One of the Kudanim sat between them and held food up for them to gnaw on. And this time there was no objection when they began to converse.

"I feel like a dog being fed scraps at table," said Thorngere. "What do you suppose this stuff is?"

"I don't know. If it's meat, it's probably the same kind we'll be providing shortly."

"You think so? I wonder. Why wouldn't they have killed us before now if that were the case? We'd certainly be easier to carry if we were butchered and divided up, don't you think? These poor little buggers are having a hell of a time with us. Did you hear them grunting and cursing on that last hill?"

"No, I was ... err,... taking a bit of a nap, I'm afraid."

Thorngere's sudden laughter made the Kudanim start, but none approached. "Ah, Balazar! Always the lazy lout. Here you are on what may very well be your last journey and you sleep through it! But why do you suppose they haven't killed us?"

"I suspect they have a little something more fiendish in mind than straight killing-they do have a considerable score to settle against me, you know."

"Humph! Remind me to stay at an inn next time I visit you: the 'score' for a night's lodging would be considerably less."

Late in the afternoon they left the stream and, well protected by a screen of hills, made off cross country, climbing ever higher through barren terrain. Ahead loomed the majestic bulk of the mountains with their snow-capped peaks, and the path began winding around huge boulders scattered about like seedling mountains. Balazar had seldom ventured this high, preferring to do his hunting in the fertile lower hills.

Topping a ridge, they made their way along its razor-backed crest as the sun began setting into the distant sea. On their right, the whole panorama of the hidden valley was open to them from the quilt-like fields along the river to the walls of Kantar itself. To the left, no more than a step from the path, the ground fell away into an inky gorge whose bottom and opposite side were already lost in shadow. But even here, in the fading light and with their heavy freight, the Kudanim marched in silence with steady, unerring step.

It was dusk when they left the ridge and wound their way down into a hitherto hidden valley. Vegetation, which had been nearly non-existent on the ascent, began sprouting along their path and before long they were passing through a deep forest of pine. Here it was already night and the carpeted floor was as silent as death under their feet. Reaching the floor of the valley, they crossed a stream on a timbered bridge and joined a well-used cart track which paralleled its course. They were now heading south again and darkness was complete all around.

After several miles they came to the shore of a lake whose still, black waters stretched away and merged with the moonless night. The track continued on along the shore but another, larger track branched off uphill to the left. At this intersection the company stopped and finally broke their day long silence. Dropping Balazar and Thorngere like logs, they flung themselves down and began chatting and laughing like magpies in their strange dialect. The leader, the old one with the feathers, walked over to a large tree and, taking up a gilded horn which hung there on a thong, blew two long, piercing blasts.

"Well," said Balazar, "we must be close. How are you feeling!"

"Oh, just wonderful! This mode of transportation has it all over sedan chairs: there are several kings I can think of whom I'd love to demonstrate it on. Seriously, though, I do have one slight problem."

"What's that?"

"My left foot. I've got such an itch! It's driving me crazy! What do you think they're going to do with us?"

"I'd rather not guess. I'm just hoping there's a chance to make a break for it when they take us off these poles."

"I've been thinking that myself. I don't think I'm tied separately from the pole. Are you?"

"No, I don't think so. It feels like they just wound us up in a continuous coil. If we get a chance, go on my signal and grab any weapon you can. We'll keep them at bay and move off slowly. Run for it and they'll have us in the back. Stand and they'll just keep coming. They don't know anything about fear."

"All right, I'm with you. But Balazar, if we don't get a chance..."

"Yes, I know. I'm just sorry you had to happen along and get stuck in the middle of this thing."

"It's funny, you know: I've never minded the thought of death in battle. But this..."

"I know what you mean." Balazar laid his head back and looked up through the trees to the night-clustering stars. He sighed and tried to compose himself for whatever was to come. But the frustration of having been bound so tightly for so long had him seething. It was all he could do to keep from screaming. Always, from his earliest childhood, he had hated being physically constrained. Even small rooms made him uncomfortable. He remembered how his father used to wrestle with him when he was small, how he would get him down on the floor and wrap his arms and legs around him until he could not move at all; and how he, Balazar, would struggle and scream and go nearly mad from claustrophobia, and how his father would laugh and taunt him until his mother rescued him. Gods! How he had hated his father for that.

But there was no mother to rescue him now. What would be their fate? Slow roasting? Boiling alive? Gradual dismemberment? It was better not to think.

Gradually, there came a low murmuring sound from the high ground in the direction of the main track. It was like a distant, moaning wind. Balazar perked up his ears. It was voices, many voices, chanting and drawing near.

"Looks like they're sending out a welcoming committee."

"So I figured," said Thorngere. "Maybe they're going to crown us kings and have us build them an empire."

"Good thought, Thorngere: hold on to it."

Soon, individual voices could be heard, wailing amid the general chorus, and in the eastern sky a glow could be seen, as from a thousand torches. Among the Kudanim around them, chattering and laughter ceased as one by one the warriors picked up the beat. Several leapt to their feet and began dancing, their lithe, fluid motions seeming to illustrate the lyrics. As the tempo quickened, the volume rose like a flood.

Presently, the head of the procession turned onto the upper track. Light from the torches cast eerie, flickering shadows among the trees and caught the faces of the dancing warriors in horrific attitudes. All were on their feet now, leaping about, waving their weapons in the air and shrieking out the verses. In moments the whole track was filled with the approaching multitude. Drums joined in, their deep-throated booming the only thing left of the original rhythm as the noise swelled to a wild cacophony. Then they were upon them.

During all of this, the leader stood stoically by the tree, horn in one hand, spear in the other. Now, raising both, he blew a long wailing blast and silence, as audible after that tumult as the whoosh of a sudden summer shower, fell over the crowd. They stood in their thousands filling the track as far up the hill as could be seen and spilling over into the trees on either side. Light from the torches brought day to the dark.

The leader addressed them then, his raspy voice rising in cadenced foreign verses. It sounded like an invocation of some kind, so metrical and precise were the phrases and at several points, Balazar thought he could recognize the sound of his own name. As he finished, the leader turned with a sweeping gesture and pointed to the captives with his spear. The yells and cheers erupted in a deafening roar.

A cart drawn by two sturdy ponies, was now brought forth and from it, several warriors pulled heavy manacles. There were four sets, each secured to the back of the cart by long chains. Balazar and Thorngere passed understanding glances between them; if they were going to have a chance, this would be it. As the Kudanim began undoing their bonds, each began flexing his muscles to revive circulation.

But there was no chance. The Kudanim were as thorough as they were resolute. Raising one end of each pole, they deftly unwound separate sections of rope that covered the captive's wrists and ankles. Thus, they were able to shackle them to the cart while they were still securely bound. The remaining coils were then removed, the poles taken away and the outlanders bidden to rise.

Thorngere was up in a flash, stamping his tortured foot and testing the chains. Balazar, though, had a bit of trouble: his right leg had gone completely asleep and when he tried to put his weight on it, it collapsed under him. The crowd laughed and Balazar's rage began to boil. Like a great glowering bear he sat on the ground massaging his leg and ignoring the pain until he was sure it was sound.

Then he erupted like a volcano, his great war cry shaking the night. Nearby Kudanim fell back in terror and a shock wave of fear rippled through the crowd. Screaming like a madman, Balazar attacked the chains, trying to tear them loose from the cart. Thorngere joined in and they started dragging the cart, ponies, drivers and all back down the path towards the bridge.

But there was no chance. The chains were too strong and a ring of spear prodding Kudanim quickly closed in around them. Shrugging resignedly, they allowed themselves to be half led, half dragged up the hill, the swirling crowd parting before them like the sea.

The track led uphill through the forest for about two miles until it leveled out onto a wide plateau backed by huge cliffs. On the far side, tucked directly under the overhanging rock, was a city ablaze with light. Through its gate they were led and along a broad avenue of neatly swept cobblestones lined with precise, well-constructed adobe buildings.

66

As he walked along, Balazar looked about in amazement. Both in style and structure this city was very like Kantar. The streets were laid out in a different pattern, of course, and the buildings were constructed on a grander scale, but the two could have been built by the same hands. Yet, as like as they were in architecture, they were as different as sun and moon in other respects. Kantar had an air of dissolution about it, as if it were slowly and irrevocably crumbling into itself. This city had an air of health and growth. It was on the upswing, still new and unstained. There was no garbage in the streets, no dog or cat carcasses, no vile smells wafting around corners, no evil shapes lurking in doors and alleyways. The lights of the procession revealed clean whitewashed store fronts, vendors' stalls still open despite the hour and little shops with awnings and wide flung doors.

Nor did the populace resemble that of Kantar. They were smaller, of course, but that was the least of the differences. It was their bearing which was so striking, and their general appearance. In Kantar, the crowds were slovenly, dressed in filthy rags and rank with the smell of unwashed flesh. Here, all but the attending warriors wore clean white togas and their faces seemed to shine. All men, they walked with heads erect and shoulders thrown back, an obviously proud people, cheering and chanting happily. Balazar had never seen the like.

"Balazar, my friend," said Thorngere as they rounded a corner and approached what had to be the palace, "has it occurred to you that you might have been fighting for the wrong side all this time?"

67

"Actually, I was thinking just that. These little people have quite a town, haven't they?"

"Ummm. Too bad we're not going to live to enjoy it."

The palace was a great white edifice built right into the face of the cliff. Its facade consisted of an immense portico topped by a triangular pediment and an elaborate frieze on fluted columns. The base extended out to form a huge stage-like platform with marble steps leading down on three sides to an open court of colored cobbles. These were carefully paved in swirling geometric and mosaic patterns. Hurrying in from all sides, the Kudanim overflowed this courtyard and filled all the windows of the buildings facing it. Still chained to their cart, Balazar and Thorngere were led front and center and their warrior guard formed a tight cordon around them. The leader mounted the steps and knelt facing the palace. The crowd hushed and waited.

There came a blare of trumpets from within. Then, to the beat of a single large drum, the palace guard marched out and formed an honor guard around the entrance and along the front of the portico. These were sparkling troops, large by Kudanim standards and dressed in bright red togas with shining helms and gold inlaid breast plates. Each bore a round shield with a stylized black panther embossed on a red and gold background. They stood stiffly to attention while the drummer played a final flourish, then he too fell silent. Another blast came from the trumpets within and all present, including the guard, fell to their knees. Only Balazar and Thorngere stood.

The King-if 'king' he was called-emerged in a white, full length toga with a deep purple mantle and cape. He was a tiny, ancient figure, bald as a stone and frail as a reed. The merest wisp of beard straggled down from his chin. Still, he walked with an assured stride and regal bearing, stopped at the edge of the portico and looked down at the outlanders.

The leader of the troop bowed low and kissed the pavement before him. Then, chanting, he repeated what sounded like the same litany as before and, rising to his feet, swept his arm back to show his prisoners. The King raised his arms and, in another formal chant, answered him. Then, with the troop leader following, he came down the steps and halted in front of Balazar. As he looked up at him, black eyes twinkled within the ancient, wrinkled mask of his face.

"Balazar," he began, his voice seeming much too large for his diminutive frame, "Oh Greatest of Warriors, I welcome you to the New City of Kantar and wish you the blessings of the Great God, Kala Atar." Then, turning to one of the guards, he said, "Release them."

CHAPTER FIVE
Another View

Open-mouthed, Balazar and Thorngere watched as their manacles were removed and the cart was taken away. Free again, at least in appearance, they stood looking down at the little king who was smiling delightedly at the effect his order had produced.

"I am Crosseus," he said, "King over all these people. I order your release as an act of trust. Strike not, then, but give me your bond and accept our hospitality."

Balazar studied the little man. Was the mirth on his face caused by their astonishment, or by some deeper, more devious joke? He could not tell. "Majesty," he said, bowing shortly, "we are obliged for your trust and, if you will freely grant that you intend us no harm, we will freely grant our bonds."

"So be it, then: thus it is spoken, thus it is done. Hence forth you are our guests. Let my palace be as your own home. But first, let me offer my apologies for the manner of your transport: you are a great warrior, Oh Balazar, the greatest ever seen by my people. As it was necessary to bring you here, so it was feared you would not come willingly. Hence, the bonds. Yet fear not: now that we can speak face to face, I swear to you that you have naught to fear from us. And when we have spoken further of these matters, you will understand the reasons for our actions. But who is this?" he asked, turning to Thorngere. "My commander, Hudarin, tells me that in the dark his warriors could not tell which of you was you, Oh Balazar, so alike are you two in size and stature."

"He is called Thorngere, Majesty, and is a warrior like myself, just come from the distant north lands."

"Then we bid him welcome as well and offer an especial apology for our late treatment. Being a stranger to our lands, such was indeed a poor welcome. I hope, Lord Thorngere, you will allow me to make sufficient amends?"

"Majesty," said Thorngere, also bowing, but more graciously than Balazar had, "since you have made such a good beginning already, I shall be most happy to allow you the opportunity."

"Well spoken," nodded Crosseus. "But now, gentlemen, you must be weary from your journey. After you have freshened yourselves, we will eat and speak further."

Crosseus led the way up the steps and between the files of guards into the palace. Though the main door was double his height and, in proportion, seemed grand indeed, Balazar and Thorngere instinctively ducked their heads as they entered. Inside, they found themselves in a large atrium with marble inlaid floors and a fountain in the center. This was a square pool in which a large panther, beautifully carved in flawless obsidian, leaped towards the vaulted ceiling with water spewing from his mouth and claws. All around, the walls were hung with woven tapestries, among which Balazar recognized scenes from both this city and Kantar. One particularly old and faded one caught his eye immediately: it showed the walls of Kantar with the broad river running past lined with quays and-moored securely to them-ships!

Crosseus stopped before the fountain and bowed low. "Again, let me bid you welcome, Oh Great Warriors. My home is yours. The servants will escort you." Clapping his hands then, he left them. Soon, a flock of tiny Kudanim women appeared and led them deep into the palace, into rooms which were carved from the living rock.

"Ho! What's this?" cried Thorngere as they entered a room with a large steaming pool in the center.

"Baths, my Lord," said the first of the women. "We are to cleanse you after your long journey." She was a raven-haired little beauty, about the size of a five year old child but with the obvious charms of a fully developed woman. Smiling mischievously, she stripped off her toga with a single, lithe motion-leaving only the skimpiest of loincloths to cover her hips-and stepped down into the pool. Giggling, the rest followed suit. Splashing about and laughing, they beckoned to the two reluctant giants standing uncertainly just inside the door.

"Tell me, Balazar, did I faint just before they executed us? I mean, is this a dream or am I really seeing what I think I'm seeing?"

"Unless we both fainted at the same instant," said Balazar, "I'd have to say it was real."

Thorngere shrugged. "In that case, how about a bit of a scrub?"

Balazar looked from his friend to the tiny women in the pool to his own sweat and grime encrusted form. "Well, I'm fine but since you smell like sheep dung, I guess I'll have to go along to save you embarrassment."

"Ha! It's you who'll be embarrassed," laughed Thorngere, stripping off his jerkin, "once we're out of these togs!"

"We'll see about that, Butterknife!"

Naked, the two men leaped into the steamy water. Though it was deep enough to cover the breasts of the women, it came only to mid-thigh on them.

"Oh," said the raven-headed one, grabbing Thorngere by the hand and pulling him down into the water, "you lords are very great indeed!"

Soon the pool was a-froth with suds as the women worked nimbly over the two men. "Hey, Balazar," Thorngere called after rinsing his head and shaking his blond mane like a great hound, "these little wenches are adorable. What say we split a couple of them?"

"Split they would, too," Balazar laughed. He was sitting now with the water up to his chin while two of the women lathered his head and beard.

"Not to worry," said one with an arch grin. Ducking under the water, she began to fondle him. Balazar gasped and choked on a mouthful of water. Thorngere roared with laughter and, picking up the raven-headed one, set her on the edge of the pool.

"Look at this little doll, would you? She's beautiful! Have you ever seen anything so well put together on such a small scale?" Coyly, the woman smiled and shook her pert little breasts. Indeed, the Kudanim women were lovely. Standing a good head shorter than the males, their limbs were perfectly proportioned, their skin soft and smooth and their faces like miniature portraits. "By the gods!" Thorngere roared, "I just may try one!"

Once out and dried, the women rubbed them with scented oil and brought in two huge togas for them to wear. "We had to guess at the size," one explained to Balazar. "Fortunately, though, we made two, thinking you might like an extra. Now we shall have to make two more!"

They fit as if made to order. The women then brought in mirrors of polished steel and carved bone combs and began smoothing the two tangled manes. When they were finished and about to withdraw, Balazar stopped them. Positioning one so that he could see into the mirror, he began pleating the long strands of his beard.

"I haven't seen you do that in years," said Thorngere.

"State occasion," Balazar said without looking up. "Besides, to tell the truth, this place kind of reminds me of home."

"That's right, you were a whelp of the Valerian aristocracy, weren't you?"

"Me? Only a dog soldier's bastard, I'm afraid. But Valeria was famous for her hot baths. They had great medicinal properties, you know: cleansed the soul as well as the body. People used to come from all over the world to soak up a cure. Worked, too. You never got to Valeria, did you?"

"Not to stay. My father was planning to send me to the philosophers there-to cure my stupidity, I suppose-but Fantar did for them before they could do for me."

Balazar only grunted at this and they sat in silence until he was finished. Then the women led them into an adjoining chamber furnished with soft couches and small tables. They poured wine for them, bade them rest until the king's summons, and left.

Once alone, Thorngere jumped up and inspected the room closely. "Do you really believe what's going on here?" he asked when he was satisfied there were no secret entrances or spy holes.

"Not really. What do you think?"

"Well, it's very odd, that's what I think."

"Umm. You know, though, they might just be on the level. They haven't been doing very well with me fighting against them. Maybe they want to buy our services."

"Yes, that was my first thought. But why like this? Why not in the field under a flag of truce. It's not like you fought with an army."

"I know, I know. But these are a strange people. I told you about the way they fight: maybe they don't believe in truces. But look, we haven't been roasted yet, so let's just bide our time and see what's up. This might even work out to our advantage."

"How do you mean-beyond the obvious advantage of keeping our throats uncut?"

"I'm not sure yet. But did you see those tapestries by the fountain? The one with the ships? I'm not sure how that got there or what it means but it's the first indication I've had in over two years that anybody in this valley knew anything about the sea. And if these people..."

"Bah," said Thorngere, "you're dreaming. That tapestry was at least two hundred years old. Besides, the river still runs past Kantar no matter what these people know. I still say we head out for the mountains first chance we get."

Balazar started to argue but at that moment sentries entered and announced that the King was ready to receive them. "I wonder who's for supper?" Thorngere quipped as they followed the guards through the maze of corridors.

"Just be thankful it's not us."

The King's audience chamber was a model of opulence. A large, rectangular room with ceilings high enough to dwarf even Balazar, its floors were tiled in brilliantly colored mosaics, its walls covered alternately with tapestries and painted murals, and its ceiling a-swirl with bands of bright color.

At the far end was a raised dais. The King sat there on a large throne of carved wood with gold inlay. The arms were in the shape of panthers and as Crosseus sat awaiting the approach of his guests, he absently stroked their lifelike heads. On either side of him were two man-sized chairs of plain design and obviously hasty construction. Attendants and members of the Royal Guard filled this end of the chamber and lined the walls. As the two Outlanders, spotless in their white togas and gigantic among that company, reached the dais, Crosseus rose and accepted their short bows with a casual nod.

"Gentlemen," he said, "I hope you have found our baths to your liking?"

"Oh, definitely," said Thorngere with a twinkle in his eye. "It's the little things in life which bring the most comfort, don't you agree?"

Crosseus laughed at this. "Ah, yes! I see, I see. You have an excellent wit, friend Thorngere. My people love good wit and I am sure they will love you as well. Lord Balazar, of course, has already established his place in the honor and respect of this land. But come, sit by me and we will sup."

As the two Outlanders took their seats, a train of male servants entered carrying small tables, platters of vegetables and fruits and jugs of wine. "You will not be disappointed in this fare, I hope," asked Crosseus? "You see, we eat no meat of any kind."

"No meat?" Balazar exclaimed. "But the Kantaran have always said..."

"You will find, Oh Balazar, that there are many things the Kantaran have said which are not true. For one thing, they cannot even rightfully claim that name. But more of that later. First, let us eat."

They fell to with a will then, Balazar and Thorngere discovering that they were quite famished after their ordeal. Plate after plate of the exotic concoctions found safe haven in their bellies and not a little of the wine. When all was done and the debris cleared away, they each sipped an after dinner cup quite contentedly and missed the meat not at all.

"Now, your Majesty," said Balazar, "you have kept us waiting long enough. A short time ago we were going, we thought, to certain death. Now, we find ourselves welcomed as kings, royally entertained, and intensely curious. Please: enlighten us."

"Yes, it is time," said Crosseus. He had been leaning back in his throne, cleaning his teeth with a golden pick. Now, he sat up and composed himself for speech. His bald head shone under the torches and he stroked his long, wispy beard with an ancient, wrinkled hand. "To understand this land, Oh Balazar, and you too, Friend Thorngere, you must know of its history. My people have suffered much, undergone many trials and, down the long path of the generations, it has only been through our dedication to honor and duty, through our perseverance in times of turmoil and war, that we have been able to survive and grow and build such a city as you see around you. We are a small people, it is true, but our hearts are great, as is our sense of purpose and hope. Though the Kantaran, as you call them, have for years preyed upon us and sought to destroy us utterly, we have endured: yes, even thrived. Our gods are harsh in their demands upon us but rich in their rewards. Though little, we are blessed."

Here Crosseus broke into a chanting prayer in his own language and spread his arms to the heavens.

"But to the story: For many generations- perhaps even from the beginning of time-our people dwelt in peace and comfort in the city you call Kantar, but which, in our language is called Kudan. We reaped the harvests of our fields, fished the waters of the river and the deeps of the sea and traded in our ships with other peoples, great and small, up and down the coast. Our woven cloths were renowned and our work in metals and statuary much sought after. We were a rich people, a happy people.

"But the city of Kantar of today is not the city of those times. It was a great city then, of cobbled streets, shining edifices and splendid halls. It is the Iblis-the people you call Kantaran-who destroyed

78

the city of those days. They are a plague upon us and seek to destroy us. They are a brutish people, ignorant of all culture and utterly incapable either of sailing ships upon the sea or erecting even the simplest of dwellings. As you yourself know, Oh Balazar, they live in horrible sloth in a decaying city and, abomination of abominations, feed upon the flesh of those who once succored them; those who, in fiendish ingratitude, they turned upon with the horror of war and sought to remove from the face of the earth!"

Here again, Crosseus broke into an impassioned prayer, one in which the name Kala Atar figured prominently.

"The Iblis, for that is their true name, came down from the northern mountains, a defeated and utterly wretched people, in the time of Corinon, my ancestor of the seventh generation. There were very few of them then, no more than two score; the bedraggled survivors, from what they said, of a once proud race. But what of the history they related to us is true and what made up to beguile us, the gods only know. They appeared at our gates, half-starved and sick, with only the rags on their backs for possessions.

"We have always been a kind and generous people, Oh Balazar and Friend Thorngere. We took them in, fed them and cared for them, gave them houses and portions of our fields. We tried to teach them our crafts and our ways. But though they grew and multiplied under our care, they failed utterly to blend into our life. They were-there is no other word for it-stupid: incapable of learning either trade or trust. They could hoe a field and make wine, that

79

was all. And all the wine they made, they drank and then lay about in filth and drunkenness. Gradually, we came to use them only as servants because they were fit for nothing else.

"Nor was it long after their arrival that contention arose between them and the people of the city. In the second generation, a leader rose among them-a man named Chulan. He came before Corilon the King-my ancestor-and demanded the return of their cattle which he said had been confiscated when they arrived. He said his people could not live on the fruits of the earth and sea alone, but that they must have meat.

"Now, Corilon was perplexed for he knew nothing of these things and he spoke to Chulan thus: 'Of cattle we know nothing, friend Chulan, for since you had none when you came, none could we take. But neither have we any and so have none to give. We live, as we always have, on the gods' gifts; the fruits of the earth and sea. Of these we give gladly that you also may live.'

"But Chulan and his people did not believe. They thought we had taken their cattle. The truth is that if they ever had any, it was the mountains, or perhaps their old enemies, who took them. Yet they lamented loudly and complained. They refused to work and fell more and more into drunkenness. Still, we endured them with kindness and patience for they were a homeless people, wretched and hopeless. We pitied them. They demanded that we sail in our ships and bring them cattle. But this, of course, we could not do: Kala Atar expressly forbids that the people feast on flesh or take an unwilling life except in war.

"It was then that the murders began-or disappearances, I should say, for at first we did not know what was happening. We suspected them from the first, of course; they being so loud in their discontent and such things being hitherto unheard of among us. We thought they might be holding our people hostage and that they would then make more demands. But then, when we discovered the true nature of their abominations-Kala Atar komen hatar salan dumalai!-we rose up against them and drove them from the city.

"But in our wrath we, too, committed a great sin: one for which Kala Atar has been exacting penance ever since with the very plague we sought to eradicate. You see, they were not then a people great enough to justify war. Yet, in the expelling of them, we killed a small number-komen hatar subai, Kala Atar-and consigned their bodies to the fire instead of to the rightful earth.

"The remaining Iblis fled into the hills and took up the forging of crude weapons and the making of war upon us. Though they sowed not, they reaped the fruits of our fields. Though they sacrificed not to the gods, they feasted upon the flesh of our people. And thus, they multiplied and, year by year, came down more heavily upon us.

"It was in the time of my grandfather-whose name I bear-that they rose up in strength against us and, through treachery and their greater size and strength, drove us from our own city. It was our turn then to flee into the hills and many were the trials we bore. Our ships were lost to us, burned by the Iblis who know naught of the sea; our fields taken over and their fruits denied us. We had nothing but

81

that with which we fled. Many, many were those who went down to death from hunger in that first year.

"But we were a great people yet. We came to this valley, carved out a new city, new fields, built boats to fish in the lake below, and we endured. We thrived and multiplied and, in time, began making war in earnest-and with the blessing of our gods-on our perfidious enemies. That war has continued down through the years, Balazar, Oh greatest of Warriors, and as I sit upon this throne, it will be won!"

Visibly wearied by his narrative, Crosseus fell back into his chair and took a long draught of wine, his hand trembling as it held the cup.

"So now," Balazar said, "you would like to retain our services instead of having to compete with them."

Sighing and wiping his brow, Crosseus sat forward again. "In short, yes. But we come not to that yet. Were it only that simple, we would have tried to do so long before now. But let me explain:

"You, Oh Balazar, are a great and mighty warrior, the greatest my people have ever beheld. Many, many are the foes who have fallen before your sword and this has earned you great honor among us-greater even than you can know.

"You see, when you first came to do battle against us, it was learned from spies that you were called Bala Azar by the Iblis. In our fright and amazement at your prowess, it was believed that Bala Azar was an Iblian bastardization of the name Kala Atar, Most High and Greatest of our gods. It was believed-and still is by many-that you were He, come in person to inflict His penance upon us."

Balazar was astounded. "But why did your warriors fight me if they thought I was a god?"

"Who dares deny the Great One's bidding? By appearing before us armed as a man, it was believed you were bidding us to fight. Is it not man's duty, above all, to obey the will of his gods?"

"Good god!" said Balazar.

"Yes, Kala Atar is indeed a good god. He has given you much strength, though you knew it not. Anyway, it has only been of late that we learned you were not the God but a simple outlander, fighting for hire. It was this knowledge which prompted your, ah, abduction."

"Well, you may rest assured, Majesty, that I am not this Kala Atar, flattering though the association may be. I am simply a man like other men and, as you yourself said, a warrior for hire. Thorngere is also of the profession. But you speak of honor and duty Crosseus: although we fight for hire, we are not without our own such codes. I tell you plainly now that, though you may purchase our services-they go to the highest bidder-you will not force them from us. If you think we will fight for you because the alternative is death, think again. Our arms are free now and it is up to the gods to decree what price you would pay to subdue us again."

"This is as it should be," said Crosseus with a short bow. "You are a true warrior born and deserving of all honor given you. Both of you. But there are no threats here and no need for any. You are our guests and as free as your bonds. When Hudarin found two and not one of you, his people

83

could not carry you and your arms too. But even now a party of warriors approaches the Old City through secret tunnels to retrieve them. When they return, you may don them and go where and when you will. We ask only that you hear us out and treat with us as we do you."

"Fair enough," said Balazar. "Then you need fear nothing from us. But you must also know that I was paid very highly by the Kantaran-the Iblis, as you call them."

"This also we know," said Crosseus with a wave of his hand. "But it grows late and I am an old man. Let us speak of these things another time-when you are armed and know the truth of my words. Tomorrow, with your permission, I would show you our city that you may know us better and of what we speak. Afterwards, will be time enough for other matters."

"So be it, then," said Balazar and the two rose to go.

"Oh, by the way," said Crosseus, the twinkle returning to his eye, "if the women of the baths did please you...?"

"Ah," said Balazar, "we thank you for your kindness and generosity, Majesty, but we are weary and..."

"Now, now, hold on there," said Thorngere. "We don't want to appear inhospitable. I mean, after this wonderful reception, it seems the least we can do... "

They were led to adjoining sleeping chambers where Balazar found a newly constructed bed of more than ample size. Just the sight of it brought a great weariness swirling to the surface of his brain and, though there was much to ponder, he no sooner stretched out upon it than he fell fast asleep.

Next door, however, Thorngere met with a different reception. His chamber, too, sported an outlander sized bed, but sight of it roused sensations other than weariness for, sitting coyly upon it were none other than the three tiny wenches who had so ably assisted him in the bath.

"Well, well, well," said he, "what have we here?"

CHAPTER SIX
The City of New Kantar

"Ah, Balazar, it was incredible, I tell you, just incredible. You wouldn't believe what those little wenches can do!"

"I believe already, I believe! Now, will you stop? Fifteen times now you've you told me how great they are. I believe!"

The two outlanders sat at table in a graciously appointed chamber near the front of the palace, awaiting the appearance of Crosseus to break their fast. In the interim, they sipped a piping hot, chicory flavored brew the servants had prepared. Upon awakening, they had been bathed and oiled again and given clean togas. Mocking Balazar's insistence on braiding his beard, Thorngere had oiled and twisted the ends of his huge moustaches into points which stuck out well beyond his ears. He was in festive spirits after his night's entertainment, and felt himself called upon to cheer up the rather more somber Balazar.

"What happened to the Balazar of old," he mocked, "Who could fight the whole day, out-drink and out-wench his comrades through the night and still be in the front rank with the dawn?"

"He's sitting right here," growled Balazar. "And he's about ready to tie your ears together with that silly moustache."

"Touchy, aren't we? What got into you last night while I was getting into..."

Balazar waved in dismissal. "Ah, I don't know." And, indeed, he didn't know. It was just a feeling. There had been dreams during the night, many dreams. But of their substance he could recall nothing. They had just left him feeling depressed and moody. "I just wonder, that's all."

"You wonder, I'm wonderful! Look, Balazar, yesterday at this time we thought we were heading for the cooking pot. Now, today, we're not only alive and healthy, we're being treated like royalty. So what have you got to complain about? Old Crosseus there even said he'd give us back our weapons. If that happens, they can't touch us. And even if they don't, there's obviously something cooking here. All we've got to do is play along for awhile and then, first chance we get, slip off into the sunset."

"And do what? Go back to Kantar and re-open the butcher shop? Swim out to sea? Or die of exposure in the mountains? No, Thorngere, I'm beginning to wonder if our best cards might not just be in our hands right here, and that we might want to play them very carefully."

"You mean actually fight with these little monkeys? You're crazy! They couldn't stand up to a stiff breeze. We'd just be signing our death warrants."

"Not necessarily..."

"Oh, come on, Balazar," snapped Thorngere, irritable himself now. "Surely you weren't taken in by that line of 'past glories' drivel Crosseus spat up last night!"

"No, no, of course not-not all of it, anyway. But there were parts of it that did make sense."

"What?"

87

"Now, wait a minute," said Balazar, holding up a hand. "I'll grant you that Crosseus exaggerated some last night-he has his own axe to grind, after all-but men in that kind of situation usually don't weave tales out of whole cloth. They just bend the truth to suit their own purposes. And a lot of what he said-no, let me go on-a lot of what he said did make sense. I can recall my teacher when I was a boy telling about the days of old when a race of tiny men in swift ships sailed the Inland Sea and traded with many cities. So strange were they, and so fine were their crafts that people thought them spirits. So there may be truth in what Crosseus says. And I'm thinking now that maybe I should have seen it before. It might have made a difference."

"What do you mean, 'seen it before?'"

"Let me give you an example: when I moved into my house in Kantar, I wanted to have the doors raised. Well, I looked all over the city for a carpenter and couldn't find one who'd do it. I had to do it myself! But it never occurred to me then to wonder who the hell had built the city if there wasn't a single carpenter willing to fix a door. I thought they were just lazy. But, now that I think of it, in all my time in Kantar, I've never seen any building going on. Not even common maintenance! Just a couple months ago, the roof collapsed on a building down by the river. Two or three people were killed. And, do you know, they not only didn't fix the building, they didn't even bother to drag out all the bodies. The ones they could see they pulled out and tossed in the river; the rest, they just left. Raised a hell of a stink. But, do you see what I'm getting at?"

"No," said Thorngere. "Because even if every word Crosseus said last night was the God's own truth, it still wouldn't make one iota of difference to our situation here. But I do see what's getting at you and I don't like it."

"Yeah? What's that."

"You're feeling guilty, that's what. You always were a bleeding heart despite your loutish demeanor. You've been going merrily along, slaughtering these people like beef and now, all of a sudden, you find out they're not only human, but apparently a damn sight more human than the people you were working for. So you feel bad. You want to make amends...

"Well, I say that's rubbish," said Thorngere, his quick temper rising. "And dangerous rubbish to boot. You were paid to fight and you fought. End of story. The rest is none of your concern. But-and this is my point-our hides are still on the line here. And a man who is all down in the dumps over some silly philosophical nonsense is apt to be of little use in a fight. And, by the Gods, if you let me down when it comes to it, I'll crack your skull before they do! I don't care one bit who wins this little war here. All I want to do is get the hell out of here and get back to my own war. Our war. Or, have you forgotten our friend Fantar?"

"Ah, Thorngere, my worthy and most excellent friend," said Balazar, his face breaking into a grin. "As ever, you rush foolishly to the front without thought for your flanks or rear. Fantar is precisely the man I am thinking of. Indeed, I have thought of little else for many years now. So, hold your skull cracking and hear me out-you'll find it's a much easier, and far safer way of finding out what's in my mind."

"The gods would be confused trying to find out what's in your mind. But speak plain."

"Not now. I think I hear the King. For now, just keep your eyes open."

Moving with a brisk step and jaunty air, Crosseus entered at that moment, flanked by members of his Guard. Simply but resplendently dressed this morning in white tunic and purple mantle, his ancient fingers were adorned with gems, and around his neck lay a heavy necklace of plaited gold with a large emerald set in its center. On his shining pate, a golden circlet served for a crown.

"Good morning, gentlemen! Good morning," he said, acknowledging their nods with a broad smile and bidding them keep their seats. "The blessings of the day be with you both. I trust you rested well?"

"Ah," sighed Thorngere with a rueful smile, "I'm afraid I hardly rested at all."

"Don't let him get started, Majesty," said Balazar, "or he'll wear you out, too."

"I'm afraid I was worn out a long time ago when it comes to business such as that," chuckled the king. "But how about some food? I trust you still have your appetite, Friend Thorngere?"

Indeed, he did, and as servants brought in platters of fish and loaves of steaming hot bread, all three fell to with a will.

During the meal, Crosseus pressed the two outlanders for details of their backgrounds. Balazar explained that he was the sole surviving son of a family of lesser Valerian nobility and that Valeria itself was a small but advanced kingdom on the shore of the Inland Sea, far to the north, which was now under control of the spreading Fantaran Empire. Thorngere, however, always guarded when it came to his past, would say only that he came from mountainous lands in the extreme north, and that he had been a wanderer and mercenary from early youth. And, when Crosseus asked how both had come to the valley of Kantar, he was told truthfully enough, except that Thorngere substituted a shipwreck for the more ignominious tale of his being tossed into the sea. It was, of course, a minor point.

"But tell me this," Crosseus continued. "Both of you men are of such great stature-are all your people so large? Our legends of old speak of great men, but we always assumed them to be of Iblian size."

"Well," said Balazar, "neither of us is uncommonly large, but we are, perhaps, larger than most. We are warriors, after all."

"Yes, I see. And the Iblis, then-they would be considered small by your people?"

"Oh, yes. On average, I'd say they would run about a head shorter."

"Amazing! And we? What would your people think of us?"

Balazar hesitated for just a second. "Could they see what you have accomplished here, Majesty," he said, "they would think you very great indeed."

"Ha!" Crosseus laughed. "You have missed your calling, Oh Balazar. You should have been a diplomat. But what have you to say, Friend Thorngere?"

91

"Well, Sire, from what I have seen of your lovely women, I would have to say that physical stature has little relation to... shall we say, depth of feeling?"

"Ah, well put! Well put, indeed," laughed Crosseus, his aged lips parting to reveal scattered teeth. "You, sir, should have been a poet! But come. The sun is over the mountain by now and we have much to see."

He led them out of the palace and down the great steps to the courtyard where a sedan chair and two files of brightly helmed Guardsmen waited. "I hope you will not take it amiss that I should ride while you must walk? I am an old man, you see, and confess I tire easily. Besides, we have no chairs large enough to accommodate you-unless, of course, you would prefer the method used yesterday?"

The outlanders laughed politely at Crosseus' joke, but neither thought it very funny.

By day, the City of New Kantar was even more impressive than it had been by torch light the night before. Everything was immaculate, from the well cobbled streets and freshly whitewashed buildings, to the courtyards and gardens within each building complex. Nowhere was there the least sign of neglect or decay. Most of the buildings were of stone faced with adobe, and even the beam ends which protruded between floors were lacquered and polished. Neither Balazar nor Thorngere had ever seen it's like and, between them, they had seen all the greatest cities of the known world. New Kantar was simply impeccable.

Built under the rearing cliffs, it was surrounded by a semi-circular wall of great height and thickness, like a wheel in which the palace and temple complex formed the hub. The main avenue led from the palace to the west gate and was crossed, midway, by another grand avenue running perpendicular to it from the north to the south gates. Leading off these two main thoroughfares was a grid work of smaller streets which, except in areas directly adjacent to perimeter wall, divided the entire city up into neat, rectangular blocks. Each block, in turn, contained a single rectangular building complex with openings on all four sides and a large open courtyard within. Crosseus explained that most of these were occupied by individual companies of warriors and that the city as a whole was sectioned off into battalions and organized like an armed camp.

"You see," he went on, "most cities grow over time and simply spread out, maze-like from their original center. We, however, were fortunate in that we were able to organize the entire city and build from scratch. Thus, we could profit from all our past experience and did not have to labor under past mistakes."

But not only was the city built according to plan, that plan itself included some ingenious aspects. Most cities of the time used the centers of the streets as sewers and garbage collectors. New Kantar, however, not only had a battalion of warriors assigned as garbage collectors (it was a rotating duty, Crosseus pointed out), but it also had an underground sewer system. Crosseus explained that they had experimented with this kind of thing in the old city but that, because the city encompassed several hills and was already fully built when they started, the scheme had proven impractical. However, he added with a smile, those tunnels which had been built had also proven to be of great value in the war as the Iblis were apparently ignorant of their existence. "It was by means of them that we were able to invite you here," he said.

The most amazing thing, though, was the water system. Every building in the city had running water-this was a thing unheard of in the outside world-and each building also had its own set of heated baths. This had become possible by accident, Crosseus said. When they began quarrying stone from the top of the cliffs, they noticed that the rock was quite impervious and that, when the rains came, their quarry tended to fill. In order to keep working, it had been necessary to drain it via a tunnel which had later converted readily into a supply line and the old quarry into a reservoir. "Also," said Crosseus, "should the Iblis attempt to enter the city through the sewers-they drain into the lake, you see-we can flood the entire system."

Balazar and Thorngere were impressed. Neither had any idea that such things were possible, let alone already in existence somewhere in the world. But as the tour progressed, Balazar became more and more perplexed by certain things he noted-or, rather, didn't note. For one thing, though crowds gathered wherever they went, they were composed exclusively of men. And the only children he saw were companies of young warriors in training barracks. He saw no female children and no women anywhere. Still, he kept these observations to himself until they had gained the wall and from its top, looked out over a barren plain which stretched to the distant forest. Then he spoke.

"Lord Crosseus," he said, "your city is indeed a marvel, but I am puzzled. I see no women, no children and while you say your people eat only the fruits of the earth, I look out here and see no fields whatsoever."

Crosseus smiled like a gambler holding trump. "Your eyes are keen indeed, Oh Balazar. But remember, we are a people at war. Were our fields spread out here and we besieged, what then would be our fate? And if our city was divided up into family homes as was old Kantar, how could we keep discipline or effectively gather and move our troops? But come. I will show you how we have answered these questions."

They went back the way they had come but, on reaching the palace, went around it to the base of the cliff where a huge double gate guarded the mouth of a tunnel. "Here, Balazar, you will find the answer to one of your questions." They entered and Balazar saw it was honeycombed with doorways and other passageways leading off on either hand. "We are a very disciplined and organized society," said Crosseus. "Our very survival depends upon it. Thus, our women and small children live here, where we can best protect them. But come, there is more."

The tunnel continued on, straight and level for nearly a mile, lit along its length by torches. Crosseus explained that fresh air was provided by ventilation shafts which led to the surface all around the quarry. At the far end, they came to another set of gates which the guards swung open to the blinding light of the sun. Squinting in the sudden glare, they stepped out into an incredible scene.

They had gone completely through the mountain and now stood on the verdant floor of an immense valley, ringed all around by sheer cliffs. All about them was alive with green, growing life. Fruits, vegetables and grains of every type flourished there, each in its assigned area and all tended by Kantaran slaves under the guard of Kudanim warriors.

"We do not treat the Iblis as kindly now as we once did," Crosseus said, enjoying immensely the looks of utter astonishment on the faces of his guests, "but, still, I think we treat them better than they treat us!"

"Your Majesty," said Balazar, "we are speechless with wonder. This morning, when you asked how our countrymen would see your people, I spoke from politeness. Now, I say from the heart, you are a very great people indeed!"

"We have worked hard on our city," Crosseus replied, bowing at the compliment, "and feel justifiably proud. But the major credit must go to the gods, for it was they who arranged the mountains so and they who grant the life-giving rains. It was they, too, who led us here in our times of peril. It is to them and to Kala Atar most of all, that the praise for whatever greatness we have achieved must rightly belong. But come, let us go back to the palace. I am sure men of your 'greatness' must be hungry by now."

CHAPTER SEVEN
Other Appearances

After the meal, for which they had baked fish and again enjoyed the hot, chicory brew, a messenger entered and spoke to Crosseus in his own language. He looked pleased at the report and turned to his guests. "Soon, gentlemen, we may speak of business." With this, he turned towards the entrance and clapped his hands twice. Surrounded by two files of Guardsmen, bearers entered carrying a large table which they set down before the window. The Guardsmen flanked it as the bearers withdrew and stood to attention. Upon the table, shined and neatly laid out, was all of Balazar's armor, including his great curved sword or falchion, and another set for Thorngere. "Here, Oh Balazar," said Crosseus, his voice rising into the cadenced rhythms he used for official pronouncements, "here are your arms as I promised you. Your sword is a great one and though my warriors feared to touch it- so many of their kindred has it sent to Kala Atar - they have brought it hither. Wear it now in peace and trust among us, and go, a free man and warrior born, wherever you will."

"The courtesy you have shown me, Lord," Balazar replied, bowing shortly from the waist, "and the great things I have witnessed in your city make me ashamed now that I ever drew that sword against you. We thank you for the honor and trust you have shown us and, as I am sure Thorngere here will agree, freely renew the bond we gave when you first released us: that was given as one takes a part in a play. This is given from the heart. In fact, were I a free agent now, there would be no question but that I would bind myself to your service, as you indicated was your desire."

"But how are you not free now?" asked Crosseus, perplexed.

"It is but a point of honor, Lord, but I am bound, by oath, to serve the Kantaran-those you call the Iblis."

"Ah, I see," returned Crosseus. "Make not light of honor, Oh Balazar, but this oath, is it not of a contractual nature, and based upon a fair exchange of obligations?"

"Ah, now I see, Majesty! So you know about my recent difficulties with Haradin as well."

"The shadows are deep near his walls."

"Then it is but a matter of negotiation."

"Have no fear on that score, Balazar," Crosseus laughed. "In case you have not guessed, our mountains are also rich in gold and precious stones. But these things must be dealt with in council, with all my assembled chieftains and with scribes in attendance. Arm yourselves now, like warriors, and come before me in the council chamber when I summon." With this, Crosseus rose and started to leave. At the door, though, he turned. "By the way, how much was it the Iblis were paying you?"

"Three cunae per head-before Haradin tried to cheat me."

Crosseus snorted. "They are as miserly as they are depraved." Pulling his mantle about him and giving his head a majestic toss, he left them.

"Well," said Balazar as the two donned their arms, "what do you think now?"

98

"I've seen better blades," said Thorngere, drawing his and testing its balance. "kind of hefty on the business end."

"They make good cleavers-my own design, you know. But don't change the subject."

"What subject is that?"

"You know damn well what subject. Don't be obstinate."

"All right, all right," said Thorngere, shoving the sword back into its sheath, "I'm impressed. These little buggers have built quite a town. But I don't see why that should change anything."

"You still don't think these people could build ships?"

"Well, from what we've just seen, they probably could. But I haven't seen anything to convince me they can fight."

"Well, I've got my own doubts there. But I still say the potential of this place-the whole valley, I mean-is worth the risk."

"Sure, it would be a great place, like you said the other night. We could feed and train an entire army in here with Fantar none the wiser. So, let's do it! Let's get out of here now, come back with a few good men and take it!"

"Damn it, man, I tell you, there's no way out of here but by the way we got in-by the sea! And by your own account, that means having a fast ship to outrun Fantar's cutters. And the only way I can see to get a fast ship is to help these people win their war and have them build us one. Besides, why make enemies of these people when they obviously would make such valuable friends? Think of how much help they could be if we did start fitting out an army."

Thorngere walked over to the table and poured himself more wine. "All right, Balazar, what you say makes sense. And if I thought these people had a chance in hell of standing up against the Kantaran, I'd agree with you. But you know yourself what kind of fighters they are-or aren't! If we go marching into battle with troops like these, we'd be slaughtered. On the other hand, if we follow my plan and go out and get some men, we can still ally ourselves here and then stand a good chance of winning."

"Sure, if we could get out." Balazar too, poured himself some wine and tossed in off in exasperation. "But we can't get out, I tell you! There's no way over those mountains."

"No way, huh? Who was it this very morning who said there was truth in what Crosseus told us last night? Well? And didn't he say the Iblis came from those mountains in the first place? And if those idiots made it over-with their women, mind-don't you think two strapping fellows like us could?"

To this, Balazar had no answer. Glowering, he paced back and forth, slapping his hand on his thigh. "Besides," said Thorngere, thinking he was delivering a final shot, "there's no such thing as an impassable mountain. Believe me, I've been climbing them all my life. I was born on one. I guarantee I can get us through."

"Well, maybe you can," said Balazar. "Maybe you can," and he resumed his pacing. But his movements were more solemn now, not so agitated, as his thoughts went deeper. Thorngere sipped his wine and watched his comrade with expectation, sure that he had won the debate. Finally, Balazar turned to face him, his own face set and determined.

."Thorngere," he said, "you may well have the right in this and you may say that I'm acting out of guilt or shame, or something, but I'm going to stay and fight with these people. You say I was only doing my duty in fighting against them-and you're right there, too. But I feel I've done a great wrong and I must help set it right. It's not just that I have slaughtered so many-that's just war. It's that I have delivered their corpses to be eaten. I've eaten them myself! When I thought both sides were engaged in the same practice, it didn't bother me-customs of the country, and all that. And I didn't have a great deal of choice in the matter. But now I see that it has all been one-sided and that, to my lights, makes it a great sin. And it's on my head. Now, you have not been involved in any of this and I have no hold over you. You do what you will but I am going to stay here and fight."

From the look in his companion's eye, Thorngere saw that further argument was useless and that it was his turn now to make a decision. He made it quickly.

"Well," he said, "I'm with you then. I don't want it said of me that I left a boon companion in peril. But do let us hope the gods protect fools!"

"They have up till now," said Balazar and they both laughed,

The business portion of the matter was soon transacted. Summoned by a Guardsman, Balazar and Thorngere were led to a small council chamber

101

adjacent to the great hall. Crosseus was there, seated at the head of a large table, flanked on either hand by a group of venerable counselors, among whom was Hudarin, the aged chieftain who had commanded their abduction. He raised his fist in greeting and smiled broadly.

Crosseus, now wearing a golden crown and a mantle of furs, rose and motioned for silence. "Lords and counselors of the People," he intoned, "we are met here today to witness and pledge an agreement between ourselves and these two outland warriors, who are fighters for hire. It is our purpose to acquire and bind them to our service in our great struggle against the Iblis, most infernal of peoples."

Quelling the stir of approbation this announcement occasioned, Crosseus turned to the two outlanders who now stood facing him at the other end of the table.

"Balazar, Oh Greatest of Warriors, and Thorngere, Friend of Balazar and Warrior

strong, hear this, our offer unto you: upon your consent to lead us in our strife, you will each receive quarters of your choosing within the city, sustenance and servants included, and a sum, in gold, of two hundred Cunae per month. Should you then lead us into battle, you will receive for every Iblian man taken or killed, by any hand under your command, the sum of twenty Cunae to be divided between you as you see fit. And, should your efforts be successful and we once again gain possession of our ancestral city, you will receive as an additional reward, as much in gold and precious gems as can be borne by the cart which brought you hither. On this you have the sacred word and bond of

102

Crosseus, Lord and King over all Kantar. What say you?"

"Majesty," said Balazar, bowing before the king for the first time, "your terms are most generous. For my part, I accept them gladly."

"Friend Thorngere?"

"I too," said Thorngere, bowing as well, "will be your loyal servant in this work."

"So let it be written, so let it be done." Quickly, a scribe produced a copy of the agreement and all present, beginning with the three principals, affixed their signatures. Wine was then brought in and with prayers, libations and a toast to victory, the ceremony was completed.

More wine was brought in and tables of food and a reception commenced with much gaiety all around. Led by Crosseus, Balazar and Thorngere were introduced to all the military leaders and chief magistrates, such a profusion of titles and names they were at a loss to keep track. All treated them with utmost deference and respect, even awe, and on no face could Balazar discern even the slightest trace of hatred or malice. This seemed strange to him for not only did he expect a certain amount of reservation-he was wearing, after all, a freshly turned coat-but it had been just two days since he had been amidst a similar press of Kudanim under considerably different circumstances. None of this seemed to matter, however, and the crowd soon became boisterous.

Introductions completed, Crosseus led them back to Hudarin, the aged warrior who had conducted their abduction and who, it turned out, was the leading chieftain of the army.

"Now, gentlemen," said Crosseus, rubbing his hands in evident satisfaction, "I will leave you with Hudarin here, our noble Commander in Chief. He will see to your quarters and pay, and will henceforth act as your Chief of Staff."

Hudarin watched the king depart, then turned and smiled a warm, gap-toothed smile at the two outlanders. "There, gentlemen," he said, "you have a perfect example of the privileges of rank: our dear King allows nothing-no matters of state great or small-to come between him and his afternoon nap. But allow me to congratulate you both on your appointments and to offer my own personal apology for the inconvenience necessary in bringing you here."

"No apology is necessary," said Balazar. "Besides, I think the greatest burden of that journey fell on the poor warriors who had to carry us. For myself, I found the trip rather comfortable."

"Yes," said Thorngere, "that was definitely the softest rope I have ever been tied with," and all three laughed politely.

"But seriously, Lords," Hudarin went on, "let me assure you of my support as well as that of the army. For long generations we have been making war on the Iblis with little success. Now, with two great warriors to lead us, we are convinced that victory is at hand. And we are ready and willing to make any sacrifice to attain it. You have but to ask and you will be obeyed."

"Thank you," said Balazar. "And in return, you have my assurance that if there is any way for victory to be had, we will have it, or die in the attempt. Now, as for instructions, there is much we must learn before we can hope to lead you effectively. As the King suggested, we will see to our quarters now. But in the morning-at dawn, in fact-we will inspect the troops. Have them in full battle gear and prepared for review. Afterwards, we will meet with all senior officers and staff down to battalion commanders and their assistants."

Snapping to attention, the aged Hudarin struck his fist to his chest in salute. "I hear, Warlord, and will obey!"

Hudarin was wrong on one point: the departing Crosseus did not retire to his chamber for a nap. Instead, he halted in a small antechamber just off the throne room where, aided by his servant, he removed his crown and robes of office, all his jewelry, even his richly adorned tunic. In its place he donned a plain white toga, and bereft even of a cloak, exited through a rear door, looking every bit the common, aging man.

With slow, wearied steps, he wound his way through hidden corridors and passageways, mounting with heavy tread several stairways, and working his way ever upward and inward towards the very heart of the mountain. His face, as he passed under the torches along the way, gradually transformed itself, his brows furling, his cheeks and mouth sagging, the lines and creases of his age seeming to etch themselves deeper until, by the time he reached his destination, he no longer looked the wise and regal king of a great and industrious people, but an ancient, care ridden wretch, one gripped to the very bowels by a horrible dread. His hands developed a palsied twitch and his step, not strong since he started, so faltered now that he more than once had to stop and lean against the wall for support.

Finally, his tremulous feet led him through a curtained arch and into a brilliantly lit chamber whose furnishings and decorative splendor made his own great chamber look like a kennel. Light in a thousand colors spilled through crystal panels in the ceiling and swirled about like an underwater paradise. Rainbows danced and twirled on the floors, over delicately carved furnishings, gold, silver, and marble statuary, and across ornately paneled walls in ever-changing, ever-blending, ever-hallucinating bands. Crosseus, ancient and enfeebled, his features distorted and mauled by the light, fell to his knees and pressed his forehead to the floor. There, he waited.

After a time, a voice arose from somewhere in the swirling, unplumbed depths of the room. "Why, what is this?" It was a male voice, high pitched and sarcastic, but speaking a delicately articulated Kudanese.

"Don't you know?" said another voice, female this time, but in the same, scornful tone. "This is Crosseus, His Nothingness Himself."

"Ah, yes, the mongrel king," returned the first. "I should have detected the scent. What would you, hound?"

Crosseus tried to speak but his voice cracked. He coughed to clear his throat and began again. "I would see the Queen, Lord." He spoke without raising his head.

"The Toy King would see the Queen," mocked the voice. "What say you, Seris, should this insult

106

be tolerated, or should we have him flogged and dismembered?"

"Enough, Koltar," said the female. "You know he is expected. Come, Crosseus. Salonis awaits you." The two figures emerged from the deep pools of light then, and led Crosseus between them. Though he kept his head sunk between his shoulders and dared not glance to either side, he towered over his guides even as Balazar towered over the Kantaran. They accompanied him across the great chamber and down a resplendent hall, lit all in blues and greens, until they came to the threshold of a huge set of ornately carved double doors. Here, they delivered him into the hands of a female attendant and left him.

Preceding him, this woman entered a domed chamber, lit all in gold and red and announced him. "Mistress Salonis, the Warrior King Crosseus."

"Let him come forward." The voice was cold and of unquestioned command. Crosseus came forth but dared not raise his eyes. When he reached the dais upon which sat the Queen's golden throne, he prostrated himself and touched his lips upon the first step. "Well?" Her voice echoed in the chamber.

Trembling and utterly subservient, Crosseus stole a glance at the figure of the Queen. Though of the same stature as all Kudanim women, she was of immense girth. Flaming red hair pillowed her head like a halo and her eyes, in the light, seemed to flash sparks of red fire. "It is done, Mistress," he said.

"They are engaged?"

"As you bade. But please, I beg of you," Crosseus whimpered. "I fear I have offended Kala Atar with this work. Let me go to him."

"Be still! You are my servant before Kala Atar's. And my servant you will remain until I give you to him." Then, in a kinder though hardly softer tone, she continued, "but fear not, old one. You do a great service here, one for which Kala Atar will smile upon you. Just play your part as I have bidden and all will go well. This dark one, Balazar-he is a great lumbering fool, is he not?"

"Indeed, Mistress. As pompous as he is large."

"But the blond-I am told he already begins to breed? That is good. See that the other does so as well. See that they both have all they can bear.

CHAPTER EIGHT
A Bard Sings

That evening the great audience hall of Crosseus was made ready for a banquet. Long tables were set up, one on the dais before the throne and others stretched in parallel rows down the length of the hall. Cloths of white linen with gold and silver embroidery were laid over these and centerpieces of many different flowers set in delicately ornamented vases placed at intervals between ornately fashioned candelabras. Oblong shaped plates, glazed in brilliant patterns of color were set out to serve at least a hundred guests. Places were set along the outside of the tables only, so that all seated would face inward. In the space between, thick carpets were laid and at the far end of the hall, stools were placed for musicians. Last, in the corner between the dais and the right hand row of tables, a single stool was set for the single use of the chief entertainer of the evening.

The guests, many of the same who had attended the reception in the afternoon (some of whom were still showing the effects of the wine there) assembled shortly after the beginning of the evening watch, all bathed and oiled and dressed in their richest finery. Crosseus, the two outlanders, and Hudarin received them at the door, and servants ushered them to seats each according to his rank. Assembled were all the chief dignitaries and military officials of New Kantar and many were the gemmed rings and richly jeweled necklaces and bracelets among them. All wore brilliantly white tunics and cloaks of various colors and lengths designating their offices. Aside from Crosseus and the two outlanders, who flanked him at table (and had some difficulty fitting their knees under it) others on the dais included Hudarin, Commander-in-Chief of the Army, Koltus, Chief Administrator of the City, Maltinus, Chief of Engineering and Architecture, Valencius, Hudarin's Chief of Staff, and three of the King's principal advisors, Tarmin, Fabrinan and Delcinius. These were all grave men, well advanced in years and rigid with formal deportment. Along the right hand row of tables were ranged the various military commanders down to the battalion level and along the left hand row, a retinue of senior civil officials. Among the whole there was not a single female.

The guests sat sipping wine and chatting among themselves until a large gong was sounded and Crosseus rose to speak. He looked pale and wan in his finery, despite earlier claims of having had a delightful nap, and chanted a short benediction to Kala Atar before launching into an introductory speech citing the occasion and lauding everything in sight from the honor and formidable presence of the outlanders themselves to the very artistry with which the tables had been set. During the more tedious portions of the speech, Thorngere, who sat to the king's left, caught Balazar's eye behind that worthy's back and with various smirks and winks, set him to choking in trying to stifle a giggle.

"But there is one other thing, honored guests, Chieftains and Lords here assembled," Crosseus said towards the close, "of which we must make mention and devote special praise. As you all no

110

doubt know, our outlander companions here are eaters of meat." There was some coughing and murmuring among the crowd at this which Crosseus silenced with a wave of his hand. "Well, Kala Atar, most High and revered of all the Gods of Kantar, knows this well, and it was through his designs that a most special offering of welcome be made to them. As the invitations to this banquet were being sent forth this afternoon, at the very moment, in fact, when the messenger delivered the invitation to Coxius here, our Eighth Battalion Commander, who was at work with his men in the new quarry-at that very moment, I say, a young pony which was being led along the pit stumbled and, pitching headlong onto the rocks below, gave up its gift of life. This death, coming as it did at such a moment, gentlemen, can only be taken as a sign from the Great God himself, a sacred dispensation. Thus, without the breaking of a single taboo, it pleases me, honored guests and new leaders of our cause, to give you... meat!"

The gong sounded again and two servants entered holding overhead huge platters heaped with steaming roast equine which were set with great ceremony and accompanying applause, before the two outlanders. There was more than the two of them could eat in a week. Other servants, a whole parade of them, followed then bearing platters of more traditional fare and, at the word from Crosseus, the musicians began to play and all fell to with a will.

"Well, are you pleased?" asked Crosseus, seated once more and turning his beaming face from one outlander to the other.

"Oh, grateful," said Balazar, already stuffing his face. "Very grateful indeed, your Majesty."

"And you, Friend Thorngere?"

"Majesty," Thorngere quipped, "Your timing is perfect: I can't remember when I've felt more like a horse's ass!"

More speeches followed the meal, standard fare all of them, honoring Balazar and Thorngere and boasting of imminent victory. Hudarin spoke of the discipline and courage of the Kudanim warriors and how, with the aid of the two Warlords, the next banquet would be a victory celebration in the old city itself. Koltus, the Administrator, spoke of the city's self-sufficiency in case of siege and quoted long statistics on the amount of stores laid by. Maltinus, the Architect, told of plans already drawn for rebuilding and modernizing the old city once it was retaken. It was dull stuff, most of it, through which both Balazar and Thorngere had to stifle many a yawn but which, nonetheless, was encouraging in one respect: though this war had dribbled on for ages, it now seemed that the Kudanim were at last serious about winning it.

Next however, was a long series of toasts, for each of which it was the custom to quaff an entire cup of wine, and by the time the entertainment started, the party was beginning to liven. Bit by bit the stern masks of authority and self-importance which the great chieftains wore began to melt away. Here an eyebrow raised, there a wooden, disapproving mouth flashed a quick grin, here again a hard eye twinkled and there, most astounding of all, one particularly stern and ancient minion actually laughed out loud. This latter seemed to act as a general signal and it was as if a fresh breeze had swept stale clouds from the room. The last toast-to Victory and Kala Atar-was met with wild cheers and from then on the room was in a constant uproar of merriment and excitement. Even Crosseus seemed to perk up and his voice-it was he who gave the last toast-positively vibrated with boyish energy.

Once the ice had been broken there seemed to be no stopping these little men in their pursuit of festivity. They were like schoolboys let loose on holiday. Wine flowed like a river and it seemed all the servants could do to keep up with demand (though from the increasing stagger of a few of them, it was evident they were finding some time for a bit of quaffing on their own). The band struck up a lively ditty and several of the younger officers jumped up and began dancing a kind of jig. A troop of acrobats entered and had no sooner begun their routine of tumbling and gymnastics than they were joined by several of the guests who had from somewhere come under the impression that their own reelings and floppings qualified them to join in. Others began singing a rousing chorus of some song or other (not the one the band was playing) and one gentleman, feeling slighted at not having the opportunity to speak before, now got up onto his table and began delivering a harangue on virtue and morality. He was quickly dragged down, however, and force fed about half a jug of wine. This apparently occasioned a revolution in his thinking for he was soon back up on the table composing an impromptu ode to revelry. In this endeavor he was not only allowed to continue, but was applauded most heartily.

Not to be outdone and finding his own natural high spirits responding to the occasion, Thorngere vaulted the table and joined the tumblers in the role of stanchion and springboard, and was soon flipping them high in the air like children and catching them again as they plummeted, kicking and squealing back to earth. Then he did a few flips and handstands of his own and was cheered wildly on all sides. Balazar, however, did not join in but kept his place beside the benignly smiling Crosseus, feeling it incumbent upon himself to maintain at least some shred of dignity as guest of honor and only other representative of the larger race. Then, too, he was not quite as agile an athlete as Thorngere and thought it wise to avoid a competition.

A juggling act followed the tumblers but had little luck with their balls as a game of leap frog kept hopping among them. The dancers who came next fared even worse as their members were bodily dragged off and replaced by drunken guests. A singer was not heard at all, but through it all the band played on and everyone seemed to be having a marvelous time.

Then, when the pandemonium was at its height (there were none now in their seats except Crosseus and Balazar) and it seemed that the only thing left for the riotous celebrants to do was tear down the hall itself, the great gong was sounded again and silence fell like a shroud over the whole crowd. Meekly, their faces once more studious and grave, they resumed their places and sat, their hands folded before them, like attentive school children. Even Thorngere caught the signal and, casting a confused

114

and slightly abashed glance at Balazar, resumed his seat as well. Crosseus rose.

"Honored guests and gentlemen all, I give you Teukonis the Teller."

A very ancient man was led in. Stooped and half blind from cataracts, he shuffled up the aisle between the tables with his hand on the shoulder of a boy and took his place upon the single stool before the dais. He was a very tiny man, the smallest by more than a head of all the company present. And this also was different about him: where most of the Kudanim had little, if any facial hair, this ancient wore a long white beard, very thick and full, which was tucked into the belt of his tunic. Once seated, a servant came forward and placed in his hands a six stringed lyre of polished hardwood. Deathly silence reigned throughout the hall as Teukonis plucked and tuned his instrument and on every face was written reverence and awe. His preparations complete, the old man looked up and even through the cataracts, Balazar could see there was fire in his eyes.

"Crosseus," said the Teller in a schoolmaster's tone, his voice surprisingly rich for such a tiny creature and filling the hall, "two days ago you asked of me that I translate portions of our Great Song into common speech for the benefit of these outlanders here, should your planned negotiations bear fruit. I told you then that such a translation, besides verging on blasphemy, was a foolish and impossible task-especially so in the time allotted. I tell you so again. Had I a hundred times two days, a thousand times, such a task could not be done. Trying to force the rhythms and inflections of the

115

Great Language into those of common speech is akin to forcing the foot of one of these outlanders into my shoe." A ripple of laughter interrupted him at this and, true performer that he was, he took it as his due and paused before resuming his speech. "Still, you have insisted and I, moved as well by other forces, have done my best to comply."

"Worthy Teukonis," returned Crosseus, "well do we know the difficulty of the task we set you, and the more do we honor you for your efforts. We did not expect success-for as you say, that would indeed be impossible-but only that you would capture some of the flavor and substance of our Great Song so that these honored guests could know and understand us a little better. And we are sure that of all the Tellers in this realm, past as well as present, only you could come close to success.

Teukonis acknowledged the compliment with a haughty toss of his head, then struck a resounding chord upon the lyre. The music swelled up, filled the hall and seemed to electrify the very air. After a few bars which set the tone, the Teller added his own clear melodic voice and began the song:

Sing in me Thetis, Oh daughter of Quin,

And Goddess of Song, that tale of sad Crosseus,

A King great in wisdom, and greater still

In the love of his clan: Tell how he met harsh fortune

At the hand of Kala Atar, Most High of Gods;

Tell of his Devil Driven Minions, the Iblis,

Most demented and wasted of all the Earth's races;

116

Tell how this Crosseus was beguiled and betrayed,
How, bleeding and bent with life-crushing woe,
He led his shorn flock to the Cave Under Hill
Where the Great God Dwelt and where a City was built.
What was his sin, this most vaunted of Kings,
A man skilled and wise in all the world's ways
Yet humble and heart-honed to duty's cruel Call?
Excess of kindness and trust thrust him down,
And withered the juice of a great people's loins.
'Out of heart, out of pocket,' sings the Sage.
And this, it is said, stoked the High God's Rage.

Teukonis' song went on, harmonic and fluid, his rich voice pushing the words like clouds across a gentle sky, and all present came under the spell, their eyes distant and mellow, their bodies swaying softly to the rhythms of the lyre as if brushed by that same dreamy breeze. It told the same story, essentially, as Crosseus had told the night before, but told it in the glory of song and made it come alive. Here Crosseus of old was no longer an ancient memory, the long dead bearer of a still living name. Once again he lived and breathed before them as he paced his hall, received the homeless Iblis, gave wealth to them from the bounty of his heart, and then writhed on the bitter blade of betrayal.

It was a story enhanced, no doubt, by time and the poet's art, but it was potent nonetheless and Balazar, too, swayed with the teller's lilting rhythms. But after a time his mind drifted and he began to sway not to Kantaran visions, but to

117

deeper, stronger ones of his own. Many times since his arrival in New Kantar, he had been struck by the familiarities-with feelings almost like dejà vu-between New Kantar and Valeria, his ravaged home. He saw them everywhere, in the styles of dress and architecture, in the efficiency and order of the city, at the baths and this banquet, and now, under the hypnotic rhythm of the song, all these things came together and he was thrust into a reverie of distant Valeria. How many times in his youth had he sat in Hall like this and listened to similar singers sing similar tales?

Ah, Valeria, he sighed. Sweet, fallen Valeria. The jewel of the Inland Sea. Was it there still? Was anything left at all? Or had Fantar and his 'popular' army razed it completely, leaving only a pile of rubble and stone? It had been a great city once, perhaps the greatest the world had ever known, a marble chimera on a golden plain, nestled between snow-capped peaks and the blue sparkle of the sea. Its ships had plied all the ports of the world bringing home wealth and vast stores of goods: silk from Palmeria, grain from the great plains of Dulcai, spices from the east, gold and silver from the furnace lands of the south. None could match Valeria. Scholars and poets, philosophers and merchants flocked there. Nowhere were there richer markets, finer statuary, airier or more pleasant abodes, happier or more contented people. Nowhere was there a library its equal or a body of law more just. There was not even an equal for its mineral baths which, it was said, cured even the ravages of old age. Nor was there anywhere else a High King like Valerius. Valerius Everreigning, King of the

118

Eye. Until Fantar came with that ragged, starveling host at his heels.

"To arms! To arms! A great host approaches the city!" Balazar could still hear the alarm. He had been in the baths when the messenger came, a chubby, cherub faced lad, splashing and laughing with his friends. Little did he know then that it was to be the last time.

Still wet and holding up his breeches, he had rushed home to find his father already armed for battle. "Ah, my son," his father had said as he bent to strap on a polished greave, "an evil day has befallen our city. That dog Fantar howls at our gates with a wild pack at his heels. He howls for blood and meat but we shall give him only bones-his own to chew on in hell! But come, my son," he said, leading Balazar aside, "I have important work for you. You must take your mother and go..."

"No, father! I must fight with you."

"Oh, no, my son. You are too young. You must..."

But Balazar had stopped and stood square and tall before his father and looked him in the eye. "I lack but three months of my majority, father. You must let me fight-especially now. All my friends will fight and I will be branded a coward if you send me away!"

And his father had stared hard at him, his face wrenched with that anguish only a father can know who loves his son more than himself, and knows, too, that the boy must become a man. "Yes, my son, I know you are near a man's estate, and that you can bear a man's arms. But you are also the King's son and you must bend to a higher duty. On you must

119

fall the protection of those we most dearly love: Arm yourself, therefore, and go to your mother, gather the women and children of the court-No, do not argue with me, Valerian! Go with your mother. Should the god's will be against us this day, you must preserve our future. You must lead your mother and the other noble women to safety."

Thus he had commanded, but young Valerian had not obeyed. Instead, he had gone to his friend, a boy named Balazar, and had commanded him to the task he was to have done. Then, in Balazar's armor, he had gone out to test himself in battle.

And oh how proud that Balazar had been, marching in the ranks for the first time in a man's helm, the great Falcon banner of Valerius fluttering over all and the long ranks stretching out across the plain. How his bowels had churned with dread and excitement! How his fingers shook! And then the advance, Fantar's raging hordes sweeping across the plain towards their tightly phalanxed line, the dust whipping about in a swirling cloud, the yells from thousands of throats filling the air! Oh, how his heart had pounded! What glory, what majesty was here!

Then the ranks closed. He picked his man, raised his arm to strike... and pitched forward into a blackness from which he had never fully emerged.

Now, in the great hall of Crosseus in New Kantar, Teukonis' tale wound down and a hush fell over the hall. He had told how his people had fled from their defeat and lived to rebuild and renew. Balazar, too had fled, but as a lone survivor, and not to rebuild, but to fight and fly and live always under an ill-defined but ever nettling shame. None had

120

ever accused him-indeed, there were none alive who really even knew him-but it was there all the same: that feeling of failure, that nagging thought that he could have done something, that he should have done more, even if it was only to die. That he was not worthy.

And now, another thing began troubling him as well. Over the many years since Valeria's fall, and despite the upheavals in his life, Balazar had settled into a pattern, an identity, a history. He was who he was, things were as they were. Even his isolation in Kantar had not changed the fundamental fabric of who and what he had become. Now, another, older pattern, long repressed and sometimes even denied, began to emerge and reassert itself. Like lava, it oozed up through the cracks and lay glowing in his mind, hot and explosive.

Balazar heard hardly a word of Teukonis' tale but he appeared as moved as the rest when, in that brief, stunned silence between the end of the song and wild applause, he reached up and wiped away the mist from his eyes.

"You weave a strong spell," he said to the wizened little figure when Crosseus summoned him to the dais. "I have not met its like since I was a lad at home."

"If such spells are to your liking," the little man retorted, "perhaps you should have stayed at home."

Balazar started at this rebuff, then decided to ignore it. "Would that I could have, Teller. Unfortunately, like the people in your song, I, too, was driven from my home. Had I remained, I fear I would have been dead long since."

121

"That may be," Teukonis replied. "But had you died then, you would have been free to claim your honor. It is only we the living, who have not yet been Called, who must live in constant struggle, and fear, and uncertainty-and have Him still there to face. But who knows what might have been? Or what is yet to be? Had you remained, perhaps you would have prevailed and have risen to become a great king. Perhaps there is yet a kingdom before you. Perhaps only death." And with this the little creature turned and shuffled off leaving Balazar feeling exposed and shaken.

"Well, I'll give you one thing," said Thorngere. "These little fellows certainly know how to throw a party!" It was quite late. He and Balazar were making their way through the maze of the palace to their quarters. Both were tipsy and weaved a bit as they walked but, like the old soldiers they were, staggered in step. As they neared Thorngere's door, they could hear giggling and a rustling on the bed from within. "And hey!" said Thorngere, "it's not over yet!"

"Wait a minute," Balazar said. "First, tell me what you think."

"What I think?" said Thorngere, rolling his eyes. "Balazar, my friend, I think you think too much. You're always taking things apart to analyze them, then wondering why they don't seem the same when you put them back together-if you can get them back together. Now me, I know what I like and what I want, but I don't have to tip things upside down to see why they're right side up. You know that if I had my way, we'd be several miles north of here by now. But we're not. You said you want to do this thing and I'm with you. So, let's just do it. Besides," he added, hearing more giggles and squeals from his room, "there are other things to think about at the moment!"

Balazar left him and, shaking his head ruefully, made his way on down the corridor to his own quarters. Though flushed as well from all the toasts, re-toasts and final toasts, his mood was still somber after the Teller's tale and the surprising events of the past couple days.

As he neared his chamber he could see a dim light splashing into the corridor. A single candle there guttered upon a small bedside table and flickered eerie shadows about the walls. Balazar stepped into the room and stopped. There, curled into a tiny bundle in the center of the bed and fast asleep, was another of the Kudanim serving wenches. Looking down upon her, at her sweet, cupid face nestled in a cupped palm, at her child's dimpled knees drawn up, at the loose hair lying wispily across her brow and flowing out over the pillow, all thoughts of sleep left him. But it was not lust that was awakened. As sweet as these bits of wenches were to look at, they aroused no fire. They were too childlike and, to his cursed imagination, reminded him too much of the dead children of Valeria, cut down before they could grow and now, without growing, somehow matured into a grotesque adulthood. The sight of them mocked and pained him; mocked his massive power and total impotence, and dug fresh tissue from old wounds.

With a snort, Balazar cursed his morbid brain and stole softly from the room. Fresh air was what he wanted! Something to clear his brain, dispel this fog of soiled memory. With a determined stride he left the palace, mounted the wall and walked the circuit of the ramparts, the guards snapping hasty salutes and wondering at this huge apparition passing their posts. He stopped at its western extremity, looked out over the plain beyond, and drank in the cool, velvety darkness of the night.

By the gods, he thought, this was what he needed. Clean, free air! He had had enough of lost thoughts and lost days. Tomorrow was a new day! Maybe there were things he could do, both to expiate his sin and help those poor lost children of Valeria. At least there was a chance. Besides, he now had an army to command! Perhaps Teukonis told a better tale than he knew!

BOOK TWO
THE WARLORD

CHAPTER ONE
A Fearsome Sight to Behold

It lacked an hour of dawn when Colinus, newly appointed Sub-Chieftain of the Fourth Battalion, rose from his cot in the chill grey light and by the glow of a single candle, began attending to his armor. Though it had been polished and buffed to a high sheen by his servant the night before, Colinus was still too new to his rank, too set in the old habits of self-sufficiency, and too excited by the prospects of the day ahead to be satisfied with any ministrations performed by another. One does not spend more than twenty of his thirty odd years in absolute awe of such official regalia to be negligent of it on the very first occasion one has to wear it. So, sitting on a stool in his tiny room and wearing only his night shift, Colinus polished and buffed and polished again, the work warming his chilled bones and kindling his imagination with the events of the day ahead.

Not only was this to be the first time he would stand before the battalion as Sub-Chieftain in ceremonial review (as if that were not thrill enough), it was also the first time he would see up close and perhaps even speak to the new Warlord of the city, the gigantic outlander Balazar-Bala Azar the Great One, Bala Azar the Scourge of the People,

Bala Azar the Butcher of Armies, Bala Azar who now came to lead them to victory.

All the battalion was a-buzz with it. All the city, in fact. Bala Azar had come. Bala Azar would lead them. The Iblis would fall before him like wheat before the scythe. They would take the Old City, honor would be redeemed. There were even some who, despite official pronouncements to the contrary, still believed him to be the God Himself, Kala Atar, finally propitiated after all these long years, and come to shepherd His people.

Of course, as Sub-Chieftain of the battalion, it was Colinus' duty to quash such rumors: the man's name was Balazar, and though gigantic, he was but a simple outlander, in no way a God. Nor the other, Thorngere. They were but men, even, he had been informed, rather inferior men when it came to brains. And there would be no instant victory. The war, if successful at all, would be long and hard, with many called to Kala Atar. That was the official line. But still, the name Bala Azar came so readily to the tongue after all this time, and the association with the God were so enticing, that it was hard even for him not to feel a twinge of excitement at the prospects, or to deny all credence to the rumors.

Dawn came late to the city tucked in under the western side of the high cliffs, and the sun later still, but as Colinus finished his work and held up his breast plate to survey it, a curious thing happened. A single shaft of sunlight, perhaps the first to clear the mountain, reflected off something to the west-perhaps something atop the wall or even something on the western hills across the valley-shot back through his window opening, struck the very center of his new beaten steel breast plate with the delicate gold inlay, and shattered into a thousand glittering gems of colored light. It was there and gone in an instant, but so strange was it, and so blinding its momentary flash, that Colinus' heart leapt: surely it was an omen, a private revelation of some greatness to come, sent by the God himself.

In a worse state of nerves now than before, Colinus bellowed for his servant, who was still asleep on his pallet outside the door and, with his aid, quickly donned his armor. First came his best tunic, pure white with the double stripe of Sub-Chieftain embroidered in green around the sleeve; then his finest sandals with the boiled leather thongs. Over them went leather grieves, reinforced with bright metal scrollwork. Next, a jerkin of padded leather to protect his chest beneath the metal plate, and a skirt of heavy leather leaves. Then came the plate itself, belted on and harnessed at the back (and Colinus imagined he could feel a tingle where the light had struck), his sword with its carved bone hilt and inlaid scabbard, secured at his side by a double wrapped sash, and over all, his half cloak of green. Last came his steel helmet, leather lined and sporting a feathered plume which designated his rank. All this was ceremonial gear, of course, made to his very own physical specifications and of the highest quality craftsmanship. None of it was ever to be worn in battle.

Snatching up his shield, which, like his breast plate was of laminated leather covered with metal, and feeling bereft without his spear-senior officers did not carry them-Colinus raced out the door. He was late. Already he could hear barked commands

127

from the courtyard as the battalion fell into ranks. Rounding the corner at the end of the passageway, he clattered through the outside door and onto the cobbled yard-and stopped dead in his tracks.

There before him, ranged in orderly ranks, stood the entire battalion dressed not in the shiny plate of ceremony, but in the leathern gear of war. And staring directly at him, his face clouding in a deepening scowl, was Simplinius, Chieftain of the Fourth Battalion.

Colinus was out of uniform. Here and there, titters erupted from the ranks and he swooned with mortification.

"Sub-Chieftain!" Simplinius' voice was clipped and hard, his face twitching with rage, barely controlled. Snapping to attention before him, Colinus could not lift his eyes. "Where do you think you are going?"

Though he worked his mouth, Colinus could not speak.

"You are aware, Sub-Chieftain," and Simplinius' voice took on a sneer, "of the difference between battle gear and ceremonial gear?"

"I,... I,... Yes, Sir."

"And I presume you are also aware-since you yourself read it to the battalion-that the order explicitly stated battle gear, not ceremonial gear?"

Quickly, like the shadow of a passing bird, a look of utter bafflement crossed Colinus' face. "Yes, Sir... I,.."

"You are a fool, Colinus!" And Simplinius' voice was like the hiss of an adder. "Sub-Chieftain, indeed! You have exactly one minute to get back

128

here in proper uniform-and I mean Warrior's uniform, not officer's, ex-Sub-Chieftain. Now go!"

Colinus spun on his heel but, at that instant, a great drum roll sounded from the city walls. "Wait!" said Simplinius. "That's the signal. There's no more time. You'll have to fall in as you are. But mark my words-you'll not live out this day!"

His life all but over, Colinus fell in beside his grizzled commander and as they marched out of the compound, he prayed for the earth to open and swallow him.

The sun was just peeking over the cliffs when Balazar and Thorngere left their new quarters. At the door, they were met by Hudarin and his assembled staff, and also a large troop of the Royal Guard.

Hudarin stepped forward and saluted smartly. "Good morning, Lord." He was dressed as they had first seen him, in leather jerkin and feathered cap. "As you ordered, the army is assembled and awaits your inspection."

"Very well, Hudarin," Said Balazar. "But who," and he gestured towards the elaborately armed Guardsmen, "are all these other .."

"Little dandies?" supplied Thorngere.

"They are ..."

"We are the Royal Guard!" interrupted a scar-faced officer who now stepped forward, his shoulder bumping Hudarin aside as he did so. The older man stumbled but did not fall. Balazar eyed the newcomer coldly.

"Hudarin," he said, "who is this man?" But again, before Hudarin could speak, the other interrupted.

"I am Cormin, Chief of the Royal Guard and Commander of this detachment." Balazar ignored him.

"Hudarin, I asked you who this man is."

"As he says, Lord," said Hudarin, his clipped voice betraying his fury. "He is Cormin, Chief of the Royal Guard."

"Cormin, eh? Well, Cormin, is it always your habit to interrupt your superiors?"

"Hudarin is not my superior," the scar faced one sneered. "I report directly to the King."

"The Royal Guard, my Lord," Hudarin explained, "is independent of the army."

"I see. But then, if you are not part of the Army, Cormin, what are you doing here?"

"I have been instructed by the King to command these troops as your personal bodyguard."

"Our bodyguards?" barked Thorngere with a loud laugh. "And just what are you going to protect us from?"

Balazar cast Thorngere a silencing glance then turned back to Cormin. When he spoke, his voice was level and steady, like a sword. "Cormin," he said, "listen to me now and listen carefully. If you were sent here by orders of the King, I will not dispute your presence. Nor can I make your Guard a part of the Army. But if, as you say, he placed you here in the capacity of personal guards, then I am going to assume he has placed you under MY command. And if, while under my command, you ever behave with such insolence again-to me or Thorngere, or Hudarin, or anyone on my staff-I will have you flogged. And if that doesn't serve to curb your tongue, I will personally cut that tongue out. Am I understood?"

For a long silent moment, Cormin tried to meet the murderous glare of the huge man before him. Then, his eyes dropped away and his face paled. He swallowed hard. "I hear and obey," he muttered.

"'Hear and obey' what?"

"Lor... Lord Balazar."

"Very well. Chief Hudarin, you may form up these troops and we will proceed with our inspection."

"I don't like the look of that little bugger," Thorngere whispered as they marched off towards the western gate.

"Nor I," said Balazar. "But watch your famous wisecracks, will you? We've got enough enemies already."

Colinus' prayers were not answered. Though he prayed hard all through the streets of the city as he marched beside Simplinius, and even harder as they passed out through the west gate and to their assigned place on the plain beyond, the earth did not open and swallow him whole. He was still very much above ground and very much in evidence. How could he have been such an utter fool? How could he? Had it not been he himself who read the order to the battalion at the previous night's assembly? How could he alone have misunderstood the instructions-he, the one who gave them? That he had given them correctly was obvious: everyone else in the battalion, in the entire army, in fact, was appropriately dressed in leather caps and jerkins and carried wooden battle shields. He alone, of all that host which now spread in formidable array across

131

the length of the plain, stood out like a silver icon among a group of wooden figurines, dressed in his best ceremonial gear. How could he possibly have been such a fool? Standing there in front of the entire army, a pace behind and two paces to the left of his commander, Colinus prayed not only for the earth to open, but for a deluge, an earthquake, for the cliffs above the city to suddenly crack and tumble down, for any kind of catastrophe at all which would avert this horrible one which was in the process of overtaking him.

"Simplinius," he whispered. "Sir? Please, I beg of you. I am Called. Let me leave this place and answer my Call in peace. Don't make me die here of humiliation!"

"Hush," growled the commander without turning his head. "We are both Called, fool-you for your stupidity and me for being stupid enough to promote you. But I will not allow either of us to slink off and die like cowards. The humiliation already IS: the least we can do is bear it like warriors."

Just then, trumpets blared atop the wall and three files of Guardsmen emerged from the gate led by their commander, Cormin. Following came the General Staff led by Hudarin and then, towering over all and seeming to dwarf the very gate and wall, the outlanders themselves. At the sight of them a murmur of fear and awe arose from the army. Bala Azar the Butcher had come. Closing his eyes to the unbearable sight, Colinus prayed for a swift death and tried to keep his knees from folding beneath him.

At the harsh commands of Cormin, the Guard executed a column left, then a snapping right flank and halted in station before the army. The staff, with slightly less pomp but an accustomed precision, took station before them. The two Warlords with the diminutive Hudarin between them, and marching in the privileged rout step of senior commanders, strolled to the foremost rank of all. The trumpets ceased then and silence, like a breath of wind, settled over the army. Eight battalions, each a thousand men strong, stood in formal array across the breadth of the plain, their faces to the city, each figure as stiff as iron, each face as rigid as stone.

At that moment, as if guided by the God himself, the great shadow of the cliff which every morning receded from the plain as the sun rose, inched its way past Colinus, and the sun, striking full on his armor for the first time, set it ablaze like a shower of diamonds. To the outlanders and their staff, who still stood in shadow, the bright flash was startling, and to the unimaginable horror of Colinus, those outlanders, with Hudarin in tow, immediately moved towards him.

Balazar stopped before the young Sub-Chieftain and inspected him closely. "Hudarin, who is this man?"

Hudarin, in turn, repeated the question to Simplinius who replied, "His name is Colinus, Lord, Sub-Chieftain, Fourth Battalion. But he is a fool, Lord, who has disgraced himself and his City."

"Speak not so hastily, Commander," said Balazar. "Men often appear as fools to their fellows who act under the guidance of a God. Hudarin, where came he by this fine armor?"

133

"It is ceremonial armor, Lord," said Hudarin, perplexed by the question.

"And who has such armor?"

"Why, all do, Lord. That of the ranks is not so ornate, of course, but all are issued gear for ceremony."

Like a large tailor adjusting the outfit on a small manikin, Balazar bent down and fingered and poked and tapped at Colinus armor, testing its thickness and quality. Colinus, too, bore the inspection like a manikin, neither flinching nor blinking his eyes though on the inside, there was a loud roaring in his ears and the mere presence of the huge man before him was so overwhelming that he almost lost control of his bladder. When Balazar was finished, he straightened up and tugged thoughtfully at his beard.

"This is very fine armor, Hudarin. How is it that you never wear it?

"Why, such finery is too costly to waste in battle, Lord. Besides, the valor of our troops is its own armor."

"Thorngere, can you believe this? For over two years I've been slicing up these flimsy shields and jerkins like brushwood and all the time every man Jack of them has had armor like this sitting home on the shelf!"

"Would it have made any difference?"

"Well, at least it would have dulled my sword. But against the Iblis? Who knows? Commander," said Balazar, turning again to Simplinius, "this man you called Fool may have just saved the army. Hudarin, hear me! Except for this man, your whole army is out of uniform!" Snatching a spear from a warrior in the ranks, Balazar strode several paces beyond the edge of the still creeping shadow and drove it into the earth. "You have until the sun touches this spot to get all these men properly armed. I ordered battle gear and such it has just become!"

There ensued a general stampede with officers screaming and warriors stripping off leather gear as they ran, and all in a great press to be the first through the gates. Balazar and Thorngere, stood amidst the roaring surge like huge trees in a river at flood, and grinned like boys. Colinus, trying vainly to keep his place and stay stiffly at attention, was buffeted and bumped along like a log caught in the rapids. Twice he was almost submerged and, on the whole, was glad to have on the armor he did. The Guard stood like an island, unmoved and untouched as the crowd swirled around them.

The sun was still descending the shaft of the spear and the edge of shadow still some distance from the head when the last of the returning warriors, running barefoot with greaves and sandals under their arms, hurried to their places. After a few more moments of flurried dressing and adjusting within the ranks all was again as still as before. Only now, where there had been the dull, lackluster brown of boiled hide on breast, shield and helm, now the whole line bristled and glistened with forbidding steel.

Resuming his place before the staff and Guardsmen, Balazar raised his voice and addressed the troops: "Men of New Kantar," he shouted, his voice echoing in the still morning air, "Look around you. No longer are you a skin clad rabble. The gods

135

have brought you the arms of warriors! Now you are an army of men! Now I will lead you to victory!"

A great cheer went up from the army and Colinus, chief agent of that God or, indeed, a fool crowned by chance, swelled with pride as he stood stiff before his battalion and roared with the rest.

"Oh, what splendor!" mocked Koltar. "Have you ever seen such a sight?" He and his companion, the female Seris, were atop the cliffs behind the city, looking out at the scene on the plains beyond. They were sitting well back and out of sight, just behind a large crack which started about three feet from the edge and ran full thirty feet along it. Koltar was a wiry, pinch- faced little man with a pencil thin moustache, curled at the ends, and with large, luminous eyes. Raising his voice, he called melodiously to the Queen who was sunning herself on a small couch near the quarry. "Salonis? Oh, Salonis, dear! You should come and see what those huge Oaf-landers have done. They've dressed all your pretty mongrels in their feast day finest and are marching them all over the plain. Are you sure you know what you're doing? They look dangerous to me."

The Queen turned her head lazily and waved a half-eaten apple. "Let them play, Koltar, dear. Let them play. But you two, do stay back from the edge. You know it's not safe."

"Oh, decidedly unsafe, Madame," chirped Koltar. "Why, Seris here is positively salivating at the mere sight of those two brawny morons-though I am sure that you, my Queen, would be impervious to such crude specimens."

"Impudent scamp!" snapped the Queen and flung her apple at Koltar's head. It missed by a wide margin, sailed over the edge and down the whole face of the cliff to splatter at the feet of a drowsy Guard on the palace portico, far below. He jumped as if he'd been slapped and stood stiffly to attention.

Koltar laughed and turned back to the scene on the plain. "What's this he's doing now? What? Oh look, Salonis, look! They're killing each other! They're killing each other!"

137

CHAPTER TWO
Hidden Arms and Instructions

"I should have known," spat Balazar. "After all I've seen, I should have known." He sat slumped in a newly constructed chair, with his elbows on a newly constructed table in the newly ordained supreme headquarters building, and propped his chin on his hand. Around him rang the sounds of continuing construction. Thorngere, positioned likewise, sat at his side, and Hudarin, at a smaller table across from them, sat sheepishly like a withered child held after school. All three had earthen cups of steaming chicory before them. Balazar and Thorngere drank sporadically from theirs, but Hudarin only clutched tightly to his as if to keep his hands from trembling.

"Well, I don't see how," said Thorngere. "I mean, the way these people are disciplined, who would have imagined...?"

"I should have imagined-I've fought them long enough, haven't I? I just thought that because I was always alone it was different, that honor was involved or something. I never guessed the real reason. By the Gods! Do you realize that we'll have to start from absolute scratch?"

"Excuse me, Lords," said Hudarin, his voice hardly more than a whisper, "but I still know not of what you speak."

"Battle lines, you ass!" Balazar snapped. "Line, square, phalanx, wedge! Anything but mass hysteria!"

Hudarin looked blank. Incredible as it seemed, the Kudanim, despite all their apparent sophistication and efficiency in military matters-in all matters, in fact-knew absolutely nothing of standard battle formations, as Balazar and Thorngere had just discovered in the abortive review. The troops had marched beautifully, had executed column turns, flanking turns, to the rears, and even oblique marches with exquisite snap and precision, but when Balazar had divided them into two groups, ordered battle formations and a mock advance, their crystalline column formations had dissolved like heated snow and the two masses had swirled together like two sluice streams in utter chaos and confusion. And before Balazar could separate them, there had even been some carnage.

It had been an incredible mess. At first, on his order to form battle lines, the four battalion commanders on each side had stared at him incredulously. Then, turning to their men, they had screamed orders to charge, whereupon the warriors, first singly, then in pairs, then in stampede, had rushed each other in a mad and furious melee. Six were dead and a score wounded by the time Balazar and Thorngere got them apart. Enraged and disgusted, Balazar had dismissed them and ordered all commanders and sub-commanders to appear before him in the new headquarters building at the end of the forenoon watch.

"But we did battle!" Hudarin shot back, his own ire rising now as he recalled the senseless sacrifice ordered by this ignorant outlander. "Who ever heard of an army ordered to attack itself!"

"Ah, Hudarin," Balazar sighed and rubbed his face with his great hairy paw, "I did not order battle-only battle formation. Obviously, the concept is foreign to you. And I'm sorry for the misunderstanding. I should have known. But why do you attack like that? I would have thought-I did think, in fact-that the merits of a more organized attack would have been obvious to you people-you're so marvelously organized everywhere else.

"Kala Atar governs battle, Lord. He steels each warrior's heart with courage and calls him to the test. And when he meets it, the God Calls to him those who have proven most worthy and grants them the honor of his presence. Today was magnificent Lord! All the warriors were flush with pride and anxious to please you and the God. I only do not understand why you set them against each other..."

"There is much we must seek to understand of each other, Hudarin, much we both must learn. It will take time. I am only sorry for the dead whose wives and mothers will now curse me."

"Wives, Lord? Warriors have no..." Hudarin bit off his words in mid-sentence and, took a huge gulp of chicory. Balazar, who had again covered his face with this hands, seemed not to notice the remark, but Thorngere started at the words and eyed the little man suspiciously.

"Ah, enough of this," snapped Balazar, straightening himself. "The dead are dead and we have much to do with the living if we are to have any hope of facing the Iblis in battle. Tell me, Hudarin, where did that fancy armor come from?"

"Why, as I said, Lord, each warrior is issued a set. But it is so costly and the honor of our warriors so..."

"Yes, yes, I know that part. What I want to know is where it came from-where it's issued from. You have a central armory, a store house?"

"Why, yes, Lord. It's..."

"Good, very good! Let us go and inspect this armory before the commanders assemble and see if there are any more little surprises lying in wait for us."

As they threaded their way through the building, accompanied by the inevitable Cormin and picking up more of his Guardsmen at every turn, they passed scores of workmen busily engaged in raising doorways, moving partitions and constructing furniture large enough to accommodate the outlanders. Everywhere were banging hammers and wheezing saws and the pleasing scent of fresh cut pine. Outside, the bulk of the Guardsmen fell in with them and with Hudarin in the lead, the entire procession marched across the palace courtyard. Ringed as they were, Balazar and Thorngere looked like teachers escorting a group of tiny players to the dress rehearsal of a school play or, more, like great statues of men being born erect to waiting pedestals.

Like the Palace, the armory was dug into the base of the cliff on the side opposite the long tunnel to the fields. Two large wooden doors guarded it but both were swung wide to admit light and allow smoke to escape, as inside a group of smiths were already hard at work on their anvils repairing the various dents and cuts the recent combat had occasioned. Leaving Cormin and his Guardsmen outside, and accompanied only by a pair of orderlies, the three leaders pushed their way through the billowing smoke and entered.

The outer room was entirely given over to blacksmithing and leather work and was lined with benches and anvils, and the walls were hung with tools. In the center a huge forge pulsed and glimmered with a fierce heat as four men worked the bellows. Lighting torches from this, Balazar and Thorngere followed Hudarin through a door into a long, low-roofed chamber roughly hewn from the living rock. With only enough room left in the center for a narrow aisle, the whole was crammed with arms. Ducking under low ceiling beams, Balazar inspected everything. Divided in half, one side of the room contained ceremonial gear, and the other leather battle gear. There were rack upon rack of spears, shelf upon shelf of helms, row upon row of breast plates, grieves, leaved skirts and shields, and literally piles of swords and scabbards. There were no surprises. But at the very back of the room stood another set of double doors, barred and locked.

"What's this?" Balazar asked.

"That leads to the private armory of the Guard," said Hudarin. "I don't have a key."

"Fetch Cormin," Balazar snapped to one of the orderlies. "You have a key to this room?" he asked when that worthy appeared.

"I do," said Cormin, his smug face seeming to twitch in the flickering torch light.

"Open it, then."

"I beg pardon... Lord, but I have no orders to admit you."

142

Reacting with catlike agility, Thorngere grabbed the little Guard Commander by the rim of his burnished breastplate and hoisted him up to the ceiling. "You have two choices here, little man," he hissed. "You can either produce that key-in which case I will put you down-or you can refuse-in which case I will use you as a club and beat the door down. Choose quickly."

The key produced, Thorngere tossed Cormin a little way towards the exit and politely bade him wait outside upon their further pleasure. "Don't like that little bugger," he muttered and turned to fit the key into the lock. For his part, Cormin stalked to the outer armory, hands clenched into fists, frame trembling, and eyes glowing with rage.

The inspection team found the inner, private armory of the Guard even more crammed with weapons than the outer one. Only here there were no leather vestments. All steel and all burnished to a high sheen with inlays of gold filigree and silver scrolls, the massed weaponry caught the torch light and set the entire chamber ablaze. Only in the back right hand corner did the shadows remain, and here Balazar stalked.

"Ah ha!" he said as he bent, threw back a protective tarp. "Exactly what I was hoping to find."

"Oh, my Lord!" exclaimed Hudarin.

Back in his barracks room, Colinus moved about like a man walking on air as he awaited the summons to council. 'A man who acts under the guidance of a God...' 'This man may just have saved the army.' The words of the great Warlord echoed in his head like the refrain of a lively tune and his feet, pacing impatiently back and forth, kept time. He,

Colinus, an agent of the God, a savior, a hero. Oh, what a thing!

His armor once again buffed to a high sheen after the dusty morning's drill, he had no thoughts of his recent near calamity, or that of the army for that matter: such were the fortunes of war. Besides, the grandeur of his reprieve had swept all that quite away. Only, he thought, that he had passed through a trial by fire, had faced certain death with unblinking (well, almost unblinking) eyes. Now he was a new man, cleansed and purified, tempered like the finest steel to be a strong arm in the service of the God, in the service of the Lord Bala Azar-Balazar. And that, after all, was what really mattered.

The summons, when it came, was not yet to council but to the quarters of his chieftain, Simplinius. His billowing sails suddenly luffing, Colinus took a deep breath and marched up the passageway to the commander's door. It was open and Simplinius faced him from behind his desk. Stiffening himself, Colinus stomped in and slapped his fist on his chest in salute.

"Sub-Chieftain Colinus reporting, Sir!"

"Shut the door, Colinus." Even without his great plumed war helm, Simplinius presented a fearsome figure. Stern and grizzled with close-cropped, wiry hair and a long scar running across his forehead and down the side of his face, he had a visage like a stone mask and his eyes, the color of granite flecked with obsidian, were cold and remorseless. He had been chief of the battalion for as long as Colinus could remember, longer even since way before he himself, as a lad fresh from the

Rite of the Knife, had been inducted into the battalion as an orderly-and though outwardly quiet and unassuming, he had always been held in fear and awe by his subordinates.

Rumor had it that in his youth he had been a great hero, had brought in six prisoners after the rest of his company had been slain. His ragged scar was said to be the result of that encounter and his Chieftainship, granted at an extremely young age, his reward. Oddly, though, after such a meteoric start, the chance for further promotion-to division command, army staff or even higher-had somehow eluded him. He had been given the battalion and that was it.

Though Colinus had no solid information on which to speculate, he believed there was some black mark on Simplinius' record, some grudge held against him which kept him down. He was like a knight on a chess board who had made one dramatic move, captured one important piece, and then was left static and unused on his spot while the rest of the game swirled around him. Now, close to retirement and the Call, hope of another move was nearly gone. But whether he was embittered by this, content with it, or had simply grown callous to it all, Colinus had no way of knowing. He only knew that Simplinius' implacable eyes were resting on him and that there was no warmth in them.

"You feel yourself lucky, no doubt-bright in the light of a rising star?" Simplinius' voice was flat, belying the affected poetics.

"Sir," said Colinus, the words coming out in a tumble, "I have no idea how what happened today happened. Nothing was planned. I was as bewildered as you. It just..."

"Just answer the question, Sub-Chieftain."

"Well, yes sir. I must admit, I do feel lucky, sir. Very lucky."

"Well, if I were you I would not trust in the light of rising stars: they wink out as fast as on, and when they go, they leave you in a darkness blacker that before. Now, because your reprieve came directly from the lips of our new, Troll-like Warlord, I can do nothing to circumvent it. But understand this: I do not buy one bit of that 'acting under the guidance of a God' business. As far as I'm concerned, you're merely a fool who has been saved by chance. And I do not like having a fool as my second in command. So I'm watching you, Sub-Chieftain. Give me but the slightest excuse and you'll be broken to the ranks. Give me a slightly bigger excuse, and you won't BE at all. Understood?

"Yes, sir."

"Very well." Simplinius fell silent here and looked long and hard at his subordinate. When he continued, his tone and his face had softened. "I want us to be in complete understanding in these matters, Colinus, because, frankly, I like you. I always have. That's why I promoted you in the first place. You have a certain flair, a dash and an enthusiasm which is refreshing. You also, apparently, have exceptional luck. But these things can be dangerous, very dangerous if relied on too heavily and exercised without circumspection. I want to help give you that circumspection: I intend, in fact, to put your head on a swivel so that maybe you won't get stabbed in the back. Now, stand easy.

146

We've some other business to cover before the Council.

"You are aware, of course, of the instructions propagated among the battalions regarding these Outlanders?"

"Of course, Sir."

"Well, there are others which I am instructed to pass on to you regarding this Council and any others which you or I or any of us might be required to attend. In fact, these instructions cover any occasion in which we have dealings with the Outlanders. These come from the highest source-you know who I mean-and any violation will result in immediate death. Am I understood on that point?"

"Yes, Sir!"

"Very well. Now, pay close attention: first," and Simplinius marked off one finger, "you are to keep your mouth shut. Under no circumstances-I repeat, under no circumstances-are you to volunteer information. If asked a question directly-and it is one which does not conflict with any of these instructions-you are to answer it simply and directly but offer no additional comment.

"Second," and he marked off another finger, "you are not to mention, under any circumstances, the name of our Most Holy and Revered Queen, Salonis. Under no circumstances! Die before you allow that name to pass your lips. Understood?"

"Yes, Sir!"

"Third," Simplinius now held three of his left hand fingers in his right fist and shook them at Colinus. "Third, you are not to make any mention of our Pure Bred Lords, any mention of breeder slaves, any mention of the Rite of the Knife or any mention

147

at all of anything that transpires in the great caves under hill. Are all of these things understood?"

"I hear and will obey, my Chieftain!"

"Good. Remember that violation of any of these instructions is to be considered an immediate Call. Now, let us go."

"Uh, Sir? One question?"

"Yes?"

"About the war. Now that we have the Outlanders, do you really think we can win?"

Simplinius shot him a look of scorn and headed for the door. "After what happened today? Don't be so naive, boy. Now, come!"

The carpenters had been amazingly efficient in their work and by the time the chieftains assembled, no trace of them or of their trade was visible. Not so much as a single shaving or speck of sawdust was left; only the scent of fresh pine mingled with the odor of paint in a remarkably altered building. All the doors had been enlarged to nearly twice their original height, partitions had been moved or removed for greater spaciousness, even a complete suite of giant sized furniture had been assembled. In the council chamber itself, which took up most of the ground floor, a huge table, and behind it two huge chairs with massive arms, stood at the head of the room. Before these was a smaller, normal sized table and the rest of the room, auditorium-like, was ranged with simple chairs now rapidly filling with the upper echelon of the army.

As Colinus followed Simplinius to their places, he could feel the tension in the room. Typically, councils were relaxed, even rather boisterous affairs: men lounged about, talked and joked with friends, laughed and drank. Then, when they got down to business, it was like old comrades-which, of course, was what they were-turning to familiar chores.

This assembly was different. There was no lounging, no jokes, no laughter, not even any real conversation. The men sat stiffly, hands clasped in front of them, eyes staring straight ahead. What conversations there were, were hurried whispers; one man leaning quickly to another and, just as quickly, leaning back. It was, thought Colinus as he too sat stiffly beside Simplinius, like the first day of school when he was a child, when all the boys sat in fear and anticipation of the Master who was to come.

With something very like shock, Colinus' eyes registered the huge table at the head of the room. It was immense, like the frame of a small building sitting there! How could mortal men possibly be so large as to sit at it comfortably? Though he had seen both outlanders at close range only that morning, and had seen Balazar from a distance once before-standing atop his cart and scanning the horizon (and Colinus was unashamedly thankful that Balazar's eyes had not, on that occasion, scanned him)-the sight of that table, standing in juxtaposition with the normal furniture around it, brought home to Colinus for the first time, the awesome stature of the men who would soon sit at it.

It also brought home something else, something which his own giddy thoughts had hitherto obscured. While he had been so relieved at his own reprieve and the effect it had on him, he had not even begun to consider what effect the Outland

Warlords-or that nonsensical tragedy of this morning-would have on the rest of the army.

Now, looking around at the faces of his fellow officers, he saw exactly what that effect was. There was fear, of course. From the snatches of conversation he had heard it was plain the men were confused by the incident and fearful that it was somehow their fault. But something else was apparent in their expressions as well: acceptance. These men were waiting for their leader!

Somehow, during that morning, and despite the bloodshed that ended it, Balazar had taken command. It was that often startling difference between expectation and reality, between fancy and fact. No longer was the great outlander going to come lead them: he was the leader. And every face in the room showed it. Colinus realized that, policy and instructions aside, the simple truth was that when the Warlord-this Bala Azar-issued a command, it would be obeyed.

CHAPTER THREE
A Council of War

When they came-when He came-preceded by Hudarin and the General Staff, an audible gasp filled the room and everyone leapt to their feet. He was huge! Both of them were huge. Bigger even than the table implied. Though the door sills had been raised, both had to duck as they entered, and as they strode across the floor, their heads seemed to graze the ceiling. They were giants! Balazar's right arm alone looked as big around as Colinus' chest, and one of his legs would make two of any man in the room. And his sword-that great butcher's blade which had claimed so many-how was it possible for any mortal to wield such a thing? Colinus doubted he could even pull it from its scabbard, let alone swing it. And Thorngere was just as big, though slimmer and more defined. They were simply awesome. And, when Balazar spoke, though it was in a quiet, almost officious tone, his voice rumbled like thunder and the walls seemed to shake.

"Gentlemen," he said, "we have much to cover today and, in the days ahead, much to do. But first, let me say this: if there is any blame for this morning's mishap, let it be mine. All of you-and I mean warriors as well as officers-behaved with great courage and discipline in obeying orders which must have seemed crazy to you. They weren't crazy: you just didn't understand them. And I should have realized you would not understand them. So the fault is mine.

"But hear this," he said, his voice rising now until they could feel its force. "The fault will be mine only once! Beginning today, this very afternoon, you will be schooled in these things. And starting at first light, you will begin drilling your troops in them. You will work at them day and night until you drop, and then you will sleep and work at them in your dreams. And when you can do them in your sleep, then you will start to become a fighting army! That's what you want, isn't it? To become a fighting army?"

"Yes, sir," said several small voices.

"What?"

"Yes, sir!" said the room.

"What?"

"Yes, Sir!" they all yelled and, for some reason, Colinus felt like grinning.

"Good. Now, though you may not realize it, time presses heavily upon us. So listen well and learn quickly." Motioning them to be seated, Balazar nodded to a pair of orderlies at the door who dragged in a large piece of polished slate which Thorngere helped prop up on the large table. Taking a lump of chalk, Balazar began to lecture.

"The very first thing you must learn is that an army moves as a unit. You know this is so on parade: now you must learn how to do it in battle. And since you are so good at drilling on parade, the battle part should only be a matter of extending your thinking rather than altering it-except perhaps in one particular. Hudarin here has told me how it is your belief that the God, Kala Atar, steels each man for battle individually. Well, I tell you now, you have misunderstood his Will." Balazar paused to let this

152

sink in and Colinus saw the shock register on the faces around him.

"No self-respecting God would treat his people so-especially not if he considers himself any kind of tactician. And I'm sure that a God such as Kala Atar, who is wise enough to inspire the building of this great city and to foster a people as bold and honorable as yourselves, never intended such a thing. In fact, I'm convinced that he has been prompting you in the right direction all along. You can see it in your buildings, in your organization, in the very structure and discipline of this army. The problem is that you, who have followed the God so well in some things, have missed the most important point of all: he has not been steeling you individually, he has been trying to steel you all together, but you have been too thick headed to listen!" Again, Balazar paused as the shock on his audience's face turned to consternation.

"I have heard much talk of Kala Atar's anger towards his people. Well, I can see no better reason for it than this: what sense is there in fostering a people and trying to lead them to victory over their enemies when they insist on fighting like fools?

"Look at the results such tactics have gained you: for over two years you have been using them to make war on me. On me alone! And how many of your comrades have I sent to the God? Me! One man! Granted, I am a bit larger than you," and here there were a few titters from the otherwise stunned audience, "but I tell you now and I tell you true: had you ever thought to attack me en masse instead of one at a time, I would long ago have been stalking the halls of hell." Voices and exclamations arose in

153

the hall like a sudden wind, but Balazar overrode them.

"I think that all this time Kala Atar has been using me to try and teach you that. I think that is why He dashed my ship on the rocks, why He guided me into the mouth of the hidden river, and why He prompted the Iblis to send me to war alone against you. All of it has been to point out to you, through necessity, the advantage of numbers.

"But you have been fools not to see! And Kala Atar knows you for fools. That is why he is angry!"

Balazar swept the room with his gaze, trying to meet every eye. The assembly was stunned, shocked, frozen. Never in their lives had they heard anyone so blaspheme the God. Yet here was this outlander, not only proclaiming the most incredible heresy, but doing it in the God's name, and, as Warlord, with the authority of the King and, apparently, with the blessing of the High Queen herself! Colinus kept glancing nervously at the ceiling as if he expected the hand of the God to rip it away and expose them all.

"For generations," Balazar continued, "you have believed that Kala Atar has withheld victory from you to punish you for a transgression committed by your ancestors. But that is not it. If Kala Atar punishes you, it is not by withholding victory; He punishes because you have failed to gain victory! You have failed to follow His prompting and earn for Him His just revenge on enemies so depraved and evil they devour the very flesh of His people. That is why the God is angry.

"But I also tell you that He has not lost faith in His people. My presence here, as well as

154

Thorngere's, proves that. When you did not learn from experience and necessity, He first guided Thorngere to me and then both of us to you to take you by the hand, to show you the path to victory, and lead you along it. Just as he used this officer here," he said, pointing at Colinus, "to show me a better way to arm you, so with the debacle that followed did He show me that I needed to teach you the art of war. So thus it is: through obedience to me will come victory and through victory will you please Kala Atar."

Turning quickly to the slate, Balazar drew a series of rectangles in line. "This, then," he said, "is a battle line. There are many variations depending on enemy disposition and terrain, but this is your basic pattern: a structured front consisting of individual units, or phalanxes. It presents a solid front to the enemy but, as it is composed of individual links, is flexible enough to either concentrate or envelope. It can advance or retreat, shift fronts, even fold back on itself and present an impenetrable barrier on all sides. Each square, or phalanx, is made up of ranks as follows:..."

The lecture continued for an hour and a half. Like a coach describing plays to a football team, Balazar explained everything forwards, backwards, from the inside out and from the outside in. Alternately using his chalk and bodies from the audience, he showed them how a shield wall worked in the front rank, how the ranks behind used their spears, how the rear ranks moved forward to fill in gaps left by the fallen, and how with various lateral or filtering movements, reserve units could reinforce any part of the line, extending it or deepening it as circumstances warranted. He took each segment and broke it down into its component parts, giving each its name. He described all the evolutions of these formations in detail, listing the commands necessary for an army in column to form the line on various fronts and then those necessary to get them back into column. These latter he went over again and again, drumming them in. When he had been through it all, he took everyone out to the inner courtyard and drilled them for over two hours: he shouting commands and Thorngere, running around like a window dresser, arranging stray bodies like so many small manikins. And when they were done there, Balazar took them back inside and went over it all again.

Colinus' head was swimming. All his life he had been marching, was more at ease marching, in fact, than in walking alone. But these evolutions and convolutions, these to the rears, lateral rights and lefts, these command front rights and command front lefts were enough to make his very helm spin! And the things he had to remember! He felt like a raw recruit again. Several times during the drills he had gone striding off confidently on command only to be snatched off his feet by the uproarious Thorngere (who seemed to be having a marvelous time despite Balazar's growing rage) and plopped down where he should already have been, and he wondered how any of this could possibly be of use in battle. How could men fight when they were all jammed together, constantly bumping into each other, tripping over each other, tromping on each other's feet or, worse, wandering off aimlessly like so many chickens pecking for grain? And what would be the result if they tried to do these things with drawn weapons?

Out of it all there was only one thing which was becoming increasingly clear: this Balazar was not the bumbling oaf everyone seemed to think he was. On the contrary, he knew precisely what he was about and why he was about it. Nor was Colinus the only one on whom this notion was dawning: as they broke off the drill and straggled back inside, he heard several remarks indicating that his own budding impression of the Warlord was fast becoming the general one. And as he took his seat for the beginning of the reiteration, he reflected that Kala Atar must be a very wise God indeed.

Finally, Balazar dropped his chalk. "Are there any questions?" His audience, stupefied after hours of lecture and drill and lecture again, sat mum. Only Hudarin rose to speak.

"Lord, these things are all new to us and will take time to sink in, but I wonder as to their effectiveness. You said that if we had used these tactics against you, you could not have stood before us. But as you said, you are only one man. What would happen if we used them against the Iblis who, while not as large as you, are still considerably larger than ourselves? And what I especially want to know is what would happen if they came against us similarly disposed?"

"Ah, Hudarin, my man," said Balazar, clapping his hands, "you could not have asked a more perfect question to lead me into the second part of this afternoon's program!" A small groan arose among the assembled chieftains but was quickly silenced under Balazar's scowl. "As for the second part of your question, Hudarin, I do not believe there is the slightest possibility the Iblis will come against you in a disciplined line. They are an ignorant, slothful people who not only know nothing of discipline or tactics, but are incapable of learning them. You know that already without my telling you. Aside from that, they are also cowardly, so if they come against you at all, it will be as rabble, and probably drunken rabble at that.

"However, you do make a good point about the size difference, and how you will fare against men so much larger, we will have to see. I only know that without such tactics as these, you stand no chance at all. So, they are an improvement at the very least. Still, I would not be overly confident leading you into battle if this was the only advantage I had to offer. It is not. These tactics will only be used by part of the army. The rest are going to have some new toys to play with and learn an entirely new way of making war. Orderly!"

At his command, an orderly trotted in carrying a bow and quiver of arrows. A gasp went up among the chieftains. "Ah, yes, I know," said Balazar, picking up the bow and knocking an arrow, "a cowardly and dishonorable weapon. Hudarin has told me. But I tell you this: the biggest dishonor in war comes from losing and with this weapon... " and Balazar suddenly drew the bow and sent the shaft zipping close over their heads and into a beam at the back of the room. It stuck there with a thud and reverberating twang. "With this weapon, we will win! With this weapon, we will overcome your stature and beat your enemy. It is not dishonorable. It is a key to victory and that is very honorable indeed. Is that clear? Good. Now, have any of you ever used one?"

From the corner of his eye, Colinus saw Simplinius' hand jerk in his lap. But then it was stilled. No other hand moved.

Balazar grunted. "Well, you will have to learn and learn quickly. Now, Hudarin, how many horses are there in the city?"

"Horses? Why, I have no idea, Lord. We use them for plowing, and pulling carts, and dragging blocks from the quarry, and the like, but how many I don't know. What do you want...?"

"Find out. Further, I want them all. Your plowing is done until the time for winter crops, and you have enough city built already. Gather them all together and build a paddock either in the outer city here or just outside the walls. I want it done by morning. How many of you can ride a horse?" This time a few hands went up. "Good. You men are instructors. At muster in the morning, we will begin selecting others. I intend to form a corps of mounted bowmen to act as the wings of the army. With them softening up the enemy first, and then hounding their flanks while our phalanx goes to work, no Iblian host will be able to stand against us. Are you with me?"

To Colinus, all the early confusion and drudgery of the day was suddenly swept away by this vision of a new kind of warfare. In his mind, he saw a great plain and a horde of terrified Iblis cowering before the stinging darts of flying horsemen, and then falling utterly under the feet of the inexorably advancing phalanx of New Kantar. It was glorious and Colinus suddenly found himself on his feet shouting with the other chieftains, "Aye! Aye! Aye!"

For the first time all afternoon, then-for the first time ever, in fact, so far as Colinus knew-Balazar grinned, his white teeth flashing from under his black beard and his eyes beaming bright. "All right," he said, "there are only a couple more things and then you can go. Hudarin, what is the purpose of these raids you people are always sending out?"

"Well, Lord," said Hudarin, perplexed at the question and clearing his throat while he formulated his reply, "they have always been a matter of policy so I never thought much about them. But I would say their purpose is twofold: first, to do what damage we may to the enemy and, second, to secure the slaves necessary for our agricultural and other work."

"That's what I thought. But since we now have a much better way of hurting the enemy, and since slaves can't plow without horses, there is no reason to continue them. Therefore, they will cease immediately."

"But Lord!" sputtered Hudarin, jumping to his feet. "We can't possibly stop the raids!"

"I beg your pardon?" From under his shaggy brows, Balazar's eyes blazed and his voice had an ominous ring.

"Well, uh... We just can't. I mean,... err... it's just not possible, Lord. We've always had the raids, Lord... They're policy, highest policy..." Hudarin faltered, his hands fluttering before him like dying butterflies.

Colinus watched sadly. He had wondered how long it would be before someone ran head on into

Instructions. Hudarin just had. How could he explain that the raids were ordered by the Queen herself? And what would Balazar do if Hudarin tried to stand against him? There was no way out. If Hudarin tried to explain, it would mean his Call. Yet if he allowed Balazar to stop the raids-in disobedience to the direct orders of the Queen-that, too, would mean a Call. Either way, Hudarin was doomed.

Knowing nothing of the reasons but sensing the struggle, which was going on in the little man's breast, Balazar overruled him as gently as he could: "Well, Hudarin, this may not be as bad as you think. Sit down and I'll explain."

Hudarin sat. Under his breath, Colinus uttered a prayer for the old man's soul.

"Now," said Balazar, "while these raids of yours do succeed in capturing slaves, they also serve to provide the Iblis with their meat supply. Stop the raids and you cut it off. You begin to starve your foe and, not incidentally, save a few of your own lives. Not a bad deal. But that's not all: once you cut off their meat supply, you force the Iblis to come out looking for it. That means that instead of having to do battle on their terms, we can do it on ours. We can pick the time and place. You see, Hudarin, this is essential to our overall strategy.

"Now, to make sure we get the Iblis where we want them, we're going to need a whole network of outposts and messengers to keep an eye on the country beyond the valley. When the Iblis come, we will see and prepare. Then, with a few well-chosen decoys, we'll lead them into traps-that should provide you with more than enough slaves, Hudarin.

161

Enough even, to pull the plows themselves! And after the Iblis have lost a few of these hunting parties, they'll come out in force, and when that happens we'll have a very large surprise ready for them. But, we'll need a good man to set up the outposts and take charge of the messengers. Thorngere, you've been loafing all afternoon. I give the honor of the choice to you."

"Leave it to you to give me the hard job!" said Thorngere, rising. "This is such a stalwart company. But I think for my money I'll take this lad here; he seems to be under a lucky star."

If anything else was said, Colinus did not hear it, so loudly did the blood pound in his head when he saw the great finger of the blond giant point directly at his own chest.

All were dismissed then, with Colinus ordered to return with his gear and move into the Headquarters building. Balazar, however, motioned for Hudarin to remain and sat down by him when the hall had cleared.

"Hudarin, I am sorry to have caused you embarrassment before your comrades, but as Warlord..."

"Yes, I know, Lord and I am sorry to have troubled you. I should have been more discreet. But you see, this is not solely a military matter."

"I see. Then perhaps we had better discuss this with the King."

"That would be... wise, Lord."

162

CHAPTER FOUR
Behind The Scenes

"Well, Colinus," Simplinius said as the two marched through the cobbled streets toward Fourth Battalion Headquarters, "it looks as though I'll have to appoint a new Sub-Chieftain after all. I congratulate you." The remark brought no response and Simplinius shot the younger man a quick glance. Though he marched erect and kept step with his Chieftain, there was about Colinus an aura of abstraction, almost of gloom, as if his head, belying its physical reality, was actually sunk between his shoulders in deep thought. Men who have been habituated by a lifetime of military posture are often able to generate such a duality of appearance: while their bodies perform their duties with machinelike efficiency, their inner selves are apt to be somewhere else entirely like an independent shadow. Thus it is possible, for example, for a man to stand in ranks at stiff attention with his eyes open and staring straight ahead while he is actually sound asleep. For another, equally habituated, such as Simplinius, these effects are easily discernable: for while the form is erect, the shadow or aura is curled at its feet. "You do not seem exactly elated at your promotion, Colinus. You are troubled?"

Though his body marched on, Colinus' aura started: "No, Sir... Well, a bit, Sir. I thank you for your congratulations, but..."

"But you are concerned about the dangers."

"Yes, Sir. I mean, look at poor Chief Hudarin? How long did it take him to run afoul of

Instructions. And he, I am sure, is a much wiser man than I."

"Yes, poor old Hudarin." Now it was the turn of Simplinius' aura to change: it stroked its chin and gazed off into the shadows. "Did you know he and I were made lieutenants together back in the old Sixth? He was always a good man, Hudarin; steady and true as the path of the sun, though I always thought there was a bit of the fool about him. You must remember a thing about Calls, Colinus: before they can be obeyed they must be heard."

"Sir?"

"You will think me an old cynic for this, Colinus, but remember that I am an old cynic who has survived. Calls do not always speak with the same voice. Sometimes they are loud and cannot be ignored, as with Hudarin before the whole council today-and not to mention before that weasel Cormin who was lurking the whole time just outside the door. But at other times, they speak only in whispers, and a man who has honor in his heart and for whom duty is not a rigid absolute but a goal to aspire to... well, in certain situations, a man might not hear such a whisper."

All of Colinus, aura as well as man, stopped short at this and gaped at his commander. "But sir!" he whispered, "That's heresy!"

Simplinius laughed out loud and then quickly glanced around to see if they were observed. They were not. "Not really, Colinus. It's just an acceptance of reality. No man is perfect. Yet if we all accepted the Code literally, we would all have obeyed the Call long ago. Look at yourself this morning: total disobedience of a direct order, witnessed by the entire army. Your Call was so loud it echoed off the very cliffs. Yet I don't notice you developing any shortness of breath."

"Yes, but Lord Balazar, Sir, he..."

"He provided you with a convenient excuse. But you know yourself that such an excuse, provided by an Outlander is not valid."

"But he is Warlord!"

"I know who he is-he has certainly made it clear enough. But you know as well as I that, technically speaking, his excusing you is not an exemption."

Colinus stiffened again to attention. "I understand, Sir, and will obey!"

"Nonsense! You'll do nothing of the kind. Look, all I'm saying is that, though technically incorrect, you took advantage of a reasonable opportunity to choose life over death. You temporized, that's all. There's nothing wrong with that. It's perfectly natural. Didn't I do the same thing? Surely, as your immediate superior who bears full responsibility for your actions, such a Call as yours should have included me. But I'm still healthy, aren't I? And I assure you, I intend to stay that way. All I'm saying is, use your judgment. If you are going to be working closely with these Outlanders, you're bound to violate Instructions in one way or another. It's almost a sure bet. Just keep an open mind and an eye out for witnesses, and don't go immediately from tripping over your tongue to falling on your sword. Now, let's go: I've worked up an awful thirst."

As they marched on, Simplinius could sense that Colinus' mind was eased and that some of his native enthusiasm was again bubbling to the surface. As they rounded the last corner and neared the barracks door, Colinus spoke again. "May I ask you another question, Sir?"

"Speak."

"Well, I was wondering about your reaction to the council, Sir, and whether-with Balazar as Warlord and with all these new tactics, Sir-whether you think we might not have a better chance for victory now?"

Now it was the turn of Simplinius' shadow to belie his carriage. On the instant it ducked furtively, glanced over its shoulder, and eyed Colinus conspiratorially. "Report to me in my quarters when you have finished your packing, Sub-Chieftain," said the body, which had not flinched or even hesitated in its determined stride, "and we will speak further of these matters-over dinner."

With the aid of his orderly, it did not take long for Colinus to gather his few belongings. Possessing only a meager outfit, and not having been of senior rank long enough yet to have obtained any personal effects (such were forbidden to all below Sub-Chieftain rank), one moderate sized trunk sufficed for all but his armor. This was tenderly wrapped in oil cloth and secured together in a bundle on his shield. After instructing his orderly to transport these things to Army Headquarters (at which the boy's eyebrows nearly flew off his forehead) Colinus, freshly bathed, dressed in a simple white tunic and cloak of office, and bearing only a short dagger at his side, proceeded to the quarters of his soon to be former commander.

He found the door open as before and Simplinius again at his desk. He too, however, had bathed and replaced armor with tunic, and his unruly hair was plastered wet to his skull. As Colinus stomped in, saluted and announced himself, he noticed that on the other side of the room, which was quite large, Simplinius' orderly had already arranged a table with plates of steaming fish and was at that moment pouring the wine. "Sub-Chieftain Colinus reporting as ordered, Sir"

"Oh, stand at ease, Colinus," Simplinius returned affably. "You're here to celebrate your promotion, not to face a tribunal!" The two men went to table then and, after a single toast to Colinus' continued good fortune, fell to with a will. When the plates were cleared and a fresh flask of wine brought in, Simplinius dismissed his boy: "You may leave us now, lad. Post yourself at the end of the hall and, should anyone wish to see me, inform them that I have left orders not to be disturbed."

"I hear and will obey, Sir."

After checking that the young fellow had posted himself far enough down the hall to be out of ear-shot, Simplinius returned to the table and poured them both more wine. "Now, Colinus," he began, twirling his glass before the candle light, "you have asked for my reaction to the council and my thoughts on our chances for victory. The first part of that question is simple and can be answered shortly. As for the second, I should like to tell you a story, a true story, one which happened to me and which I have not breathed a word of to a single soul in nearly thirty years. I tell it to you as a precaution because your growing association with the Outlanders is putting you in much greater danger than even you realize-and I tell it to you only on the condition that you give me your vow, here and now, on your honor as an officer and a warrior, not to repeat a word of it to any soul, living or dead. Do I have your vow?"

"You do, Sir, and on my absolute honor, not the equivocal kind you spoke of earlier!"

"Point scored and accepted," said Simplinius, his usually stern features breaking into a grin. "So, about the council. I was, frankly, impressed. This Balazar is obviously not the fool he has been taken for around here. He is both quick and decisive-as well as being a veritable mountain!-and knows well how to command. His ploy of inserting himself directly between us and the God, while obvious, was not without effect among the others and, overall, I think, succeeded. But the fact that he was intelligent enough to think of it and articulate enough to implement it so facilely, indicates that he is, in fact, a force to be reckoned with. As for his mass battle tactics and the strategy of cutting off the raids, they make obvious sense. If he is allowed time to implement them, and is not stopped by other factors entirely, they stand a good chance of success."

Colinus here started to interrupt, but Simplinius stayed him with his hand. "Hold, Colinus. I know what I have left out. I am not yet finished. About these 'new' weapons: first, know that they are not new. We have known about them since long before our expulsion from the old city. In fact, they were once used quite commonly to hunt birds, and with a length of twine secured to the arrows, to skewer salmon and other fish when they came upriver to spawn. The Iblis, too, know about them-learned how to make them from us, actually-but either their eyesight or coordination is bad, because they never managed to shoot them effectively. In any event, bows have been around for a long time. There is even an old tapestry hanging in Crosseus antechamber which depicts archers shooting fish in the river. It was from that I got my idea.

"You see, Balazar is not the first to have thought of using archers in war to equalize the size differential between us and the Iblis. I myself trained a company and would have used them to good effect, had not other forces intervened."

"What happened?"

"I was very young then," Simplinius continued, his eyes fixed on his slowly turning glass and his voice growing remote, "and ambitious. It was shortly after my 'heroic' promotion. Everyone said I was the youngest man ever to be given a battalion-I was just twenty three at the time-and was destined for great things. I let all that talk go to my head, I suppose. Anyway, I thought of using bows and arrows, but I didn't want to just suggest the idea: I wanted to demonstrate it. All for my own 'greater glory' you understand. So, when the occasion presented itself, I studied the tapestry closely-Correlius was king then, but you probably don't remember him-and then experimented with different designs and materials. The best I found was a stave of the Yactus tree reinforced with leather wrappings. Then, I set some of the armorers to making them in secret-I believe they ended up

169

making enough to outfit half the army!-and, using the pretext of long marches, took a chosen company down the valley and trained them. They proved quite adept and within two months, most of them could hit their mark at over a hundred paces. Meanwhile, I scouted the country closely around the old city and laid plans for an ambush.

"Finally, when all was ready, I went to the king. It was my hope that he would come out and observe my show. I gained an audience, but did not get to see the king alone: Procin, who then commanded the Guard, was also in attendance and listened eagerly. The king said he was impressed with my idea and that I should go ahead with my plans, but that he himself would not be able to observe. Instead, he would send a reliable representative who would give him a full report.

"That representative turned out to be none other than our own Cormin, a sneaking weasel of a man even then, who by various underhanded means was already quickly working his way up through the ranks of the Guard. He hated me for my prominence, and I him for several reasons which have nothing to do with this story-suffice it to say there was no love lost between us and that I was not pleased to see him arrive on the evening we were to set forth.

"And I was especially not pleased to see him arrive, not alone, but commanding two full companies of Guardsmen. 'Orders,' he said. The Guards were to provide extra protection for my men in case anything went amiss. I protested, but in vain. I had my orders, too, and we set out.

"The ground I had chosen was a soft valley between two wooded hills about two leagues distant from the old city. I stationed my men under cover on the upper slopes and, at first light, sent out a small party as bait to lure the Iblis into the trap. Cormin split his men and put them on the crests behind mine. Then we waited.

"The plan worked to perfection. My scouting party showed themselves before the city and immediately about fifty Iblis came out in pursuit. My men led them like sheep into the ambush, staying just far enough ahead of them so that by the time the Iblis entered the valley, my scouts were already back up the slopes and ready to greet them with the rest of us.

"The Iblis came on fast, trotting down the valley like dogs, panting and drooling on the scent of meat. When they were dead center between us, I ordered a volley from one side. My men were excited and not used to firing downhill, so most of them overshot, but still, five or six Iblis dropped in their tracks and the rest instantly panicked. They behaved exactly as I hoped they would and, instead of running back down the valley, immediately started rushing up the other slope, away from the arrows. That's when my other volley hit them, right in the face. Though this, too, was mostly overshot, the effect seemed to paralyze them. They started scurrying around in aimless circles down there between us and seemed not to know what to do.

"That's when Cormin made his move. Jumping up from cover he began yelling to my men: 'They're beaten now! You've got them!' he screamed. 'Forward! Take prisoners! Attack!' And my men, confused and excited, rushed to the attack with the Guard hot on their heels.

"I started in too, but before I could take a step, I was seized by two burly Guardsmen and held fast while another quickly bound and gagged me. Helpless, I watched what followed. As my men rushed in, all eager for glory and forgetting their new weapons, the Iblis recovered their wits and rose to meet them. Confidant in their numbers-we had them outnumbered by six to one-and not dreaming of treachery, my men attacked at a run with the Guard right behind. But as the lines met and the fighting began, instead of attacking the Iblis, the Guardsmen began cutting my men down from behind."

"Simplinius! Is this true?" Colinus was aghast.

"Quite true, Colinus. Caught in two lines with the Iblis between and the Guard all around, my men were slaughtered to a man. Not one escaped and none were given quarter. And when it was over, do you think the Guard fought the Iblis? Not a bit of it! They stood there, looking over their work and then, without so much as a word, let alone a blow, parted: the Iblis dragging off corpses for the stew pot and the Guard to gather up the bows and escort me back to the city."

"But why, Simplinius? Why?"

"Because the bow would have given us victory, and victory is not Policy, that's why. Though why that is, I do not know. I do not even know why I was spared, though my guess is that the king could not abide quite that much treachery. All I know is that on the way back to the city Cormin said I was spared because of my former heroic service, but that

172

if I ever breathed a word about what had happened, or sought reasons, I would meet such a death as had never been imagined. And I was in such a state of shock and confusion that I went along, and when I did begin to think again, it was too late. There was nothing I could do except cause my own end. So I kept silent. But it was shortly after this that rumors began about the Iblis using bows and how such weapons were cowardly and not worthy weapons for a warrior."

"Simplinius-Sir-I am astounded! For what reasons would the King, even the Queen, not want...?"

"I know not Colinus. But this I do know: if these Outlanders seriously intend to lead us to victory, then they and all who serve them are in peril."

Accompanied by a very tremulous Hudarin, the two Outlanders found the King in his personal chambers, enjoying dinner in company with his architects and discussing plans for the new amphitheater being built down by the lake. On being told there were grave matters to discuss, however, he dismissed the architects and bade the military trio be seated.

"That won't be necessary, your Majesty," said Balazar. "And we apologize for taking your time. It's just that we seem to have run into a little problem here which Hudarin feels we should discuss with you. It won't take long, I'm sure."

"The time is of no concern, Lord Balazar," returned Crosseus. "I am entirely at your service. Pray, do be seated. Now, what is this 'little problem?'"

"Well, in a nutshell, Your Majesty, I've just ordered the raids on old Kantar stopped and it is Hudarin's opinion that I have overstepped my authority."

The king jolted as if he'd been struck and his spoon clattered onto his plate. "You've what!" Quickly, however, he mastered himself and even managed a small smile. "I see. And what, if I may ask, Oh Balazar, is the reason for this?"

As Balazar quickly sketched out his strategy, Crosseus stroked his wispy beard and listened intently. "Well," he said when Balazar was done, "I must admit the plan has merit. But, there are other issues to be considered here. As I'm sure Hudarin mentioned, these raids provide us with much needed field hands, not to mention depriving our enemies of manpower. They are also almost a tradition, our one means of striking back... But, let me meditate on this overnight and advise you in the morning."

"Well, you see, Your Majesty, that's the problem: the orders have already been issued."

"I see," said Crosseus, contemplative again. "And you went along with this, Hudarin?"

"I..."

"He had no choice, Lord."

"I see. Well, I shall still have to consider this. It is a serious matter."

Momentarily, Balazar's eyes flashed angrily. Then he, too, mastered himself and spoke mildly: "Certainly, Your Majesty. As you have made me Warlord, so can you unmake me..."

"There is no need to speak so, Balazar. You are as I have named you, rest assured. Nevertheless, this has long been a matter of policy and I must meditate

174

on it and pray to Kala Atar before I can give my full blessing. Rash council is not good council, Balazar. We will speak further of this."

The three left him then, but instead of meditating, Crosseus stripped off the ornaments of his office and again made the long trek up into the bowels of the cliff. His path was longer this time, however, for the Presence he sought was not within but on the very top of the cliff, taking her ease in the soft evening air by the side of the great quarry. She sat on a reclining couch, eating fruit, and was surrounded by a group of richly dressed, equally diminutive men and women. The Teller, Teukonis, sat beside her strumming his lyre. Escorted by servants, Crosseus approached bent low and fell to his knees before her. When he explained his errand, Salonis exploded into wrath.

"How dare that oaf contravene my policy! Why did you not stop him?"

"Majesty, I was not present. It was done at a military council." Crosseus was trembling, speaking very fast.

"And what of that worm Hudarin? Was it not he who was to control these Outlanders in military matters?"

"There was nothing he could do: the Outlander simply ordered it in open council. It would have been death to disobey."

"It IS death to disobey! And death he has earned. Now, go back this instant and stop this madness!"

"Majesty, if I countermand his order, the Outlander will leave. And that will foil our plans."

"Fool!" In disgust, Salonis threw a half-eaten apple into the quarry, her fat arm rippling violently. "I've half a mind to slit your throat with my own hand!"

"As you wish, Majesty." Crosseus cowered lower, his voice muffled in the earth.

"Salonis, if I may be so bold...?" It was Koltar who spoke.

"What?" she spat, turning a savage face upon him.

"Well you needn't bark-I'm not one of your mongrel pets, you know," and he turned away in affected pique.

"I beg your pardon, Koltar, but as you can see, I am upset. Please, what is it?"

"Well, it just occurs to me that this needn't be a rock in the road at all, so to speak. Simply send a message to Chubar and buy some time. After all, time is our major objective. This could even work to our advantage. How much time do we need from them: a month? Two months?"

"Hmmm. Yes, you may be right, Koltar. Crosseus, go tell this dolt Balazar that you have decided he may go ahead with his plans. And you, Koltar-since you've been so bright and convincing-you may go yourself to Chubar."

"I, Lady? Myself? But it's such a long and arduous journey. And I have the new valve to work on in my lab. Surely, others would be better suited to the task?"

"You, Koltar. Shave off that ridiculous mustache and leave at first light. But tell me Crosseus, are the Outlanders breeding well?"

176

"The fair one-Thorngere-is, Your Majesty. But Balazar-I am afraid he has sent away all who have come to him."

"That fool! Talk to him, Crosseus, convince him. Otherwise I shall have him killed outright and we will make do with the other. That's all, you may go," and with a flip of her hand, she dismissed him.

"Ah, pardon me, Majesty, but what of Hudarin? Truly, he had no choice and he has served you well?"

"No, he is Called. Someone must pay for disrupting my plans... But bid him use poison, small doses over several weeks so that he seems merely to be wasting away from some illness. I don't want to arouse the Outlander's suspicion. Now be off or I'll have you whipped."

"Well, Balazar, old friend," said Thorngere, "I hate to admit it, but I'm impressed."

"With what?" said Balazar, stuffing his face with vegetables. The two were at dinner in their new quarters, the table between them heaped with food.

"With how you handled things today. I never saw you do anything like that before. It was like... like you knew what you were doing."

Balazar grunted and reached for the horse meat. "I wish I'd known enough about what I was doing to keep those little buggers from killing each other."

"You couldn't help that. And they did obey your orders-that's the important part. But what I'm talking about is later, in the council: where did you come up with all that strategy stuff? That was great."

"Come up with it?" Balazar stopped chewing and looked up in surprise. "It just made sense, that's all. You would have said the same things."

"Well, some of them maybe. But it was good, that's all. If we had some real men on our hands instead of this crowd of runts, I might even think we had a chance."

Balazar put down his spoon and looked straight at Thorngere. "We not only have a chance, my friend: we are going to win. Believe it."

"If the king will let you."

"Humph."

"You don't see a problem there?"

"No, I think his 'meditation' is just a way to save face. What else could possibly be so important about those raids that Crosseus would risk losing us so soon after he got us?"

"Maybe he thinks he can turn you into a puppet."

"Ha! He'd have to stand on a pretty high stool to make me dance!"

The two lapsed into silence then, concentrating on the important work at hand. But Thorngere kept stealing glances at Balazar, as if his old friend had become something of a stranger.

CHAPTER FIVE
Koltar's Ride

Freshly shaved, and dressed in the garb of a Kantaran child-though not at all in a childish humor-Koltar left his chambers high inside the cliff and made his way through a back passageway to the Queen's private stables. These were built cunningly into the rock on a shelf just below the summit so as to be hidden from view on all sides. Squinting in the morning sun after the semi-darkness inside, Koltar cursed the two Kantaran grooms who saddled a pony for him in feverish haste. Grabbing the reins, he leapt on, dug his heels savagely into the beast's flanks and raced off on his mission.

He did not take any of the routes used by the warriors on their raids of the Old City. Instead, he headed directly south along a path hollowed out of a natural declivity in the back side of the cliff. Like the stables themselves, this path was hidden from view on either side by solid walls of rock. A few miles south, the ridge below which New Kantar was built joined the mountains which encircled the entire land. Turning westward here, Koltar followed another well-defined path along the slopes, past the head of the lake and over the other ridge which fronted the city. Here his path descended into the foothills and, still hidden from view, curved in a large semi-circle all around the plains, turned north and approached the Old City from the back, the side away from the river.

The ride was long, near fifty miles, and though he had stopped to rest himself and his pony several times during the course of the day, the poor beast was reeling when the trip was done. Nor had the long hours in the saddle improved Koltar's mood. Reining up in a hidden grotto about half a mile from the city walls, he unsaddled and tethered the pony, then flopped down himself in the fast fading light to eat the meager rations he had brought along.

Koltar's ego was smarting from the messenger duty. He had been used to these trips as a youth, indeed, had even enjoyed the dash and excitement of them. But since he had reached his man's estate, had finally fathered a son and had taken his place not only as a leading noble of the city and nephew of the queen, but as one of the leading designers and inventors as well, such things were beneath him. But there was no appeasing the Queen these days. He realized full well that she was facing a crisis which threatened the very life of the city, and that she bore a tremendous load of responsibility, but still, there seemed little provocation for her continual outbursts of rage and little rationale for her maltreatment of those around her. Each day seemed worse than the last. And it was not only him she was abusing: ordering Seris whipped the other day for lightly suggesting that the First Born be allowed to sample the favors of the Outlanders as well, having a mongrel servant drowned in the quarry for daring to serve her an apple with a soft spot in it... These things were not like Salonis. She had always been a stern ruler, but a fair one. Indeed, as Queen, she had always been compared in patience with her grandmother who had borne the great building and, in wisdom, with her great grandmother who first conceived the city. But now she was like neither, was, rather, showing the temperamental signs of her great grandfather, the last king-he who had gotten them into all this trouble in the first place.

Briefly, Koltar wondered if such character flaws could remain hidden for several generations, only to reappear, and made a mental note to look into it. But then, this irascibility of Salonis was not something which had developed over time, like a growth or a tumor. No, it was a thing which had emerged in response to external pressures, like the leaves on certain plants turning to follow the path of the sun (except in this case she seemed to be turning away!) All the while the first outlander had been active-this Balazar giant-she had been slowly developing signs of distemper. But that was nothing: stress, anxiety. Then, when reports came of another outlander making his way to the Old City from the mountains, she exploded. But whether this was simply a natural reaction to increased stress (he had done load tests on various kinds of rock and knew about such things) or whether there was something inside her which was just now coming out, or even a combination of the two, he did not know.

It was interesting, seen dispassionately, assuming one was not made a victim of it and sent off cross country like this on a mere whim like some Sonless youth. No, it was interesting despite that (Koltar could be very objective in such matters), but like the question of continued Breeder potency, like the question of potency itself, he had no notion yet how to probe it. Valves and conduits,

181

mining and agricultural technologies, these things were easy compared to the questions of life.

Reclining on a soft mossy hillock and chewing on a grass stem as he pondered these things, Koltar suddenly realized that he had fallen asleep, that the sun had gone, and it was past time to signal. Well, he thought, he would just have to rattle the cage and hope to draw attention-hopefully the right attention.

Rising, he walked rapidly to the head of the little grotto and, squeezing through some brush beside an outcropping of rock, entered the mouth of a tunnel behind. Inside, it was pitch black but he knew the way and walked easily, sliding one hand along the wall. The tunnel extended for a long way through many curves and corners, but ever uphill. At the third turning, he knew he was under the city walls and, a few turnings after that, saw ahead a light shining from the chamber beneath the palace. He was in luck: they had left a torch. Perhaps?-but, no: entering the chamber, he saw that the gate to the stairway was locked. Had he made the signal, this would have been open. Now he would have to call and hope someone was in the palace basement. There was not much risk in this as only Chubar's most trusted servants were allowed there, but still, if someone else got lost and wandered down, or was just lurking round (the place abounded with thieves) and found him down here-well, perhaps the disguise would work, perhaps they would think him some child locked up for punishment. Perhaps they would not notice the tunnel mouth. Perhaps, perhaps. Perhaps they would see him for what he was, break down the gate and carry him off for supper, too!

Hearing a scuffle of footsteps from above, Koltar thrust his head between the bars and called out softly, "Halloo! Halloo!" The steps approached and presently the figure of old Galdomere, Chubar's head wine steward, appeared at the top of the stairs.

"Why, blast me if it isn't young Koltar!" this ancient said as he hobbled down one belabored step at a time. A blow to the head in his youth had partially paralyzed his left side-and numbed his wits, as well-and this, plus his age, caused him to move very slowly. "What brings you here, Koltar? I haven't seen you in a dog's age. Why ever didn't you signal? Something told me, something told me, though, that a messenger would come tonight. I knew. You see the torch? Yes, I put the torch there, indeed I did. I knew!" Each of these sentences was delivered a step at a time and all the while he was fumbling in the pouch at his belt for the keys. When he reached the landing at the bottom, he had them. "You're lucky to have caught me, Koltar, lad. Why ever didn't you signal? Chubar's at table: just sent me down to breach a new cask, otherwise you'd have slept the night here." Pushing open the rusty gate, and taking Koltar's arm in his grandfatherly fashion, Galdomere pulled him out into the light. "Here, boy, let me have a look at you. Why, bless you, lad, you haven't grown an inch in all these years! How's that possible? It's got to be fifteen years since, yet look at you! Just as fresh and sprightly as ever. How do you do it, boy?" he said, holding Koltar up, and turning him this way and that under the torch.

"Will you just shut up for a minute, Galdomere! And put me down!" Koltar snapped and shook himself free. "In the first place, I didn't signal because I forgot. In the second place, I am not a boy; and in the third place, I have important business with Chubar. Now, will you take me to him or not?" Standing with his fists on his hips, Koltar delivered this lecture much like a spoiled child and Galdomere received it like an abashed grandparent.

"Well, I didn't mean to dally, boy. I'm just so glad to see you, and you know I don't move so fast any more, and, well..."

"It's all right, Galdomere. I'm glad to see you, too. But now, let's go."

Koltar followed as the old wine steward shuffled slowly and awkwardly up into the basement, and thence through various back passages to Chubar's private apartments. Here, Galdomere poured some wine for him and withdrew, promising to tell Chubar he was there.

Settling himself into a roughly hewn wooden arm chair which was much too large for him, Koltar began to wait. And a long wait it was. The first quarter hour slipped by, then another and another. For a while, Koltar tried to amuse himself with his various speculations, but waiting being everywhere the same, he soon became bored and hopping up, began to pace the room and examine things without really caring to look at them. It had changed little in the years since he had last seen it: the crude wooden furniture still bristled with splinters; the wall tapestries were a bit more faded and showed a few more tears; the earthen pitcher and cups which adorned what served as a side board were of the same sloppy craftsmanship. The room was sparse and clean, but devoid of either color or taste. That it was the private sitting room of the city's leader only reaffirmed in Koltar's mind, how crude and backward these Iblis were.

Tiring of this as well, he climbed back into the chair and soon fell asleep. Footsteps and the slamming of a door awakened him and he started up to see Chubar standing over him.

"Well, Koltar! Galdomere said it was you: must be important, indeed, if that little slut of a Queen sent the likes of you. Why didn't you signal?" Chubar was a tall, lean man with a complexion like candle wax and the eyes of a snake. His hair was completely grey now and had thinned considerably since Koltar had last seen him. But he could tell at a glance he was the same pit viper he had always been.

"I didn't leave till late and so arrived after dark," Koltar lied, assuming his most off-hand and condescending manner. "But yes, it is important. If you would care to seat yourself, I will explain."

"Just spit it out and be done," snapped Chubar. "I have important guests waiting."

Not being at all quick, but drawing his tale out in a most circumspect and elaborate manner, Koltar described the situation with the Outlanders and the problem of the raids. During the course of this monologue, Chubar did in fact seat himself, but when he heard that the raids were to be stopped, he leapt again to his feet. "What!" he shouted. "This is madness! Impossible. I only agreed to this idiot plan in the first place because it was more convenient than killing the swine. But I'll brook no disruption of supply. You hear me?"

185

"I hear you quite well, Chubar. You needn't shout. And if you'll just bear with me for a moment... This disruption of supply will only be temporary, a couple weeks at most. If you will but hold your people back, these Outlanders will see the folly of their plan and we can get back to business as usual. If not, they'll go storming off and we'll have real trouble on our hands."

"Real trouble? You want real trouble? I'll give you real trouble: cut off my meat supply and you'll see what real trouble is. Hold my people in check? Impossible! Oh, I can see very well how this little plan would cause you no trouble: you'll be out a few slaves and some skins. Big deal! But you're talking about starving this whole city. Impossible! Even if I wanted to, I could no more hold my people back than I could stop the tide from filling the river basin. No, no, my young friend, you go right back and tell that little whore if things don't proceed as usual she'll have more real trouble on her hands than she ever dreamed of!"

"I'm afraid you don't understand the delicacy of the situation, here, Chubar," said Koltar, trying his best to remain level headed and objective...

"You're the one who doesn't understand," Chubar snarled and grabbed Koltar by the front of this shirt and hoisted him up to eye level. "We've been playing at war for a long time now, our two cities," he hissed, revolting Koltar with the stench of his breath, "but you mark me well: if you continue with this folly, you'll find out what real war is! Now get out of here!" and he flung the hapless Koltar halfway across the room towards the door. Scrambling to his feet, Koltar scuttled the rest

186

of the way on his own and barely avoided being kicked into the back hall.

But no sooner was he out the back door of Chubar's apartment, than another figure, who apparently had been listening all the while, stepped in through the front.

"You heard, Haradin?" said Chubar, still breathing heavily from his exertions.

"I heard. And you had better hope you convinced him, Chubar," said the merchant, pointing a level finger at the Law Giver. "It will go ill with you if the people have no meat."

"Me? Who was it talked me into going along with this idiot scheme in the first place? Who was it complained about the market being glutted, about falling prices? Who was it I heard wailing that this new Outlander would cause his ruin? Who, Haradin, who?" And Chubar advanced upon the merchant, teeth bared.

Jogging the last few miles along the cliff road after his pony died beneath him, a reeling and exhausted Koltar reported the fearful news to the Queen: that Chubar meant war. Contrary to his expectation, however, Salonis received the news with seeming indifference, only sighing wearily and turning again to her breakfast. "You had better get some sleep, Koltar," she said, her mouth around a fig. "You look all done in."

"But Majesty..."

"Have a fig, Koltar, they're delicious." Picking an especially succulent one, she held it out to him. He took it but did not eat.

"Chubar means to make war, Lady! Real war!"

"Oh, Koltar, you're such an infant when it comes to some things: for all your brilliance at inventing things, you have no concept of how to deal with people. I have dealt with Chubar for years. Believe me, I understand him. He will bark loud and long, but he will not bite. He will hold his people back. He knows who has the upper hand here-who has always held it. Now go and get some rest. There was no need to kill a good horse."

CHAPTER SIX
Stirring up the Stew

So, Balazar got his way. The raids stopped, construction on the new amphitheater stopped, quarry work stopped, non-essential agricultural work stopped, even garbage collection was put on a bi-weekly instead of a daily basis. All the resources the city could command-animal, human, and material-were placed at his disposal, and with an air of confidence and dispatch that surprised even himself, he set about arraying them for war.

Under the cliff, at the northeast end of the wall, a huge paddock was built to stable the two thousand odd horses for the planned cavalry, and in the wall itself, a new gate was constructed to provide access to the city. At the armory, craftsmen were put to work night and day refurbishing old weapons, hammering out new, and manufacturing field equipment for the day when the army would take up the march. Now useless leather jerkins were converted into field packs, heavy cloth was woven, waterproofed with pitch, and sewn into tents. Tripods and lightweight pots were forged for cooking over open fires. And, as luck would have it, Yactus wood, the essential material for bow and arrow making, turned out to be a common material used in building, so that a ready supply of seasoned staves was already available: and from them, bows by the hundreds and arrows by the thousands flowed weekly from the cliff carved armory.

In the hidden fields behind the cliffs, and in the vast storerooms below, agricultural workers and

Kantaran slaves worked steadily preparing and packing rations. Each warrior would carry three days' supply on his back, and enough to feed the entire army for a month was readied for transport with the baggage train. Meanwhile, on the great plain outside the city walls, the army drilled, and drilled, and drilled some more.

With a thoroughness and efficiency which impressed even his most ardent detractors, Balazar oversaw it all. Among the smiths, it was joked that not a weapon was made he did not try, nor a tent sewn he did not set up and sleep in. The agricultural workers swore he sampled every sack of grain, every basket of fruit, salted himself every fish that was caught. And among the army, officers as well as men, infantry as well as cavalry, outposts as well as administration, he seemed omnipresent: especially on those occasions when mistakes were made. His orders were crisp and decisive, his grasp of situations quick and intuitive, and his treatment of the men fair and just. Though his discipline was stern, it was no more than they were used to, and they came to see him, in very short order indeed, not only as a great warrior in his own right, but as a very competent commander. Within two weeks, despite the arduous dawn to dusk pace he kept them at, the army was his to a man, and they bent to his will with a will of their own.

No less, though in a different way, did Thorngere impress the troops. Though he confined his labors to the army itself, in him they found the perfect complement to Balazar: where the Warlord was stern, and often unapproachable, Thorngere was open and flexible; where Balazar made them

190

feel their lacks and work to overcome them, Thorngere praised their strengths and gave them a joy even in the worst of their labors. He was, in short, a great friend to them. In him they were able to see the human side of these huge outlanders, and this in turn enabled them to overcome their innate sense of awe in order to work under them. Kala Atar, they felt, was a wise God indeed to send such a pair to lead them. Few doubted either the God and his choice, or that victory would soon be theirs.

To the great Warlord himself, however, the picture looked not so rosy. As he worked day and night, putting in himself longer hours than he demanded of any, Balazar was always aware of fleeting time, of the need for haste. Better than anyone, he knew how the Kantaran would react to losing their meat supply and knew, too, just how quickly they would react. His leaving alone had to put a great hole in their supply, and now, with the raids stopped, it would not take long for salted and smoked stores to be used up and for hungry mobs to begin roaming the streets. What crimes and defilements they would commit among themselves he did not like to imagine, but he knew beyond doubt that by month's end, they would be coming out in force. He had to be ready to meet them.

Yet the difficulties seemed insurmountable. Of his two battalions of horse archers, only a mere handful of officers had ever ridden a horse, and none had ever handled a bow. Of the horses themselves, which ranged in quality from colts barely away from their mothers' teats to ancient relics hardly able to totter about, very few-fewer even than the number of officers able to ride them-had been saddle broken. To weld this amalgam of untrained horses and men into an effective fighting force within the span of a few weeks seemed utterly impossible. His best hope was to push them to the point where the men could at least stay aboard their mounts, propel them in approximately the same direction and-may it please the gods-be able to launch an arrow or two from their backs. But even this was a lot to hope for. What he needed, and what he sorely felt the lack of, was a trained commander to guide them. Neither he nor Thorngere were adept at cavalry tactics, and certainly neither of them were proficient enough with the bow (though both at least knew which end of the arrow to knock the string) to train others. The officers who could ride were able-barely-to break enough horses themselves and train others in breaking so that, after a couple bone jarring weeks, most of the horses were suitable, but the archery training lagged considerably. Three battalions of men, two of horse archers and one of foot, practiced daily at the several hundred targets set up on the plain, yet after two weeks, hardly an arrow had pierced them, while the ground in all directions was as chewed as a newly plowed field. Two men sent to collect arrows had been wounded, one severely, and another man had somehow managed to skewer his own foot. Balazar cringed at the thought of having to rely on these men to blunt the attack of a Kantaran host: they would be extremely lucky if they could reach the host, let alone harm it.

But just as there was no leader to effectively train and guide these men, so there was no other choice but to use them. Though the army itself was adapting quickly to the new formations-much more quickly than Balazar had thought possible-he still doubted their ability to stand up to an enraged mass of men twice their size. However, his reservations on this score were somewhat lessened by a discovery made by Thorngere. This happened early on in the training when Thorngere set out to demonstrate the effectiveness of a shield wall. To do so, he had armed himself and a company of warriors with blunted wooden weapons and lined them up before the assembled host. Explaining the defense to all, he then set out to demonstrate it by attacking the line himself. Clowning about, as usual, he pawed the earth, shook his wooden sword at the opposing line, and uttered a great series of war cries as he strode up and down before it. Then, in a mad rush, he attacked and began raining heavy blows on the raised and interlocked shields of the totally terrified warriors.

At first their line bent and gave way but then, as a spearman in the second rank thrust at Thorngere's head over the shoulder of the man in front of him, and as Thorngere raised his shield to parry the blow, the swordsman in the front rank dealt him a nasty thwack in the groin. Thorngere went down, clutching the offended organs and groaning loudly, much to the delight of the assembled host, who assumed he was still clowning. But clowning he was not. However, by the time he recovered, his anger had turned to excitement as he realized the utility of such a ruse in actual battle. Here was the exact technique needed to exploit the size difference between Kudanim and Iblis and to use the Iblis' larger size against them.

193

As he explained to Balazar later while soaking his bruised and battered beloveds in a hot bath, the Kudanim were perfectly positioned to strike low blows. With spearmen in the second rank thrusting high, and swordsmen in front striking low, there was no possible defense. An Iblis parrying high would be struck low and one parrying low would be struck high. With cool heads and proper training, Thorngere proclaimed, the Kudanim phalanx could mow the Iblis down like wheat.

But though he was cheered by this-in fact, he had a good laugh at his comrade's expense-and though the technique was immediately incorporated into the training regime, Balazar still fretted. Nor did his worries stem entirely from the misguided bumbling of his fledgling cavalry. Other things of a much vaguer nature-and perhaps made weightier by their very vagueness-preyed on him as well, and kept him up night after night, pacing in his chamber when all but the watch were asleep.

Part of it, of course, was simply his newness to the loneliness of command, and his own long standing doubts as to his fitness for it. Who was he, after all, to walk in here out of the blue-worse, out of the black of enmity-and take over command of an entire army? Though he had been raised to command from cradle to near adulthood, and trained from the time he could toddle to eventually succeed his father and assume a very powerful throne, his subsequent experience, which was now of slightly longer duration, had done nothing to reinforce that early training, and much, on the contrary, to counter it. Not only had he never commanded more than a single company of

194

swordsmen-and that only a few times-he had never once been on the winning side in any battle. The majority of his fighting experience was as a simple soldier of the host, standing in vain before the crushing armies of Fantar and then, with the host reduced to rabble, fleeing for his life. No crowns of laurel had ever adorned his brow, no revels of victory ever surrounded him, nothing even of hope had ever attended him since that awful day long ago when, in cowardly disobedience of his father's command, he had exchanged royal armor for common and had lost everything, including his name, in his vain quest for glory. Did he now, lost and nameless for so many years, presume to lead this other people along a path he himself was unfit to tread? Though his early training allowed him to cast an impression of assurance and confidence, and though the pragmatic side of his nature allowed he had no choice at the moment but to command, his heart shrank from the task and thumped with dread at the thought of another defeat.

But that was not all. If he felt a charade within himself, much more did he feel the charade without. Though he had as yet no facts upon which to base his suspicions, indeed, had nothing even with which he could name them, he still felt like a man who stands on the apparently firm surface of a bog and feels the earth sag and shift beneath him. Something there was which was not right. That much, and only that, did he know. While on the surface all seemed solid and direct-he was commissioned as Warlord at a certain price to lead the Kudanim to victory over their traditional enemies-currents below the surface seemed aimless at best, contrary at worst.

There was Hudarin, for example; hale and hearty one day, ready to march forth and fight, then on his death bed the next day and in his grave a few days after that. Granted, Hudarin had not been young. Granted, Death cared not for appearance when he swung his scythe. Still, there was the question: why Hudarin then, and how so fast? Balazar had visited the late Chieftain in his quarters only hours before the old man died, and his parting words to the new Warlord echoed ominously.

He had found him in his bed, already bone pale and plainly in sight of death. His cheeks were sunken, his body listless, and his eyes vacant and distant, as if the object of his sight was not of this world. He had little to say and seemed hardly to recognize Balazar. When asked about his illness, he only moved his head and sighed something about age, and time, and the call of the God. Only when Balazar was turning to leave did he bestir himself. Reaching out then, he grabbed the great butcher's wrist and pulled himself up onto one elbow. "Balazar," he said, his voice hoarse and rasping, "greatest of warriors, you claim to have come at the will of the God to lead my people to victory. Know that I accept that and that my heart is with you in this quest. But know this also and beware: God's will is fickle and his path like that of the winding snake. Tread carefully, therefore and look not only to your front. Kala Atar haman sutar-my blessing go with you." And he fell back, spent. Hours later, word was brought of his death. Though he had only known him briefly, Balazar grieved. Hudarin had been an honest man and a good leader. His presence would be missed as his warning went unexplained.

Then there was Cormin, that distasteful little prig who shadowed his every step, and Crosseus himself, the man at whose direction Cormin apparently moved. What was Cormin watching for, and what purpose could Crosseus have in setting him on? To see whether Balazar was keeping to his end of the bargain? Proof of that needed no watch dog. To keep him and Thorngere from escaping? Why should they want to escape if all was on the up and up, and how could a few pint sized Guardsmen possibly stop them if they did? Could Cormin be greatly exaggerating his authority from Crosseus? Or did Crosseus really think Balazar needed a bodyguard?

Twice Balazar had gone to Crosseus to complain of Cormin's hounding, but neither time could he gain any satisfaction. Instead, Crosseus had waved the issue aside, speaking vaguely of the requirements of honor and the need for proper pageantry in the display of power. Then he quickly changed the subject to, of all things, Balazar's pleasures! As if that had anything to do with anything. He was concerned, he said, that Balazar continued to send away the women sent to please him. Was Balazar not happy? Did he, perhaps, have different tastes?

This line of questioning mystified Balazar. Why should a king whose people were at war concern himself with his head general's sexual pleasures? Was he King or procurer? His interest, said Crosseus, was in seeing Balazar honored as was his due, that the interests of the war could best be served in this way. And how could Balazar tell him that the reason he sent the women away was that they reminded him of children: more, that they reminded him of the dead children of Valeria who, had they been allowed to live and grow, would now be his loyal subjects? How could he explain that, far from arousing his lust, these lovely little women only exacerbated his own sense of failure, that in his mind their mature loins and breasts on children's frames had become horrible symbols. It was as if his own illegitimate growth and maturity had been superimposed on the stifled ghosts of Valerian children to mock and curse him. He didn't really understand it himself, but how could he possibly tell the king that the women of his city made him nauseous?

And why should the king care? Balazar's job was to lead the army, not bed the women. Wasn't it?

The subject of women itself further disquieted him for, other than the ones sent to himself and Thorngere, he rarely saw any. He had supposed, when Crosseus first explained about the women living under the greater security of the cliff, that there must be some arrangement for spouses to meet-or for lovers, or paramours, or whatever they called them, if these people did not go by the marriage system-similar to the one he and Thorngere were experiencing. But that would necessitate either the women coming out or the men going in, and he had seen no evidence of either. Now, he thought, perhaps these people had an entirely different system, perhaps they mated by lot on feast days or something. That was possible. In his travels he had seen many different peoples and many different customs and knew better than to expect any kind of standard behavior. But he had gotten no satisfactory answers to his questions in this area, either, and the seeming total lack of intercourse-of any kind-between the male and female members of the population continued to trouble him.

As did other seeming contradictions: their incredible discipline and organization on the one hand, for example, and their utter lack of battle tactics on the other; their possession of the bow and their failure to utilize it; the same with their metal armor; their generations-long insistence on pursuing the war by means which only served to prolong it; all of these things, these seeming blind spots, set against the technical wonder and architectural achievement of the city itself; in short, their apparent genius on the one hand and obvious density on the other. In truth, as the weeks went by and his impressions were reinforced by further interactions with members of the army, he began to think it inconceivable that these people could have built such a city. They just did not seem that bright.

One other thing troubled him, perhaps more than any of the others because, as a thing he saw daily, it was more tangible and evident: since these people ate no meat, and kept no herds of cattle or sheep, where did they get their leather? Were it a scarce commodity, he could assume it was attained from the occasional and natural demise of a horse. But, as it was, that sporadic source could never begin to explain the quantities available. So where? Had Hudarin lived, Balazar would have asked him. But there was no other in whom he felt the confidence or had enough rapport to pry.

Which was another thing: though he had the cooperation and respect of all, and felt every day the growing admiration and dedication of the army to himself and his leadership, there was still a distance between them. Officers obeyed his commands with alacrity, even with enthusiasm, but they volunteered nothing; men cheered but did not speak. Valencius, Hudarin's replacement as Army Chief-now Army Chief of Staff-was a cold fish, effective but distant, and the rest seemed to follow his lead. In every encounter with anyone, the business at hand was ticked off one, two, three, and that was it. "I hear, Warlord, and will obey." No suggestions, no asides, no common civilities, nothing even beyond the formalities of position. He told himself that he had to expect some distance-the loneliness of command and all-but still, it seemed at times, as if he was not dealing with men at all, but with toy figures, carved in the shape of men and somehow imbued with the ability to move and speak.

All these things troubled Balazar and kept him up night after night when the duties of the day were past, pacing about his chambers or sitting before his vacant hearth (the weather had been furnace hot of late) and starring into the long dead ash. But as there were no embers, neither were there answers. In fact, there were hardly even questions, for in Balazar's mind, these things revolved like bits of meat and vegetable in a great simmering caldron of stew; surfacing for an instant here, sinking there, perhaps popping up again along the other rim, or rather, being replaced by another, identical bit with no way to count or tell. It was all a-swirl, a thing which nagged at the back of his brain but which yielded no insights, no ideas. Yet, neither would it let him go. Balazar's mind, while sharp and decisive when it came to matters of practical reality, was not of the kind that moved hastily through the realms of abstract thought. Rather, it was thick and ponderous, moving like a great barge down some sluggish river, gathering bits of this and that along the way, but unable to sift or sort them until it had reached some distant and as yet unspecified port. But slow though it was, it ignored nothing along the way and, as it plowed constantly on, gathered an ever increasing momentum which no force save death itself could stay. That distant port, wherever it was and however long it took to reach, would be reached, as surely as the river would reach the sea.

It was in the midst of one of these great evening mulls, as the fateful month neared its end, that Balazar was interrupted by a timid knock on his door. Opening it, he was surprised to see, standing stiffly at attention on the threshold, the little figure of Colinus, the former battalion sub-chieftain who had been appointed commander of outposts and messengers. Though Balazar was kept well informed of the status of the outposts, it was to Thorngere that Colinus usually reported. This night, however, as Colinus quickly and apologetically explained, Thorngere was "otherwise engaged" (which was not unusual) and had sent him here. As he, Colinus, needed to be away before first light, would Balazar, he wondered, mind receiving his report in Thorngere's stead?

"Not at all," said Balazar affably, "Not at all. As a matter of fact, I could use a bit of company... I tend to fret and worry too much when I'm left alone of an evening." He was curious, too, for Thorngere had often mentioned how sprightly this little fellow was and how effectively he had set up his network. Ushering him in, Balazar bade him stand at ease, offered him a glass of wine-which was gratefully accepted as Colinus had had a long ride-and motioned him to a small chair set beside the hearth near his own. "Sit you down, lad, and tell me what's up."

Overwhelmed at this gracious reception and somewhat tongue-tied in the presence of the Great Warlord (he had only dared come here because Thorngere, through a closed door and amidst grunts and giggles, had ordered him to) Colinus began stammering out his report: increased hunting parties coming out from the old city, growing turmoil within, but as yet no large scale movement in this direction. The parties were small and unorganized and confined themselves to searching along the lower ends of the streams coming down from the mountains. As yet, none had ventured as far as the mountains and only a few into the foothills.

"Good," said the Warlord. "The longer they fool around down there, the longer we'll have to prepare for them when they do head up. But tell me more about the city: what's going on there?"

"They're getting desperate, Lord. Supply has all but run out and they're beginning to riot in the streets. Chubar has been counseling patience, but the other night a mob broke down the gate of Haradin, the meat seller, and rampaged through his house."

"Good enough for him. I hope they slit his throat and cooked him!"

"Well, he wasn't harmed from what I hear, but there have been reports of Iblis being murdered at night and eaten by their fellows."

"How do you know all these things?" asked Balazar. "Thorngere has told me what a good job you have been doing, but I'd like to hear about your network first hand."

That Colinus had indeed been working to good effect was evident as he began to explain his system. In the short month since the council meeting, he had set up more than thirty observation posts at strategic points around the old city, and a system of messengers and signal stations leading back like a huge funnel to his own command post just this side of the western ridge. All were kept deftly hidden and runner's paths were marked out along ways that would offer the least chance of discovery by the Iblis. As a result of the system, no body of Iblis could leave the old city and march more than a mile or two before Colinus heard of it, many miles away. In addition, he had set up an observation post high in the hills south of the city which could command a view of all within, and he had commissioned several of the younger warriors who could safely pass as children to infiltrate the city itself via the old tunnel system and bring out first hand reports. The stock of information he had gained by these means was considerable. "I even know who the thieves are in town," he joked.

"You don't need a network of spies for that!" Balazar laughed. "All you have to do is close your eyes and point. But this is good, Colinus. Thorngere obviously made the right choice when he picked you. You're doing a fine job and I won't forget it when the time comes for rewards. But tell me, now, in your opinion, how much time do we have before they get desperate enough to come out searching in force?"

Colinus considered for a long moment before answering. "That's hard to say, Sir. They're an impulsive lot and don't seem to act under any kind of plan. Even their hunting parties are disorganized: whenever they feel like it, any old group of men will grab their weapons and dash out the gate. And then they spend more time bickering among themselves than looking for us. So, it's hard to say. It could be next week, it could be tomorrow. All they need, I think, is for someone in authority to stand up and say, 'Let's go.' So far, as I said, Chubar has been holding them back, but why he should want to do that and how long he can continue to do it, I don't know. Will we be ready when they come, Lord?" Colinus trembled inwardly as he asked this, for not only was he stepping out of bounds militarily-interrogating a superior officer, THE superior officer-but he was also violating Instructions and risking a Call. But he was also finding this bearded monster to be a very likable fellow, and that sort of made the question slip out. Besides, he wanted to know.

For his part, Balazar eyed the young officer cautiously before venturing a reply. Had it been another man asking this question-one of the toadies on his staff, or even the King himself-he would have given his stock reply that there was much to do but that all would be well and victory was assured. Such was simply good policy for a commander. But this Colinus was an interesting chap: sharp, inquisitive, perhaps a bit overeager, but also quite personable, and all in all, considerably different from the usual stone-faces Balazar had to contend with. And he might prove useful. Balazar needed a man from the city in whom he could confide-and from whom he could gain confidences as well. Plus, this Colinus offered the additional advantage of spending most of his time away from town and out from under the general scrutiny of Cormin and company.

"Well, we're certainly getting more ready every day," said Balazar and, reaching for the decanter, poured them both more wine. "And I have to commend the effort everyone has shown. But I do have to admit that I'm worried." Swirling the wine in his goblet, Balazar stared into its depths and let silence settle into the room.

Colinus, in contrast, strained forward in expectation, his face etched with concern. "May I know why, Lord?" he finally asked.

"I need leaders, Colinus-a leader, anyway: one who knows what he is doing with a bow and can train cavalry. Here's the situation: as you know, the whole strategy is aimed at delaying a major battle until we can prepare for it. As far as the army is concerned, that preparation is going marvelously well, better than I hoped. The men can get in and out of line blindfolded now, and I'm sure they have enough discipline to stand like rocks once we're engaged. But without a strong cavalry and effective archery, I fear they will have a difficult time against opponents so much larger than themselves. So we need an equalizer... Especially if we are pushed into action too soon. Yet, ironically, the only delaying action we can fight-ambushes when the Iblis finally come out-require archery as well.

"Do you see what I'm getting at? I had hoped to use the archers to gain time for the army to prepare, but now it turns out the army is fine and it's the archers who need time. And there is no way to gain it. When the Iblis come, I have got to put archers against them. But as things stand, the archers couldn't hit an Iblis with an arrow unless they ran up and beat him with it. And if you put that archer on a horse! By the Gods! you can't imagine what a mess that makes. Have you seen any of the cavalry drills lately?"

Colinus shook his head that he hadn't-but he had been hearing stories. Balazar continued:

"Well, if it wasn't so serious, it would be funny. Imagine a whole column of horses, standing quietly with riders at their heads: all is calm and orderly, just as it's supposed to be. Then the order to mount is given and it's like somebody hurled a rock into a hornet's nest! Horses and riders spewing out every which way! Horses bucking, riders screaming, bodies flip-flopping all over the place. I swear, it's enough to bring tears to your eyes! Takes them a good half hour just to get back where they started." Balazar chuckled at the fanciful scene-which was, in fact, not the least fanciful-and even Colinus dared to smile. But then Balazar started forward, his face sober.

"Trouble is, Colinus, it's not funny at all. The survival of this city depends on those people. They're trying their damnedest, but they don't know where to start. And neither Thorngere nor I have the experience to teach them. Given time, we could all figure things out, I'm sure. But we don't have that time. So I need a leader, someone who at least knows how to use a bow. But I'm afraid I won't get one of those either."

Colinus, of course, knew of just such a man and ached to tell the Warlord so. But, mindful of his oath, he kept his mouth shut, though it caused him actual physical pain. It was not his place to volunteer another. He had no doubt, though, that once appraised of the need, Simplinius, true warrior that he was, would immediately step forward and do his duty. He would speak with him.

They talked till quite late, this huge and for some reason unusually affable Outlander and his diminutive subordinate, until long after Colinus had gotten over the flattery of it and had, in fact, had more than enough of it. He had been awake since long before dawn that day, as he had for many days, and when he finally made his way down the corridor to his own meager quarters, he was reeling from exhaustion and not a little wine. Much too far gone to try and see Simplinius that night, he fell onto his cot fully clothed and was instantly asleep. Only in his dreams did his spinning brain try to assimilate the amazing occurrence of his having spent a quiet evening of comfortable conversation with the great Bala Azar himself. And in those dreams it seemed not at all strange that the two had become quite close friends.

CHAPTER SEVEN
Insight and Conjecture

Colinus was up again before dawn. Dousing his face with cold water to chase out the fog, he set off towards his old barracks in search of his former commander. Strangely though, Simplinius was not in his quarters. Nor did his orderly, whom Colinus found still asleep on his pallet by the door, have any idea where he might be. Making his way as quietly as he could through the sleep stilled halls, Colinus looked into the officer's mess, the general mess, the Battalion command center, even the new sub-chieftain's quarters and the lieutenant's dorm: Simplinius was nowhere to be found. Not wishing to make his search too obvious by awakening others, and having his own duties to concern him as well, Colinus made his way to the new stables, saddled his horse himself-from absolute ignorance he had become quite proficient at this during the past few weeks-and left the city via the paddock gate.

It was that hour of the morning when one first detects a hint of the dawn to come. Still pitch dark, there was just that beginning glimmer of grey in the sky, of not yet light, but diminishing dark. Around him, damp mists swirled as he guided his horse slowly over the uneven ground and the silence about him was like a presence. Every sound, the step of the horse, the creak of the saddle, his breath and that of the horse, even his own heartbeat seemed at once muffled and amplified, as if they were encased in some soft-walled cocoon. It was that time of early dawn, according to the stories of his youth, when ghosts made their way home from their nightly haunts, that time when they were most forlorn over their loss, when they realized they could no more face the day. He rode cautiously, not frightened, but not brazen either, and peered intently ahead for the first sign of the road he intended to intersect.

By chance, his path led him across the archery range, and when the first target loomed into view-a large canvass effigy of a warrior stuffed with straw and propped up on a pole-it startled him so he jumped in his saddle and the horse shied. Quieting the beast, he altered his course slightly to follow their line to the road. The second target came up swiftly and then the third. As the fourth came into view, however, he noticed something else as well, something smaller and half shrouded in mist which seemed to cower before the target, something which moved as the noise of his own approach became audible and darted behind the bulk of the target. In that instant, however, he recognized it.

"Simplinius?" he called softly. "Is that you?"

"Colinus?" came Simplinius' voice in reply.

"What are you doing out here? I've just been looking for you." Dismounting, Colinus led his horse forward to where Simplinius stood, still in the shadow of the target. But the Simplinius he saw then bore little resemblance to the Simplinius he knew. Even in the half light, or perhaps because of it, it was apparent that a dramatic change had come over his former commander. The face which stared back at him from under the disheveled hair was not the composed, commanding face of a battalion chieftain, but the wild-eyed, haunted face of a man in torment. His whole form, in fact, reflected this change. Wearing only a short night shirt which was torn and smudged, his feet were bare on the damp earth and his limbs were scratched and stained. And he sagged visibly, like a man who has just regained his feet after being knocked down by a blow and is about to topple again. "Simplinius! Sir! What is it? What's wrong?" Colinus exclaimed.

"Ah, Colinus! That it should be you who finds me thus!" Leaning back against the target, Simplinius slid to the earth and buried his face in his arms. Colinus squatted beside him and placed his hand on his shoulder.

"What is it, Sir?"

"First them, now you," Simplinius whimpered, his voice muffled by his knees. "All condemn me. It is just. Would that I had died before and not had to face them now?"

"Who, Sir?" Colinus shook his head trying to dispel this sight that was so strange and abhorrent to him.

"My comrades, Colinus!" Simplinius wailed. "All those old faces. They leave me no peace! They sneak into my chamber at night, fill my dreams with loathing. They pull me from my bed, drag me forth into the night, heap shame and abuse upon me, throw me to the earth and make me beg and crawl. Now they have brought you, too. All will condemn me!"

Suddenly, Colinus understood. There were ghosts in this night. "Simplinius," he said, "you know where your duty lies." He meant the remark kindly, but his voice sounded harsh.

210

"You mustn't speak, Colinus! You gave me your vow, your promise!" Clasping the younger man's knees, Simplinius pleaded: "I can't, Colinus. I cannot. Don't you understand? For thirty years I have lived with this fear. Now I am frozen. I can do nothing. Nothing!"

Colinus was torn. While his heart felt the suffering of his former commander, the warrior in him was also repelled at this display of weakness. Pulling away, he stood over Simplinius who fell to his knees and buried his face in the earth. "I will not speak, Simplinius. I will keep my vow. But, listen to me now," he said, his voice sounding as cold as the mists themselves. "All my life I have admired you and sought to make myself in your image. You have been my leader, my chieftain. More. You have been like a father to me. Many times I would gladly have died at your command. So it grieves me deeply to see you thus. But you know the peril we are in, Simplinius, and you know where your duty lies. Do not fear death, Simplinius. Fear failure." And with this, Colinus leapt onto his horse and spurred away.

Reaching the road, he kicked the horse even harder and raced blindly off, seeking to put as much distance as possible between himself and the spectacle he had just witnessed. Across the plain he dashed, and plunged down through the forest and along the lake. But as he neared the bridge, his horse heaving beneath him, he realized that it was not the darkness or the mist which blinded him, but his own tears. Slowing the horse to a walk, he lay across the neck of the sweating beast and gave himself up to wracking sobs. Of its own accord, the horse stopped and for some time the two remained there, each gasping for different reasons.

Finally, Colinus sat up and collected himself. Wiping his nose and face on his cloak, he closed his eyes and breathed deeply. He was amazed at the chaos of emotion both the interview and his reaction to it had aroused in him. Never before had anything like it ever happened to him. It seemed as if the guiding star of his existence had suddenly winked out, leaving him alone and bereft. But as his mind reflected on the image of the once proud Simplinius pleading on his knees before him, his anger subsided and he began to wonder if he had spoken too harshly. Looking out over the quiet lake where the mists still hung in the growing light, he wondered, too, if the whole thing might not have been a dream. Had the figure he stumbled upon really been that of iron-hard Simplinius, or that of some night demon sent to confuse and defeat him? Could the Simplinius he knew really crumble like that from fear?

Looking out, it seemed that the mists themselves were like fear, lurking, ever present and incorporeal in the back of one's mind, rising in the night to fill one's dreams, retreating but never quite dissipating with the dawn. What a thing it must have been, he thought, for Simplinius to live with that fear for so many years. How much fear could a man bear? How long would it take for any man to become lost in such mists? And what would happen then, with the coming of dawn? He began to pity Simplinius, and wished he had been more comforting, more supportive. Duty, he thought, should not totally quell compassion.

About to turn his horse back, he was arrested by the sound of running footsteps from the bridge ahead. Riding forward to investigate, he found one of his own messengers staggering towards him, reeling from exhaustion.

"Commander!" the man gasped. "Iblis! Two hundred or more. Making for the hills. They come, Commander! They come!" These words taking the last of his energy, the man pitched forward onto his face.

His whole being suddenly electrified, Colinus wheeled his horse in earnest now, and without even a backward glance at the fallen messenger, raced off towards the city, his voice already raising the alarm.

As the first hint of dawn lighted his east window, Koltar leaned back in his chair, stretched and rubbed his red-rimmed eyes. On the table before him were piled many papyrus scrolls and stacks of older clay tablets over which he had been pouring throughout the night and for many days previously. They were the accumulated records of the city, private journals, official records of births and deaths, tables of agricultural yields, accounts, all the raw data from which history is derived. Koltar, however, was not engaged in writing history, at least, not in the formal sense. In fact, he was not even engaged in the investigation which had first led him to these records, for once into them, he had stumbled onto information relating to another area entirely, one which was infinitely more fascinating: that of potency.

Koltar's room was spacious, hollowed out of solid rock high on the eastern side of the cliff and looking out over the fertile fields of the hidden valley. Had it been furnished in the usual fashion of New Kantaran aristocracy, it would have been luxurious indeed. But such was not Koltar's bent. Instead of couches, thick rugs, wall hangings and decorations, Koltar had tables piled high with the materials of his various projects. So crowded was the room, in fact, that his sleeping space was restricted to a small couch in one corner.

Even among his contemporaries, Koltar was considered an eccentric, for he rarely indulged in their indolent pastimes. Indeed, unless his work took him out, or he was ordered out to attend the queen, he rarely left his chamber or his work. Possessed by an insatiable curiosity, he delved into one subject after another and often came up with startling and useful innovations. It was he, for example, who had developed the water powered grinding wheel which milled their grain, he who with various kinds and shapes of crystal, had devised the lighting panels in the queen's chambers, he who had discovered the fertilizing effect of compost when spread on the fields. Though the term was not even current and empirical methods of approach a millennium away, he was, in simple fact, a dedicated man of science. In this he followed his father and his father's father back to long before the leaving of the old city. It was in large measure due to their compounded efforts that the new city was what it was.

But this new project had taken him far beyond the realms of engineering, architecture, and agriculture, and was so absorbing him that for some weeks he had left off all other work. His new valve, which utilized the principle of a threaded seat and which, when perfected, would replace the slide and cog valves now in use throughout the city-as soon, that is, as he could stop the damn things from leaking!-lay gathering dust on the next table. Likewise lay his astronomical charts, his experiments with various kinds of levers, his new metallurgic process, and his scrawled attempts at formulating the relationship between circles and their radii.

This thing had started as a whim. His reflections on the queen's temperament in the hidden vale outside the old city had prompted him to ferret out some of the old journals left by his predecessors in hopes of gaining more information on the characters of her mother, grandmother and great-grandfather. Though he suspected the whole idea would prove groundless-or at least, far beyond his ability to research and analyze it-he did know that various characteristics of plants were passed on from one generation to another, and on that basis, thought the effort would at least be interesting. He was looking specifically for references to these leaders' behavior under stress and had in mind an attempt to compare their day to day moods during known historical events.

What he found, unfortunately, shed very little light on the temperament of his subjects. However, several references in another area entirely had caught his eye and within a few days had so absorbed his attention that his original project had been forgotten. The first thing he noticed was an entry by his own grandfather during the first years of exile from the old city, when the people were living in the hidden valley and beginning to tunnel into the back side of the cliff. It ran thus:

"Celis, dear wife of my heart, delivered today: another daughter. In three years here, that makes three daughters in a row. When will I father a son to continue my name? Nor am I the only man with such troubles: many are the daughters born among the people, but few are the sons."

Then, a few days later:

"I have taken a rough count of births since we came to this valley and am shocked: of the nearly one thousand children born during the past three years, less than one hundred have been male. Is this a new curse from the God? How will our race continue if this persists?"

What startled Koltar about this entry was not the God's curse. That, and its ramifications had been a critical issue all his life. What startled him was its connection with their arrival in the hidden valley. Legend held that the curse was the result of abominations committed on the Iblis-killing some and then burning their bodies rather than burying them-and that losing the old city was also part of the punishment. But might it not also be possible that there was more to it than a simple, superstitious curse? Might it not have something to do with the valley itself? And if this was the case, might it not also be something reversible?

This thought was an astounding one to Koltar, one of immense proportions, and sent him on a feverish search through the accumulated records of his people to find out more. For it was the Curse, that single, seemingly incontrovertible fact of drastically reduced male births, which formed the

216

central core of New Kantaran culture. It drove the entire system devised over the generations to sustain the race. Remove the Curse and there would be no need for the breeder slaves, no need for the mongrel army, no need for the horrid infanticide of mongrel females, or the castration of mongrel males, no need even, of the entire Iblis population in the old city! Without the Curse, there could be war, real war, fought to win, instead of this hideous body trade which had gone on for generations. And if that war could be won, there could be real peace! Perhaps even renewed intercourse with the outside world! Koltar's head swam with these thoughts and he dug and dug and dug.

Two things, he thought, supported his thesis right from the start. One was that there was no mention of any such Curse when the people were still living in the old city. Yet there were many years between the abominations and their actual expulsion from the city. Second was the well-known fact that Iblian breeder slaves themselves became victims of the Curse after living for a time in the valley. Freshly captured, they produced male and female offspring in roughly equal proportions. But after a time (was there a way of determining how long?) the number of males dropped off sharply and the slave, no longer useful, had to be replaced.

But, Koltar reasoned, if there was a Curse from the God on the New Kantaran people, why did it extend to their Iblian slaves as well? Could the God so hate his people that he set his Curse even on those who unwillingly helped them survive? That did not seem to make sense to Koltar. The breeder

217

slaves produced only mongrel warriors and never, ever mated with first or second born pure bred women. The two breeding systems were totally separate, as were the two orders of society. So what could the God have in mind? Had he anything in mind?

If not, if there was no curse, then what other cause could there be? From his studies of physics and chemistry, Koltar had deduced a single law: like occurrences produced like results. Thus he knew, for example, that two stones of equal weight and composition would displace the same amount of water when immersed, even though they were of different shape. He knew, too, that fluids would always seek not only their own level-this was the principle behind fountains-but absolute level as well, no matter how their containers were inclined. This principle was used in building. Thus, he reasoned that if the curse was not in effect in the old city, but affected all in the new, it must be because there was something fundamentally different in the way of living between the two. His first thought, of course, was food.

Meat he eliminated quickly, for his people had never been meat eaters (though he did wonder if this fact might have something to do with their small stature). But the rest of the diet was harder to pin down, and it was this task which had caused him such labor. It would, in fact, have been impossible but for one incredible discovery: during that long ago conflict, even as the Iblis were breaching the outer defenses and the people were fleeing with whatever possessions they could carry, someone had had the presence of mind-or perhaps lack thereof-to grab a record book of recent agricultural yields. Thus, Koltar was able, bit by bit, to assemble a comparative list of harvests by kind and amount. Measuring these against known population figures, he was able to chart a general diet pattern. It was hard and frustrating work and thus far he had established few essential differences: the first years were lean, of course, but beyond that, the crops were basically the same, relative yields were the same (except, he noted with pride, when his fertilizer came into use!), methods of preparation were the same. The diet, in fact, seemed identical.

On the table before him now was the long scroll of his nearly completed list and, rubbing his eyes once more, he leaned forward to check through it once again. Was there anything he had left out? Anything he had failed to consider? Wheat, oats, soybean, barley, carrots, potatoes, peas, squash, the list went on and on, the figures for the many years entered in long columns. All danced before his weary eyes. It was no good. He was too tired. Already the sun was peaking up over the mountains and splashing through his window. Staggering up from the table, Koltar stretched and rubbed his aching neck muscles and turned towards his make-shift bed.

But he was not yet destined to lay upon it, for at that moment his door was flung open and a messenger entered in great haste. "You are wanted by the Queen," he announced, neglecting even the proper ceremony. "Now!"

The Queen! At this hour of the morning? Something horrendous must be afoot, thought Koltar. But as he dashed out the door, he determined that if she had it in mind to send him off on another ridiculous mission, he would... Well, he didn't know exactly what he would do, but she would certainly hear about it!

To his surprise, the Queen was neither still in her bed nor lounging on a couch when he entered her chambers, but was striding back and forth before her own dais in great agitation. With every step her great bulk quivered and shook, and this only increased his own sense of the urgency of the occasion.

"That fool Chubar!" she shouted at him before he even had a chance to bow.

He tried to slip in a "Good morning, Majesty," but she cut him off at the "Good..."

"Stifle yourself and listen to me, Koltar. About two hundred Iblis are approaching the western ridge-apparently with Chubar's blessing-and that great fool Balazar is leading the army out to meet them. I should never have let this farce go on! Something has got to be done, and done now! You go to Cormin and tell him I command him to accompany the Outlanders."

"But Salonis, dear, what can Cormin do against the whole army?"

"He knows what to do and when he sees you, he'll know it is from me. Now ask no more but do as I tell you. And be quick about it!"

Who could argue against reasoning as subtle and persuasive as that? Quickly, Koltar scurried to do the Queen's bidding.

CHAPTER EIGHT
Ambush

"Remember, none must escape. None!" Shaded from the hot mid-afternoon sun by the foliage overhead, Balazar moved cautiously along his line and reiterated this basic instruction to each of his officers. "None must escape." It was an essential point, the pivot upon which rested his entire strategy for gaining badly needed extra time. If they could get them all, the Old City would hesitate, wait for news, would fear the unknown. But if even one man escaped, then the entire city would erupt in wrath and Balazar would instantly have an army to face. And he did not yet feel anywhere near ready to do that.

Across the valley, also hidden by trees on the opposite slope, Thorngere likewise counseled his troops. Of the lot, these two were the only ones who moved. The rest, two full battalions of archers, sans horses, crouched under cover with weapons in hand and waited nervously. In the valley between, the tall grass rippled softly in the light easterly breeze, and the only thing that passed was the occasional shadow of a lofty cloud, or the darting shape of some bird. In fact, it was a wonderfully peaceful scene: the quiet valley and tree-lined slopes, a serene late summer afternoon, the deep blue vault of the sky. It was a timeless day like countless others that had passed before and countless more that would follow after this one particular day became history.

Yet, for those hidden on the slopes, it was a time fraught with tension and fear, for soon, they knew, that smoothly undulating grass would be trodden down by hundreds of Iblian feet, the wooded slopes would spit forth a multitude of stinging shafts and the lovely valley would erupt with the roar and blood of battle.

Satisfied with his dispositions and that all understood their tasks, Balazar made his way back to his command center where a messenger was just finishing the rugged climb up the back slope. "What word?" Balazar demanded as the little warrior gasped for breath.

"They're on the move again, Lord, about a mile distant by now and headed this way."

"Well, finally," said Balazar and waved the messenger away. These Iblis did not march like any army he had ever been in, he reflected. Not that he expected them to. But they moved slower than even he expected. All the hustle and hurry of the early morning hours, the muster of troops, the quick sketching of instructions which were already well planned and rehearsed, the chaotic dash of the cavalry to reach the appointed spot before the enemy, the worry that the infantry would not catch up in time to reinforce-all that energy and hustle seemed wasted now, for the Iblis sauntered leisurely along like a group of picnickers, stopping to rest more often than aged women, detouring like sightseers, and quarreling like badgers. Five full hours had Balazar's archers been lying in wait, the warriors nervously plucking their bow strings and craning anxious necks to look down the quiet valley. For two hours, nearing two and a half, the infantry had been on station behind the screening hills to the east and the extra battalion of foot archers, whom Balazar had not even planned on taking part in this action, were cooling their heels under cover at the head of the valley. All that there had been time to do, and still the Iblis dallied. What worried Balazar now was that the long delay would take the edge off his troops, that lethargy would set in from excess tension and that they would be unable to mount a determined attack.

Cursing under his breath, Balazar strode back and forth, trying to relieve his own impatience. It was strange, he thought, that after all the battles he had been in he should feel so like an untried youth again before this one. Of course, part of it was that he had never borne the responsibility of command before. But there was more to it as well. Ever since he had taken command he had felt things stirring in himself that he had thought crushed and wiped away years before. Gradually, he was coming to feel that he had stepped back in time, that he was not simply a common mercenary, rapidly approaching the nether end of his prime and with a long history of defeat and despair behind him, but was again a young man on the threshold of life: a young prince of the blood, even, ready to reach forth and grasp the scepter. This feeling alternated with his usual mood of self-scorn and mockery-when he would chide himself for these pretensions and feel his failings even more keenly-but more and more his negative side was giving way to the positive and he found his thoughts more taken up with what could be done than with what should have been done. He was beginning to look ahead.

Sometimes now he would notice his calloused sword hand and it would seem like it was no longer just a hammer of death, but an instrument of power: power which could be a force for life.

Subtly, the act of command, that charade he had so flippantly described to Thorngere, was transforming him. In playing a part, he found himself becoming the part because, ironically, the only models he could summon for the character he wanted to play were first his father and more importantly, his own hidden self. By playing himself, he was becoming himself, and strange as it was for a man of his history and condition, Balazar was beginning to hope.

But even this did not tell the complete story behind his anxiety as he waited to send his troops into action. The bottom line was that it had become very important for him to win this battle, and not just important strategically. Strange as it seemed-stranger even to him than the other feelings he had been experiencing-was the fact that he, the man who had mercilessly slaughtered hundreds upon hundreds of these little warriors, was becoming quite fond of them. And it was not just a belated sense of guilt.

Oh, they were a stiff necked lot, cold and distant, reserved in the extreme-except for the occasional one like Hudarin or that lad Colinus-but still, they were not without some fine qualities. For one thing, they were tough. Even though they were very small, they still made admirable soldiers. They had discipline, tenacity, verve, and most of all, a sense of honor Balazar found particularly refreshing after his years among the conniving Iblis. Yes, he

224

thought, they were good men, overall. Among them he had yet to spot a coward or a malingerer. They were men who would make any leader proud.

Chafing at the bit, however, Balazar stalked down the slope to the edge of the trees and scanned the mouth of the valley: nothing but grass, blue sky and the serene panorama of gentle hills beyond. Damn, they were slow! Shaking his head at the expectant faces peering down at him, he returned to his post and resumed pacing.

It had been a day of surprises: the alarm which, even though expected still came as a shock, like the sudden death of a long sick friend; then the fact that the cavalry were able to stay aboard their mounts after all and even maintain a reasonable formation; then that what's-his-name coming along (much good he would do at this point!); and then, most surprising of all, just when he had reined in his own horse at the edge of the plain to let the troops pass down the forest road, the emergence from the city of none other than Cormin at the head of a well mounted, well riding troop of Guardsmen.

It was not the appearance of Cormin which surprised him-he had expected that and was only just then beginning to think he might have gotten away from the little sneak for once-but the fact that they were mounted and riding like they had been born to the saddle. The rest, of course, was predictable: Cormin's insistence that the honor of the Guard demanded they be allowed a place in the line; his refusal to be deterred by Balazar's counter commands, claiming that the King himself had ordered their involvement. Not even his own easy acquiescence had surprised Balazar as much as their appearance mounted. How had they learned to ride like that? And where had they kept the extra horses? This was definitely something to be looked into, if there was time. For the nonce, however, he had stationed them far down the valley-telling Cormin he had "the honor of the point"-where, if his plan succeeded, they would be completely out of the way.

But at the moment, he himself was beginning to feel out of the way, and he wondered if there was any possible way the Iblis could miss the valley. Thorngere had inspected the sight after Colinus picked it and had reported it was the only reasonable path for the Iblis to follow. But when, Balazar wondered, had the Iblis ever behaved "reasonably?" Feeling the battle itch in his very palms, Balazar squeezed the hilt of his great falchion and tried to be patient.

Lying flat on his belly, Colinus inched his way to the top of a small knoll and peered through the tall grass. There they were, about two hundred yards off to the northeast and headed this way. Colinus' stomach flopped nervously at the sight of them and he crushed his body even closer to the ground. It was not fear he felt, so much as an erupting excitement that made it hard for him to keep still. All the planning and hard work was at last coming to fruition. Hopefully. The enemy was on his way and there was no way they could avoid the trap. What happened then would have to be seen.

They were about two hundred in number, mostly men from the city guard, and marched-or rather, straggled-along in a loose mob, keeping no formation, having no scouts or flankers out, and maintaining a leisurely pace. It was clear they expected no trouble. Their swords were sheathed and those who carried shields had them slung over their shoulders. To Colinus, they looked more like a group of farmers coming in from the fields than a war party out on a raid, and as they neared, he could hear several voices raised in some kind of quarrel. He could not quite catch the conversation, but could pick out individual words and could see the speakers gesticulate as they talked.

The leader-or, at least, the man in the lead-was a rotund, flabby looking fellow, bald as an eel, who looked as though he would have trouble getting up from table but, nonetheless, strode easily along and obviously had considerable strength beneath his layers of fat. He wore a bright red tunic which stood him out from the rest, and it was to him that most of the angry words were addressed. He replied with abrupt, forceful gestures, but did not stop or face his accusers.

The man just behind this leader shouted again and Colinus jumped to hear the name "Haradin" clearly over the intervening distance. So! It was Haradin who led this raid, he thought. Balazar will want to know of this and, without waiting to discern the nature of the argument, Colinus inched his way down the back side of the knoll and, once safely out of sight, leapt up and sprinted off.

From this side, the valley appeared to be the only opening in a long ridge which marked this part of the country. Running north and south, it was the first terrace leading up to the high ridge beyond. Though easily passable at several points by those who knew the terrain, it presented a rugged face to those who did not, and it was this fact which Colinus had counted on to lead the Iblis into the trap. Coming from the north west, their path would naturally parallel the ridge until the mouth of the valley was spotted. Then, just as naturally, they would enter it.

Colinus, however, did not head directly towards the valley, but aimed for a spot along the ridge just to the north. At this point, screened by trees and a small knoll, a small rill had cut a cleft in the face. It was in this steep gorge that the horses were hidden and it was through it that all the messengers came and went.

But as he approached it now, Colinus suddenly halted, for on the bluff overlooking the mouth of the valley he saw a red-tuniced figure-obviously a member of the Royal Guard-standing out from under cover and apparently observing the approaching Iblis. The fool! thought Colinus. Waving his arms, he caught the man's attention and waved him back. Realizing suddenly that he was exposed, the man nodded quickly and darted back into the trees. Shaking his head at the stupidity of it, Colinus hurried on.

Splashing into the little stream, he forced his way through the overhanging brush and sloshed his way upstream to where the banks opened out. Here he could see the dense crowd of horses with their grooms and as he hurriedly angled his way around them up the steep slope, he put a finger to his lips signaling the grooms to be still.

The back slope was very steep, dense with timber and thick with crawling underbrush. Twice in his haste, Colinus tripped and sprawled headlong, scratching his arms and face and ripping his cloak. But he bounded up instantly, not heeding these minor injuries, and continued clawing his way upward. He was winded by now, gasping raggedly, and his legs felt like lead, but as he neared the summit, he put on an additional burst of speed.

In truth, Colinus realized his mission was not that important. Whether Haradin was leading the raid or not was of little consequence and besides, Balazar would learn of it soon enough in any case. But the long building momentum of his excitement had overcome Colinus and he was not thinking of such things right now. He was not thinking of anything, in fact. His need for action had become its own reason and he dashed madly onward and upward, not because he had something important to do, but because it was tremendously important that he do something. Though nearing middle age by count of years, in his heart Colinus was still very young, and much too impetuous.

Just below the summit, and still well behind the line of warriors crouching in wait above him, Colinus turned sharply and began sprinting full tilt along the line, aiming for Balazar's command post in the center. But he had only taken a few steps when one of his feet was again snagged by an obtrusive root and he again pitched headlong. This time, however, his head smashed full force into a sturdy tree trunk and he knew no more.

Word was passed that the Iblis were entering the valley and the whole line became electrified with tension. Moving cautiously, Balazar made his way down to the edge of the trees and peered around a thick trunk. There they were!-sauntering casually along, not in the least aware of the trap they were walking into. Looking across the valley, Balazar could see Thorngere, likewise crouched and watching. Thorngere acknowledged his readiness with a nod and Balazar raised his arm behind him, signaling his own troops, and the last few moments of waiting began.

The Iblis came on, chatting among themselves, their shields still slung over their shoulders, oblivious. They were half way up the valley now, almost there. A scant hundred feet more and the trap would spring. Beneath his thick moustache, Balazar felt his lip curl into a savage grin as he watched. Like sheep, he thought. Just like sheep. Throughout his massive body his muscles twitched in anticipation. Always it was like this before a battle, his body like a spring wound too tight, ready to explode. They were almost there. Fifteen feet. Ten feet. Balazar's raised arm quivered. Five feet.

Then they stopped. Stopped and like nine pins, scattered and flopped down onto the long grass. They were taking another break! Casting shields aside, they stretched themselves out like picnickers after a big meal! Balazar could not believe his eyes. Not only were the fools walking into his trap, they were lying down and making themselves quite comfortable in it.

Balazar waited until they were all quite cozy, then stood and signaled his line forward. On his side, Thorngere did the same. Two thousand warriors with arrows nocked and bows at the ready, stepped from the trees in unison and began marching down the slopes. The Iblis, suddenly discovering themselves utterly surrounded and vastly outnumbered, were too astonished to move. They just sat, or laid there, and looked around stupefied. Stopping his troops about fifty paces away, Balazar moved forward alone, his great falchion drawn before him.

"Get to your feet, slowly," he said, his voice a calm, deadly growl, "and leave all your weapons. Any who try to run will be shot down."

"Balazar!" called one of the Iblis. It was Gafton, the old sergeant of the gate. "Why have you turned on us?"

"Just do as you're told, all of you, and you won't be harmed." Slowly, men began to rise and unbuckle their swords.

Then, suddenly, one from the center of the pack made a dash back towards the mouth of the valley. The others watched in silence as he ran, zigzagging for all he was worth, head down and arms pumping. A bow string twanged, an arrow streaked, and the figure crumpled, skidding through the grass, a long shaft sprouting from its back. The bowman, head erect and eyes glowing with a fierce pride, said not a word, but knocked another arrow and stood at the ready. That's the one, thought Balazar, suddenly remembering the man's name: Simplinius.

Among the prisoners Gafton wailed and fell to his knees. "My son! My son!" he cried and started crawling through the paralyzed ranks towards the body. Striding after him, Balazar caught him up by the collar and yanked him to his feet. But the old sergeant crumpled again to his knees and looked up, anguish squeezing tears from his eyes.

"Why, Balazar? Why? Why have you betrayed us?"

"Be silent, Gafton. Don't be a fool like your son."

The Iblis were disarmed and bound quickly. They put up no struggle. Astounded by the sudden ambush and terrified by the sight of so many arrows, they submitted meekly and soon stood in long lines, their hands bound behind them and their necks lashed to long poles.

"Well, my friend," said Thorngere as the prisoners began marching off, "this little plan of yours seems to have been a smashing success. I doff my cap to you, Sir-you are a great Warlord indeed, to have conquered such a host... Say, what's this?" Both looked up to see the battered figure of Colinus stumbling down the northern slope. His helm was gone and his face and chest were covered with blood. Running to him, the outlanders caught him just as he was about to fall.

"Good lord, lad," said Thorngere. "What happened to you?"

"It's over?" cried Colinus. "I missed it? Ohhhh!" and his knees buckled beneath him.

"Steady, lad," said Balazar. "you didn't miss much-in fact, it looks like you've had a worse fight than any of us. What happened?"

"I... I hit a tree," Colinus stammered. But before he could finish his explanation, the two outlanders burst out laughing.

"Was it at least an Iblian tree?" Thorngere wanted to know.

"Judging by the wallop, it must have been an Outlander tree," said Colinus, unable to suppress a grin himself. "But, did you get them all?"

"Every single one," said Balazar. "They just walked in and sat down in our laps."

"Even Haradin?"

"Haradin? Where?"

"That's what I was running to tell you. Haradin was leading the raid! You didn't get him?"

"Are you sure, boy? Sure it was Haradin?" Grabbing Colinus by the shoulders, Balazar shook him despite himself.

"I heard him called by name. And he wore a bright red tunic! You didn't see him?"

"Cormin!" Balazar roared to that worthy who, as usual, was lurking nearby, "one has escaped. If you want to be useful, take some of those great riders you've got and go fetch him."

233

CHAPTER NINE
The Plot

Rising early, Koltar dressed hurriedly, hollered to his servant for a cup of chicory, and went immediately to his work table. Outside his window, there was just light enough for him to work without a candle and he bent urgently to his lists. There was no telling how much time he would have. For the past three days, ever since the outlander had led the army out, he had had no time to work at all. No sooner would he grab a minute to sit down than someone would burst in with the latest news or, worse, announce he was wanted by the Queen.

Wanted by the Queen! After three days he was sick of the sight of the Queen. Hour after hour he had been forced to sit with her, holding her hand, listening to her woes, being stung by her viper's tongue, consoling her. At times, he thought she might lose her wits completely, so wrought up over this business had she become. "Oh Koltar," she would wail. "Oh dearest, dearest Koltar, what am I to do? I have led my people to the executioner!" They were hideous, these displays, very unseemly. The whole business was hideous and he was disgusted with it. But she couldn't say he hadn't warned her, that much was sure.

The problem was that this outlander, Balazar, had consistently refused to behave as expected. In the beginning, Koltar could grant that something had to be done. In his position as chief butcher for the old city, Balazar had proven himself much too proficient. He was unbalancing the market and undermining the whole system of trade. But Koltar had never really felt comfortable with this Warlord charade and had only agreed to it when news of the other Outlander's arrival threatened complete economic chaos. Salonis, however, had been convinced it would work. "Why just kill him?" she asked. "All reports indicate he's an ignorant, slovenly oaf, less intelligent even than the Iblis-why not use him, use them both? They'd make excellent breeders."

So the two were to be taken, given the royal treatment, empty titles and lavish promises, then allowed to glut and breed themselves into impotency. After that, they could be disposed of in the usual manner.

But it had not worked out that way. Salonis had underestimated the outlanders' abilities and the attitude of the mongrel army. Who would have thought, after the slaughter this Balazar had wreaked among them, that the mongrels would turn around overnight and follow him? Ironically, the opposite had been the Queen's major worry, that they would do away with him before he could be used effectively. She had been quite in error on that, quite in error on the whole thing, in fact. She had offered this Balazar the illusion of power, hoping to corrupt him with it and he, like an alchemist, had turned the illusion into reality.

Now he had taken the army and marched on the old city. The Queen was quite right to be upset about that. If the army was slaughtered-and there was every expectation that it would be-then the Iblian horde would immediately head this way and wipe out everyone. On the other hand, if by some

235

miracle, the mongrel army succeeded in wiping out the old city, then where would future breeders come from? Where would the cursed Kantaran aristocracy get the men needed to till the fields, harvest the food, build the city?

No one outside the inner conclave of the new city and a few top men in the old knew how dependent the two cities were on each other, how, despite the nominal fact that they were at war, disaster to one would automatically spell disaster for the other. Contrary to the popular belief (which was itself necessary), the war between the two cities was not a struggle for dominance at all, but simply a method of trade: the new city traded cold meat for the warm bodies which bred the meat and, on the side, traded gold for workable hides. It had all worked very well, this symbiotic hostility. Until this Balazar had come along.

So the Queen was right to be upset, Koltar reflected, but why did she have to take it out on him? Especially now when he might be on the verge of unlocking the key to the whole problem? If she would only let him alone to do his work, then it might not matter what Balazar did. Who knew?-it might even prove preferable that he win! But the Queen would not let him alone and he could not work. Even now, when he had gotten up early for just that purpose, he was unable to really concentrate, but drifted off, instead, into political speculation. It had not been a good three days.

"Chicory!" Koltar bellowed to his servant who seemed unusually tardy this morning.

"Coming, my Lord," said the Iblis, entering at that moment with a steaming cup. "But you had better drink it fast, Lord. I just saw a queen's messenger headed his way."

"Damn!" said Koltar as the messenger did, in fact, enter and summon him to the Queen. Koltar took two quick gulps and dashed off. So much for work this day!

He was not surprised, this time, to see the Queen up and dressed: she had not been getting much sleep either. He was surprised, however, to see both Cormin and the mongrel king, Crosseus, attending her. She sat, in stately array, upon her throne in the crystal-lit room, and Cormin stood at her side. Before them, on his knees and obviously broken in spirit, was the king. As Koltar entered, Crosseus was sobbing and wailing.

"I cannot bear it, Majesty! All my sturdy warriors led to the slaughter! I did my best, this was not intended, I know it was not. Oh, Majesty, grant me my Call, I beg you!" He went on in this vein with Salonis and Cormin, quite mute, staring down at him. Then Salonis nodded curtly to Cormin who stepped down from the dais, and with one quick stroke, slit Crosseus' throat. Gurgling blood and tears, the old king clasped his hands, looked adoringly at his Queen, and expired.

"Did you call me in here to witness that?" snapped Koltar, carefully stepping around the widening pool of blood.

"No," said the Queen. "I had not even intended it, but the old fool had quite lost his reason. Cormin," she said, turning to the blood spattered regicide who instantly snapped to attention, "if this plan of yours works, I'll appoint you his successor."

"It will work, Majesty," said Cormin and bowed low.

"What plan?" asked Koltar.

"One which I should have expected from you, Koltar dear," said the Queen, her voice honeyed with sarcasm. "But since-despite my pleading for counsel-you have chosen to let that vaunted brain of yours lie idle, others-principally Cormin here-have had to do your work for you."

Koltar raised an eyebrow and coldly appraised the figure of Cormin who stood, knife in hand and feet in blood, over the crumpled remains of his former king. "Well, Salonis dear, if you find this mongrel so worthy a counselor, perhaps you should take him into your royal bed and see what lies idle then."

"Ah, such a wit we are this morning!" sneered the Queen. "But enough! The plan is this: Our great Warlord and his bosom companion are even now encamped with the army outside the old city, offering battle. Soon, I have heard from Chubar, the offer will be accepted. Now, what Cormin has suggested is that he arm a hundred or so of his Guardsmen as common soldiers and, in the heat of battle, infiltrate the ranks surrounding the two outlanders-according to their plan they will fight together as shock troops-and cut them down."

"Oh," said Koltar. "That's a novel plan indeed! Have you perchance forgotten, though, that over the past two years, literally hundreds of mongrels have tried that very thing with Balazar alone and that he remains quite healthy in spite of it?"

"They were never Guardsmen!" blurted Cormin.

238

"You overrate yourself, dog," sneered Koltar. "And you assume a tone not at all to my liking."

Cormin bowed his head in submission. "I beg your pardon, Lord. But..."

"No, you have a good point, Koltar," said the Queen, "One I brought up myself and which has occasioned your presence. Crude and stupid though these outlanders are, they are great brutes of men and it is quite possible that they could fight their way out of such a trap-even against your sturdy Guardsmen, Cormin. So we must ensure they do not. Among your vials and potions, Koltar, have you not something which would induce a slow paralysis?"

"A number of poisons could have that effect, Majesty"

"Well, that's it then! Before the battle, Cormin here, acting under the aegis of our dear departed Crosseus, will propose a toast to victory and give the outlanders wine tainted with this drug of yours. How long would it take for such potion to do its work?"

"That depends on the amount taken and the size of the person. You would also need sufficient wine in the mix to disguise the taste."

"Could it be arranged so these two great hulks would be affected, say, within an hour or so?"

"Oh, certainly. To have it act quicker would be the problem."

"Good!" said the Queen. "Fetch it, then."

"One question, Majesty: if this plan works, what happens to the mongrel army after the outlanders have fallen?"

"Well, I expect they'll be thoroughly beaten and our friends the Iblis will have themselves a great feast. But I also expect the majority will escape. After that, we can get back to business as usual. You don't agree?"

"Actually not. I think the risks here are considerable and, besides, I'm not at all sure we should go back to 'business as usual.' I've been doing some research and I think..."

"Oh, Koltar, you think too much. And you know you don't have any head for politics. Besides, if this plan is to have any chance of success, it must be acted on quickly. Now hurry and fetch your poison."

"But Majesty..."

"Now, Koltar!"

So Koltar fetched. But he did not hurry. That woman could be so exasperating at times: so apparently reasonable one minute, so absolutely stone-headed stubborn the next. And to speak to him like that in front of a mongrel! She just... just lacked all sense of propriety sometimes.

In his quarters, Koltar pulled down the potions he needed and carefully measured appropriate doses into two vials. Still, something about this whole thing did not seem right, and as he headed back-still not hurrying-he tried to unravel the snare of his thoughts. It was not just the killing of the outlanders. That would be done at some point in any event. And the Queen probably was right about the outcome of the battle: with the field around them littered with meat, there was no way the Iblis would mount a determined pursuit. So things would go back to 'business as usual.' But such business! And to actually have to lose a battle in order to win just seemed to rankle him. It was like trying to quench a thirst with salt water.

Suddenly, Koltar stopped dead in his tracks, not even aware that he had just entered the Queen's antechamber. Salt water! That had to be it. Of all the items in the two diets he was comparing, that was the only difference. In the old city, they had eaten fish from the tidal river or the sea. The Iblis still did. But here, the fish were caught in the fresh water lake. That had to be it. He had no idea how or why, but if his putting fertilizer on plants made them grow differently, was it not reasonable to assume that something in or not in the water could affect the way fish grew? And, in turn, affect the people who ate them? Of course it was. It had to be.

But then another through struck him: if this was the case, if the change in fish was the cause of the curse, then victory in the coming battle was essential. They had to regain the old city. His mind running feverishly now, Koltar began to pace. How could he prove this? What evidence could he gather? Unaware, he passed by the very door to the Queen's chamber.

"Koltar!" Her voice jerked him up like a fishing line. Running in, he began, in a rush, trying to explain both his idea and why they must not kill the outlanders. But in his haste, he garbled it and Salonis, her quick temper flaring, silenced him in no uncertain terms. Cursing at him for the delay, she jumped down from her dais, snatched the two vials from his hands and gave them to Cormin. "Be off now, and quickly," she commanded. "Do your work well and remember my promise." Bowing every step, Cormin backed hastily away from the august Presence.

"Salonis, you must listen to me..." Koltar began again.

"No!" screamed the Queen. "You will listen to me!" And in a long tirade which recalled every instance of his insolence towards her as well as innumerable other sins, some of which he had long forgotten, she banished him from her sight.

It was one of those absolutely still mornings, the product only of late summer when all nature seems to have come to a complete standstill. Not a breath of air tickled the tall grasses or the various crops spread across the plain, and the sky was a solid, unmoving blue. Even as the sun rose, it seemed not to move but to hang, suspended. From his position atop the crude earthworks of the Warrior camp, Balazar scanned the scene before him in search of movement. There was none. It was like the world had been painted, the perfect reproduction of an instant which would stretch on unaltered in the slightest detail, through eons of time. Across the four or so miles of fertile plain, with its polygons of ripening crops, Balazar could see the crumbling walls of the old city shimmering in the stilted haze. The gates were shut fast and upon the walls there was no indication of life. It was like looking at the ruins of some grand and noble edifice, now dead and derelict.

Why didn't they come?

Often in the past, Balazar had looked upon the city from this distance and had thought how vulnerable it looked. A determined army, he had believed, with only the simplest siege equipment could quickly breach those walls-in places they were merely piles of rubble-and a stout assault easily take the town. But then he had been looking at the city from an Outlander's point of view, as someone like Fantar, with a full sized army would see it. Now, with only the tiny Kudanim-the real Kantaran-at his back, it looked quite different. With such an army, direct assault would be futile. Worse, it would be suicide. Without the protection of their massed line and preliminary work by the cavalry, there was no way his warriors could stand up to the larger and stronger Iblis. In an assault they would be slaughtered. Literally.

But how long could he wait?

At his back, the early sun was already beginning to bake the land and the heat seeped through his armor and into the massive muscles of his back and shoulders. It was a relaxing, soothing warmth, the kind that slowly steams away tensions and cares and makes one want to just bask and loll in it. Around him, the whole panorama of the valley seemed to reinforce this feeling. Nothing moved, all seemed drowsy, at the very point of drifting off into a sweet sleep. Balazar stretched and shook himself. It was ironic, he thought, that the best time for this kind of work was when you felt least inclined to it.

Were the Iblis just too lazy to fight?

Lifting his eyes to the high cliffs separating the old city from the sea, he followed their line to the north and around to the great mountain peaks which encircled this land. The stillness was indeed an illusion for soon, he knew, those ragged peaks would snag the first of the great gales sweeping in from the sea to the northwest. The great black clouds would catch there like ships run up on reefs. Their bellies would be ripped open and their cargoes dumped. Soon, even while the valley was still in harvest, those peaks would be choked with snow. Woe be, he thought, to any man foolish enough to try those mountains this time of year. He was glad he did not have to. When this war was won and the Kudanim reinstalled in their ancestral home, he and Thorngere would build a boat. They would sail out and return with friends. Slowly, they would build an army, a real army: one capable of meeting Fantar.

But first this war must be won and, judging from the events of the past few days, that was not going to happen soon. Time, he knew, was the great trickster in warfare. It was either the greatest of allies or the greatest of foes, depending on how one used it. Years before, in long dead Valeria, the king had ill-used time-to his doom-by hastily marching out and engaging Fantar when he should have stayed within his walls and awaited his allies. With Haradin's escape, Balazar had been determined to avoid the reverse of that fate by moving as quickly as he could. He had been certain that once word of the ambush reached the old city, the Iblis would pour forth like boiling water and that he would have to face a major battle almost immediately with untried troops. So, when efforts to catch Haradin failed, he had moved his army on the double, thinking he would be fortunate even to be able to pick his own ground.

But time had been an even more devious trickster than he thought, for after all the haste, nothing had happened. That Haradin had reached the old city was certain, for it had not been three hours before Cormin returned with the distressing news that Haradin had jumped one of his men and made off on his horse. Cormin had given chase, of course, but had not been able to overcome Haradin's lead and had seen him enter the city's gate.

So word had indeed gotten back, but for four, going on five days now, nothing had happened. The infantry had come up, a fortified camp had been constructed along a line of hills at the edge of the plain, even the baggage train had arrived with tents and supplies, and still the Iblis sat tight inside their walls. Twice a day Balazar had sent his battalions out to demonstrate before the walls. They had razed crops and taunted the Iblis, but with no result. In the meantime, screened from view by the low hills, his cavalry had drilled and drilled, and spent long hours practicing their archery.

Though he was grateful for the respite-under the leadership of Simplinius and the pressure of imminent combat, the horse archers were improving dramatically-Balazar was still intensely frustrated by it. Why didn't they come? Reports from the scouts (Colinus himself had just returned to duty with a stern warning from Thorngere not to argue with any trees) indicated that the city was on the verge of chaos, that people roamed the streets day and night salivating like dogs. Cannibalistic murders were widespread and the guard no longer even tried to drag away the charred bones of victims. There was rioting, looting, savagery on all sides, yet no one ventured outside the walls. How could it be that an entire city of people starved for meat made no move to attack an army that was composed of it?

Turning his back on the plain and the old city, Balazar climbed down from the embankment and made his way through the crowded camp to his headquarters. Why didn't they come?

Of all those in the Warrior camp, only Cormin knew the full answer to that question. Lounging in his tent, sipping a mixture of wine and mineral water, he was also the only man in camp that morning not yet armed and on alert. Through the open flap he saw Balazar return to his tent and the soft smile on his face turned to a sneer. 'Soon, oh great Warlord,' he thought. 'Soon you will meet the God,' and he raised his glass to him in silent salute.

For the past few days, Cormin had made it a point to ingratiate himself to the two warlords. He had even gone so far as to apologize to Balazar for his early hostility, saying he had at first suspected their allegiance, but that now, seeing in what regard the King held them, and after watching their progress with the army, and especially now after the success of the skirmish, he had come to realize how loyal and valuable they were, and wished to make amends. In his dealings with them, he had let no chance slip to compliment them. He laughed at Thorngere's jokes, nodded sagely at Balazar's counsel, and kept his watchful minions at a distance.

Naturally, he said nothing of the fact that it was he who warned Haradin of the ambush, and he who had given him the horse on which he had made his escape. Nor did he mention that it was due to his counsel and the plans he had afoot that Chubar held

246

back. These things, he thought, the great warlords would learn either too late, or not at all. And when they were safely disposed of, he, Cormin, would return to the city as King.

Preening himself with these thoughts, he did not at first notice the messenger who entered, and started as the man snapped to attention and slapped his chest in salute. About to curse him, he held back when he saw that this was the very man he had been waiting for.

"All is ready?" he asked instead.

"Yes, my lord. I spoke with Chubar himself last evening. He sends his compliments and assures his cooperation. They should come forth any time now."

As if on cue, the alarm was suddenly sounded from the battlements and the camp erupted into a flurry of activity. The Iblian host was at last coming out! To arms! To arms!

"Well, my dear Catalus," said Cormin, rising and throwing off his robe, "it appears your timing has been perfect. Help me on with my armor."

CHAPTER TEN
Treachery

Colinus was trembling with excitement as he dashed to the Warlord's tent for final instructions. About him, the streets of the crowded camp were a chaos of armed warriors running to formations. Up and down the central street, battalions were forming, the men darting to their assigned positions, aligning themselves and snapping to attention. Second by second the ranks swelled and bristled with spears and shields, helms glistened in the sun. 'This is it!' thought Colinus. 'The moment of victory! We're going to win at last!' But as he ran, he was very careful to watch where he put his feet.

Just outside Balazar's tent he met Simplinius who was just then dismounting, having ridden in from the cavalry station behind the hills. The two officers looked at each other, their eyes glistening with excitement. Clasping forearms and shoulders, they wished each other well in a mute salute: no words were needed. Then, they quickly entered the tent.

Within minutes of the alarm, all commanders were assembled and Balazar, huge and awesome in his black armor, spoke. "We all know our parts here. Let us only remember them. Battalion commanders, keep your alignments and let none of your men rush forward. Keep uppermost in your minds that our strength lies in the solidity of our line. Simplinius, wait for my signal before you attack. We must make sure the Iblis are far enough out from the city to be committed to the attack.

Until then, keep your men behind the hills. Infantry archers, make sure the horsemen are out of the way before you fire. Any questions?"

"With your permission, Lord," said Cormin, resplendent in the red and gold armor of the Royal Guard. "The King presents his compliments and has sent this flagon of wine from his own table to toast the impending victory. May I offer his toast?"

"By all means, Cormin. But make it fast."

"It will be fast, Lord. In fact, the wine is already poured," he said, handing the warlords each a large golden goblet and cups to the officers. Holding up his own, he began, "In the words of the right and true King of all the Kantaran People, then, may your arms be the thunder and your swords the lightening that rains death down upon our enemies. To victory!"

"Wait!" cried Simplinius. "No such toast would be complete without a prayer and offering to the God. May I lord?"

"By all means, Simplinius," said Balazar. "You were quite right to mention it."

Simplinius chanted to Kala Atar, and under the searing eye of Cormin, poured fully half his wine onto the ground. All the rest, including the outlanders, and finally Cormin, followed suit. "Now, to Victory!" cried Simplinius.

"To victory!" all cried and drained their glasses.

"Now, to arms!" cried Balazar.

Now the great panorama of ancient warfare began to unfold on the plain outside the old walled city. From its gates poured a great mass of Iblis; men, women, even a few older children. Seven

249

thousand strong they came, enraged by hunger, wild from drink and riot, they came in a swirling, rushing, roaring mob, their ranks bristling with every conceivable weapon from swords and spears to clubs, rakes, and staves. At their head, armed in flaming gold and marching under the banner of the city, was Chubar the Lawgiver. Long of limb, evil of face, he stalked forward with his naked sword held high. "Onward," he cried. "Death to the outlanders! Death to the vermin!" and the crowd roared in reply. Beside him marched Haradin, armed with a great cleaver and intent on butcher's work.

Across the plain, emerging from the raw earthen embankments of the Warrior camp nestled among the first of the rising hills, came the army of the new city, marching to the beat of drums. No disorder was here, no roiling, rushing mob, but the steady, cadenced precision of well trained, professional soldiers. Battalion by battalion, their burnished arms glistening under the pure sun, they came, all aligned, all in step, all treading as one. Four hundred yards out from the gate, the lead battalion wheeled left, the next right and, in perfect balance, they formed their line, each unit marking time until all were set. Then, as one, the line began to advance.

Balazar had structured his battle line as simply as possible by developing it from the existing structure of the army. Its basic unit was the hundred man company, under the command of a Lieutenant. Arranged along a twenty man front, five ranks deep, this unit linked with others on either side to form a battalion front. This provided both strength and flexibility. Each battalion formed a front of six companies with four behind in immediate reserve, and the entire line was four battalions long with the fifth in apparent reserve. It was in this last battalion that Balazar marched with Thorngere by his side.

The strategy, too, was simple. Horse archers were to ride out first from the flanks and engage the enemy with long range missile fire, hemming them in as they did so, and directing their advance. Once in range, a battalion of foot archers, deployed in front of the battle line, would take up the fire and the horse archers would fall back to protect the army's flanks. As the host neared, the foot archers were to fall back through the ranks of their fellows, but keep firing over their heads into the faces of the opposing line. The horse archers, too, were to keep up their fire, and as the armies engaged, were to begin an enveloping movement.

But it was for when the armies engaged that Balazar had kept his surprise. At that moment, his reserve battalion was to rush forward and smash into the enemy center, breaking it and splitting the ranks in two. This, according to the plan, would force the Iblis to retreat, and by applying pressure along the whole line, it was intended that the retreat be turned into a rout. As this began, the enveloping horsemen were to fan out along the line of retreat and harry the fleeing Iblis. But they were not to cut them off. On this Balazar was quite adamant. "Surround them," he had said, "and they will fight to the death. But, leave them a way to flee and they will panic. They will not be able to mount any kind of coordinated defense, and we will be able to advance with them right into the city."

In formation, then, and with this plan of action drilled into every man, the army of New Kantar proceeded with its steady advance. There was no rush, no cheering, just the drums and the steady stomp of booted feet. And towards them rushed the Iblian mob, already stringing out and losing what cohesiveness it had as its weaker members fell off the pace.

As Balazar marched, he and Thorngere towering over their fellows, he kept watch to the north where the tiny figure of Colinus sat atop his horse and measured the distance between the Iblian rear and the gates of the city. When he judged a mile had been covered, he turned and spurred his horse back towards his own lines. Seeing this, Balazar turned and waved his great falchion high in signal to Simplinius. "Now, Thorngere," he said, "we shall see if we've honed a cutting edge, or just ruined a blade."

Out from behind the screening hills came the cavalry. It two files, each a thousand men strong, they trotted down the forward slopes on either side of the camp and started across the plain. Sweeping wide around the flanks of the army, they spurred to a gallop and let out a loud cheer as they went by. The army answered, but only once, and kept on with its relentless march as the horsemen, like winged warriors, soared off towards their prey.

But however majestic and inspiring the sight of this flying host might have been to their fellows afoot, it was not without its comic side. No men had ever worked harder at their task, or with stronger will than these brave pygmies, and few, if any, had ever succeeded so well in so little time. Yet they were far from expert, and though in the main they stayed aboard and held their formations, some still had their troubles. As the pace of the columns increased, they began to leave debris; riders tossed from their saddles like apples from a bouncing cart. Others, losing control of their mounts, went hurtling off this way and that, clinging madly to their horses necks, their rear ends flapping behind them like pennants. It was one of these who had the misfortune to become the first casualty on that grisly day: flying out from the center of the column like an arrow, this poor fellow went plunging straight into the ranks of the enemy and was immediately hacked to pieces.

On the whole, however, the riders kept together, and as they came into arrow range of the enemy horde, they slowed to an easy canter and, sweeping around the Iblian flanks, loosed their first volley. It was a ragged volley to be sure, and the loosing of it caused not a few to lose their seats as well, but the shafts went up nonetheless, and when they came down among the densely packed foe, they also drank blood, and the first screams of pain filled the air.

Circling one clockwise and the other counter-clockwise, the two columns swept completely around the enemy's rear, loosing volley after volley as they went. Now it was the Iblis who began scattering debris, a debris not of bruised and limping warriors still capable of fight, but of dead and writhing wounded.

As the horsemen first approached, the Iblis had started to rush them, separating from their center and spreading wide across the plain, and Balazar feared the intended herding effect would work to the contrary. But as the first volleys scored home, and as the columns continued to circle at a pace too fast for the Iblis to counter, they drew back and sought protection from their shields. This was effective, as the small bows of the horsemen were not powerful enough to carry through the thick hide, but the ragged aim of the bowmen and the varying direction from which each volley came, more than countered this. Iblis shielding themselves to the right as a column swept by would be skewered by overshoots from the left, and vice versa.

The overall effect was devastating. Round and round went the archers, spitting feathered death from every direction, yet never coming close enough to be attacked in return. The Iblian advance slowed, yawing first this way, then that, then colliding with itself in confusion. Some sought to run forward, some back, some on the flanks sought safety in the center, while those in the center, where the rain of death fell just as heavily, sought safety on the flanks. All, it seemed, wanted desperately to get somewhere other than where they were, and the result was a milling, stumbling, screaming chaos of rage and fear. And still the archers circled, still death zipped and hummed and stuck, and still, to the heavy beat of their drums and with a cadence as steady as a parade, came the advance of the Kudanim army.

Now Chubar, no longer so resplendent with blood pouring down his cheek from a glancing arrow, sought vainly to rally his troops. They had come to a complete stop, the whole mass writhing like a huge beast in mortal agony. Pushing his way through the confusion, dodging the hail of shafts sent purposely his way, Chubar waved his sword and yelled for order. But the host was near panic and his shouts were drowned out by thousands of others. It was a full three miles back to the city, but he knew that in moments the entire host would break and stream back towards that refuge. It would be a slaughter.

Turning then, he saw that the Kudanim army had now approached within a quarter mile of his front. Here was a foe they could strike. "Kill!" he screamed. "Kill the Vermin! Kill, kill, kill!" Near madness himself, he rushed towards the enemy lines. Haradin followed him, as did his standard bearer and his own corps of guards. Sensing movement with purpose, the Iblis, by ones and tens, hundreds and then thousands, took up the chant and joined the charge.

"Kill, kill, kill,!" they shouted, their chorus taking on a marching beat. "Kill, kill, kill," and the great mass, churning and roiling, turned from agony to rage and rushed to meet Balazar's half-sized line.

There was no stopping them now. Here was that great trickster Time, up to his usual pranks. Had Balazar's line been but a few hundred yards closer, had they marched just a bit faster and been able to hit the Iblis at their point of greatest confusion, they would have caused an instant route and the day would have been won. Had they been slower and further away, the cavalry alone would have done the job. But they were in precisely the wrong place at this precisely right time: close enough so the sight of them turned the Iblis panic into battle madness, close enough to be reached on that same adrenaline rush, and just far enough away to allow the whole moving mass of Iblis room to achieve optimum momentum. From being on the cusp of a stunning victory, the brave little men of New Kantar would now have to fight for their lives.

So headlong was the Iblis charge, that the volleys of the foot archers checked them not at all. Here was no new terror but only more of what maddened them in the first place. So though the shafts flew and struck, and though men fell from them, their fellows paid not the slightest heed. They were beyond caring for any life, beyond fear. All they could see was the enemy within reach before them and all they cared about in this world was to drain his blood. Eyes wild, faces twisted into mad, grinning, gasping masks, the mass rolled on like something from a nightmare with six thousand throats bellowing a single roar.

Had they hit with any kind of solid front, their crazed momentum alone would have carried them through Balazar's line like a tidal wave smashing a rickety fence. But they had no front. They struck raggedly, unevenly, and the great wave dissipated. As the leaders rebounded and fell, they impeded those behind and the momentum of the charge was obstructed and absorbed by its own mass. Balazar's line held. But though the momentum had been checked, the force that drove it had not and, as more and more Iblis reached the line, the fight began in earnest.

Balazar's sturdy warriors worked with a methodical efficiency that was a marvel to see. Confronted by a maddened horde twice their size, they locked shields against the onslaught and fought back as coolly if this were another drill. On impact, the spearmen in the back grounded the butts of their weapons to form a living abatis. Then, as the work began, they struck high while their fellow swordsmen in front struck low, just like in practice, only now the effect was murderous. Instinctively raising their guards to deflect spear thrusts, many an Iblis felt the quick sting of a swift, sharp sword slicing into his midsection and the horrific whoosh of his intestines spilling out onto the ground. Grasping vainly at the blubbery, slippery mess and dropping to their knees, their necks were chopped with the next swing and their corpses toppled over into the bloody mud.

But Iblis were not the only ones to die. Kudanim fell as well-with head wounds, mostly-though in surprisingly fewer numbers than their foe. And when one did go to meet the God, another immediately stepped forward in his place. The shield line held and gradually, began to push forward.

From his vantage point in the rear, Balazar watched with swelling pride, waiting for the moment to land his hammer blow and turn the tide. Thus far, everything was going according to plan. On the wings, the cavalry was breaking off in companies to fill their quivers from wagons Colinus and his messenger force had brought out from the camp, and from behind the line, the foot archers were steadily arching their arrows over the men in front and into the faces of the enemy. Over all, the din of battle, the crash of steel, the grunts and screams of sweating and dying men rose up in a great chorus which to Balazar had the aura of a melody. His breathing was heavy and his great muscles flexed and reared as he itched to join the fight. Beside him, Thorngere was prancing like an anxious stallion in sight of a mare and as the two crossed glances, they grinned uncontrollably.

"What do you say, old friend," said Balazar, raising his voice above the din, "time to get our feet wet?"

"More than time, I say!" and with great shouts, the two Warlords led their men forward.

Driving through their own ranks, Balazar's reserve battalion crashed into the center of the Iblis line, directly opposite the banner of Chubar. As he came on, Balazar could see that long figure, his pointed face exulting now, slashing away at the warriors before him. And at his side, working in tandem with him and swinging his cleaver with good effect, was Haradin the meat seller. The two were guarding each other, Chubar going high, Haradin low, and between them they effectively warded off all damage and were wreaking considerable havoc.

"There!" shouted Balazar and pointing with his sword, drove with Thorngere directly towards the murderous pair.

But Chubar saw them coming, and having no wish to cross swords with their like, drew back with Haradin behind a screen of his own guard. It was these that the two Warlords met and these who first tasted their steel. Swinging his falchion on the run like a sledge hammer, Balazar smashed through the upraised shield of the first Iblis he met and split his skull. Blood and brains spurted up as the man went down and Balazar, feeling the gore splash onto his face and tasting it on his lips, roared out a war cry and raged on. The blood madness was on him now and he fought with invincible fury.

Thorngere, too, tasted blood, as he slashed the head off the first to come within range of his great sword and the two of them stormed ahead like farmers run amok with their scythes at harvest. All before them were brutally hacked and the air around them rained splattered blood. It was like they were slashing their way through a field of cane, for though the men before them tried to back off, the press of their fellows behind was so great they could not move and they died in panic, trying vainly to run. The two Warlords opened a great circle around themselves which the little warriors at their heels were quick to exploit and soon, a great dent began to form in the Iblis center. But though they advanced as quickly as they could, they could not quite reach the two enemy leaders. Chubar and Haradin melted into the press and stayed out of range, waiting.

To Colinus, standing atop the supply wagon in the rear, the sight was unbearably thrilling: the sturdy battle line tightening around the Iblian host like a belt; the resupplied horsemen pouring in arrows by the thousand and even now beginning their envelopment; the two great Warlords towering over all and wreaking unbelievable slaughter. Colinus had never really seen the Great Balazar at work-nor Thorngere either, for that matter-but now he saw that the stories told of his prowess were no exaggeration. The speed and brute power of the man was incredible. No wonder the warriors had thought him a God! In the heat of battle now, he had slung

259

his shield high on his shoulder and wielded his murderous falchion with both hands. The huge blade rose and fell with the regularity of a woodsman's axe, every stroke counting a death, and even from this distance and over all the intervening tumult, Colinus could hear it strike. Thwack! The blade rose in a graceful arc and then, thwack! disappeared in a blur. Rose and fell, Thwack! And at the height of each swing, the huge figure of the Warlord seemed to hang for a second, etched against the swirling background, the great muscles bulging, the half turned face wearing a horrible grin. Then, thwack! the blade would come down and none could stand before it.

If an Iblis tried to parry with his sword, it was his own sword that was first driven back into his flesh. If one blocked with his shield, that shield was smashed without slowing the blade. Or if, by some chance the shield held, the arm behind it was smashed and the force of the blow drove the man almost into the ground. Nor did any so struck rise again to their feet, for their heads were smashed as well.

Nor was Thorngere any less impressive. Leaner, golden-tressed, his musculature more sharply defined than the other, he was perhaps a bit fleeter of foot, but if there was any less power behind the blurring blows of his great sword, it showed only in that the bits of wreckage he hewed did not fly quite so far.

Watching them, Colinus felt like a spectator at a boxing match, his body unconsciously mimicking their moves, his teeth gritting with vicarious satisfaction. He itched to get into the fight himself, but knew that this could not be. He had his orders. His duties now were the price he had to pay for keeping the army informed. Because he and his men had been out scouting, they had received none of the training the others had, and if they went into the fight now, they would only be in the way. Colinus had known all along that it would be this way, he understood it and had, he thought, resigned himself to it. But still, it was hard now to stay put when there was such glory to be won only a few hundred yards away.

Within his sight at that moment were scores of men he had known and served with all his life-the grave Simplinius, riding proud and bold now at the head of the cavalry, loosing the best of all the arrows; Paudalis, his long-time rival for the sub-chieftain's spot, who had taken the battalion from Simplinius and now worked bravely by the side of the Warlord himself; Catalpus, his bunk mate and fast friend from the training battalion, now sub-chieftain of the third and rallying his men calmly under the onslaught; Dagris, Hoplis, Bordulius, and many more-what stories they would have to tell! And what would he say? That he had enjoyed the sight very much? That he had bravely stood up in his wagon to watch despite the jittery horses? That he had been untiring in his efforts to hand out arrows? That, at some risk to himself, he had actually drawn near the fighting? Oh, it was too much! How he longed to get in there and swing. Unbidden to his mind came the words of an old marching song from his youth: "Come death, take life, Call me to my Joy in strife."

Unable to bear the sight of his shame any longer, Colinus turned away in time to see a very curious sight. Coming out from the camp at quick time was a full company of impeccably dressed, obviously fresh troops. At their head, resplendent in his Guards armor, rode Cormin. This was very curious indeed. Watching them approach, his face must have indicated his puzzlement, for Cormin rode over to him and with scorn on his face announced, "I discovered these cowards lurking in camp-hiding in their tents like women! But they'll see some fight, you can be sure of that!" Then he rode off again, and with curses-which he had not been using before-drove the malingerers into the line directly behind the Warlords.

'Malingerers?' Colinus thought. They certainly did not look like malingerers. Quite the contrary, they looked like rather sturdy troops, and in fact, seemed rather anxious to join the fight. What was Cormin up to?

But just then, Colinus was interrupted in his reflections by yet another curious thing: in the midst of that absolutely still and pristine day, a strong west wind had suddenly arisen. Lifting his eyes to the cliffs behind the city, Colinus started at the sight of a great billowing mass of storm clouds rolling in from the sea. Already, with the wind, the temperature had dropped perceptibly and the storm front was coming on fast. It would not be long, he thought, before the battle lines were drenched in rain. One of those freak summer storms. Weather this time of year could indeed be treacherous.

Jolting suddenly as if his whole body had been electrified, Colinus leaped down from the wagon and began sprinting towards the fighting lines. Malingerers indeed! "Balazar! Balazar!" he yelled. "Thorngere!" But he had no sooner entered the lines than something heavy struck him from behind and he pitched onto his face among a litter of corpses. For the second time, he failed to deliver a crucial message.

With the rising wind, the storm came on fast. In minutes the sky was a solid mass of roiling black clouds, and the wind was tearing at the standing crops. But none, or very few, of the men on either side of the goring lines noticed until, with a sudden crash of thunder, the deluge hit them. It did not start with a sprinkle, or even a spatter, but came on full force at once, a blinding, obliterating downpour, the sound of which drowned out even the din of the battle. So sudden and so shocking was it that the battle lines suddenly broke and fighting ceased completely as stupefied warriors on both sides looked up astonished. Then, shaking the water from their eyes, they continued with the fight.

But it was in this instant, when Balazar too looked up at the heavens, that the first wave of dizziness hit him. His eyes suddenly blurred-and not from the rain-and his legs seemed to give way. He staggered back, almost losing his balance. It passed as quickly as it came, but as he shook his head to clear it, he saw Thorngere suddenly sag and lean on his sword.

"Thorngere!" But then, Thorngere too started up as the fit passed and the two locked glances, their eyes narrow with suspicion.

That was the last thing Balazar clearly remembered, for the dizziness came again, and the

263

rest was a swirling nightmare. Thorngere was there, he knew, but where that was he was no longer sure. Attackers suddenly seemed to be coming from all sides, Chubar and Haradin now closing with the rest, and he was somehow aware of being back to back with his friend, defending both sides. And moving. Instinct told them to break away, and as they fought now on instinct alone, so they moved with it. There were voices too, ugly shouts, and one, louder and clearer than the rest-it was Cormin's-calling them traitors and cowards.

"The Gods have sent the storm as a sign of their treachery!" he yelled. "Kill them! Kill the outland traitors! Kill them!" And with these words echoing in their dizzy brains, the two Warlords tried to fight their way clear.

They knew not who they struck nor who struck at them, only that blows came from all sides, and that their own were weak and leaden in reply. They could not even have said how they were moving or in what direction, or how they managed to stay together, one guarding the other. Something other than their minds did that, for to them, all was but a swirling, teeming, blinding, roaring dream. They fought not men, but demons and how long it went on they were never able to say.

Nor did they realize when they came to the edge of the fighting, when they broke free into the ring of cavalry. They were not aware of how one man-Simplinius-held horses for them, nor how the Guard hacked him to death as they spurred off through the rain under a hail of arrows, their shields slung over their backs as if on purpose.

264

Their bodies did these things but their brains were unaware, locked in and blanked out by a poisoned fog. And as their horses splattered off towards the river and the heavy curtain of rain closed in behind them, reflex alone kept them mounted, for they were no longer riding but simply lying across the horses' necks. Both were unconscious.

BOOK THREE
THE EYE

CHAPTER ONE
A Light in the Forest

Balazar dreamed of the battle for Valeria, of Fantar's horde sweeping down from the mountains like a great flood, filling the plain and crushing the defenders against their own walls like so much flotsam. Balazar was again young Valerian, a proud, haughty youth, heir to a great throne. Again he marched forth, his eyes dazzled by the awe and splendor of armies rushing to collision. Again came the clash like thunder, the ring of steel, the screams of men, all that cacophony of death and woe.

But then, the dream changed. Suddenly, he was alone in the midst of a dark and misty field, struggling with some great, incorporeal force. In utter silence, save for the rasp of his breath and the wild echoing of his heart, he fought bare-handed, wrestled and sweated against a thing of great weight that he could not see. All around him was black and utterly still. Only the mists, creeping like long fingers over the earth, cast a chill luminescence. On and on he fought, grunting, gasping, grasping, seeking a hold for his feet, or grip for his fingers, for some leverage to throw the thing, some chance to escape. But it was everywhere and nowhere, a thing neither of earth nor air yet seemingly of both. He could neither grip it, nor release.

Then he was on his back, the thing above him, pressing him down, smothering him. He writhed and kicked, thrust at it in vain. It was overwhelming, pushing him bodily into the muck of the earth. Dank slime oozed through his clothes, choked his pores, swallowed him. He felt it close over him like the sea, the thing above him still thrusting him down, drowning him. His mouth filled with muck, his nostrils plugged. He thrashed in panic, fought to lift his head, screamed for air...

But then, at the instant of death's victory, the dream scene switched back. Again he was outside Valeria, but the plain was dark and still. In the distance, from the city, flames rose into the night sky, screams and cheers filled the air. The weight was still there, but now when he thrust at it, it moved. He pushed it up with both arms, held it in the light and found himself staring into the eyes of his dead friend. The eyes were cold and unmoving, the face ghastly and gored, the teeth grinning. He shuddered and pushed the thing aside. He scrambled to his feet but saw with horror that the corpse arose with him. It stood before him, stiff and mottled, the dead eyes staring into his own, the dead hands rising up, reaching.

He backed away but the thing, on legs of wood, staggered after him, its arms outstretched now, the palms open, the face pleading. He backed faster, turned to flee but tripped and sprawled. He tried to crawl but a hand held his ankle, a cold, stiff hand which held him with the grip of death. It was the hand of a headless corpse whose touch froze him with fear. Other hands grabbed him, other corpses rose up, other dead faces stared. He was ringed with them, held fast by them. All that field of dead was reaching for him. And there, to the fore, was the corpse of Balazar, his friend, approaching with outstretched arms. His face was pale in the firelight, his eyes like wet stones. His lips moved, trying speech. The mouth formed the word "please," but all that came forth was blood. Then the corpse pitched forward and lay on top of him again.

Balazar screamed and snapped open his eyes. All was still and dark. But in those first milliseconds of consciousness, when they say the wandering soul of the dreamer flies like an arrow back to the body, in that first instant, the dream came with him and he thought he was back in time or worse, had gone himself to the land of the dead. It was all so clear in that moment, and yet so uncanny. Though he had wandered all the years since, it seemed now he had never really left that field. It was as if the dead really had held him and he was there still, the corpse of the real Balazar weighing him down. His shield and his burden, it had saved him from death but now it kept him from living and as he lay under its weight, he saw himself forever locked in a kind of living death. Balazar-Valerius-closed his eyes again as a great sense of despair flooded through him. He wished never to open them again but to sink down under the weight, yield to the death that had eluded him years before.

Then a drop of water splashed onto his face and startled him into full consciousness. He snapped his eyes open again and this time saw a huge tree limb etched against a star studded sky. His brows furled in perplexity. Where was he? There were no trees on the plain of Valeria. Even then, a passing breeze

268

shook the bough and others around it and he could hear a rustle of leaves, the shower of rain drops on a forest floor. But if this was not Valeria, then what was this weight which was most surely crushing him into the earth? Turning his head, he saw it was a horse whose corpse bristled with arrows.

Other visions came then and with them, the certainty of memory. Again he closed his eyes with despair. He knew where he was now, how he had gotten here and why. Even as he struggled out from under the horse and discovered himself-miraculously-unscathed, he cursed himself for a fool in not seeing Cormin's game before his final move. But as he tried to sit up, he was racked by convulsions and, rolling to his side, vomited wretchedly. It was in the midst of his gagging and retching that he felt his shield bumping about on his back, and when he was again able, he pulled it off and inspected it. Like the flanks of the horse, it was studded with broken and bent arrows. That, at least, explained his escape: instinctively, he must have slung it over his shoulder as he mounted. But what of Thorngere?

Balazar staggered to his feet but was felled again by a wave of dizziness. The poison was strong in him still. On hands and knees, he shook his head clear and looked around. He was in a forest, in hill country, some distance north of the river by the looks of it. He remembered pouring rain and vicious figures attacking him, remembered clinging desperately to the horse's neck as it pounded away, but how he had managed to cross the river, or how far he had come since, he had no idea. He saw then, some fifty yards away at the bottom of the hill, what appeared to be a short log with many branches. Half crawling, half stumbling, he made his way to it. It was Thorngere.

He lay on his face, arms and legs sprawled, and did not move as Balazar neared. His shield, too, had been slung over his shoulder-a life of danger breeds safe habits-and like Balazar's, was stuck with arrows. Thorngere, however, had not been quite so fortunate: one arrow had struck lower than the rest and protruded now from the flesh of his lower left side. Balazar knelt beside him and laid a hand on his shoulder. It was cold to the touch, but not cold with the touch of death. The rain only made it chill and beneath the surface, life still pulsed. Sighing with relief, Balazar bent in the dim starlight and examined the wound.

Thorngere's luck had held. The arrow had first struck one of the straps of his harness which impeded its force. Still, it had bit deep, burying the head and nearly two inches of the shaft in the wound. Gently, Balazar grasped the shaft and tried to pull it out. It would not come. The arrow must have been spinning, or twisted on impact so that the barbs on the head were not aligned with the surface cut. Balazar tugged again, more firmly this time and watched for a reaction from Thorngere: he was still solidly unconscious and did not flinch. 'If it's to be done,' thought Balazar, 'it's best done now.'

With utmost care, he bent the shaft to one side and slipped the tip of his dagger into the wound, probing for the head. It was as he thought, twisted nearly at right angles to the surface slice. Grabbing the shaft again and trying to guide the barb with the tip of his knife, he pulled again, twisting counter-

270

clockwise this time. The arrow moved a bit, then snagged again.

There was nothing else for it. To pull harder would mean ripping the flesh or, worse, losing the head entirely. He would have to cut. Working swiftly, he sliced down along the shaft, heedless of the blood which now flowed profusely. Thorngere groaned but did not stir. With the wound widened, Balazar was able to slip a finger into the wound and guide the barbs out. But he had made a bad wound worse and he shook his head at the gaping hole that was left.

He let it bleed for a bit-that being the best way he knew to cleanse a wound-then staunched it with cloth torn from his tunic and bound it by passing other strips around Thorngere's waist and tying them at his side. Then he made his comrade as comfortable as possible and sat by to wait.

Around him the shadowed forest was still and silent, save for Thorngere's even breathing and the plop of raindrops on soggy humus. Occasionally, a gust would sweep in from the sea with a long whoosh and the trees would shake like great dogs, showering him with spray. Cold water dripped off his battle cap and he shivered as it ran down his back. He felt utterly wretched. Still groggy from the poison-its effects wafted across his mind like patches of fog drifting across an open sea-he sat hunched over his up drawn knees, stared at a patch of wet leaves between his feet and tried to order his thoughts.

Cormin had tried to poison them, of course. That much was obvious. He had been a fool to trust the little bugger even for an instant. But why then?

It didn't seem to make any sense. He had fully expected an attempt of that sort to be made sometime, but figured it would come after the battle, when the old city had been won and there was no longer any need for his services. But why during the battle? Why deliberately sabotage your own army at the moment of victory? It didn't add up. Even if Cormin was not acting under the orders of Crosseus-if, say, he had some plan to usurp the throne for himself, which would be perfectly in keeping with his character-wouldn't he still have profited more from victory than defeat? Why steal a throne which was tottering on the brink of destruction when one could as easily steal a secure one, flushed with new won power? Even a fool could see the advantage in that. Or had Crosseus ordered it? But again, to what purpose? Surely, they could not have thought the army would win without them. Balazar shook his head in mystification. It just made no sense at all.

And what had happened to the army? Obviously, judging from the arrows he and Thorngere had carried away, it had turned on them, thinking them traitors and had, no doubt, been encouraged in that belief by Cormin. But then what? Surely the Iblis would have taken good heart at seeing the two outlanders flee and would have pressed the fight with renewed vigor. Could the army have stood? Again Balazar shook his head. He had seen too many battles where even the flight of lesser leaders had caused a general panic. They had not stood. The only real question was how many had managed to survive. As for the battle itself, that could be marked down as another item in the long ledger of his defeats.

His defeats. How many did that make, he wondered? How many cities ringed the Inland Sea? He had fought and lost before them all. But how many major battles? How many minor ones? How many skirmishes, ambushes, inadvertent encounters? How many battles at sea before the indignant ocean spat him out into this god-forsaken land? He had lost count long ago.

For that matter, how many times had he sat like this, weary and beaten, chilled to the bone without so much as a cloak to cover his wretched hide, watching over the body of some wounded comrade and gauging their chances of escape? Too many. He felt like an actor who has for too long dragged himself through the same weary part, uttering the same dreary lines night after night, dying the same dismal death. Only the stages changed.

His thoughts were taking a dangerous turn, and he fought to redirect them. One did not think of defeat when beaten: it only made the burden of it that much heavier and lessened the chances for survival. That was the old lesson. A lost battle could be left behind and the way prepared for a new one. But a beaten spirit fled with one and killed more surely than any enemy.

Balazar tried to rally himself, tried to turn his eyes and spirit forward. But the only path he could see led north into impassable mountains, and from those steep sides, his weary imagination slid back into gloom. From how many defeats could a man flee and still survive? Did the effects perhaps accumulate, one adding to another until they weighed the spirit down? How much could his spirit bear? At what point would that final lintel of hope crack and the stones of defeat come crashing into the very heart of his soul?

That weight was heavy on him now, heavier than the horse under which he had lain, heavier than that corpse of Balazar whose name he had also borne for so long, as heavy as all the corpses of all the men he had killed and seen killed in battle, as heavy as the walls of every town he had fought for and seen fall. He felt as if all those falling stones had landed on him, as if he had dragged away from each city with a huge mound of rubble mounting steadily on his back.

And for what? What had he accomplished with all these years of struggle and defeat? Was there any essential difference in his situation now than on that long ago night outside Valeria? Only that he was older now, much older, that the mountains he had to cross were higher, and that the hope he carried with him burned dimmer, much dimmer. Only that he was now much further away from accomplishing his goal than he was then: only that he had started out with nothing and had lost steadily ever since.

And that goal? Just what was it he had been trying to do all these years? Win back his kingdom? Yes, but not only that-that was the end, not the means. His mind snowballing out of control now, Balazar thought back again to that night, saw again the smoke and fire, the flower of his people wilted and sprawled grotesquely along the path of Fantar's conquering feet, felt again the shame of accidental life in the face of inexorable death.

Death would have crowned him. Life had left him unworthy even to bear the name of King. Had he been a coward to flee? Vain to seek proof in life for what could only be realized in death? A fool to seek a crown which only fit a skull, a scepter for a skeletal hand?

His hope had been the fool's hope of youth. He had thought that by proving himself a King, he and his kingdom would be redeemed, that the force of his life and spirit would lift his name from the dust of death and ignominy. He saw himself now as he had trudged up those first mountain slopes, his war gear bloody and too large for his frame, his child's brain filled with visions of a great rising, of a tide sweeping him back into power. He saw now that a King without a kingdom is less even than a man without a name.

Suddenly the nausea hit him again and his sight started to swim. He fell back onto his elbows and tried to clear himself with deep breaths. But they seemed to echo in his ears and his brain took up a cadenced, ringing beat. The wind seemed to wallow in the trees and the leaves whispered with voices. Balazar thought he was going to pass out, when suddenly, everything stopped and the night became as quiet and pristinely clear as wine in a crystal goblet.

"Valerius." A voice came to him, so low it seemed to reverberate through his brain and he was not sure whether he had heard it or just thought it. Then it came again. "Valerius?" Higher this time, rising in question. Balazar sat up. There, up the hill encased in light and standing beside the fallen horse, was a figure robed and hooded in imperial

275

blue. The voice came again, calling him, but seemed to come not just from the figure, but from everywhere. Balazar rose.

"Father?" His own voice was a whisper and his feet did not seem to touch the earth as he moved up the hill.

"Valerius Everreigning," came the voice, strong now with command. Balazar approached the figure and knelt.

"I am here, Father." Curiously, he felt no fear.

"Why are you here?" The voice was deep and loud, filling the whole forest now and welling up like the rumble of an earthquake echoing in a distant cavern.

"Why?" Balazar looked up, not understanding, but the figure gave no further explanation. It stood, a dark, noble form, frozen in soft light, its face shrouded by its hood. Not even eyes were visible. "What do you mean? I am here because I live."

"Why do you live?" The voice was questioning, not accusatory. Balazar peered deeper into the shadows of the hood, seeking the eyes, a mouth, a face.

"I live to fill your place."

"You have forsaken your people."

"Father! I have not. My people are dead. I... I... Father, let me see your face."

The figure threw back its hood then and Balazar started as if he had been struck. The figure wore a golden crown, but the head was not his father. One eye was covered with a leather patch and the face was twisted in mocking laughter.

"Fantar!"

276

In that instant his tortured soul flared up. He was consumed in the seething fires of a rage which boiled up like lava and exploded through his brain. Bursting to his feet and drawing his sword, he rushed blindly, insanely at his mocking foe. Snarling and screaming, he struck a two-handed, shattering blow. But its target was no longer there. The great blade buried itself three-quarters deep into the trunk of a large tree, and snapped at the hilt.

Drained as suddenly as he had become enraged, Balazar stared stupidly at the haft in his hand while the shocked tree showered him with spray.

From behind he heard a "tsk, tsk, tsk," and spun to see Thorngere sitting up and grinning at him. "Such a temper you have, my friend," he said. "Behold, the great Balazar whose wrath doth make the very forest weep!"

Balazar opened his mouth, but all that came forth was a gurgle. He took several steps in Thorngere's direction, then pitched forward and fell flat on his face.

"Did I say something wrong?" Thorngere muttered. Wincing, he climbed to his feet and tried a step, but was immediately felled by a wave of dizziness and pain. "Whoa," he said, supporting himself on his right arm, "things are not so good here-me stuck in the back and drunk as a lord, and poor old Balazar running amok in the woods. Must have been one hell of a party!"

Crawling the rest of the way, he rolled the burly warrior onto his back and brushed the wet leaves from his face. Balazar's half lidded eyes were upturned in their sockets. "Ah, Balazar, my friend, or King Valerius, if that's who you truly are-you always did take things too seriously."

Then he too sat by and took a turn at waiting.

CHAPTER TWO
The Butcher's Last Stand

The first grey haze of dawn was flitting among the high leaves and early birds were beginning to rustle and chirp when Balazar finally stirred. Thorngere was carving steaks from the dead horse when he heard a groan. Stuffing the bloody meat into a saddle bag, and using a forked stick as a crutch, he hobbled back to his side.

"So, you're back among the living."

Balazar lay flat on his back, staring bleakly at the foliage overhead. He did not feel like one of the living. "I'm not so sure," he said. "Seems like there's more of me dead than alive, and that the rest shouldn't be far behind." He sat up with a grunt. "How about you?"

"Feels like I've been stuck with something sharp and nasty."

"That's probably good. I pulled an arrow out of you a while ago."

"So I guessed. But I don't know whether to be angry they shot me or pleased that they finally hit something."

Balazar grunted, then retched. "I feel like I've been clubbed in the stomach... Whatever Cormin put in that wine was pretty potent stuff."

"Certainly made us the heroes of that battle, eh?"

"Poor buggers. I'll bet it turned into quite a rout. But what I can't figure is why Cormin would have turned on us then-we were winning, for god's sake!"

"Well, he obviously had a different set of plans. But there was strange stuff going on there anyway. We're better off out of it."

"I should have seen it coming. It's my fault. I'm sorry I got you into it." Balazar hugged his knees and stared at the ground. What was left for him? Inside, he felt hollow, totally empty; and yet heavy, like it was more than he could manage to hold himself upright, like the weight in his dream had gotten inside and was pulling him down. He wasn't sure he could resist any longer. Or that he even wanted to try.

"Well," said Thorngere, trying to sound cheerful, "you're not the only one who swallowed his wine-I mean line! But it's over and done. The thing to do now is get the hell out of here."

"Or go back and finish the little bastard."

"You're not serious."

"Well, it would be pretty stupid, I suppose. But damn it all! Things were going so well there. That's what really gets to me. For the first time in-what, fifteen years?-it seemed like things were finally getting on track. This valley would have made such a staging area!-and now we're back to nothing."

"As me dear mother used to say, 'as long as you've got the skin you were born in, you haven't lost everything.'"

"Yeah, but there's more to things than their skins. Sometimes I think I'd be better off without mine."

"That's coward's talk."

"It's not cowardly to honestly admit defeat."

"No, but it is to give up without a struggle."

"Without a struggle? By the gods, man, what else have we been doing since before our beards were grown? I'm sick of the bloody struggle. There's no end to it. No way out. I don't know. I probably shouldn't even be talking this way."

"That's right, you shouldn't. Besides, who says we're beaten? This valley can still make a staging area. All we've got to do-like I told you before-is slide on over the mountains and find some folks our own size to stage it with. We might even be able to come back and give Cormin a taste of his own medicine."

Balazar looked hard at his friend, and suddenly grinned. An idea had occurred. "I think you're right, Thorngere! You're definitely right. Except for one thing-you'll never make it over those mountains."

"Oh, not this again... Shhhhh! Listen." From the south, quite near and approaching fast, came the swish and plop of horsemen riding through the sodden forest. "Come on!"

They had just time to crawl under some bushes before the first of the riders appeared. There were perhaps twenty-five in all, guardsmen by their cloaks and armor, and all well mounted. When the leader saw Balazar's horse lying up the slope, he spurred his mount and the rest followed, clattering by within feet of the hidden outlanders. The leader dismounted by the fallen beast and called for the others to fan out. They did, but strangely, none came back down the hill: all went either east or west along the ridge, or disappeared over the brow to the north.

Soon a voice called back from beyond the hill. "Dalgrin! Here. The other horse."

"Dead?" the leader called back.

"Yes."

"Any sign of them?"

"No, sir."

"Well, at least they're both afoot now. Come on. They're probably headed for the mountain gate. Hurry, we can probably overtake them-King Cormin has promised great rewards if we bring them down!" Swiftly, Dalgrin remounted and cantered off to the north, his troop converging behind him.

"Fools!" Thorngere muttered. "We should have stood up and told them which way we'd gone-that would have really confused them! But did you hear what he said? 'King Cormin?' So that's what that little weasel was up to. I'll bet he took over the palace as soon as we left with the army."

Balazar shook his head in disgust but said nothing.

"And did you hear what else he said? About 'the mountain gate?' Do you want to tell me now there's no way through?"

"All right," said Balazar, crawling out from under his bush and brushing himself off. "I will grant you that the weight of evidence seems to indicate there is a way through the mountains. And I will grant you that under normal circumstances, we could probably make it through. But look at you! You've a hole in your back the size of my fist, and you can't even stand up without leaning on that stick. There's no way you can go mountain climbing until you're healed, and by then the snows will have already covered the high ground. Add to that the fact that we don't have enough rations for a hike like that, and that even if we did make it through, it would take us god knows how long to reach civilization on the other side. And besides all that, just where do you think that cavalry troop is headed? No, my friend, I still think the mountains are a bad plan."

"And I suppose you have a better one?"

"Well, one that has a chance to succeed anyway. You saw the way that search party spread out? They're so convinced we're headed to the mountains, they didn't even look anywhere but in that direction."

"So?"

"So that's our answer. If they're looking to the mountains, we'll head for the sea. There's a spot in the woods not too far from the river, by the old city, where I felled some timber a couple years ago on my first attempt to escape. There's not enough for a raft yet, but what we can do is float them downriver one night and hide out in the tunnel or on the beach on the outside-if there is any. That way, you can rest and heal, and fish for our suppers. I'll sneak back inland and get more timber until we've got enough to make a proper craft. What say you to that?"

"What about Fantar's galleys that you were so afraid of?"

"Well, we can pick our time. Once we're ready, we can watch from the cliffs until we spot some merchant shipping heading south, then sail out and hitch a ride."

Thorngere's brows furled and his mind raced trying to come up with a reasonable objection to this plan, but it made too much sense. It was the obvious thing to do, except for one thing...

"All right, Balazar. All right. Your plan makes sense. You always do make sense. But if you're going to make that decision, you had better do it with all the facts."

Now it was Balazar's brows that were furled. "And those are?"

"Well...," Thorngere hesitated, then took the plunge. "I haven't exactly been honest with you. You see, I didn't get here from the sea like I said. I came down from the mountains-that's how I know there's a way."

"Then why in the world didn't you say so before?"

"Because I know..." Thorngere felt his pulse quicken, his heart thudding like a drum. "Because I know who you are,... Your Majesty."

Balazar opened his mouth, but no sound emerged. He stared, too stunned to speak. He sat, mouth open as Thorngere quickly sketched out what had happened: his mysterious summons, his ship waiting south of Zagorbia, his trek into the mountains, Volkmir's lair-at the mention of whose name Balazar started like he had been stuck with a pin-his charge to bring Balazar-Valerius-back, and of course, The Eye.

"The Eye!" Balazar exclaimed. "My god, man! Why did you tell me none of this before?"

"Ah, it was wrong, I see that now. But Volkmir insisted I say nothing. He went on and on about you having 'to come to it of your own volition' or something. He's a bit of a windbag, you know. Anyway, I was supposed to come up with some devious means of getting you up into the mountains, but you've been too pig-headed to go! But you're right, now: even without the Guard, I'm afraid this hole in my back would put an end to me before we made the top."

Balazar's brain was swirling. Volkmir not dead but waiting for him? The Eye, there, waiting for him? It was like a door to a crypt had suddenly swung open to reveal, not darkness inside, but light!

"And I thought it was just the dead of Valeria that called to me..."

"Excuse me?"

Balazar didn't respond but sat, for a long moment, staring into space. Then abruptly, he rose and pulled Thorngere to his feet. "All right. Let's go north, then and see if we can't get some of Volkmir's potions into you before the vultures clean your bones."

"What about the Guard?"

"We'll just have to see how they fare against 'Balazar the Butcher'! But as for the other matter, I think it's best if we don't say anything for now. That will have to be between Volkmir and me, all right?"

"All right."

"Good, then. And now, my devious friend, since you do know the way, perhaps you wouldn't mind telling me how far it is?"

"I was five days coming down-three to the gate and two from there to the city. The trail follows a stream that has cut a gap in the cliff face. That's probably why they called it 'the gate.'"

"Well, then we had better get started. If I have to carry you it could take us twice as long to get back."

For three days they marched through rugged, uninhabitable country. Dense pockets of forest yielded to rubble strewn ridges, and hills snarled with brush and brambles, which in turn, plunged into more forest. So thick were these woods that at times the sun could not pierce the canopy of leaves and the two outlanders lost their way, wandering in the gloomy maze of great trunks and clinging vines. Then, suddenly, they would emerge into the light and discover themselves faced with a rocky cliff fifty or a hundred feet high, or a field of bramble so thick and broad they must waste hours circling it. What trails there were, they avoided, preferring to make their way across country, hacking through where they could not walk, crawling where they could not hack, detouring where they could do neither, and always having to re-chart their course on every height.

They headed roughly north, towards mountains which loomed ever higher and more forbidding before them. Always they seemed so close that they must rear up out of the earth just beyond the next hill. But always, when that hill was crested, there was another hill and the mountains still beyond.

It was an exhausting, bothersome march. Insects swarmed about them, brambles tore at them, vines clung to them, rocks kicked at them, snakes hissed at them, game fled from them, and all the while the great trees looked on impassively, offering no advice at all. Three times they saw parties of guardsmen riding along distant ridges, and once, as they stepped from the forest at the base of a small cliff, a band clattered by directly overhead. At night they dared no fire, but sat huddled under whatever protection they could find and ate sparingly of raw horseflesh. The dried rations they had found in the saddlebags were saved for the worse ordeal to come.

At first, Thorngere thought the march might not be too bad. As he walked, the area around his wound seemed to grow numb and for most of the first day, he walked quite easily, using his forked crutch like a walking stick. But as the afternoon wore on, a dull throbbing began, and he found it harder and harder to hold himself upright. They stopped early and Balazar made him as comfortable as possible. But the throbbing increased and the wound grew in Thorngere's mind until it was a huge red, pulsating thing. He had nightmares of wolves and jackals tearing at his flesh. In the morning, his whole lower left side was swollen and red, and Balazar had to help him up, and then help him along. Their pace slowed, and Thorngere hobbled through a waking nightmare.

Balazar spoke very little, beyond encouraging Thorngere and occasionally cursing the terrain. There was none of their usual banter. Thorngere knew his revelation had rocked his companion and in his easier moments, he watched him to see if he could gauge a reaction. But he only saw a very silent, contemplative man, intent on a difficult task.

For his part, Balazar was glad of the silence, for there were few words he could put around his surging thoughts, and those were mostly of doubt, anger, frustration, and even fear. How could he become Valerius again after all these years? And what would it mean? What would he do? What would he say to Volkmir? But then, hadn't he really been Valerius all along, at least on the inside? He'd always known it. So how could a name change him?

287

Or would it? On the other hand, why had he not been Valerius? Why had he hidden his identity? Had it really been simple necessity, as he had always told himself, or had it actually been cowardice: had he been afraid of who he was? Round and round went his thoughts in a dizzying circle, so that, except for Thorngere's wound, he was even glad the march was so difficult, for it forced him to concentrate on something other than himself and helped vent some of his agitation.

Toward the middle of the second day they finally got some indication of progress. They had just climbed a high, barren ridge and were standing in the shadow of a huge boulder, scanning a panorama of sheer grey walls that confronted them. The closer they came, the more the mountains appeared impassable. Panting and exhausted from the climb, Thorngere leaned on his stick and wondered where, in the vastness before them, he would leave his bones. For he was beginning to fear that despite Balazar's help, he could not make the assent. Then Balazar nudged him and pointed off to the north east. There, dim in the distance, was what appeared to be a gap in the mountain face. Thorngere nodded, and they set off. He would make it that far at least.

Traveling was somewhat easier in this direction, for they were no longer running against the grain of the land, but like tiny boats in a granite sea, were quartering the waves of ridges and crests of cliffs. Thorngere's wound eased a bit as the afternoon wore on. Keeping a sharp eye out for Guardsmen, they moved quickly along the ridges and picked opportune spots to cross the valleys in between. Overall, the land rose steadily and the intervening forests began to thin, the great trees falling away and low scrub filling in. The second night they camped, again fireless, by a little stream, and Balazar washed and redressed Thorngere's wound. The cool water was so soothing and Thorngere so exhausted, that it put him instantly to sleep.

But Balazar sat long, staring into the night, his tired brain still whirling, refusing to stop. What had Volkmir meant that he had to 'come to it of his own volition?' What else had he been trying to do all these years? Or had he? Was there something to what Volkmir said? Certainly, his reaction to Thorngere's news had not been what he expected: he felt more dread at the prospect than anticipation. And it was also true that he had grown accustomed to thinking of himself as Balazar, not Valerius. Even when he thought of that great future day when Fantar should fall, he saw himself as a man in the ranks, not as the king leading the way. The king was always... Was always who? His father? But surely, his father was dead. And since the father was dead, who else was there who could even become king if not himself? No one, that's who. So why did he not see himself so? Because he could not believe it? Because he feared it? Was he, Balazar, who had faced death a thousand times, afraid to become a king? Afraid to become himself?

Balazar was not aware of falling asleep but when he opened his eyes in the dawn, they happened to focus on the trunk of a small tree next to his head and on a large red beetle that was clinging there. It looked odd, strangely translucent

289

and idly he reached out and flicked it with his finger. It shattered and he realized it wasn't a beetle at all but only an empty shell. The beetle, or whatever he had become, had discarded it. How convenient, he thought, for the beetle to assume a new life by just climbing out of his old skin and flying away. But then, he wondered, what might it be like for the beetle? What terrors did he face when he realized he was coming apart? Dismissing the speculation he rose to check on Thorngere.

His wound was worse. The swelling had increased again during the night, and he was starting to sweat with fever. He seemed vague and listless, ate little and when they broke camp, Balazar had to help him along as they walked, and rest even more often. By mid-morning, their tacking trek had brought them eastward, and as they topped a small ridge, Balazar discovered they were almost directly opposite the suspected gap and that it was indeed the mouth of a mountain river. A long valley wound up beyond it into the distant heights and on the near side of the mouth lay a wide alluvial plain.

Balazar was impatient to be off now and literally carried Thorngere down the far slope. But they still had a considerable distance to travel and it was not until late afternoon that they mounted the edge of the plain and stood at the very base of the mountains. These rose to incredible heights, their tips lost in cloud. Stretching as far as the eye could see in either direction, they presented a solid grey wall which rose, unbroken to the very heavens. If there was any way through, Balazar thought, the valley before them had to be it. And between them and the mouth of that gate-like valley lay but a mile of flat, brush covered plain.

They had stood for but a moment looking into the depths of that green swath which cut back into the barren grey rock, when the noisy clatter of hooves startled them into motion.

Balazar and Thorngere lay in the scree and rubble on the slope just below the lip of the plain and watched as the Guardsmen rode by. There were about thirty of them, riding easily in double file, their red cloaks billowing out behind them and their burnished armor glistening in the late afternoon sun. Having mounted the plain just to the south of the outlanders, they rode by at close range and made straight for the head of the valley.

"At least none of them are carrying bows," said Balazar. But Thorngere had not noticed. He was lying on his stomach, fast asleep, his face pressed to the earth and his heavy breath blowing up tiny bits of dust. Balazar watched him for a few moments, then, as gently as he could, carried him to some nearby bushes and arranged him comfortably. Then he slid Thorngere's sword from its scabbard and put it in his own.

"Let's see if Bala Azar can still work his old magic," he muttered, "or the Butcher still do his business," and started off after the Guard, dodging from bush to bush.

As the riders approached their destination, other Guardsmen appeared from hiding within the valley itself. These clustered about the newcomers and Balazar could hear the babble of their voices through the soft evening air as they went through the ritual of changing the guard. Then the relieved

291

Guard spurred their mounts and rode out the way the others had ridden in-straight towards the hidden outlander.

Balazar pressed himself into the bushes, gripped tight to the hilt of Thorngere's sword and waited for the alarm. But no alarm came. Again, the Guardsmen rode harmlessly by, and when they had disappeared over the rim of the plain, Balazar resumed his approach.

The new guard apparently cared nothing for stealth. Instead of hiding and lying in wait as their fellows had done, these openly went about setting up camp, some gathering a huge pile of brushwood for a fire, others paddocking their horses in the lush grass by the stream, still others clearing smooth places for their sleeping rolls. None, it seemed, paid the least attention to their guard duties: until Balazar suddenly stalked out into the open, his shield and naked sword at the ready.

"Guardsmen of New Kantar!" he shouted, marching steadily towards them, "Bala Azar the Butcher brings you greetings from the God! Come, if you are not cowards, and pay Him homage!"

The Guardsmen in and around the camp froze, and every eye watched, mesmerized, as the huge outlander stalked to within forty yards of their fire, then stood facing them. No one moved a muscle.

"What's this?" Balazar yelled. "Is the famed Guard of New Kantar afraid to face a lone warrior? You must get your courage from your new King, that piss-willy Cormin." And he laughed a loud, brassy laugh, the sound echoing from the mountains, like the beating of a huge gong.

But then the script that Balazar had been so used to playing changed. The Guard did not rush out one by one to be slaughtered by the Butcher. Instead, their captain, who had been sitting on a rock by the fire, casually got up and strolled-it was almost a saunter-out to face the outlander. He was a trim little man, just approaching his middle years, and wore his authority, like the gold braid on his helmet, with a casual grace. He kept his eye fixed on Balazar as he approached, and as he stopped within sword's length, Balazar could detect no sign of fear in him.

"I am to inform you that King Cormin has ordered you found and brought to New Kantar to answer for the murder of King Crosseus," was his only greeting. "What say you?"

"The murder of Crosseus, eh?" Balazar shook his head sadly. "Makes sense, poor bugger. But I think you'll find, my good Captain, that the answer to that is Cormin himself. As for you, I'll not kill you now, since you've been brave enough to stand here before me. But I have business in those mountains yonder: will you stand your troops aside, or contest my passing?"

"You already have the answer to that, 'Warlord'... And where is your loutish friend?"

"Oh, he's off napping somewhere. I didn't feel the need to wake him for such as you," said Balazar, a grin spreading over his face.

"No, he's not," said Thorngere, hobbling up on his stick. "He's right here, ready to join in the fun!"

"You shall both be wearing other grins presently," snapped the little Captain, "when I take your heads to Cormin!" And with that he turned on his heel and marched off, spouting orders as he went. In moments a dozen Guardsmen had formed a battle line-Balazar's own style battle line, with locked shields and bristling spears-and marched out, en masse.

"This isn't the way you described these little encounters," said Thorngere, readying his stick like a club.

"I know. It appears some fool has been teaching these little guys how to fight. Are you OK?"

"I'll do-for as long as it's necessary, anyway."

The fight was short but furious. Instinctively, Balazar moved to defend the wounded Thorngere and for a time, the two were able to hold the Guardsmen at bay. Standing back to back and turning slowly, Thorngere with his stick and Balazar with Thorngere's sword, they managed to kill several and kept a circle around them clear for a time. But these Guardsmen did not fight like the Kudanim of old, and this was definitely not another slaughter for Balazar the Butcher.

While the ring of Guardsmen kept them hemmed in, a second wave of six rode in and attacked on horseback. Balazar unhorsed one, but as he swung at a second, the horse reared and kicked, his hoof catching Balazar in the head. He spun from the blow, knocking Thorngere down, and then crashed on top of him as a spear, thrown from yet another horseman, slammed into his back, just below the right shoulder.

Another spearman closed in for the kill. Balazar tried to raise his shield, but blackness swept over him. He did not even see the arrow that caught the guardsman in the throat just as he was about to strike.

CHAPTER THREE
Visions of the Eye

Thorngere saw it, and as he wriggled out from under his sprawled companion and struggled to his feet, he saw another arrow, and then another, zipping in from the bush in quick succession and taking down two more of the riders. Grabbing his sword and his crutch, he returned to the fight as still more arrows flew with deadly effect. The last two horsemen, starting off in the direction of the hidden bowman, were knocked down within a dozen paces, each with a long shaft piercing his body. Then a footman toppled, kicking and gurgling, skewered through the neck. Then another. The rest, seeing their backup fail and the tide turning quickly against them, faltered and began backing away.

Thorngere lunged at one, driving his sword through the man's breastplate and into his chest. Quickly snatching up and throwing the man's spear, he got still another as the whole group turned to flee. But the arrows were quicker. Even as they ran off, two more Guardsmen pitched onto their faces, feathered shafts sprouting from their backs.

Then it was over, and Thorngere stood leaning on his stick, rasping for breath, the pain in his back suddenly acute. About him lay no fewer than a dozen bodies, among them, the courageous captain. But the plain was silent. The Guard had gone as quickly as they came.

Thorngere knelt down to examine Balazar. He was still alive, but unconscious. A large blue swelling was already pronounced on the left side of his face where the horse kicked him, and there was a nasty wound in his back, in the large muscle below his right shoulder.

"His Majesty lives?" Thorngere looked up to see a small, dark-complected man standing before him. He was carrying a bow and a near empty quiver of arrows. It was Chad, the servant of Volkmir the Mage.

"Yes, Chad, he lives. But what in the name of Ute are you doing here? And where did you learn to use a bow like that?"

"Master send me." Chad spoke with a soft, purring sound. "He worried you not back. Use bow to shoot birds for master eat. Do pretty good, yes?"

"You did very well, though your timing could only have been a bit better." Chad beamed a broken toothed smile. "Now, can you help me with Bal... with his Majesty, Valerius?"

"Oh, yes, Chad help. Chad has things. You rest, Chad take care." Darting back into the woods to retrieve his haversack, the man quickly set to work. Pulling supplies from his bag, he swiftly cleaned and stitched Balazar's wound, applied some foul smelling unguent, and bound it tightly.

"You're pretty good," said Thorngere, watching the man's deft fingers at work.

"Master show me long ago. How about you hurt?"

"Oh, it's fine... Just a little tender, that's all."

"Chad look... Ah, bandage dirty. Chad fix." And before Thorngere could really protest, and without really feeling a great deal of pain, he had his own wound properly cleaned, stitched, and redressed. Nor was that the end of Chad's talents.

Within a very short time he had collected the Guard's horses and rations, gotten Thorngere fed, fashioned a litter for Balazar-which he ingeniously lashed between two horses and even managed to get Balazar comfortably into-gathered several other useful items from among the fallen Guard, and presented himself to Thorngere, ready to leave.

"Chad," said Thorngere, as the smaller man helped him mount one of the horses, "if you can get us up that mountain as neatly as you've gotten us out of this mess, I'll begin to believe in your Master's magic."

When Balazar next opened his eyes, he found himself lying in a bed, in a stone vault, or cave. A number of candles burned in the chamber and cast a warm, flickering glow across the rough ribbed ceiling. Balazar watched it for some time, trying to collect himself and his situation. His body felt stiff and sore, and he could feel bandages wrapped tight around his chest. The side of his face, too, was swollen. The last thing he remembered were Guardsmen attacking on horses and an image of Thorngere swinging his crutch like a mighty club. Then there were vague, dream-like, glimpses of high rock walls and peaks, and clouds, and sky he seemed to be floating through. There were other dreams too; darker, murkier visions that troubled him but could not be recalled. And he was hungry. That above all: it felt like he had not eaten for a week.

A face appeared at his bedside.

"Ah, I see Your Majesty has decided to remain yet a while among the living." The face was older, more wizened, but had not really changed.

"Hello Volkmir. So it really is you."

"Without a doubt, Sire. The question is: is it really you?"

Balazar turned his face away. There was another figure, holding a tray.

"But more of that later," said Volkmir. "Right now you must rest and heal. Chad here has some hot soup. Does Your Majesty feel well enough to sit up?"

Balazar struggled up onto his elbows, pains stabbing his shoulder and head. "For hot soup, Volkmir, I think I'd sit in hell itself."

They propped him up and put the tray in his lap. His hands shook as he spooned the broth and not a little slopped onto his chest and beard. But it tasted wonderfully good and he slurped it greedily. There was bread, too, and a small cup of honeyed wine, and as he ate the shakiness left his hands and his head began to clear. "Ah! Thank you for that,... Chad is it? You have returned me to life."

"In more ways than you know, Your Majesty," said the Mage as the silent Chad took the tray and backed out of the room. "It was Chad who brought you here."

"Then Thorngere..."

"Thorngere, too. He brought you both, or what was left of you. But we can talk later. Right now I think you should sleep."

Though he had not eaten a great deal, Balazar's shrunken stomach felt stuffed, and the heat from the soup and the wine flowed through him with a drowsy warmth. His eyes blinked sleepily and his head felt heavy. Yes, sleep would be good.

"And Thorngere is..."

299

"Yes, he's fine. Was up and about two days ago. You sleep now."

Balazar slept. And when he awoke, it was so gentle that a dream-a memory, really-accompanied him, and for a few moments he lay pondering it. He had been on a hunt with his father and a party of nobles from the city. There had been a large stag, and in his eagerness, he had shot too soon. His arrow struck the beast in the stomach and it leapt away before the others could draw their bows. The King was furious and cursed him loudly before the whole party: he had always been a quick tempered man, not given to long consideration of his remarks. But he had called him inept, a fool of a boy, too slow for his age, stupid and dreamy. He would never make a man at this rate, much less a King. When would he learn?

Lying there in the flickering light, Balazar could still hear the echo of those words, empty now over the distance of the years, and wondered at the anguish they had caused him then, and at the significance of the dream now. He had run then, ostensibly to chase the deer, but in reality, to escape his father and the humiliation, and had tracked the beast, alone, for the better part of a day before finally bringing it down and finishing it off with his dagger.

He had wanted so hard to please his father. But then, the carcass was too heavy for him to carry alone and by the time he returned with a party of bearers, the wolves had gotten to it and torn it to shreds. His father was not appeased. He, Valerian, had only compounded his error. He had not only

300

wasted a magnificent animal, he had endangered the future of the entire city by running off alone...

"Good morning, Your Majesty." It was Volkmir and Chad again. With more food. Was it morning? There was no telling in this stone vault, lit only with candles. But did it even matter? He fell to with a will and when Chad lifted the empty tray from his lap, Balazar stretched himself, and felt the strength returning to his limbs.

With Chad's help, Balazar rose and on shaky legs, tottered to a stool in the corner. Chad brought water and washed him and changed his bandages, and helped him dress in a clean and mended tunic. Gingerly, Balazar began pacing about the room; he was still weak and a bit dizzy, and there was still a slight ringing sensation in his head, but he knew now he would mend.

Volkmir returned and smiled. "You recuperate quickly, Sire. Would that I still had such youth and vitality! You will soon be about your work."

"And what work is that, Volkmir?"

"Why, the reclaiming of your kingdom, what else?"

Balazar shook his head. "Ah, Volkmir, I do not believe there is to be any kingdom for me. I am not fit to be a king."

"You, not fit?" quipped the Mage. "Valerius Everreigning, son of Valerius, heir and scion of the ancient line, not fit? You mock me, Sire. If you are not fit, who is?"

"I know not who is, Volkmir, only that I am not."

"And why is that, pray tell?" said the Mage, indignation rising in his voice. "Because like a

301

sparrow chick you fell from the nest before your wings could carry you?"

"Now who mocks, Volkmir? You know as well as I that because my wings were weak-to follow your own line-that nest was crushed.

"You condemn yourself for things that were beyond your control."

"Perhaps. But that was only the first failure. Have I not hopped from nest to nest for over half a life time since? And have not all those nests been crushed? Is that not proof enough there is no flight in me? Or, to straighten your metaphor, that I am but a sparrow, not an eagle?"

"You reckon without the gods' will. Do you not suppose it possible that there are other forces at work here? That the time was not ripe for you to follow your father then? Fantar did not rise to power alone: He rose on a tide of discontent. Much there was amiss in the Empire then to fuel that flood, and had you tried to stem it, you might have simply drowned. Thus, I believe you have been acting, in part, at the Gods' will in not revealing yourself.

"But the signs have changed. Now is the time for you to step forth and be revealed, to claim your due. I see the signs, Valerius Everreigning, and I see a realm stretching forth from your hand greater and more magnificent than all your father's or his father's, back to the beginning. I see it is you, Valerius, who will be the greatest of your line, you who will unite the whole of the Inland Sea, bring about a Golden Age!"

Balazar gave the Mage a scornful stare. "Do you think you are speaking to a boy, Volkmir? One you can bedazzle with tales of golden glory? Look

302

at me, man! I am no dreamy youth. Fifteen years have I been at war. My hands are calloused from the sword, my body scarred from battle. My very soul is stained with blood. Of this you would make a glorious King?" Balazar shook his head. "Do you know that I have even been reduced to eating human flesh? No, Volkmir, I do not think this king you see is me."

"You are stubborn like your father, and like his father before him," the Mage countered. "Through your whole line that has ever been your greatest strength and your greatest failing. Will indomitable! What a thing, hey? It has enabled your line to rule for generations, to build magnificent cities, move mountains when they stood in your way. But also, *Balazar*, there are times when it has made you unable to see the clear path around those mountains.

"Tell me, what did you hope to accomplish over all those years? Did you think that by your arm alone the Empire would be redeemed?"

Balazar sat on the edge of the bed, his fragile strength ebbing quickly. "No, but I thought that if I could prove myself worthy, I could earn back my name. And my crown."

"You know that's not true. You never sought to prove yourself. You denied yourself. You sought death. Escape. Oblivion. You condemned yourself for self-preservation, covered yourself with dung and claimed the smell as your own. You say look at you: well, what else have I done these fifteen years? I have seen you-*Oh Balazar, greatest of Warriors*. For fifteen years I have watched you face death time after time. You showed no fear, but that was not courage, was it *Balazar*? No, you showed no fear of

303

death because you desired death, didn't you? He would have brought sweet oblivion, an end to your pitiful woes. That would have been the easy way. But He would not take you, would he? He passed you by. It was fate that ruled it so, and I say to you now, if you would really be redeemed, take the other road.

"You say you are not fit. I ask, is a man's refusal to leap in the sea proof that he cannot swim? Ah, Balazar-since that is what you insist on calling yourself-can you not see the fallacy here? You say you are not fit to be king, to bear the name you were born to. I say you cannot judge that until you take that name. You say you cannot swim, cannot fly. I say you must first leap into the sea, leap into the sky.

"Ah, Valerius, my pupil, don't you see what you've done? How could you win a race you would not enter? How prove your worth when you denied your self? Was Valerian ever Balazar? Then how could Balazar ever become Valerius? How could you ever wear a crown you did not claim? Don't you see?

"Besides," the Mage continued, "It doesn't matter a fig whether you're worthy or not. The crown is not an honor bestowed upon you: it's a duty. Whether you're worthy or not, whether you like it or not, you're it. You are the King. You have no choice. You are Valerius, son of Valerius Everreigning. Now, if you will excuse my saying so-age has made me sometimes rash in my opinions-I think quite frankly you should stop feeling sorry for yourself, own up to who you are, and get on with the job."

Balazar looked at the Mage intently, his mind grappling with his words. "Thorngere said you told him I must 'come to it of my own volition.' What did you mean?"

"Simply that to rule is an act of self-assertion. To lead, you must command others to follow: to be a King, you must proclaim yourself one." The Mage rose then, and pulled from his robe a large red gem fastened to a golden chain. "Here is your scepter, King Valerius. When you can bear to see your true self, take it up. Test it. Claim your destiny." Dropping the stone on the bed and turning on his heel, the Mage left him.

For many minutes Balazar sat looking down at the red gem beside him on the bed. Its many facets caught the flickering candle light and tossed it about so that it sparkled and swirled like the swift running water of a river in the sun. The Eye. From his earliest memories he had seen it glitter on his father's chest. The Eye of Valeria. Even now he could see murky shadows moving in its depths, shapes forming, beckoning. Legend had it that its legitimate bearer was granted mystical powers, that with it he could see past and future, see into the hearts of men: that its bearer was the rightful King Everreigning.

For many minutes Balazar sat looking into the large red gem beside him on the bed. Then he took it up and strode out into the late morning sun.

It was more like a dream than a vision, more a knowing than a seeing, an understanding than a thinking. At first it was frightening, standing there in the clear mountain air with the sun hot on the surrounding rocks and glinting in the stone with razor like flashes. He held it upright with the chain hanging down from his hand like a stick and wondered what to do next. Magic or not, the gem was a powerful lens. Should he look into the sun or away? What had Fantar done that cost him an eye? Into the sun seemed like him. Balazar turned away.

And at first there was nothing, except a sense of nervous silliness, so that he almost turned again. But then he noticed the reflection of a passing cloud moving along the surface of the stone. It inched across its face, so clear and precise he could see every puff and fold. Yet it did not move away with the cloud but began to rotate, slowly at first, then faster, and began to sink into the ruby depths of the gem. And his eye followed it, caught and fascinated by the flickering shadows and highlights, by the faint stirring flashes deep within the stone, and by the deepening vortex of the spinning shadow. He lost his sense of physical reality, lost awareness of sky and cloud, of his feet and rigid legs rooted upon the rock, even of the passage of time. Deep inside, the Eye began to glow and pulse, and he followed it.

But it was not a cognizant experience. He did not think "I am in the Eye." He did not think at all, but rather felt his thoughts drifting. There was a tremendous sense of space, like a vast twilight sky tinged rose by the setting sun, through which he floated, and yet a tingling sense of energy, like he could shoot off in any direction at will, like an arrow. Yet he willed not. He drifted passively, content with the feeling of space and freedom that buoyed him and open to whatever random images drifted his way.

And they were pleasant, those images that seemed at once there and not there, that drifted across his path like flotsam on a glassy sea. There was himself as a babe, tottering across a flagstone floor, the face of his mother, clear and warm, unseen these many, many years, the streets of Valeria, his room, his father's commanding presence, the thrill and spectacle of the army at muster, all a-glimmer and a-glow-these and a thousand other scenes so clear and real it was as if the contents of his memory had been spilled out upon the floor and he walked, picking his way among them. Or like the rummaging of an old trunk, long forgotten under the eaves and packed with musty rememberings.

Gradually, though, he began to sense another presence. Nothing visible, just a feeling of something behind him and he felt himself twitch and glance over his shoulder. Then it grew and took on weight and he twitched again like there was something upon his back. Then, suddenly, it was as if he had stepped off a cliff and dropped back into that drugged dream after the battle; a black dankness descended upon him with a roar, and he staggered under a heavy load; arms grappled about his chest and a hand with icy fingers groped at his face. A horrible stench scorched his nostrils.

He shouted and jumped, springing forward to throw off his attacker, then spun to face him, crouched and tense. But the man lay in a crumpled, moldering heap, a body long dead and decomposing. With his foot he nudged aside a rotting arm and disclosed the bloated, blistering face of his friend, Balazar.

Pain and grief wracked him. He knelt beside the body, his own chest convulsed with sobs. Tears gushed from his eyes and splattered onto the face. And where they fell, they healed. The skin smoothed and became fair, the lips unbarred and reformed themselves, the eyes closed and rested, peaceful as if in sleep. Again he beheld the face of a beautiful child, at the very bloom of manhood. But the rest of the body remained as it was, and as the tears left him, he straightened, inhaling sharply. 'Balazar,' his mind said, 'I am sorry you are dead. I am very sorry, but you are dead.' And he turned and stepped back into the light.

The waning afternoon sun was stretching a path of sunlight across the floor from the open doorway of the Mage's cave before he returned. Volkmir and Thorngere sat before the still empty hearth, sipping wine. Volkmir rocked himself back and forth in a straight backed wooden rocker, stroking his beard and smiling softly. He seemed quite pleased with himself. Thorngere sprawled against the cushions of a large upright chair, tapping his foot and looking anxiously towards the door.

"And you're sure his head is all right?"

"Oh, yes. He was up and walking about fine this morning. The dizziness was quite gone."

"I never saw anyone stay out so long from a kick in the head. I had to tell him, you know."

"Yes, so I gathered."

"It was the only way I could get him here."

"Yes, I know. But it's all working out exactly as I hoped, even if not exactly as I planned."

"Do you think...?" But at that moment the patch of light in the doorway darkened as a large figure

308

entered, then grew again behind him as he crossed the room and stood before them. He looked even taller than usual, standing there, even more imposing. Around his neck hung a large red gem on a golden chain.

"Ah, Thorngere, my friend," he said, "I'm glad to see you're coming around. I was beginning to think at the last there that you had gotten into some more of Cormin's wine."

"Me! And who was it I saw break his sword attacking a tree, and then get his head kicked in trying to hug a horse?"

"Must have been somebody else. But listen, as long as it appears you're going to be with us awhile, perhaps you wouldn't mind helping me plan a couple little projects? If you went from here to the Hidden Valley, you must have come here from the north, right? And if I know you, that means you would have sailed up from Dulcai and left a ship hidden along the coast somewhere south of Zagorbia? And probably left a few of your disreputable friends aboard?"

"Unless they've all died of drink or the pox by now," Thorngere quipped. But just then the great gem caught a shaft of light from the doorway and flashed brightly into his eyes. He winced, and looked again, more closely, at his friend. There was something new in his eyes, a kind of benign amusement. And he added, "Your Majesty."

"Good, good," said Valerius, "because we need to get back to Dulcai. I've got an idea or two that just may fix our little friend Cormin there... Volkmir," he said, turning abruptly to the Mage,

309

"did you know my father never consulted the Eye when Fantar attacked Valeria?"

"No, Sire, I did not know it, but I am not surprised: he did not believe in other powers, only in himself. Nor do I know what the Eye would have shown him. But I know what counsel I and his other advisors gave."

"Which was?"

"To keep within the walls and summon his allies."

"Then it was unanimous. Strange, isn't it, how differently my father and I have been alike?"

CHAPTER FOUR
The Return

Dressed in the ragged garb of an Iblian child, Koltar sat fishing just inside the great cavern by the old City that led out from the hidden valley to the sea. Casting his line, he noted with satisfaction that it immediately began drifting upstream. That meant the tide was definitely on the rise, bringing a fresh flood of salt water in from the sea and with it, more fish. Ebb and slack tides were not good times to fish, and he had found that it even took a couple hours of the flood before they really started to bite. Adjusting himself more comfortably against the hard rock wall of the cavern, he settled in for business, making sure his feet were braced for instant action, and that he maintained a solid grip on his pole. Some of the fish in here were quite large and he did not want to risk losing another pole, or worse, getting dragged in himself.

Still, business seemed slower than usual today, and as the minutes dragged by, Koltar's attention began to wander. To his right, just inland of the cavern entrance, where the woods were steadily encroaching on the old tow path, the afternoon sun played delicately on the new green leaves, and the lush grasses lining the river bank swayed and dipped to a balmy breeze. Upstream, where the river broadened as it crossed the fertile plain, he could just make out a number of Iblis plowmen and their teams, rutting up the field of last year's great battle.

Spring had come suddenly this year, he thought, but then recalled that he had this thought

311

every year. Disliking the forced confinement of winter, he usually fretted and chafed so, and was so impatient for it to end, that when it did, he was shocked and surprised. And delighted. When spring came, the leaves seemed to burst from the trees, the grass and flowers to erupt from the newly fecund earth. It was a violence of rebirth and it always made him dizzy with joy. This year especially, for it meant he could at last begin the experiment he had been planning for so long.

He was convinced that the potency problem-that great Curse of the God which had afflicted his people for generations-was in some way related to the change in diet the people had experienced when they were forced to flee from the old city. And the most obvious change he could identify was the switch from salt water fish caught here by the old city, and the fresh water fish the people now caught in the lake below the new city. But whether the change was due to the lack of salt in the fish, or the addition of something else that was in the fresh water, he did not know. All he knew was that when men-be they pure bred Kudanim or Iblis slaves-moved from the old city to the new, their ability to produce male offspring dropped sharply. The problem was not with women. When mated with newly caught Iblis, they produced male and female offspring in equal proportion. But after a season or so, the offspring of those same males became almost exclusively female, just as had been the case with the pure bred nobility for the past three generations. In his own case, for example, he had mated with at least fifteen different women since reaching maturity, and had produced ten daughters before being blessed with a single son. And he was luckier than most.

So the question was two-fold: if the curse was caused by some mysterious difference between salt water produce and fresh, how could he prove it? And more importantly, could it be reversed? For if it could be reversed, his people would be saved from almost certain extinction. Exactly how that could happen, given the current state of affairs between the two cities, he did not know. But he did know that nothing would happen-that 'nothingness' would be inevitable-if he could not prove his hypothesis.

And how could he do that? Talking and theorizing had gotten him nowhere: even the more intellectual of his pure-bred compatriots had given but scant lip service to his ideas, and none were willing to take on the enormous risks involved in putting them to the test. So he had determined to do it himself. As soon as the weather broke, he had moved himself here and set up housekeeping inside the cavern on the old tow road by the river. He brought enough dry goods to last the season, and for fresh vegetables, planned to filch at night from the fields of the Iblis (and herein lay his greatest risk, for if he were caught and identified he would immediately become fresh meat for them). As for the rest, he would eat fish from the sea. At the end of the season, he would return to the New City, mate with as many females as he had the energy for (and after two weeks away, that already seemed a most inviting prospect!) and hope to count on a favorable issue. Assuming, of course, Queen

313

Salonis did not have him immediately beheaded for his long unauthorized absence.

Still nothing biting. What was going on today? Were the fish celebrating a holy day? Pulling in his line, Koltar checked his bait and was about to cast again when something caught his eye from deeper within the cavern. It was a shape, on the water. Dropping his pole, Koltar flattened himself against the cavern wall as a ship materialized from the gloom and glided past him into the bright spring sun of the hidden valley.

It was a large, oared ship of the kind he had seen on old tapestries and read about in his chronicles, with a curved prow and a great bow ram slicing the water ahead. Its mast was unstepped and lay flat along the length of the vessel and out over the stern, with its yard and bundled sail all neatly lashed and secured. Along the rails hung a double row of shields and many men-huge men!-clustered on deck, manning the long sweeps or keeping watch on the channel ahead. But none made a sound. As silent as an apparition, the great ship slid by within yards of him. Behind it came another, and behind that, yet another shape congealed in the gloom.

As the bow of the first ship crossed the line of shadow at the cavern's end, its decks suddenly blazed with color and light as the sun swept across the shields, cloaks, arms and faces of the crew. And as the stern slid into the light, the sun struck like gold upon the polished armor and purple cloak of the great black bearded man at the helm.

Bala Azar! The outlander had returned!

There were four ships in all, and as each passed out of the cavern, its crew swarmed with block and tackle to re-step the mast, and then broke out grapnels fore and aft. Unmindful of his own safety, Koltar dashed along the bank in their wake, very much like a boy indeed, until he suddenly emerged from the woodsy undergrowth, and the rearing sight of the old city's walls brought him to his senses. Scuttling quickly back into the bushes, he found a convenient spot and settled in to watch.

Majestic as a flock of swans, the four ships glided up the river on the tide with hardly a touch of their oars. Nearing the bank by the city's main gate- in the exact spot where ships were pictured tied up in the old tapestries-anchors were dropped on the outboard side and grapnels flung ashore. One by one the ships were snugly kedged up alongside the bank and gangplanks run out.

All this was done in mute silence, the crews practiced at their work and wasting no movement. But then, with the four ships moored and the gangplanks laid out like shop doors open for business, a sudden trumpet blared from the lead ship and about two hundred huge, heavily armed warriors swept ashore and formed a cordon along the bank. The great warrior, Balazar, ablaze in gold and purple, stalked out to their head and stood to wait. By his right hand stood a flag bearer waving a red banner with what appeared to be a golden lion on it, and by his left hand stood the other outlander, the golden-tressed Thorngere. On Balazar's chest glittered a large red gem.

But the trumpet was not needed to raise the alarm in the old city. Already Koltar could hear the clamor of shouts and orders, and before long, a stream of Iblis issued from the gate. Their guard

315

came first, breaking what order they had as they left the gate and all tried to rush, pell-mell to the front. Then followed a motley mass of warriors, hastily armed and in no formation whatsoever, and behind them, swelling their ranks and lining the ramparts of the city itself, the old, the young, the women and the infirm-so many, it seemed to Koltar there could be none left in the city at all. Like dark wine pouring from a keg they flooded the green sward between city and river, but stopped abruptly short of the thin but immensely intimidating line of warriors standing guard before their ships.

They stopped, and stood, and stared, a full fifty paces separating them from the outlanders, and as the flood of bodies leaving the gate fell to a trickle, a hush fell over the vast crowd like an audience awaiting the start of a play. Then the great voice of the outlander rang out, clear even to Koltar, nearly half a mile away.

"People of Kantar," he shouted, "I am Valerius, High King Everreigning of Valeria and all the Inland Sea. I bring you greetings from the great world beyond your shores. Fear you not! We come in peace."

He paused and a murmur of voices rose and swept through the host like the low growl of some suddenly threatened beast. Then several voices shouted, "Kill them! Kill the outlanders!" and many shook swords and spears. But none dared a further step in their direction.

Then, from the dense crowd, emerged a small troop of more disciplined guardsmen, and in their midst, looking harried and a bit disheveled from being buffeted by the crowd, came the ruling contingent of Chubar, Haradin and their closest retainers. As these approached, Valerius stepped forward and greeted them with a short bow.

"Greetings Chubar, Law Giver of the People, and Haradin, my old friend and, shall we say, former employer? I am glad to see that you both managed to escape unharmed from the recent troubles."

"You! You are no King!" snarled Chubar. "What do you want here, Outland dog?"

"I am as I say I am, Chubar," replied Valerius evenly, the official smile gone from his face. "And we come here in peace. We wish only the use of a small bit of your land for a time, that we may set up a temporary camp-it will be of use to us in business we have outside."

"You'll do no such thing in this land, you traitorous devil!" Chubar shouted. "What you will do is get back on those ships and sail out of here, or I'll see all your hides stretched to dry along my walls! I should have had you flayed and burned years ago, you barbarian!"

For a moment or two there was complete silence as Valerius glared at the wild-eyed Chubar and he grimaced back. Then, without warning, and with astonishing speed, Valerius stepped forward and kicked the Law Giver square in the groin. Hard. Chubar grunted as the force of the blow lifted him completely off the ground, then crumpled into a ragged heap at Valerius' feet, his eyes rolled back in his head.

Picking up the senseless Chubar by his collar, Valerius held him out to his startled companions. "Haradin!" he commanded, his eyes flashing

317

dangerously now, "Take this weasel back to his den before I slit his throat," and with a flip of his arm, he tossed the Law Giver several feet in his direction. The man landed like a rag-doll and Haradin hurried forward and dragged him away.

Now Valerius pulled out his sword and raised it high. This was not the large, cleaver-like falchion of old, but a shining, double-edged broad sword with a jewel encrusted hilt, a gift from Volkmir the Mage. "People of Kantar," he bellowed, "Hear me! Your Law-Giver, Chubar, has scorned our offer of peace. Yet I say again, we come in peace. But we have also come to stay! We will build our camp there by the river, and we will sail our ships in from the sea. Leave us in peace and all will be well-we will offer you no harm. But if you would contest our presence, if you think you can drive us back into the sea, try it now. We stand ready for you."

A great silence now settled over the plain, Valerius and his few but massive Outland warriors standing to their arms on one side, the Iblian throng in their thousands on the other. No one moved. No one spoke. Even Koltar found himself holding his breath as minute merged into minute and the tableau etched itself ever deeper into his brain. But then, just as the tension seemed unbearable, from somewhere on the walls or in the crowd, an infant howled-a long, lusty howl, the kind only a mother's milk can quell-and the crisis seemed to pass. The Iblis shifted and stirred, their voices murmuring. Then slowly, irresolutely, ashamedly, they began shuffling away. And Koltar knew the outlander had won.

318

Like dispirited fans after losing a big game, the Iblis went back to their homes, the plain draining of people in a slow-motion reverse of the way it had filled. Going last through the gates, the Guard pulled them shut behind them. Only then did the outlanders move. Reboarding their ships in their own cinematic reverse, they pulled in their gangplanks, hauled in their lines and kedges, and sailed another mile upstream where they went ashore on the opposite bank and began building their camp.

Work on the outlander's camp proceeded with the same vigor and efficiency as their ship handling. The leaders laid out the dimensions and marked the gates, while one group began felling nearby trees to construct an abatis, and the rest took up mattock and shovel and began digging a great trench around the perimeter and piling up the earth on the inside. The camp was rectangular, with provision for square towers at each corner, and double-back gates in the center of each wall. Later, a palisade would be constructed between the trench and excavated earth which would be piled up inside to form a parapet.

They were still hard at it when, just after dark, Thorngere was attracted by a commotion at the newly fashioned main gate. A guard was holding a small Iblian child, still dripping wet from apparently swimming the river, and struggling vainly to escape. The guard had his hand clamped over the boy's mouth to keep him quiet.

"What have you got there Olaf?" asked Thorngere.

"It's one of their brats, I caught, Sir. 'E says 'e wants to see the King."

319

"Oh, really! He must be a very determined lad. But the King is pretty busy right now. Why don't you take him and..."

But the end of Thorngere's sentence was cut off by a yelp from Olaf as the boy managed to get his teeth around the man's little finger.

"I am no child!" Koltar blurted as the offended hand was yanked away. "Put me down and let me speak!"

At a nod from the startled Thorngere, Koltar was set down. Though he was certainly dressed as a small Kantaran child, Thorngere thought, the voice was too full, too masculine, too... commanding.

"Who are you then?" he asked.

"My name is Koltar," said the little man. "I am a noble of the New City and I have an urgent need to speak to your King Valerius. There is much we have to discuss."

Bending closer, Thorngere peered into the little fellow's face. "I'll be damned," he said.

CHAPTER FIVE
The Mission

Thorngere rode in sulky silence behind Valerius and the tiny Koltar. Behind him, strung out in single file along the narrow trail, marched another twenty or so of their old comrades. On his right, way off to the west, the late afternoon sun was sinking towards the cliffs and the sea, and on his left, beyond the precipice of the ridge, the valley of New Kantar was already filling with shadow. They had come this way once before, Thorngere recalled, under rather different circumstances-he and Balazar had been tied to poles at the time-but he was not so sure that the end result of this mission would be any different from what he had expected then. At the prompting of this Koltar, they were on their way to the New City on what Thorngere believed was not only a fool's errand, but a dangerously foolish one.

Why stick your hand in a beehive if you didn't need honey? That's what he wanted to know. There was no reason to go to New Kantar. They had agreed on that from the start. Let the treacherous little buggers go hang! That was his opinion. What could the Kudanim do to them? Nothing, that was what. The only reason they had ever managed to get in and out of the old city was through the drainage tunnels, and there would surely be none of those in their camp. So what could they do? Attack the camp? Sink their ships? Ridiculous.

So there was no reason for this "diplomatic mission," as Bal... as Valerius called it. To Thorngere, the best plan would have simply been to complete their camp so it was secure from Iblis treachery, then get on with the business of preying on Fantar's shipping. The plunder from this, they could sell at a discount in Dulcai, and then, by spreading the word that Valerius was alive, gradually build up their power until they could do something really effective. There was no way the Iblis could stop them and there was no need to involve the Kudanim, or Kantaran, or whatever they called themselves-Mongrels, if you believed this Koltar.

And Thorngere wasn't sure that he did believe Koltar. Oh, the little bugger was convincing, all right, and the tale he told certainly had logic to it, but it was just too astounding to be true. That the two cities were not really at war at all, but only engaged in some obscene trading arrangement? That Cormin wasn't really a King, but only a puppet appointed by the Queen? That the Kudanim weren't really even Kudanim at all, but castrated half-breeds? It was disgusting, that's what it was: too sick to be true. But Valerius bought it: hook, line, and sinker. And now he had totally discarded their original plan and agreed to go along with this Koltar. Or had that been his plan all along? It was hard to tell just what Valerius knew, or what he was thinking since he got that Eye. It had changed him so. "Ah, I see," he had kept nodding as Koltar went on and on. "Yes, that would make sense, that would explain it."

"Well, I don't buy it," Thorngere had countered when the little guy first proposed going to this Queen. "Even if this isn't a 'real war', who would sell their own people to be used as meat?"

"You would," said Koltar, "if it was the only way your race could survive. But that's not the point. I agree that the whole business is despicable, but it was going on before I was born. Before my father was born, even. And it was going on because we had no choice... until now."

"But if I understand you," Thorngere had pressed, "then these 'mongrels' you send out to feed the Iblis are in fact the children of your people."

"They're half-breeds, yes. But we don't exactly send them 'out to feed the Iblis.' We send them out to do battle. To defend the New City. Don't your young men go off to war? And don't some of them die? The only difference in our case is that the enemy eats our dead-and we're certainly not responsible for that!"

"No, but you are responsible for artificially continuing the war."

"What artificial? What choice have we ever had? With our male population shrinking every generation, we would have been overcome and devoured years ago. All we did was use their men to build our half-breed army. If you will, we offered the half to preserve the whole. But we never really had any choice in the matter."

"Yes, but to castrate them..." Thorngere had shuddered.

"How else could we control *their* breeding?" Koltar had countered. "It was that or die ourselves. As I said, we never really had a choice. Until now, don't you see? For the first time in generations we have an opportunity to stop this thing. If, with your ships, you can bring beef into the valley, they will have no reason to eat us. And if I'm right about the fish, and we can set up some sort of trading arrangement, then we won't need them as breeder slaves: we'll be able to rebuild our own population. That's why it's imperative that you talk to Salonis."

"And that's what I still don't get," said Thorngere. "Why?"

"Because if you're going to stop a war," said Valerius, "you have to stop both sides."

But Thorngere was still suspicious, and the very hairs on the back of his neck tingled with a sense of impending danger as they set up camp that night just below the ridge, in a small dell tucked into the forested hillside. Thorngere made sure a good watch was set, then managed to speak with Valerius apart from the rest, and told him of his fears.

"I don't think we need to worry," Valerius responded. But he was thoughtful about it, as if he had thoroughly considered the issue before but was willing to consider it again. He was like that these days; so calm and serene, not like the volatile Balazar of old. He listened more and seemed even more respectful of others than before. It was unsettling, especially considering who he was and what that large red stone around his neck meant. It was as if he really needed others' opinions. Thorngere could see that people were drawn to him by this, but it seemed most un-kingly to him. "What advantage would they get from killing us now?"

"They tried it before, didn't they?"

"Well, yes, but that made perfect sense when you put it in the context Koltar supplied."

"But that Cormin is a treacherous weasel."

"No doubt. But he only took advantage of circumstances-circumstances which have now changed. Besides, we now know that Cormin is not really a king, and neither was Crosseus: they were simply appointed to lead the mongrels. The real power is this pure bred Queen Salonis, and that's who we will parley with."

"I still don't like it."

"Well, I appreciate your instincts, and I agree there's danger. We'll stay on our guard, of course, but I still think it's worth the risk."

And that was that: Valerius thought it was worth the risk. In the old days, Thorngere would have told him to bugger off-they might even have come to companionable blows over it. But he couldn't do that now. Now, his old friend Balazar was Valerius, and even though he had yet to regain his kingdom, Valerius was High King. As he tried vainly to get a few hours' sleep, Thorngere realized he was still having a bit of trouble getting used to that.

The servant bent his head low and averted his eyes as he knelt and offered up a tray of sweetmeats. "Ah, here's my Pretty Mongrel," said the Queen. "And what have we here? Let's see, we'll take one of these and one of these, and there: you may take the rest away."

"Thank you, madam," Colinus murmured. Still bowed and with face averted (all he had seen of Her Magnificence were the painted toes of a fat and rather hornily-calloused left foot) he backed away to resume his station. This was at a discreet distance behind and to the left of the Queen's couch. Beside him stood the wine steward, a long-time veteran of

325

the Queen's service, whose vintage features evidenced just the slightest smirk as he stared impassively off into the misty reflections of the morning sun on the water in the quarry. 'I'd like to pop a cork in your eye, you old crock,' thought Colinus, knowing how the man would tease later, when they were off duty. 'Pretty Mongrel, indeed!'

Colinus, it seemed, had become one of the Queen's favorites and "Pretty Mongrel" was but one of several pet names she had for him. "Cutey Cur" was another. But "Handsome Gelding," which mocked the sacred Rite of the Knife, was perhaps the worst. But all were humiliating, as was the way she taunted and teased him. When he was on duty she would accept service from no other, and sometimes she even made him sit beside her on the couch and ruffled his hair and chucked him under the chin like a boy. He, Colinus, warrior born and former sub-chieftain of the Fourth Battalion! It was hard to bear. But then, his very life these days was hard to bear. And what was the alternative?

After the battle, Colinus had come to his senses just as the army broke in panic and fled back to the New City. Knowing his life was forfeit if he tried to resume his old place, and not knowing where else he could go, he had sought refuge by sneaking into the palace itself. In the confusion surrounding the death of Crosseus and ascension of Cormin, he had boldly presented himself to the Queen's chief steward and said Cormin had ordered him there. To his surprise, the man had not batted an eye but had given him a place in the servant's quarters, issued him a fresh tunic and assigned him-miracle of miracles-to wait on the Queen herself! He had even coached him on his duties lest he blunder and the Queen have his throat slit.

His one fear, of course, was that Cormin would recognize him and have his throat slit anyway. But this fear proved groundless-he was apparently far too tiny a fish to have even attracted the notice of such a shark as Cormin. But what he heard transpire between Cormin and Salonis made him wish his throat had been slit. He knew there had been treachery against the Warlords, but to what extent it reached, he would not have guessed in his wildest dreams. That his city, his Queen would be in league with the Iblis! It made him realize his entire life had been a sham. And that made him wretched.

Many times, he had thought of actually obeying that long ignored Call and of flinging himself off the cliff, or doing something equally lethal such as purposely looking at the Queen. But he did not. Something held him back and he did not believe it was simple cowardice. There was something in the memory of Simplinius, something that said there might yet be hope. But what it was and when it might come, he had no idea.

Nor had he any more time to ponder, for just then two things happened in such rapid succession that they were forever afterwards linked as one event in Colinus' mind. The first was that the Queen shook her arm and called to him, apparently for the second time. "Come, you Mongrel," she snapped. "Do you not hear your master's call?" And the second was that the instant those words left her mouth, someone sounded a long, wailing blast on the great gilded horn down by the lake.

"That should let them know we're here," said Valerius, letting the horn swing back on its lanyard, "though I suspect Cormin knows already." They were in the small clearing by the lake where, the year before they had been untied and shackled to a cart for their final assent into the New City above. This time, however, no crowds flocked down to meet them, and as they mounted the hill and emerged from the forest, the plain stood empty and the gates of the walled city, tucked in under the cliffs, were closed and barred. They dressed ranks here, broke out the old Valerian flag-this, too, a relic from Volkmir-and marched in parade formation across the plain towards the city.

They had covered but half the distance when the main gates swung inward and a party of horsemen clattered out. They were guardsmen, dressed in their red tunics and armed with bows, and at their head, resplendently dressed and riding under his own black and red panther banner, rode Cormin.

"Welcome outlanders!" he called, reigning in at a safe distance. "And welcome to you, too, Lord Koltar-we feared you had fallen afoul of our enemies." Behind him, his troop fanned out in a semi-circle, bows at the ready.

"There is no need for weapons, Cormin," said Koltar, advancing on him. "These men come in peace to take council with the Queen."

"Forgive me, Lord Koltar, but this Balazar has not the reputation of a man of peace."

"My name is Valerius, King Cormin. I am heir and rightful High King Everreigning of Valeria, a kingdom on the Inland Sea, far to the north. As

Lord Koltar says, we come in peace to take council with your Queen."

"And what council would this be, oh High King Everreigning?" said Cormin, a sneer only thinly disguised in his voice.

"It would be unseemly," returned Valerius, honey thick on his own tongue, "To address private counsel in so public a forum, as I'm sure Your Majesty understands."

"Surely. But you must also understand-as I am sure Lord Koltar does-that as sworn protector of Her Majesty, I must have assurances that no harm portends."

"And you have them, Majesty, on my word as Valerius and even, if you will, on my word as former Warlord of this city."

"Need I remind Your Majesty that as Warlord of this city, your last act was to desert the Army in the face of the enemy? Surely, the word of such a one cannot be expected to carry much weight."

"And need I remind Your Majesty of the circumstances extenuating that act?"

During this conversation, though their voices remained level and polite, both monarchs had been drawing steadily closer, their eyes locked ever more intently, and their bodies leaning forward in their saddles ever more threateningly. Now Koltar's voice snapped the tension between them.

"Enough of this banter!" he said. "Cormin, yours is not to interrogate King Valerius. He is here under my bond. Whatever assurances you feel you need, you have from me. Now, escort us to the Queen at once!"

329

"A thousand apologies, My Lord," returned Cormin, bowing submissively and averting his eyes to hide the fire that flared in them. "I did not intend to presume. But you must understand, My Lord, that the Queen would never condone my bringing so many armed men-especially such men as these-into her presence. What could we do against them? My Lord, if King Valerius is as good as his word, let him come alone to take council with the Queen."

"That's an insult!" snapped Koltar. "Valerius is a King. A Royal escort is his by right..."

"It's all right, Koltar," said Valerius. "I believe we can trust the People of New Kantar in this."

"Your Majesty!" said Thorngere.

"It's all right, Thorngere."

"No sir! It's not all right. I'll have Cormin's head right here before I see you go into that city with him alone."

"No need for threats, Lord Thorngere," soothed Cormin, honey back in his voice. "When I invited his Majesty, I had no intention of excluding you. Were you not also a Warlord of the City? We are happy to welcome you both. Your men can stay here-they will be amply provided for-and watch over your arms..."

"Cormin," said Valerius, "Your predecessor, King Crosseus, accepted our bonds when we were first brought to New Kantar. He had no squads of archers, yet he gave us back our weapons and bade us walk in his city as free men and warriors born. Have you so much more to fear from us than he?"

"I do not fear you at all, Outlander! It is for my Queen I am cautious. Yet you have a point. Despite your proven faithlessness, you do come under the banner of another city, requesting council. As such, I will honor your bond and allow you, as free men and warriors born, to bear your weapons. Yet I will keep my archers. Come!" Spinning his horse on its heels, he spurred off towards the city, yet was forced to pull up and wait when his guests did not follow with the same alacrity.

With care and exaggerated deliberation, Valerius instructed his men to return to the clearing by the lake and to make a temporary camp there and await further instructions. Then, with as much pomp as three lone riders and a worn banner could summon, Valerius, Thorngere, and the diminutive Koltar plodded off in stately fashion towards the city, leaving a seething Cormin and his troop to form what honor guard they would.

Guests had arrived to sit with the Queen just after the horn sounded, the usual set of pure-bred snobs who usually sat and took a late brunch with her. They were not nearly so brilliant nor so beautiful in person as they had seemed from the Fourth Battalion, and as it was considered unseemly to show any interest in anything outside their own circle, none of them paid the slightest heed to the events unfolding on the plain below. Neither, then, could Colinus and while he served them with almost as much deference as he showed the Queen, inside he was desperate to know what was going on: that horn was only to be sounded on the most serious or solemn occasions.

Finally, the meal ended and as Colinus headed off to the scullery with a load of plates, he swung wide to look out over the cliff and see what was what down below. There he almost dropped his plates. Outlanders! A whole squad of them confronting a troop of Cormin's Guard. And who were the two mounted at the front? Could it be? There was no doubt of the blond and black manes, but Balazar in gold plated armor? And Thorngere bearing a royal standard?

It had to be. Could be no other. But who was the third, a pure bred Lord? Could it be Lord Koltar? And what was this? The three of them riding off in the custody of Cormin? Whatever did that portend?

Dizzy with excitement now-or was it dread?- Colinus dashed off to the kitchen with his load. What should he do? Let the Queen know that the missing Lord Koltar had just showed up with the former Warlords? That was not his place, of course, but he had seen enough of Lord Koltar over the winter to know that if he was accompanying the outlanders, something important must be brewing. Maybe the Queen already knew, was in on whatever it was? He doubted that. He had heard no mention of anything of the kind-and he had heard mention of so many private things it was hard to believe the Queen would be discreet about this. No, she did not know, he was convinced. And surely he could not trust Cormin for the truth. So the Queen must be told. Yet it might mean death for him to speak. Was that it? Was it for this he had been waiting for all these months? Was this his fate, this why he had been placed so close to the Queen? There was only one way to know. Resolved, he headed back up to the quarry.

But messengers had already approached the Queen, and just as he arrived, she rose up angrily and stalked off, a squad of Guardsmen flocking behind her.

"What's happened?" Colinus demanded of the Wine Steward.

"They've caught the outlanders trying to sneak in and assassinate the Queen."

CHAPTER SIX
Omens

The outlanders were escorted to the breakfast room at the front of the palace-the same room where they had dined with Crosseus-and Koltar went on to his own chambers. Hot chicory and bread was served, and Cormin bade them relax until they were summoned by the Queen. But then, as he left, they heard the ominous sound of the door being locked behind him.

"Well, they've got us now," said Thorngere, leaping up and pacing. "I knew we shouldn't have trusted that little weasel!"

"Cormin or Koltar?" Valerius was sitting quietly at the table, his huge hands folded around his chicory mug.

"Either one of them. They've got us right where they want us now."

"We still have our arms."

"Yeah, but they've got bows now... We can't stand against archers."

"I don't think it will come to that."

"So you said last night. But how can you be sure? Have you seen something with... with...," and Thorngere nodded with his chin towards the large red gem on Valerius' chest.

"With the Eye? You would dare ask such a thing?" There was a gentle reproof in Valerius' voice.

Thorngere stammered. "I... I know. I'm sorry, Your Majesty. It's just that, well, you've been my friend a lot longer than you've been my king and, well, frankly, I just think we may have stepped in it this time."

"Oh, Thorngere," Valerius laughed, "That's just your feet. I've been meaning to mention them for some time now: the men have been complaining!"

"Come on! I'm serious."

"I know, I know," Valerius chuckled. "And to be serious, the answer is 'no,' I haven't 'seen' anything. The Eye doesn't work that way... at least, not in the usual sense of seeing."

"Then how can you be so sure Cormin won't try to have us killed?"

"I'm quite sure Cormin *will* try to kill us. I'm just also sure he won't succeed."

"How's that?"

"Thorngere, my friend, the power of the Eye has been a mystery to generations of men; even to many of the men who wore it. I myself have only used it a half dozen times, only enough to explore some of its mysteries. How it works, I could not explain if I wanted. It's a thing that has to be experienced... But it's also a thing that has to be trusted.

"Let me put it this way: say you've taken a ship to sea and a sudden storm comes up. The ship heels to the wind, waves crash over the bows. You glory in it, standing at the helm with the spray blowing in your face. But one of your passengers-a woman it will have to be, knowing you-is terrified. 'The ship will capsize!' she wails. 'We'll all be thrown in the sea and drowned!' You try to reassure her, tell her it's all right. But she won't believe you... perhaps you've tried to sweet-talk this one before? 'How do you know?' she insists. And, indeed, how do you

335

know? Surely, ships are lost at sea. Surely, there are hidden rocks, killing seas. Ships do break up and founder. How do you know it will be all right?

"Well, you know your ship and your crew, you know the wind and the sky. You know the waters. You have confidence in these things, and in your own ability to steer the ship and trim the sails. Yes, there is danger, but you know it is not great. You *feel* that knowledge. It is compounded from all your senses and experience. You are sure all will be well. But how do you communicate that to her?

"It's the same with us now. The Eye has not shown me the future... I'm not even sure that is one of its powers. Or, if it is, I have not yet mastered it. But I do know that I am being guided on this course, that it is the right one. And I am confident of our situation. I cannot explain why or how, I just know our little 'ship' will weather this storm."

"And what 'course' is that?"

"Well, like any mariner, my sight is confined by the horizon, but I do know a couple of things: one is that the situation here in this Valley has to be resolved, and that my fate is somehow caught up in that resolution. I don't know why-maybe it's simply because these people have no other option, maybe it's because of my earlier career here working for our friend Chubar-but I feel very strongly that I cannot walk away from this mess. If it's in my power to fix it, then fix it I will. Otherwise, well, let's not talk about otherwise.

"The other thing is poor old Balazar. I owe him something as well. After all, his name protected me for many years. Yet, my last appearance under that name ended in a rather ignominious flight. We need

336

to make amends for that and clear old Balazar's name."

"Surely we cannot bear the blame for being poisoned!"

"No, but I'm sure Cormin neglected to tell that part of the story and that the army here thinks we deserted them—or worse, led them into a trap. By openly walking back in here, I hope to amend that. And I think we will: I'm just not quite sure how."

"Well, I wish I could share that confidence," said Thorngere. But he did sit down, and did reach for his mug, and would perhaps have taken a sip had not, at that moment, the door been flung open and a file of Guardsmen marched in.

Trying to assassinate the Queen! That was impossible. Who would ride boldly up to the main gate on such a mission? It was absurd, but it would not let Colinus stand still. Down below, over the cliff's edge, he could see the army forming in the Palace square, battalion after battalion marching from their barracks in tight formation, filing into their places, standing rigidly at attention. How he longed to be with them! And how he longed to know what was going on! But he couldn't leave. The other pure-breds were still lounging about the quarry, oblivious, and there was still his duty to be done. But he could pass as close to the cliff's edge as he dared, could still perhaps see what was happening.

Below, trumpets blared. But then, someone called for him, and when he turned back again, he was startled to see a pair of Guardsmen standing at the cliff's edge, a small cauldron between them.

Colinus was mad with curiosity, but then, he was called again as, again, the trumpets blared.

At the first trumpet blast, the outlanders were led out onto the large portico that fronted the palace. Before them, the entire army was assembled and stood in rigid silence. Then the trumpets blared again and the honor guard marched out to their drum. Following them, resplendent now in a white full length toga, purple mantle and cape, was Cormin, and behind him, flanked by two female attendants and accompanied by the ancient Teller, Teukonis, came the Queen. At the sight of this regal procession, the Army dropped to their knees as one and touched their foreheads to the ground. Only the outlanders, and their immediate guard remained standing.

Thorngere eyed the Queen. She was a fat little person, neither regal nor pleasing to see, but she had, nonetheless, an arrogant nonchalance about her that betold a habit of ultimate power. For an instant, their eyes met, and he felt a chilling sensation of careless cruelty.

"Welcome, Your Majesty," proclaimed Cormin oratorically. He, too, had dropped to one knee, but unlike the others, his face was upturned, looking at the Queen with studied adoration. "The army of New Kantar is honored by your presence which will mark this day with special significance. Kala Atar komen hatar! And we would all be glad indeed, but for the duty which brings us here. You see before you, Majesty, these Outlanders whose perfidy cost so many their lives in last year's misguided attack on the Old City. They have returned, Majesty, to continue their depredations. It is my sad duty to

338

report that we caught them just this morning, trying to sneak into your complex, armed and with murder in their hearts."

Thorngere started. What treachery was this? A gasp also went up from the army, and he could see that many of them had now twisted their necks in their supine position and were peeking up at their King and *the* Queen. But then another voice boomed out, loud and deep, filling the square and echoing off the cliffs.

"That is a lie, Your Majesty!" Valerius stepped away from the circle of guards and stood so he faced both Queen and the assembled army. "I am no assassin. I am Valerius, Rightful King Everreigning of Valeria, and High King over all the Inland Sea. I approached your gates openly, bearing the Royal Standard of my people, to seek your council and bring greetings to the people of New Kantar. This mongrel would turn your eyes from the truth, Your Majesty, as your own noble, Lord Koltar will attest."

"What have you done with Koltar?" snapped the Queen, her eyes flashing angrily.

"Done? We have done nothing to Koltar. It was he who guided us here. He has just gone to his chambers."

"Majesty, Majesty," said Cormin, "I know not what spell this outlander seeks to weave with these lies, but I do know Lord Koltar was not with them when they were caught, and as far as we know, he is not within the city now. My men will attest to that. As for the rest, I think it plain these are the same two Outland dogs who killed King Crosseus and betrayed our army last year. I say we put them to death, here and now!"

No Koltar? What perfidy was this? Thorngere felt a red rage rising in him and reached for his sword. All around archers drew their bows, but it was Valerius who stayed him with an upheld hand.

"Majesty," he said, his voice still calm and deliberative in the tense atmosphere on the portico, "if we had been 'caught' as your puppet here claims, why do we still bear our arms?"

"On my head be that, Majesty," said Cormin, the boldness of his lies exceeded only by the deftness of this thought. "Though capture them we did, we could not disarm them. Our arrows can bring death, but they cannot lift a sword, and we feared that any who came near enough to do so would have simply become shields. So we brought them as they are. But rest assured, Majesty, even armed as they are, they can be struck down in an instant."

"It is true we are at your mercy," Valerius broke in. "If you wish our deaths, you may have them at any time. But I would caution you not to act precipitously in this, for if Cormin has not told you, Majesty, you should know that we did not return alone to the valley of Kantar. Even now my army is encamped by the old city. Kill us and you will no longer have just two oversized outlanders to deal with, but an entire host!"

"An army indeed! Majesty, the man is brazen beyond all belief! There are no ships, no army. These two have obviously stolen some new clothes and someone else's standard, but they are the same vermin."

340

"You may hide Koltar, Cormin, and cover a lot of things with your slick lies, but I doubt you'll have as much luck talking an army away. Majesty, if you doubt my word, simply send one of your battalion commanders-send Golamin, there, for I know him to be a trustworthy man-send him down to the lake where my escort awaits. Have him ask Boltar how many ships we came in, and what are their captains' names. Have him ask whatever you like. Then have him ask me the same questions when he returns."

"Majesty, Majesty, we do not need to waste your precious time with children's games! I can prove my words here and now, before you and this entire army, by signs as irrefutable as the very earth we stand upon."

"And how would you do this, Cormin?" said the Queen who, through all this had been shifting her gaze from one litigant to the other, and looking smug, disdainful, bored and impatient by turns. She now sounded fatal.

"I will call upon the God, Your Majesty. If I speak true and if it is His will that these Outlanders be put to death, let him send a Sign." For a moment, the Queen looked strangely at Cormin, but then Thorngere saw him glance upward. She nodded regally, and at a sign from Cormin, the Teller, Teukonis, strummed on his lyre.

Colinus heard the sounds of the lyre drifting up from below, then the Teller's strong, melodious voice raised in the chant of invocation and he could stand it no longer. Ignoring the absently outstretched hand of a noble before him, he edged towards the cliff. The Teller's voice sang on, begging the God to hear their plea and grant their petition.

What was going on? Colinus was mad to know. How could the Warlords have tried to assassinate the Queen? How could they even know about her?

Then he heard Cormin's voice, raised to a shrill pitch, and edged his way up behind the Guardsmen who were inching nearer the edge. They held small paddles and Colinus saw that the cauldron between them was filled with blood. "Give us, Oh God, a sign," he could hear Cormin wail, "that these Outlanders should die. A sign, Oh God! Give us a sign!"

At this, the two Guardsmen began splashing blood out over the edge so that it fell, like red rain onto the portico below. That's when Colinus snapped. He wasn't aware of making any ultimate decisions, or of overflowing with heroic rage. He did not feel the hand of any God. He just snapped: acted without thought, without premeditation of any kind. He simply lunged forward and pushed the two Guardsmen off the cliff. Spinning madly in the air, one Guardsman reached back to grab his assailant- or anything, really-but only managed to catch hold of the cauldron rim which tipped its contents and plummeted after him.

It happened so fast, Thorngere had no time to react. One instant Cormin was standing there chanting, his arms spread wide, his eyes closed and his face upturned and sincerely penitent. Then there was a quick scream from above, a gasp from the army, a red blur, and a great ringing crash as two bodies, a bronze cauldron, and about fifteen gallons of raw blood smashed down, the cauldron crushing

342

Cormin. Everyone was splattered with blood and the scene looked as if some huge primeval beast, after devouring several men and finding them not to his liking, had vomited them there in a ghastly puddle on the palace steps.

In the stunned silence that followed, Koltar came bolting from the palace doors, knocking two Guards aside, and raced towards the Queen. He was bruised and bloody with his toga half torn away, and he still bore a bloody dagger in his right hand. "Majesty!," he yelled as he ran, "beware of Cormin...!" but then, as he skidded to a stop and stared down at the gory remains of Cormin and the two Guards, the urgency left him and his voice trailed on like the final spatters of rain after a violent storm. "He violated his trust... He gave his word, but then he set guards over me. He lied... He..."

"He asked for a sign," snapped the Queen. "And he got one."

"Well, Outlander," she continued, nonchalantly holding out her hand for the cloak of the nearest Guardsman and using it to wipe the spattered blood from her face, "It would appear we are not yet finished with one another."

"No, Queen Salonis, I think we have only just begun."

"You know," said Salonis, skirting the puddle and stepping up close to the towering Outlander, "our tradition has it that my people were cursed by the God for taking unwarranted life, a crime Cormin was just prevented from committing. It was also said, by our warriors here, that you were the God

343

himself, Kala Atar, come to punish us in the flesh. Is this true? Are you the God?"

"No, Salonis, I am as I say I am, a man and king with many burdens. But do the gods direct men to fulfill their designs? I believe they do, that men can act as the hand of God, and I think you will find such a hand here. But I do not believe they can know it, and I do not believe their will is the God's. I think we are blind and only grope towards the light."

In the midst of the scene, a Captain of the Guard rushed up and stopped abruptly when he saw the remains of Cormin.

"What is it?" snapped Salonis.

"Majesty, pardon me," said the Captain, snatching his eyes away from the grizzly mess, "but a messenger has just come from the old city. The Iblis have attacked the Outlander's camp. They floated across the river on logs during the night and set fire to one of their ships. Now they have the camp under siege."

"Does the camp hold?" asked Valerius.

"Yes, your Lordship. The first rush was beaten off and as far as we know, the attack has not been renewed."

"Then I suggest, Queen Salonis," said Valerius, "that we proceed with our council. There are some things Lord Koltar has to say I think you should hear."

CHAPTER SEVEN
The Second Battle of Old Kantar

The forenoon sun was hot on his helm and breastplate as Valerius strode out onto the open hillside and surveyed the plain spread out below. Spring was in full bloom now and lush green grasses undulated along the hills and fields, dotted here and there with patches of colorful flowers. In the trees, buds were bursting into leaf and from the plain there arose the rich smell of freshly plowed earth. Overhead a myriad of birds wheeled and danced. In the far distance, the walls of the old city rose like a grey smudge against this gay panorama and nearer to hand, on his right and across the river, lay the still raw cut and freshly dug walls of his own encampment. It was on this that he bent his attention and was relieved to see sentries still alert on the battlements, and inside, carefully laid out rows of tents and the tiny figures of men-his own men-going about their daily business. In the river before the camp, his three remaining ships tugged quietly at their moorings, one showing the black scars of a fire on her foredeck, the others apparently unscathed.

But neither had the trouble passed, for he could also see signs of recent battle about the camp. Several still forms lay just outside the walls, and an Iblian force was still plainly visible, massing in the woods and along the surrounding hillsides. There appeared to be under a thousand of them, and even as he watched, the alarm was sounded inside the camp and men came running to the battlements. In moments, the dark mass of Iblis rushed in and the spring breeze brought Valerius the distant sound of war cries.

"Now Colinus!" he called to the mounted figure at the bottom of the slope behind him. "But remember, demonstrate only between the city and the river. If any sally out, engage them with archery but not on foot. Your job is to cause a distraction until the main army can come up."

"I hear and will obey, Sire!" Looking regal in the golden inlaid armor and purple bordered red cloak of the Commander of the Royal Guard, Colinus signaled his troops and galloped ahead, down onto the level surface of the plain. The entire Guard, a full, thousand man battalion strong, well mounted and splendidly armed, followed in tight formation.

The column swung right, heading for the river and the embattled encampment. As it drew near, someone among the Iblis gave the alarm and part of their attacking force broke off and moved to defend the ford just upstream. The others hesitated in their attack, not wanting to be engaged too heavily on their front while a threat was apparent in their rear. But at the last moment, Colinus and his column swung left, dashing along the river towards the city, all eyes in the attacking force following them.

This was as intended, for at that moment, still standing on his distant hill, Valerius nodded to a standard bearer who waved his banner wildly, and the woods and hills surrounding the encampment suddenly erupted and showers of arrows began falling among the Iblis. Like hosts of starlings frightened from their roosts, flight after flight of winged death arose from the trees and settled again onto the scurrying figures before the earthen walls, stilling them.

The group by the river sought escape across the ford but a new mounted column, Kantaran horse archers this time, dashed out from behind the screening hills upstream and cut them off. Arrows from their quivers, too, poured forth and the Iblis trying to ford the stream, toppled into it and drifted down and out to sea.

Now Thorngere-for it was he who directly commanded the effort to relieve the encampment-ordered all his troops forward and Valerius could see a second ring of attackers closing in on the first. Firing shaft after shaft as they came, they squeezed the panicked Iblis tighter and tighter against the walls. From inside the camp, Outland archers, who had not been idle, now redoubled their efforts and soon, all living targets between the two groups were extinguished. The entire fight took less than half an hour and from his hill, Valerius could hear two distinct shouts of victory: one higher pitched and a couple thousand voices strong, the other, deeper and from fewer throats, but just as joyful.

Meanwhile, Colinus' troops had reached the fields before the city just as a reinforcements for the besieging Iblis emerged from the gate. Colinus wheeled his column into line at extreme bow shot and blocked their path. The Iblis hesitated, massed themselves more tightly, and were about to attack when voices from the walls-where the results of the other battle could be plainly seen-recalled them. Angry, jeering, and hurling insults, the Iblis backed away and retreated behind their gates.

Though he tried to keep a most serious and solemn countenance as he sat his horse like a statue before the walls of Old Kantar, Colinus could not keep his face from grinning.

On his hill at the edge of the plain, Valerius had been joined by the royal contingent as the main army moved up behind him. There was Salonis herself, looking regal, if somewhat jostled, in a sedan chair, and accompanied by a coterie of her household staff; Teukonis, the Teller, also in a sedan chair, though a less regal one, and looking even smaller and more frail in the bright spring light; Maltinus, chief engineer and architect for the city; Koltus the chief administrator; and a number of other senior officials and advisors who, once the word spread that the queen was going on the march, discovered themselves to be indispensable as well.

Koltar, too, was there, but not as an advisor. Armed in diminutive plate and helm and grasping a heavy spear, he rode at the head of a two-hundred strong, mounted contingent of Kantaran nobles, nearly the entire remaining population of able-bodied pure-breds. This martial figure reined in before the royal party and snapped off a salute.

"Request permission, Sires, to lead the march on the old City?"

"Permission granted, Lord Koltar," said Valerius, hiding a smile beneath his moustaches. "And may I compliment your troops on their ardor and martial demeanor?"

"Thank you, Your Majesty. And may I say, it is more than time that the native men of this valley resumed their place at the head of its affairs." With another salute, he returned to his column, gave the

348

order to march, and led the host of New Kantar down onto the plain before their native city.

In their thousands they came, battalion after battalion, with tightly dressed ranks and brightly polished arms, looking-but for their diminutive size-as grand as any army of mankind that ever trod the earth. Out onto the plain they marched, stepping eagerly to the beat of the drum, past the site of their old camp, and wheeling left and right, formed their line of battle amidst the freshly plowed fields of their foes. Colinus and his Guard returned from the walls, taking up station on the army's left wing, and Thorngere, reinforced now with the relieved Outland troops, forded the river and took up station on the right. End to end, the forces of New Kantar extended nearly a mile and as Valerius rode down to take command of the center-leaving a company of Guardsmen to protect the Queen's party on the hill-he smiled with pride.

But of the Iblis, there was no sign. They stayed tightly locked inside their gates, and as the sun edged into mid-afternoon, Valerius ordered his reserve battalions to work re-establishing their old camp, and sent to have more of Thorngere's men help clear the dead from about the outland camp and throw them in the river. Then he turned to Koltar.

"Lord Koltar, take a party of your nobles to the gates under a flag of truce. Call for Chubar and bid him watch the bodies of his people drift down the river and out to sea. Tell him, from me, that the chance to live in peace with us has passed and that either this or fire will be the fate all his people will suffer if he continues to resist. Tell him we intend to cleanse his city with fire and sword, and call on all

349

the Iblis, very loudly, to come out from the city, lay down their arms here in the field before us, and give themselves over to our custody. Only in this way, tell them, will any be spared. Tell them they have until this time tomorrow to decide."

If the severity of this ultimatum shocked Koltar, he did not show it. Slapping his chest in salute, he rode off with a squad of brightly armed nobles under a white banner hastily made from a toga tied to a spear. Reining his party in before the walls, Koltar rode several paces in front of his fellows, and called out for Chubar in his loudest, most official sounding voice. In a few moments, the sally port in the gate opened and that worthy appeared, but not before a bit of comedy: still suffering from the blow Valerius had given him, Chubar, too, was being carried in a sedan chair. But his would not quite fit through the narrow sally port, and in trying to tilt it just so, one of his bearers tripped backwards over the sill, dropping the chair and dumping the hapless Chubar ignominiously onto the ground. It was not without much cursing and kicking, and not without finally opening the main gate itself, that Chubar finally appeared before Koltar's delegation, in state, though not in humor.

"Chubar, Law Giver of Iblian Kantar, " Koltar addressed him in his official voice, though concealing a smirk, "I am sent by Valerius, High King Everreigning over Valeria and all the Inland Sea, and Warlord of the Kantaran People. Look! Valerius bids you, look upon the bodies of your people even now drifting down the river and out to sea. Such is your fate if you continue to resist, and such will be the fate of all your people: either the river or the flames. For your chance to co-exist in peace with us has passed and Valerius bids me tell you he intends to cleanse this city with fire and with sword. You have until this time tomorrow to lay down your arms in the field yonder and surrender yourselves to his custody. Only that way will you be spared!"

Red with suppressed rage to begin with, Chubar's color rose to purple at Koltar's speech, and now he exploded, staggering up from his sedan chair and advancing on Koltar with shaking fists, and only halting when Koltar leveled his spear at his chest. "Cleanse my city, will he! I spit on your Valerius! King indeed! You tell that butcher Balazar that I will piss on his corpse, that I will personally cut off his testicles and fry them for my dinner. And as for you, my little Koltar, when I am done with you, you will beg for the fire! Cleanse my city, will you-you just go ahead and try to breech our walls!"

"Chubar," said Koltar, unmoved by the other's venom, "you above all should know we do not need to breech walls to enter your city-or to burn you out."

For an instant, Chubar's face went blank with astonishment. But then the rage spewed forth again. "We'll block those tunnels, you sewer rat!"

"You fool," Koltar spat. "You do not even know where they are!" And he spun his horse and galloped off with his party, leaving Chubar still sputtering before his gates.

Though most of the Kantaran forces spent the night under the open stars-their baggage train had not even been made up when Valerius marched them from their city, and would be another day at least negotiating the difficult terrain-provision was made for the Queen and her immediate party when the Outland camp was moved from across the river. Thus, it was in an Outland sized tent, sitting with her pudgy legs dangling high upon an Outland sized stool, and eating with Outland sized utensils, that Valerius found her in the morning. He wondered whether she had put away an Outland sized breakfast as well, but bowed to her in his most courtly fashion.

"I trust your Majesty spent a comfortable night?"

"As comfortable as could be expected after a day and a half being bounced around in that chair box like a stone in a rattle. But I do not complain-I would take twice that much bouncing and more to see such sights as I saw yesterday! I had no notion our puny mongrels could march and fight so."

"They are small and lack power, Ma'am, but as infantry they are unmatched in my experience, and given the right weapons and training, they can be formidable indeed. Had the battle last year not been-shall we say, interrupted?-I believe we would be well along rebuilding the old city by now."

"Yes, well, we can only do the right as we are given to see the right, as the saying goes... That 'interruption' may have been ill advised."

"I do not complain, Salonis. My own vision has improved considerably since that time. And who knows, in the larger cycle of things, whether we may not be further ahead as we are?"

"That I cannot say. But after three generations of this insufferable charade, it is time to cast the die. Whatever comes, I feel I am breathing free air for the first time in my life. But tell me Valerius, think you the Iblis will come forth and fight today?"

"I think it a good chance, Ma'am. Your Lord Koltar put a serious fright into Chubar yesterday, and I think the surprise we had for him this morning will convince him an open fight is his only hope."

"A Surprise this morning?"

"Yes. We sent a party into one of the secret tunnels and set a large brush fire under the palace. Chubar was driven from his bed this morning by the smoke."

Salonis laughed outright. "Oh! I'd love to have seen that! And that other surprise you mentioned?"

"Ready and waiting, your Majesty."

In the city across the plain, where the smoke still rose from the windows and gables of his palace, Chubar had indeed decided that his walls could provide no sure protection and that his only hope was to crush his foes as quickly and completely as possible. Besides, being smoked out of his bed had put him in a towering rage, and to fight would have been his choice even if other options had been available. Spurning the sedan chair of the day before, he mustered his forces and charged out the gate.

Valerius was back in his own tent, meeting with his senior officers when the alarm sounded. "All right, gentlemen," he said, "we've been through this drill enough to know what we're about. Just remember our most effective weapon is the bow—that, and our discipline. Keep your ranks tight and fire as fast as you can. Colinus, you'll fight your Guard dismounted on the left wing—you can fire more quickly from the ground—but keep your mounts close. It will be your job to keep the Iblis from breaking away to the south. Thorngere, you'll have most of our fellows with you on the right. Work your way around the Iblis left and remember, we need to keep them clear of the river banks. Any questions?"

"Aren't we going to have a toast?" Thorngere joked. But it was met with an awkward silence until Koltar piped up with a quip of his own.

"I can assure you there wouldn't be any problem this time." But then he realized what his remark had implied and blushed a deep red. The silence in the tent became even more awkward.

But Valerius laughed. "You don't know how that has comforted me, Lord Koltar. And yes, Thorngere, we should have a toast. But this time, since the mission for all of us is to win back our homelands, let us toast with the pure wine of the earth-water!"

All laughed at this and raised their leathern water bottles. "To victory, then," said Valerius, "and to homelands."

Chubar's headlong charge slowed as the distance from his gates increased and as the Kudanim rapidly deployed before him. Many among his followers knew what a close thing their victory was the previous year. Many still nursed hurts from that fight-Chubar himself was still nauseated, swollen, and sore from the recent kick he had received-and the sight of the tightly dressed ranks spreading across the fields before them slowed their advance. And as they closed to within long bow shot and a delegation came forward from the opposing ranks, they were not really sorry for a brief halt.

The delegation, all on foot, consisted of Koltar and several of his nobles, and the towering Valerius, striding among them like a giant out of legend. Chubar, Haradin, and several others came forward to meet them. Valerius spoke first.

"If you are come to surrender, Chubar, have your people lay down their arms here and pass single file into our ranks."

"Surrender? You swine! I came here to kill you!" And without warning, Chubar attacked Valerius, who had not even drawn his sword, and began raining sword blows on him. Valerius caught them on his shield, then body-blocked Chubar, knocking him to the ground. Stepping back, he drew his sword as the other leapt up, maddened beyond reason or obvious care for his life. But before they could join, Koltar jumped between them, his own sword in his hand.

"Step aside, Koltar," said Valerius, his voice fell with anger. "You can't face him alone."

"Sire," said Koltar over his shoulder, his eye on a menacing Chubar and his sword at the ready, "let me do this-for the honor of my People."

Valerius considered, then nodded. "Very well, Lord Koltar-for the honor of your people."

Chubar's eyes gleamed madly and with a snarl he attacked immediately, swinging his sword in a broad horizontal sweep. Koltar caught the blow on his shield at shoulder height, but the force of it bowled him over and he rolled along the ground like a ball. Chubar rushed after him, sword raised for the kill. But Koltar was quicker. As Chubar's sword came down, Koltar's went up; inside the other's guard, under the breastplate and into his bowels. Chubar instantly vomited blood, and as Koltar yanked his sword from the wound, Chubar's intestines spilled over him, and the Law Giver of Kantar toppled, his eyes already turned stony dead.

Drenched in blood, Koltar started to shake in sudden reaction to the violence. But as he looked down upon the vanquished body of his foe, he was suddenly swept up by a surge of exaltation. With a couple quick chops, he removed Chubar's head from his corpse, and thrusting both head and his bloodied blade high into the air, Koltar let forth a primal war cry, so loud and fierce it sounded as if it had been pent up for generations. And though he was perhaps the tiniest figure on all that field, many Iblis actually stepped back in fear.

But as the cry left him and the red mist began to clear from his eyes, Koltar was, for the second time in his life, astonished to see, sailing upriver from the mouth of the cavern, a fleet of outland ships. Eight of them there were, fat, stubby merchant vessels, led by the missing fourth outlander galley.

All eyes watched as, again, outland ships kedged themselves to the river bank and gangplanks were laid ashore. But instead of armed outland warriors pouring ashore, this time, up from the holds and onto the grassy banks behind Thorngere's screening troops, were driven hundreds of jostling, bawling cattle. To a man, the Iblis stared openmouthed at this unimaginable sight.

"Haradin!" Valerius called out. "I speak to you now as the leader of your people. Make your choice-death here and now from bow and sword, or a new life-with beef-under Kantaran rule. Choose now! Or be the next to die."

Dumbfounded, but still essentially a man of business, Haradin looked from Valerius to the cattle still stumbling from the Outland ships, then back to Valerius... and dropped his cleaver.

Once more in possession of their native city, the diminutive people of Kantar set to work in a frenzy. Fastidious by breeding and lifelong discipline, the scurrilous state of the old city seemed an affront to their very natures. They could not work hard enough or fast enough to rid it of pestilent debris, and within two weeks, a great transformation had come over the city.

Gone was the entire Iblis population, moved out and into the camp built by their former enemies and now converted by a palisade into a huge pen. Here they lamented their lot and did little to improve their circumstances, but were driven out daily, to till the fields and provide brute labor for their new masters, and at night were fed small portions of the promised beef. Gone, too, from the old city were all traces of these former inhabitants. While the Iblis were allowed to keep their personal and family possessions, huge piles of refuse and decay were collected and burned on the plain outside the walls, and the remaining liveable quarters scoured from top to bottom before the conquerors moved in.

Then began the work of reconstruction. Whole battalions were set to work repairing the walls, while others attacked the numerous derelict buildings, repairing where they could or, pulling them down entirely and using the materials elsewhere. Along the river, under the guidance of Thorngere and the more knowledgeable and equally energetic outlanders, piles were driven and proper quays constructed. Into the palace moved Queen Salonis and her staff. Out onto the fire heap went all Chubar's splintery furnishings, and down from the New City came wagon load after wagon load of her finery to transform the palace from a cheerless stone vault, to a place of beauty and splendor. And she herself seemed likewise revitalized, working night and day directing noble and army staff alike, losing weight in the process, and gaining a cheerfulness of disposition that translated itself throughout the ranks of her people. The New City, she said, would be maintained as an occasional retreat and bastion for defense, but it was here, in their ancestral home of Kantar that she would maintain the official seat of her people's power.

Haradin's complex was first burned with ritual fire, then totally razed and the ground cleared of every rock and stone which had witnessed his butchery. The remaining earth was raked smooth, planted with grass and shrubs and converted into a public garden. In its center was placed a single large rock with a marker on it, memorializing those who had been sacrificed.

Valerius and as much of his staff as would fit, moved into his own former dwelling, Valerius marveling to himself, as he toured its rooms for the first time, at the changes which had occurred in his life since the last time he had been there; so much, it seemed that even the old name Balazar felt foreign to him. Yet, as much as had been changed, there remained so much more to do. His quest now had ceased to be an idle, almost hopeless fantasy, but had become an immense, near incomprehensible job of work, and it was on this that he fixed his attention.

But a very curious incident one day underscored and helped put this task in even larger perspective for him. He was meeting over dinner with Thorngere and his senior staff, discussing a plan to increase the height of the cavern enough to allow the passage of full sized ships and galleys without having to fold down or remove their masts, when Koltar entered bearing an old musty scroll and called him aside.

"Majesty," he said, "forgive the interruption, but I believe you will want to see this. In my spare moments I have been delving into some old archives I discovered in the basement of the palace, and I came upon this: it is a scribe's record of the very first interview between our then King Corinon and the leader of the refugee Iblis, a man, oddly enough, named Chubar. The document records the tale basically as we have known it-that a small number of Iblis, totally bereft, straggled down from the northern mountains and appeared before our gates-but there is a part here I am sure you will find most surprising. May I read it to you?"

"Certainly my Lord Koltar."

"You may not find it pleasant."

"I have dealt with many things more unpleasant than musty old scrolls, Koltar. Read away."

"Very well. Here it is:

Then said this Chubar, in a dialect crude but understandable to our ears, that his people had been numerous and prosperous in the north, that they had homes and fields and counted their wealth in many cattle. But there arose a king in the far distant northlands who exacted tribute from all the peoples. He sent his emissaries to the Iblis, demanding their cattle, and when the emissaries were killed for this offence, the king set his armies upon them, killing them and driving them from their homes. 'Who is this King who so abused you?' asked Corinon. 'He is called Valerius,' quoth Chubar, 'Valerius Everreigning. And may the curse of the gods descend upon him and all his race.'"

End of Volume One

360